D1444460

Blessed is
the fruit

Blessed is the fruit

a novel

Robert Antoni

Henry Holt and Company
New York

Henry Holt and Company, Inc.
Publishers since 1866
115 West 18th Street
New York, New York 10011

Henry Holt® is a registered trademark of
Henry Holt and Company, Inc.

Published in Canada by Fitzhenry & Whiteside Ltd.,
195 Allstate Parkway, Markham, Ontario L3R 4T8

Library of Congress Cataloging-in-Publication Data
Antoni, Robert
Blessed is the fruit: a novel / Robert Antoni.—1st ed.
        p.   cm.
        I. Title.
PS3551.N77B57   1997   96-31960
813'.54—dc20   CIP

ISBN 0-8050-4925-8

Henry Holt books are available for special promotions
and premiums. For details contact: Director, Special Markets.

First Edition—1997

Printed in the United States of America
All first editions are printed on acid-free paper. °

1   3   5   7   9   10   8   6   4   2

Portions of this book have appeared in *Conjunctions* and *The Paris Review*.

para Ana y nuestro niño por venir

in memory of

Lilla Gonsalves née Scott-Johnson

(1903–1992)

and, with love and thanks, to

Velma Clarine Bootman

Blessed is
the fruit

Bolom

The world is this room.
That's all there is and all there needs to be.

Toni Morrison,
Beloved

1

Holy Mary full of grace the lord is with thee, blessed art thou amongst women, and blessed is the fruit of thy womb Jesus. Holy Mary mother of God pray for us sinners, now and at the hour of our death amen.

Holy Mary full of grace the lord is with thee blessed art thou amongst women and blessed is the fruit of thy womb Jesus. Holy Mary mother of God pray for us sinners, now and at the hour of our death amen.

Holy Mary full of grace the lord is with thee blessed art thou amongst women and blessed is the fruit of thy womb Jesus, holy Mary mother of God pray for us sinners now, now at the hour of our, of our . . . life . . .

2

Mummy she calls me. *Angel* she calls me. "Sweet sweet mummy me white angel," she whispers, sleeping, between turns of the sea. Only I hear.

Vel. *Velma Clarine Downs Bootman* in clear cursive, penciled cross the back of a brown envelope. Miss Vel on Sunday mornings to the coolie-crabboy. Girl to the no-goods on Independence Corner their golden bottles dangling from two fingers even still. She is simply Vel to me. That breath: *Vel.* My Vel.

Here beside me sleeping quietly at last. Peacefully at last. Now with Dr Curtis's needle in her hip and the bleeding finally stopped. The bawling—her terrible bawling. Lying here naked on her back with the folded rectangle of my Limacol-sprinkled kerchief resting on her forehead. The bloodstained feather pillows beaten by the doctor's little fist beneath her buttocks. Her powerful thighs spread wide, her wounded sex shoved up toward the ceiling, splayed open to the salt-soaked air. Lying here with her bent knees still pinned back to the mattress like a frog's for a schoolboy's dissection—thwarted—her supple ankles twisted round, toes downward-pointing. With the thick, yellow soles of her feet pressed flat together. Softly. Carefully. As though they were praying hands. As though she were the ebony-carved totem of some ancient African fertility diablesse.

Here beside me sleeping peacefully at last. Her belly big, round, purple as a batchaks' nest stuck to the trunk of a cedar tree (but how could I not have seen it? detected it? for so long?). Mother's breasts spilling backward toward her shoulders looking even fuller. Her small silver crucifix caught sinking between them, the obeah shard of mirror which wards off the evil eye—*maljoe* she calls it—two religions tied round her neck with a strip of yellowed fishingtwine. Lying on her back with her arms at her sides and her hands upturned and clear-palmed, black-slashed: two clean *M*s, the palm-lines. Lying here beside me looking smaller than ever in this big, whitewoman's bed. In these barren, whitewoman's sheets. More husband and wife than have lain together in this bed for ten years. For a decade of years. Sleeping peacefully at last her calm breathing occasionally falling into rhythm with the soft Caribbean Sea breathing just outside the window. Occasionally falling into rhythm with my own silent voice.

4

Mrs Lilla Woodward, née Grandsol. Madam Grandsol. Mistress Lil. To her, frequently even *mummy* (though I'm the farthest thing from motherly I could possibly imagine; though it's she who cares for me, mothers me; though, indeed, we're both the same age—both thirty-three—two Geminis, almost to the day). Occasionally she even calls me her white angel.

Naked too: a pledge made to myself since my days at the convent school (never again to sleep in knickers and a nightgown, never again to put on a stitch of underclothing). Lying here on my back beside Vel naked too, my own body loose-looking next to hers. Softboiled. Long-limbed and long-digited. Nearly fleshless, breastless. My own skin so thin it is nearly transparent save an eerie, milk-blue glow in the late afternoon light. Against the white sheets. Beside Vel. Some cartilaginous sea creature drawn twitching up from the depths. Scarcely visible save its primordial, milk-blue glow. Save its sea-grey, gargoyle-staring eyes. Blinking in the first light.

And you? How to call you? *Bolom* is the name I've heard your mummy use, when she couldn't've known that I was overhearing. There in the kitchen looking *not* into the simmering pot (as I had thought), but down at her own secretly bound-up belly. Her palms pressing flat, fingers probing tenderly as though to touch you (as I see it now). To feel your heart beating still beneath the layers in strips of ripped bedsheet, wrapped round and round, pulled tight and square-knotted. Whispering as though to herself:

"What you come to give me this struggle for, Bolom? You think we could go home in Sherman, Bolom? Onliest thing is starvation in Sherman, Bolom. Onliest *thing* is blight!"

Bolom, Bolom . . . but I know that name. Though in truth I've not heard it in donkey's ages. Not since my nursemaid Di's stories—folktale stories of the forest, and obeah, and magic—told to me from earliest infancy. *Bolom.* Mythical unborn child struggling for life, destined to die before its birth.

Yet living still. Oh, yes! Miraculously living still.

Even so. Even now.

Bolom.

3

Lying here on my back feeling the breaths of cool seabreeze drifting in over my naked skin. Past broken blinds. Splintered jalousies. Staring up at the shadows shifting slowly cross the gabled, corrugated-zinc ceiling. Crenellated waterstains. The bright orange bubbling rings of rust (a vision of myself running with a calabash in the middle of the night to catch the pelting, leaking rain, lightning cracks shaking-up the floor to knock me off my feet). Lying here studying the intricate patterns of pale-blue mildew, powdered cross the ceiling. All the little islands of fuzzy, bluegreen moss growing long the ridge where the roof meets the walls, along the rotting rafters (and how else, Bolom? with Vel not permitted inside to scrub-down the place with lye as she does downstairs? fierce yellow astringent?). And there—a miracle in itself—there stuck between two such rotting rafters in a hidden, moist corner—leafing out, big as a cow's head: a solitary fern. Maidenhair-fern. Delicate bridal lace, her spore-bearing ribbon trailing. A bouquet of petticoats rustling softly in the gentle seabreeze, in the pale afternoon light.

Lying here naked on my back in this big bed, the golden skeleton key in my hand fingering. Twitching. My right hand—as though it were the actual beads. *Let not thy right hand know what thy left hand doth. My* religion, tied round my own neck on a strip of black ribbon. For a decade of years. This solid-gold skeleton key copied by special request to the Queen's own Royal Crown Jewelers of London, Commonwealth Division. Dodgy little shop on Abercromby Road with the dodgy little monocled Englishman inside. Counting karats. The old-fashioned sort of key shaped like a sad little flag with a squashed ring at the bottom. The old-fashioned sort which turns the locks from both sides of the doors (locked-in or locked-out). Which turns the lock to this bedroom door precisely ten times a day. (Tell me, Bolom: do we make these numbers for the world? or does the world make *us* for these numbers?) First thing every morning at the sound of Vel's quiet knocking. The key in the lock turning to open the door and take the tarnished silver tray with the single cup of coffee—when we've the coffee. The small bake buttered and quartered and dribbled with golden syrup—when we've the flour, butter, the tin of Lyle's Golden Syrup. The tray balanced in one hand and the key turning again in the other, the door locked behind Vel's retreating back. Turning again an hour later—once, twice, the door open, locked again—descending the stairs to return the tray to Vel back in the kitchen.

Again in the lock turning before and after every afternoon nap after tea. Turning again last thing every evening after dinner. Or after sitting with Vel for an hour of quiet company each in a wicker rocker on the back gallery. Looking out over the calm, moon-glittering sea. Climbing the stairs in darkness now feeling my way along the banister down the hall. Bending over the key on the ribbon round my neck hanging fitted inside the lock jiggling, turning. Extracted and finding the lock on the other side of the door turning again by touch, by instinct, habit of the body. The fingers. The same key every night day and night turning again like clockwork, like time-keeping (or staving-off?), this madness with locks, with this *key*. Shut-up inside this room for another night. Lying here alone for another night in this big bed. Naked on my back staring up at the shadows shifting on the corrugated-tin ceiling. Another night. The golden skeleton key in my hand fingering. Twitching.

This master skeleton key which turns the lock also to the big double front doors downstairs. At the crack of dawn every Sunday morning for the coolie-crabboy already calling out, singsong: *"Miss Vel! Mistress Lil!"* Taking down from off his matted head the equally tattered pasteboard box emitting those mysterious rasking noises. Peering under the lid to reach in and snatch out two blue monsters. And handing them over to Vel ever-so-gingerly, one by one, held between thumbs and middle-fingers cross their backs their pink, partitioned undersides showing. Legs spidering. Shifting stalks of eyes. Modars snapping the air. A ferocious, foaming, hissing blue monster in each of Vel's hands. Big as two small umbrellas, their articulated spokes flipped inside out and stripped of their webbing. Both of us hurrying back to the kitchen now with me standing back of the pot, reaching out, holding the lid open a crack. Waiting for Vel to toss them in with me clapping down the lid one by one in the cauldron of water waiting, already boiling. And after the two monsters have been picked lovingly apart, put to simmer in their sludge of okra and dasheen leaves—green green like green, Bolom, the *definition* of green—Vel in her white church hat-and-handbag hurrying, the key in the lock turning to let her out.

With me suddenly dizzy. Faint. Confused. Slouching down in a slump to sit right there on the worn Persian rug before the locked front door. Key still in my hand. My back pressed flat, knees pulled up tight against my chest. Looking round me now at the tall, empty foyer as though for the first time. At the chandelier hanging above my head with half the crystals missing from one side (side of the sea-blast? the thin wire breaking off with a shattering of falling crystals each time Vel climbs up to tease way the cobwebs, to feather-dust). The chandelier hanging quite skewgeefied. Bisqwankee. Studying the two paint-peeling portraits at the top of the stairs: *MuMu,* my exquisite Creole grandmother, all silence excepting her eyes; *Grandpapa,* goatfaced, the French Comte. Sitting here studying the listing staircase. The buckling banisters. Looking out cross the horizon of floorboards bursting up in one place, rotting through in another. Sitting here on the worn Persian rug waiting for Vel to walk the mile or two to town to attend her church service and return (Shango? Baptist? Roman Catholic?). Wondering: *But supposing she doesn't this time? Supposing she doesn't come back?* And suddenly feeling almost *nauseous*—the overly-sweet soup, overly-rich—so thick in the air I can scarcely breathe.

Then hearing her quiet knocking at last. At last. Jumping up to my feet now my hand trembling so much I can scarcely fit the key jiggling inside the lock, turning. Open. Closed. Locked-up again inside this huge, decaying house like a couple of jumbies. A white and a black jumbie. Young, thirty-three-year-old jumbies. Sitting here at either end of the long diningroom table. Happy. Smiling now. Each with a tarnished silver tablespoon in our raised hands. Ready to eat our Sunday callaloo.

Every Wednesday morning the key in the front door unlocked for our weekly excursion to market in father's old Ford—though I've still not learned to drive it properly. Though I still refuse to get my driver's license (and why should I, Bolom? spoil the fun?). Very nearly knocking down half-a-dozen coconut palms even before we reach the front gates. Very nearly pelting down over the cliff into the river below. Vel sitting beside me, pressing up against me, *screaming* with pleasure at every turn of the wheel! Each time an oncoming motorcar blasts his horn and swerves off the pitch into the bush, cursing. Sitting there in the parked Ford a moment catching our breaths, still giddy with laughter like two adolescent girls, preparing to face the crowded market. Vel with the big basket balanced on top her head following behind me. Picking our way among all the commess—all the world bawling all together—fighting-down the marchands in my own rankest Creole, *Them two little potato there for fie-cent, eh? Them two onion, two green-fig!*

Back in the Ford again to Nelson's Grocers, where the palsied old-man no longer even bothers to mark down on his debits slate the two tins of tinned beef, pigeonpeas, two Carnation sweetmilks. A block of butter and a bag of rice and a piece of bacon. Of salted Canadian cod from the crate. Stopping on our way home to thief two colossal eden-mangoes from the tree in front the Prime Minister's house. His yard-boy chasing us off his cutlass in the air. Hurrying the Ford now straight to Huevos Beach—because *such* mangoes can only be properly eaten sitting in waist-deep water. The beach deserted in the midday heat of Wednesday. Vel stripping down in one to her bodice and me stark naked (of course, with nothing under my dress). Using our teeth to rip off hurriedly the long chamois-strips of bright red skin, floating away on the crystal water. Sinking our teeth into smooth, orange flesh the texture of *human* flesh—of a baby's bamsee, Bolom! Juice sticky running down our chins, necks, our breasts—awful, *wonderful*. Sucking the sweet, hairy seeds with all the life left in us. Till we've nothing remaining in our puffed, puckered cheeks but a couple of dry, hollow kneecap-bones.

Dressing back in our dresses dripping wet, legs caked in sand. Back in the Ford driving slowly now, ever-so-sleepily, the other motorcars tipping their horns for us to hurry up. Back at the house again with the key turning the two of us locked-up inside for another week. Dry now. De-sanded jumbies. Ready to take our sleepy afternoon teas together in the parlour (Darjeeling for me and a vile-smelling concoction of caraili or kooze-maho bushtea for Vel). Ready now to climb the stairs the key in the lock turning for another afternoon nap. Another night spent here alone in this big bed. Lying here naked on my back staring up at the shadows shifting slowly cross the corrugated-tin ceiling. This golden skeleton key in my hand fingering. Twitching.

4

Till one night five years ago when the fingers had had suddenly
enough. Enough of the feel, the touch of precious metal in my hand
hanging round my neck again fingering, for five years. Jumping up suddenly out the bed not even noticing my own nakedness, bothering to
wrap the sheet round. Pale-white milk-blue glowing in bright moonlight. The key in the lock turning hurrying down the dark hall. Down
the stairs. My hand held trembling before me clutching the key.
Following the key—the key itself. Fitted inside the front door unlocked
out onto the gallery. All the way round the house. Down the three concrete steps of the back porch stoop—the moon full, bursting, sky bright
as day. The shadow beneath the flamboyant tree in the backyard every
bit as dark and distinct. Flaming fire above in the bright night.

Following the key cross the yard already gone to pot by then, now.
Gone to bush, we say, Bolom—completely to bush. Picking my way
through tall guineagrass the weeds high as my waist, vagrant castoroil
bushes reaching up over my shoulders. Careful to circumvent the
shadow beneath the flamboyant tree—*never cross the night shadow of a
tree: there Bazil waits.* My hand held before me clutching the key.
Following the key. Through the ruined rose gardens their treacherous
thorns. Through sedge, seaoats, reeds of miniature bamboo growing
along the property's edge their razor-sharp blades slashing past my
naked thighs. Treading with bare feet over brambles and clusters of burrs
as innocent looking as ears of wheat, blood-sucking. Sinking my feet
now into cool, spongy moss. Out into ankle-deep water out over flat,
moss-carpeted stones. The gently rippling water translucent beneath the
bright moon. Its invisible lower layers shifting back and forth against my
shins with each slow suck. Each extended exhalation. Water clear
enough to see every needle-thin spike of every black urchin, stuck
together in clumps. The fluorescent purple tips of thick, pale-green
medusa-tentacles—an enormous, solitary polyp. Undulating anemone.
Water clear enough to see the dotted spines and pulsating inner organs
of every transparent minnow. Each minuscule, peering eye.

Following the key still over slippery stones out into cool water up
past my knees. Stinging my scratched-up thighs, ankles, my burr-
pierced bleeding feet. Suddenly a single hard pull of my hand holding

the key (as if the hand were thinking suddenly for itself? for the key?).
Yanking hard against the threadbare strip of ribbon round my neck:
burst. The breeze carrying it off a sliver of silver seagrass tumbling over
the surface of rippling water. The key in my hand clutching tight, tight,
drawn slowly back behind my shoulder, pausing an instant, and throwing forward with all my strength to pelt as far as possible out over the
abyss of sky-water bright-moon *but not letting go!* The hand. The key.
(Almost tumbling face-forward over slippery stones into the abyss
myself!) The fingers holding tight still. Clutching tight to precious
metal-memory after five years. Five years of lying every night alone in
this big bed. Lying here on my back with this golden skeleton key in
my hand fingering. Fingering. Refusing to let go even a little bit to
release and let fly relinquish forever golden metal-memory holding
tight still.

And following the key, the hand. Still. Again. Now. Turning round
slowly my feet heavy dragging through the water over slippery, moss-
carpeted stones. Picking my way among the clumps of black, undulating, solitary minnows pulsating greenish clouds of a million tiny,
peering eyes. Picking my way step by step slowly out of the water up
onto the slippery shore. Wet. Dripping. Stark-naked madwoman climbing up out of the water in the middle of the day-bright night. Still following the key. The key itself (or maybe the hand?). Through sedge,
seaoats, babybamboo treading clusters of burrs. Circumventing the
flamboyant's dark shadow picking my way along and then, suddenly,
stopping. Hearing suddenly—for the first time—the loud night-
insects: *screaming.* A deafening, buzzing, screaming noise interrupted
every fifteen seconds by an instant of perfect silence. Then a hollow *toc-
toc* sound. Then the screaming again.

Hurrying again through tall guineagrass; weeds; vagrant castoroil
bushes big as trees. Cross the yard up the three back steps up onto the
gallery. Round the house. Through the front door cross the foyer
beneath the chandelier stepping over creaking floorboards. Through the
livingroom into the parlour hurrying now, almost running. Yanking
open with my left hand the lower desk drawer (my right hand still not
releasing yet not yet not even a *little*). Removing a white envelope taking up the fountain pen in my *left* hand—writing with my *left* hand—
for the first time in my life. The pen in my crimped fist like a child

learning all over again to make her first childish block letters each one a different size, slanting backward, each *E* for some peculiar reason reversed:

KƎITH WOODWARD
C/O LANCASHIRƎ CRICKƎT LƎAGUƎ
LANCASHIRƎ, ƎNGLAND
U. K.

The gumflap touched thrice to my dry tongue and then finally, at last, the fingers of my right hand clutching tight one by one peeling away slowly letting go *and the key not wanting to leave my palm!* Holding tight still—the key *itself!* Holding tight to the center of my palm due to sticky perspiration? static electricity? habit of metal-memory clutching tight still to the center of my palm after five years, the key itself, holding tight. My palm spread flat fingers stiff thrust downward toward the open mouth of the envelope—once, twice, thrice—and finally letting go. Surrendering finally precious golden metal-memory locked *itself* inside the envelope, addressed, the flap stuck-down, the key inside. Finally. After five years.

5

Sitting here at the desk a quiet moment catching my breath. Willing my beating heart to soften its pounding. Rising slowly now and taking up the envelope the key inside, finally. Making my way cross the creaking floorboards through the silent, shadowy house. Slowly climbing up the creaking staircase my legs suddenly exhausted. Trembling with fatigue. Feeling my way along the banister down the dark hall and slowly, step by step, approaching the bedroom door bending over as though the key were *still* hanging on its ribbon round my neck. And realizing, slowly, step by step (the *full* implications), my hand on the cold knob: *locked*. Without even intending. Locked again without even stopping thinking locked again by simple habit of the body. The fingers. *Locked outside the bedroom inside the house.* With nothing left to do now with the key surrendered, finally, after five years. The key itself locked-up inside the envelope. Stuck-down. Addressed. The act accomplished. Done. Not to be undone.

With nothing left to do now but fall exhausted against the locked bedroom door. To slide down along the locked wooddoor surface slippery now with my own perspiration. Sliding down slowly in a heap with a *thubb* of loose, flesh wet to the flooring. Sitting there in the dark my back pressed flat against the locked bedroom door. Knees pulled up tight against my chest. Naked. Covered in perspiration salt-sea slime down my legs, ankles, feet encrusted in blood-smeared filth. Nothing left to do now but sit here holding the key, finally, locked inside the envelope without even a note, a *word* of explanation (because what else need be said that the key itself could not alone say?). The act accomplished, done, not to be undone. With nothing left to do now after five years but sit here and weep. Cry hysterically.

With Vel hearing the commotion. The loose *thubb* of my wet body falling to the flooring on the ceiling above her head in her room downstairs. Below. Jumping up from her bed and reaching under to take out the white pasteboard shoebox dumping its contents out onto the mattress: a dozen spools of thread, swatches of cloth, needles, pins, thimble, the large sewing scissors. And taking up the scissors now in her clenched fist like a weapon—a dagger—raised above her shoulder, and stepping out of her room cautiously now to see. Thinking: *What? Eh? Thief? Eh? Thief in the house?* Walking through the livingroom, foyer, climbing the stairs, making her way cautiously down the dark hall. And hearing me weeping now. Finding me sitting there in a heap on the flooring. Naked. Covered in slime. Sitting there my back pressed flat against the locked bedroom door weeping like a madwoman. Traumatized child. Crying hysterically. Looking up now to find her standing there above me—sewing scissors clutched tight in her fist raised above her shoulder like a dagger, glinting like a dagger—her eyes shining bright in the dark. Reaching up with my two arms outstretched palms upward-turned holding out the key, the white envelope, bawling:

"*Take it! Post it now! Immediately!*"

And Vel answering in a whisper, calmly, ever-so-gently:

"*Shush . . . shush. . . .* Never you mind, Mummy. I going post it, Mummy. Never you mind."

Laying the scissors down on the flooring and reaching at the same time to take the envelope now out of my outstretched palms, finally. Placing it there carefully inside the bosom of her nightgown patting it flat between her breasts. Safe. There together with her small silver crucifix, her obeah shard of mirror fishingtwine–tied round her neck. And reaching down now. Lifting me up off the flooring. Wrapping her strong arms round me holding me tight. Tight. My fatigued body trembling in Vel's strong arms. My face pressed wet against Vel's soft cheek. Weeping. Trembling. Holding me tight in her strong black arms for a full minute. For a lifetime. And then quietly, slowly, beginning ever-so-tenderly to make a soft *clicking* sound with her tongue against the roof of her mouth: soothing, matronly. A sound somehow familiar. Vaguely familiar. Rescued somehow from the memories of my earliest childhood.

Vel making her soft clicking sound and turning me, taking me down the stairs. Her arms still wrapped round me, supporting me. Step by step to the bottom slowly, slowly cross the foyer, livingroom. Slowly past the big diningroom table, kitchen, into Vel's own little room at the back (my own former childhood bedroom years before). Hugging me tight with one arm and reaching down with her free hand to grasp the hem of the sheet, flipping it up: spools of thread, swatches of cloth, pins and needles and thimble flying. Pattering. Pinging down on the wood flooring. And putting me gently now to lie down there in her own bed (my own former little bed). The sheet billowing a breath of cool air spread cross my naked, my perspiring skin. My filthy legs, feet. Tucking the cool sheet carefully round me. Walking round to the other side of the little bed removing the envelope now from inside her nightgown, from between her breasts. Placing it there on the bedstand. With me seeing the envelope (the key inside), bolting up sitting bolt-straight in the bed, bawling, again:

"Take it! Post it now!"

Vel outing the lamp. Reaching out in the dark. Pressing me back down firmly, gently against the mattress. Covering me again with the cool sheet. Vel lying down in the dark in the little bed beside me. Two of us here together in this little room, this little blackwoman's bed, blackwoman's sheets, side by side, here, together, whispering:

"Never you mind, Mummy. Never you mind. *Shush . . . shush. . . .*"

14

6

Waking early the following morning discovering myself alone. Alone in Vel's little bed, Vel's little room. And jumping up. Running into the kitchen to find her climbing up out of the window above the sink, the key in the envelope held between her teeth—clenched between her *teeth!* Climbing up out of the window above the kitchen sink like a burglar. A thief, breaking out of her own home! Walking to town first thing the following morning to post it away. The golden skeleton key locked finally inside the plain white envelope addressed in the child's script, without even a note of explanation (because what else could writing say that the key itself could not in perfect silence say better? louder? more poignantly?). The key locked inside the envelope posted away cross the sea with the front door locked (and knowing full well), the bedroom door. Every door in the house. Vel returning from town an hour later with no choice now but to climb up again through the window above the kitchen sink burgling again to get herself back in.

And on Wednesday morning the two of us together. Two chicken-thieves. One behind the other breaking out of the coop—our own coop! Vel first and then me behind her up over the sink, shoving out the big basket, shoving out *myself,* the second chickenthief, breaking out of my own coop behind Vel. And having to stop all of a sudden midway, *stuck*—my legs hanging out the window, toes pointing hard reaching toward the ground. Lying backward into the sink sprawled out cross the sill, stuck, paralyzed by a fit of laughter! *Weak* with laughter. Vel too. Both of us bursting out suddenly like two adolescent girls caught—by *ourselves*—at some secret, illicit act. A pair of wicked schoolgirls caught breaking-biche. Found out behind the forbidden bush, in the toilet stall! With me suddenly stuck, sprawled out cross the sill. Unable to do anything other than tumble myself laughing spilling out the window into Vel's waiting arms. Two of us laughing all the way to town. All the way to Nelson's all the way back home. And just when we thought ourselves too exhausted to laugh ever again—*ever* in our lives again—winded, our throats raw, bellies paining us. Just when we thought we'd gone beyond the threshold of our own girlish silliness, unable to hold ourselves back from falling into a fit of giggling once more. Two naughty, adolescent girls climbing back in through the window to get ourselves back inside the locked-up house.

Having to wear Vel's clothes now, then (of course Bolom, with all my own clothing locked-up inside my own bedroom). All her dresses hideously *bosomy*. Vel begging to take a few tucks with her needle and thread and me refusing, actually stuffing the bosoms further still with cottonwool—tottots out to *here,* Bolom! All Vel's dresses hideously *short*. The two of us giggling again at my *insistence* on trying on her little minidress, her scandalous little minidress, scarcely covering my crotch—and me of course without knickers, hips swinging like a bell! And Vel: "You *wouldn't,* you *never,* not in the public with them tottots like that all you bamsee *expose,* Mummy! I be so shame, Mummy! So shame!" Both of us laughing still.

Wearing Vel's clothes now, then, for five weeks. The feel, smell, the texture of Vel's clothes against my skin. Like living *inside* another's skin for five weeks: a bobo-soukuyant getting her skins confused. Dressing herself up every morning in the skin of her opposite. Her own twin sister. Living inside Vel's clothes, her skin, now, for five weeks.

Climbing in and out of the window above the kitchen sink for five weeks. Sleeping there together night after night for five weeks: Vel's own little room. Own little bed. Two of us together. With me sleeping *properly* now for the first time in five years. Peacefully. Such soft, easy surrender without the key on the ribbon round my neck in my fingers keeping me awake. Here with Vel beside me beneath the cool of these blackwoman's sheets. This blackwoman's little bed. Here together.

Because in five weeks the same key. Same *envelope:* unopened, the key untouched. Same envelope with the same backward-leaning childish script each letter a different size, each *Ǝ* reversed. *Without even a return address written cross the back envelope flap.* (So how, Bolom? how *possibly?*—unless somehow examining, holding up against the light, his fingers feeling the key *through* the envelope? and recognizing? realizing?) Because in five weeks the same unopened envelope, tucked inside another. The key untouched. *Unfingered.* (Not by his hand or any other as though the key itself would not permit it. Not yet.) Same unopened envelope tucked inside another. Double-skinned. The outside skin of the second outside envelope-address typed out in capital letters seemingly too *large,* unevenly spaced, somehow *childish*-looking (as if to mock my *own* childish left-handed printing; as if printed out not by the typing-machine of an adult, but by a child's *toy*), each *A* for some peculiar reason an inverted capital *V*:

LILLA GRANDSOL
D'ESPERANCE ESTATE
ST. MAGGY,
CORPUS CHRISTI,
W.I.

Same key in the same envelope on the same black ribbon hanging round my neck. After five weeks. Five years. (The key itself with its own meaningless mocking predilection for symmetry and balance, for the same meaningless numbers, repeated meaninglessly, mercilessly.) Same key turning again inside the same bedroom door. Open. Closed. Locked-up again inside the same room. Same solitary bed. Lying here on my back staring up at the shadows on the corrugated-tin ceiling. Same key in the same hand.

7

Lying here beside Vel again, now, after five years. Two of us together again. More husband and wife than have lain together in this big bed for twice as long. For a decade of years. Lying here on my back feeling the breaths of cool seabreeze drifting in over my naked body. Past broken blinds. The window with three jalousies remaining. Soft afternoon light sifting in. Illuminating patterns of pale-blue mildew powdered cross the walls. The fuzzy patches of bluegreen moss growing long the rafters. Bathing down the maidenhair-fern of delicate bridal lace. Leafing out bold-faced there in her hidden corner.

Sitting up now, my back pressed against the headboard, looking round the room as though it were somehow changed. Transformed in some way by Vel's sudden presence—by the presence of *both* of you, Bolom—here together with me in this bed. And looking round me now as though I might even detect some change in the very furnishings. These tired, ancient furnishings. Covered in dust. This navy-velvet chair cross from the end of the bed (the chair mummy always referred to proudly as the *fauteuil* chair): tattered, misshapen, the velvet worn to gauze along its back and winged arms. Bagging down from the seat like loose, wrinkled skin. On the wall above the chair the Cazabon water-colour, *Misty Savannah:* sitting on the bank of a yellow-green river dwarfed by gigantic tufts of bamboo, by so much ferocious silence, the aboriginal Amerindian lovers. Perfect; minutely gentle; memory's memory of desire. Looking round me now at the dressing table and chair in the corner of the room. The tall, triple-glass-mirror behind it, its reflection mottled to a shiny snakeskin. There on the table Mummy's wedding photograph—every bit as beautiful as her own Creole mother in the portrait at the top of the stairs—caught in a backward glance over her shoulder with her face frozen in mild astonishment, the train of her bridal gown so long it cascades all the way down the coral steps of St Maggy Cathedral. Beyond the confines of a milky-green, once-gilt frame.

Looking round me now at the bedstand to my left, elaborately carved to match the Louis IV headboard behind my back. The bed-stand with its brass lamp missing (of course: taken up to fend-off the imaginary thief, rapist, and left there on the bottom step). Replaced now by the open bottle of Limacol smelling up the room like stuffy old-age sickness. Like the neverending fevers of childhood malaria. Drowning out the last traces of Dr Curtis's ether lingering in the air. And there—on the other bedstand beside Vel—arranged carefully in size-order on a piece of green-coloured cloth: a dozen medical instruments. White stainless steel. Crude-looking. Primitive. A series of bent crochet needles, mutilated spoons, of long-handled pincers with sharp-toothed piranha-jaws at the clamping, flesh-tearing ends.

There on the flooring beside Vel the pile of her bloodstained, ruined dress. Cut away from her body by my own trembling fingers. All those blood-saturated strips of ripped bedsheet—and seeing them again with my eyes closed—my own hand working the scissors, again: Vel's dis-tended, blue-black, secretly bound-up belly *bursting* forth from beneath the severed strips of cloth. Beneath my own trembling fingers. Those strips of ripped bedsheet wrapped round and round and pulled tight and square-knotted. The same secret ritual every morning before she ascends the stairs the tray in her hands with the single cup of coffee, the little bake. All those mornings. Wrapping. Knotting. Binding up her belly so that I would not notice. Detect her growing pregnancy. Send her away, home. *You,* Bolom.

8

Alive. Still. Even against all the expertise of bush-science; obeah-science; medical-science. All the age-old wisdom. The forbidden knowledge whispered mother-to-daughter and sister-to-sister across continents, seas, time. All those doses of bush-medicine (understanding it, deciphering it now—and recollecting well enough myself, Bolom— my *own* unsuccessful attempts). Those stews of green pawpaw, castoroil, of *womb-fruit:* vile-tasting concoctions resulting in nothing more than chronic diarrhea. Still alive after all those doses of quinine tablets. Three times a day. Morning noon and night. Tiny white pills swallowed down one after the other like clockwork. (But how could Vel have purchased those pills without a prescription? binding up her belly too to beg the pharmacist? feigning malaria spells?) All those mornings of cursed obeah burntrags pressed into her armpits—her *armpits?*—of course, there on top the pile on the flooring beside Vel together with the meshed metal mask and the ether-saturated wad of gauze: two spell-bound, obeah-cursed burntrags. Still alive after all those mornings of binding up her belly. Wrapping round and round and pulling tight, tight. All those mornings without my noticing, detecting, never even suspecting.

Surviving all that, Bolom. And then, five days ago—on New Year's Day of all days—the fall from the flamboyant tree in the backyard. With me sitting there alone at the huge diningroom table, amid the spoils of our gluttonous New Year's Day feast (two of us starving ourselves for weeks in order to *afford* so much food): splitpea soup including the ham bone, fricassee chicken, rice, pigeonpeas, yam, buttered christophine. Sitting there alone at the huge table feeling absolutely bloated—wonderfully, sinfully gluttonous. And waiting now for Vel to bring to table the guava duff—*duff,* top of all that! Sitting there alone amid the spoils of our New Year's Day feast, waiting, wondering: *What in heaven's name could be taking her? Re-steaming the duff?*

And noticing through the window, through the corner of one eye: something moving about at the top of the tree. Something *big.* Sitting there half-asleep, bloated as a battleship, half-watching the spectacle for a full minute. Not surprised, startled, not even very curious. Sitting there half-watching through the corner of one eye, and thinking, calmly: *bear.* (Not *thief;* not *putu-aguti-lap;* not even anything as sensible as *monkey*—since there are a few howlers remaining in the forest.) But sitting there half-asleep, half-watching, calmly accepting that absurdity: a *West Indian* bear climbing in the flamboyant in the backyard.

Suddenly jumping up. Rushing over to the window. And seeing, registering: Vel, high at the top of the flamboyant tree. Wondering: *But how can Vel be out there climbing up in that tree when she's locked-up here with me in this house? How possibly? Unless I could've left one of the doors open by accident? Unless she could've climbed up out the window above the kitchen sink?* Thinking all this and rushing *not* to poor Vel's aid at the top of the tree, but into the kitchen to verify that suspicion: to check the window! And finding it open, of course. Vel's apron in a bundle there on the counter beside the sink. Looking out the window again watching Vel for another full minute, high in the tree climbing higher still. Questioning *not* what Vel could be doing up there—what *possibly*—but wondering instead why she didn't ask me to unlock the door to let her out the house? How she could be climbing up in that tree with her stomach so bloated? Actually wondering why she couldn't at least have waited to do her tree climbing till after we'd finished eating our guava duff? Standing there before the sink looking out the window, not comprehending a-tall, and feeling frustrated now by my lack of comprehension, and in my frustration beginning to feel *vex.* Vex with Vel for ruining our New Year's Day feast, for leaving the house without my *permission!*

Coming to my senses at last. Fumbling with the key on the black ribbon round my neck, unlocking the back kitchen door. Rushing out onto the gallery down the three stoop steps. Picking my way through all the weeds, bush, waving the branches out my face, hurrying toward the flamboyant tree. Toward Vel. Still not understanding a-tall (not until *today* Bolom, five days later). Confused, frustrated, bawling:

"What in heaven's name Vel what are you doing up there? Get down from there this instant, this instant! I absolutely forbid, prohibit—THERE WILL BE NO TREE CLIMBING! Vel! Vel!"

Not even noticing. Not even *hearing* me bawling like a madwoman, standing there on the hard dirt beneath the tree. Standing there confused, frustrated, looking up at Vel climbing slowly higher. Higher. Grasping branch after branch carefully wrapping unwrapping fingers, prehensile-toes, moving her limbs slowly, dreamily, lemurlike. With a dreamy expression on her face. As uncomprehending *herself* as I am standing there beneath the flamboyant tree shading my eyes from the bright sun staring up at Vel. Calling out still (quietly now): *"Vel? Vel?"*

And taking off up the tree myself! Climbing up behind Vel—and not even sure myself *why*, what I might possibly *do* once I got myself up there—but taking off climbing up the tree a monkey myself. Not calmly, carefully: climbing up in a mad rush grasping branches, limbs, pulling myself higher, higher. An *expert* monkey myself (of course Bolom, with all those years of childhood tree climbing). Climbing up in no time higher and higher up toward Vel, and calling, quietly, still: *"Vel, I'm coming behind you! Vel!"*

Up there beside her in no time a-tall. Up at the top of that flamboyant tree without a *single* red petal, leaf (*autumn* in the Caribbean?), two of us together like two monkeys, two howlers, Vel slightly above me arms and legs wrapped round the grey trunk just like a *bear!* (Exactly like the North American grizzly I saw once at the top of its iron pole in the London Zoo. Arms and legs wrapped round.) With me up at the top of that flamboyant slightly below Vel, reaching out slowly, tenderly, reaching out to touch her shoulder. To caress her smooth, dark skin. Whispering: *"Everything's fine, Vel. Vel . . . my Vel. . . ."*

Letting go. Unwrapping arms and legs both at the same time at the very *instant* my finger-tip touches her smooth, warm skin. Letting go. Falling backward against the hard dirt flat on her back. *Brups!* And bouncing straight back up onto her feet! *Straight* back up onto her feet again in a single smooth movement even after that fall fifty feet from the top of that flamboyant tree! Straight back up onto her feet again as though nothing, nothing had even *happened*—the fall, the tree. Bouncing back up onto her feet again unharmed, untouched. (And you too, Bolom! five months old bound-up secretly in Vel's belly unharmed by the fall too!) Walking back to the house now, then. Toward the open kitchen door. Walking *briskly* even. The shard of mirror and small silver crucifix fishingtwine–tied round her neck *bouncing* shoulderblade to shoulderblade with each stride—*that* briskly—flashing beneath the bright afternoon sun. Walking back toward the house, toward the open kitchen back door as though nothing had even happened. A-tall. With me the monkey my startled monkeyface still staring down from the top of the tree.

9

Then, this afternoon, five days later: the final, frustrated, the hysterical attempt with the sewing scissors. Vel's large sewing scissors. Here in my bed asleep as usual at that hour of the day: taking my afternoon nap after tea. And waking suddenly. Hearing her muffled cries coming from somewhere below, downstairs. Lying here in my bed thinking: *Thief? Thief in the house? Hurting Vel! Raping Vel!* And jumping up. Throwing my housedress over my head in one and taking up the lamp off the bedstand—the heavy brass lamp, held upside-down, its long electrical cord dragging behind me. Unlocking the bedroom door. Cautiously. Hearing Vel's cries louder now, more desperate. Walking cautiously down the hall. Stepping slowly out onto the landing, peering down, and seeing her lying there in the shadow at the bottom of the stairs. Hearing her bawling—her terrible, wounded cries: *"Ayeee! Ayeee! Ayeee!"* Raising the brass lamp in both hands high above my head, looking round the foyer now for the thief, rapist, thinking: *He's run? He's heard me coming and fled?*

Descending slowly, cautiously, brass lamp high above my head, electrical cord trailing behind, step by step slowly toward Vel, wounded, crying out at the bottom of the stairs. And then suddenly seeing, taking it in: all the *blood!* Whole *handprints* of rust-coloured blood along the wall at the bottom of the stairs. Footprints on the flooring cross the foyer coming from the back of the house. Vel herself: *bathed*-down in blood. Soaked in blood. Lying there wounded. Bawling. Bleeding still. Hurrying down the stairs now toward Vel and then, suddenly, stopping. Seeing it, making it out: her large sewing scissors. Lying there in a pool of glistening, wine-coloured blood at the bottom of the steps beside her.

Standing there *frozen*—my legs halted in midstride between two steps—looking down at those large sewing scissors, lying there in the pool of Vel's own blood. And looking at Vel lying there beside them—her dress black-red, soaked-through. Blood on her hands, up her arms high as her elbows. Standing there frozen in midstride for a split second—for the *eternity* of that split second. Recalling the inexplicable fall from the flamboyant tree five days before. Seeing now—for the first time—the *weight* Vel seemed to have put on during those last months—with scarcely anything a-tall to eat in the house! Standing there in that split second hearing those conversations again: Vel conversing with the simmering pot (as I had thought). And beginning to comprehend, to understand now: talking to *you,* Bolom. Seeing, hearing, reconsidering it all in that split second. Deciphering. Beginning to understand. Thinking: *But how possibly with those sewing scissors? How in all the world? My dear, dear Vel!*

Looking up. Seeing me standing there frozen in midstride between two steps, the lamp held upside-down in both hands high above my head, cord trailing behind—the look of *horror* imprinted upon my face—Vel seeing me standing there above her. And calling out to me. *Pleading* with me, Bolom. Crazed. Hysterical:

"Five months I trying to throw this child, Mummy! Five months! Trying to taking the bush-medicine, the quinine powder till me think this child was going abort me, Mummy! Trying to wearing the curse burnrag under me armpit so long but ain't doing nothing, nothing! And binding up me belly every morning pon morning so as you don't see—send me way, home—nothing but starvation home, Mummy!"

Placing the lamp down slowly on the bottom step. And reaching at the same time to take Vel up. To lift her up slowly off the flooring. To take Vel up in my arms and hold her tight, tight, covered in blood now too. Whispering:

"Shuuu . . . shuuu. . . . There, Vel. There. *Shuuu. . . ."*

With Vel pleading, hysterical, still:

"Don't send me home, Mummy! Nothing for me home, Mummy!"

Holding Vel with both my arms wrapped tight round her, supporting her weight, and turning her slowly, starting her slowly up the stairs. One step at a time. Slowly. Step by step. Whispering:

"Nobody's sending you away, Vel. *Nobody! Shuuu . . . shuuu. . . ."*

Holding her up, walking her up the stairs onto the landing, slowly down the hall. Slowly into my own bedroom, now, for the first time.

Here inside my own bedroom for the first time since Vel has come to live with me in this house. This whitewoman's private bedroom—sanctuary, cell. Here together with me in this bedroom for the first time in ten years. A *decade* of years.

Putting her gently now to lie down here in this big bed. This solitary, whitewoman's bed. Barren sheets. Helping her lie back softly now against the soft mattress, moaning, weak from loss of blood—all the *blood!* Helping Vel to lie back gently, softly, and then—in one quick motion with one quick hand—grasping the blood-soaked hem of her skirt and flipping it wetly up. Exposing her bound-up belly. All those intricate layers and layers in strips of ripped bedsheet, blood-saturated, black-red, and pressing my hand against her bound-up abdomen: hard as wood beneath the bindings.

Standing there beside the bed, looking down at Vel struggling, wounded, bleeding still. Looking down at all those strips of cloth, knotted impossibly—and suddenly terrified for Vel's life (not even thinking yet about the child—*you*, Bolom—not yet). Thinking: *Untie them? cut them through? knife? scissors?*

And turning, rushing out the room. Down the stairs. Taking up the same scissors and climbing again, hurdling steps and wiping away the blood from the scissors at the same time against my skirt. Vel thrashing about in the bed, in pain, struggling, bawling still: "*Ayeee! Ayeee! Ayeee!*" Beginning now with the hem of her dress cutting it all the way up high as her collar, and cutting through the collar. Cutting through the sleeves down along each shoulder. And pulling away the ruined, the blood-soaked dress. Out from beneath her back, buttocks. Heaping it up wetly there on the flooring beside the bed. The two wads of her obeah-cursed burntrags pressed each into an armpit. Sliding a leg of the scissors beneath the layers of intricate bindings, carefully, severing them through. Slowly. Carefully. And watching Vel's blue-black belly *bursting* out from beneath the severed bindings. Out from beneath my own trembling fingers. Piling it all there on the flooring—black-red, blood-saturated. Finally the last few strips and then, suddenly, my fingers halting. Stopping. Suddenly hearing it: the *silence*. Absolute silence. Vel perfectly still. Quiet beneath my trembling fingers: unconscious. Faint from loss of blood. And throwing the scissors onto the pile on the flooring now too, pressing the back of my hand against her soft, warm cheek with only the slow, slow, the clear pulse of a large artery at the side of her neck to assure me she's still alive. My Vel.

1 0

Taking off running down the stairs. Out the house. Jumping into the Ford and taking off bat-out-of-hell pelting straight to town. To Dr Curtis's office on Abercromby Road. With the whole world suddenly *dead, silent!* At six o'clock in the afternoon! And not understanding why Bolom, how St Maggy could be so thoroughly deserted without even a beggar, a stray dog or cat in the streets. And then suddenly remembering, realizing: *Of course, all quiet at home or in church for the Epiphany Mass.*

All except Dr Curtis, his little shiny head bent over an enormous ledger, scarcely visible behind his enormous desk. Looking up: his little red face, his watery, newt's eyes. Seeing me standing there with my dress covered in blood. The look of horror still imprinted upon my face. And recognizing me at once. (Perhaps even recalling the *same* horrified face from a dozen years before; barging into his office one afternoon in just the same way—madwoman, hysterical—feigning malaria spells, demanding a prescription for quinine tablets.)

"You must come with me at once," I say, bawl. "*At once!* My servant has wounded herself terribly—*critically*—attempting to throw a child!"

"Ah . . ." he says, thoughtfully, after a moment. And then, a malevolent spark of curiosity in the depths of his watery eyes: "Some sort of wretched implement, I may presume?"

"A scissors," I say—bizarrely, absurdly striving to match his own audacity, his own insolence. "A *large* sewing scissors!"

"Ah. . . ."

"*Come!*"

He does. Suddenly, surprisingly animated. Packing up his big black doctor's bag in one. Hurrying out behind me.

Three minutes and we're back at the house. Rushing through the foyer. Stepping over the pool of glistening, wine-coloured blood there at the foot of the stairs. Past the line of rust-coloured handprints shoulder-height along the wall. Vel there in the bed just as I had left her: perfectly still. Unconscious. Only the large artery at the side of her neck pulsing slowly, clearly. My Vel.

Dr Curtis yanking a stethoscope out his bag like a live mappapee snake. Fixing the U into each of his ears. Listening first at Vel's chest, then pressing the tiny cup to the lower curve of her abdomen. Just above her mound of coarse pubic hair, matted with clotted blood. Shifting the cup, pressing, listening. While I stand there studying the lines running horizontally cross her belly, round her hips—evenly spaced, perfectly parallel—impressions left behind by the bindings.

Both of us looking up at the same time: his little red cheeks, lips; his pale, watery, newt's eyes. Salamander face. My own look of horror.

"Dead?" I ask. Then I specify: "The *child?*"

"Quite to the contrary," he says, slowly, a little too loudly. "A good deal better off than its mother, I should think."

He pulls the stethoscope out of his ears, leaves it hanging round his neck. Lowers his voice: "Most likely she never even got near the cervix. They seldom do, you know. Especially when they're hysterical."

Each pronouncement of the word *they* strikes me like a slap cross my face. I take hold of Vel's hand—warm, limp—looking down again at her striped abdomen.

"Any idea as to her time of gestation?" he asks. "We might even give the poor woman her wish, you understand? Long as there's someone to foot—"

I cut him off: "Yes," I say. "Certainly," though I know it's a lie. Impossible. That there's no more than a few measly dollars remaining in the brownpaper-sack beneath my bed. Then I look into his watery eyes, lying again: "Three months," I say calmly. "Four at most."

"Ah. . . ."

Suddenly Vel comes to life: bolts-up sitting bolt-straight in the bed. Thrashing about. Bawling: "*Aye aye aye aye aye!*"

Two of us pressing her back down against the mattress.

"There, Vel," I say, grasping both her shoulders. Pressing her down. "There now. *Shuuu . . . shuuu. . . .*"

And almost before I can take it in the doctor removes a syringe and a tiny glass vial from his bag, breaks off the tip of the vial, and draws a clear liquid (morphine?) into the syringe. A few bubbles foaming out at the tip of the upturned needle. He pinches Vel's hip—a handful of thick, dark flesh—and from a distance of a couple inches away, tosses the syringe into Vel like a dart—just like a dart.

"Aye aye aye aye aye!"

"Shuuu . . . shuuu. . . ."

A moment later I feel the softening of Vel's shoulders, relaxing beneath me, her eyes closed, moaning softly. And Dr Curtis begins working now. Swiftly. Efficiently. Not a wasted motion of his little hands. His *horrid,* little hands. Little fingers, grotesquely *hairy*—as though to compensate the hair missing on his head. Fuzzy black tufts, two to a finger. The backs of his hands covered with scrubs of black curls.

A small mask of meshed metal, oval-shaped, removed from the black bag and fitted over Vel's nose and mouth. A piece of gauze doubled-over, fitted inside the mask, and from a little metal bottle five drops (ether?), counted aloud—*three, four, five*—dripped onto the gauze. Vel's shoulders now limp beneath my hands, the room smelling of pitch-oil. Of nail-polish remover.

A little hairy fist now *beating* the feather pillows one after the next beneath Vel's buttocks. Under her wide hips—*poff poff poff*—with Vel's wounded sex shoved abruptly up into the air, open—a flood of thick, black liquid spilling out. Covering the white pillow. Little hairy fingers grasping hold of Vel's bent knees, spreading them wide apart—*wide, impossibly wide apart*—pressing her knees back firmly against the mattress. Pinning them there. With the thick yellow soles of Vel's feet now fitting themselves together. Pressing themselves softly together—involuntarily, carefully, purposefully—even as though they were praying hands.

Removing from his bag a bottle of alcohol, roll of cottonwool. Tearing off, dousing, dabbing at Vel's wounds and dropping the little pink disks of cottonwool onto the pile beside the bed. Rummaging through his bag for a tiny cellophane package of suturing thread. Stretching it out: a length of fine transparent fishingtwine, a tiny curved needle attached at the end. The tiny needle now grasped firmly with two sharp *clicks* into the head of a long-handled clamping instrument. Held in Dr Curtis's little, hairy fingers.

Watching him begin now to suture Vel's wounds. And feeling suddenly nauseous, Bolom. *Revolted.* (Not by all the blood. Not even by the spectacle of that tiny needle piercing with a tiny pop Vel's raw, glistening vaginal flesh, the beads of bright red appearing on either side of the wound, in and out; *click click;* pulling, slipping; three little tugs of Vel's glistening flesh at the end of the length of fine fishingtwine; *click click;* in, out.) No, Bolom. Not by the suturing. Not by any of that. A-tall. Revolted solely by those *obscene,* those hairy little fingers. Unable to bear the sight of them another instant.

Turning my face away. Letting go of Vel's hand. Leaving her side. And going to sit *not* in the fauteuil chair (as I had thought, intended); but walking past it and slouching down in a slump on the flooring in the far corner of the room. My back pressed flat against the wall. Leaning my head slowly back, back, resting gently against it. And looking up at Dr Curtis suddenly far, far away. A world away. Bending over Vel, his shiny little head thrust between her spread thighs, working. Working those efficient, those obscene little hands which I could no longer see. *Bear* to see.

Closing my eyes. Forcing myself to listen to the water rolling slowly up over the rocks. The moss-carpeted stones. Retreating again. Each slow suck. Each extended exhalation. Listening to the breeze blowing softly in the flamboyant tree just outside the window. Blowing cool cross the surface of my hot shins, forearms, cross my hot beating temples, cheeks.

Sitting there on the flooring, my mind drifting, slipping back to the scene five days before. Seeing Vel again: there at the top of the same flamboyant tree. The dreamy look on her face. And taking off myself up the tree again. Climbing up behind Vel again. Not knowing a-tall why, what *possibly* the two of us could be doing up at the top of that tree on this New Year's Day, this first day of 1958. But comprehending it now, finally, five days later: trying to throw the child. Even at the risk of her own life. This child who would not be thrown. Who refused, utterly, to go away. To die: *you,* Bolom. Willing to defy your own fate. *Our* collective fate. History. Faith.

My dear, dear Vel.

My Bolom.

And jumping up. Rushing over to the bed. To Vel's side. And seeing those awful, primitive-looking instruments: laid-out carefully in size-order, spread cross the piece of green-coloured cloth. There on the bedstand beside Vel. Seeing those obscene, those hairy little hands probing deeply inside Vel. His little shiny head thrust between Vel's powerful thighs. Suddenly grabbing up the big, black, the overstuffed doctor's bag in both my hands. My own trembling—my suddenly, surprisingly powerful hands. Thrusting the bag bold-faced into his little chest. Shoving him backward. *Bodily* backward. Actually lifting him up off the flooring for an instant an enormous sea-wave lifting him up bodily into the air. Shoving him backward. Backward. Sweeping him out the room.

Throwing to the door. Bending over the key on the ribbon round my neck fitted inside the lock, jiggling, turning.

Click.

This Side of Sleep

1

Lying here on my back feeling the breaths of cool seabreeze drifting in over my naked skin. Ever-so-gently. Ever-so-softly. Taking me back to my childhood again. Dreamily. As if in a dream. Lying on my back again on the white, sandy bottom of that shallow cove nearby the convent. My breath held. (And practiced till I could hold it up a minute at a stretch Bolom, an entire minute: the *eternity* of a minute.) Lying there on the bottom submerged in cool water. Submerged in silence. My eyes open, staring up through the gently rippling pane of the surface at the watery nimbus of orange sun. At the dome of cobalt sky, the fluffy clouds drifting past. Then a cloud would eclipse the sun and the inside surface of the water would become a mirror. A rippling dream mirror: mirror of my childhood imagination. I could see my own image reflected there—my opposite, my twin sister—floating facedown on the surface of the shallow water. The tiny bubbles dribbled upward from my young, puffy lips would be swallowed up again by my twin's puffy lips. A silent, secret communication of slowly ascending pearls.

And because the face I saw reflected there was gently distorted, in the dream of my childhood imagination it could become another face, any face I chose, a stream of faces. A continuum of faces drifting slowly past: Dulcianne's, and mummy's, Di's, and now, even, Vel's.

Lying here on the white, sandy bottom feeling the invisible currents of waves brushing over my naked skin. Slow rushes, soft as breaths of air. Nudging me backward with the tips of my shoulderblades softly scrubbing the sand. Pulling me now the next way, in the direction of my tingling toes. Each slow suck. Each extended exhalation. The gentlest surge within my genitals each cool, gentle surge of warm, pulsating blood. Ever-so-softly. Ever-so-gently. Again and again with the golden skeleton key in my right hand, again my left. *Now. Now at the hour of our life, Bolom. Of our life.*

2

Lying here together now with Vel. My opposite. My own twin sister. Not face to face but side by side. Not in a dream but in reality. Though it *feels* as though it were a dream, Bolom—all this—which is always more real. Where time becomes distorted, tumbling head-over-heels in a great rush one moment, treading painstakingly slowly through thick mud the next. Where events seem softly anachronistic. Where objects appear with a special hardness, a sharpness, etched into space: this key in my hand; that shard of mirror fishingtwine–tied round Vel's neck, her small silver crucifix; those stainless-steel instruments spread cross the piece of green cloth, there on the bedstand beside her. Beside Vel. Vel who is sleeping now. Dreaming perhaps. Moaning softly. Sleeping in that seemingly impossible position with the pillows still stuffed beneath her buttocks. Her bent knees spread impossibly wide. Wide. Pinned back to the mattress. Her ankles twisted round with the thick yellow soles of her feet like praying hands, pressed together. Her arms stretching along her sides with her clear palms upturned, out-held, black-slashed. Lying here with her wounded sex shoved shamelessly up toward the ceiling, splayed open to the salt-soaked, the ether-smelling air.

Vel, perhaps, who's dreaming now. Pleasantly perhaps. Of me? Of *you*, Bolom? Then perhaps all this is actually Vel's dream? Because in that moment only a moment ago when I thrust Dr Curtis bodily from the room, shut the door and turned the key behind it; in that moment Bolom, it was as though I were the phantom of someone else's dream. (It could *not* be my own, since I'd lost even that subtle sense of control which the dreamer—except in madness—always maintains; which allows the dreamer to tell herself, even within the confines of her own terrible nightmare: *It is only a dream.*) My own strangely powerful hands responding to someone else's desires. Fulfilling someone else's needs: Vel's? Yours, Bolom? Then perhaps this dream actually belongs to *you?* This dream of your own two mothers? Of Vel. Me. Of yourself, Bolom. Dreaming yourself into existence. Thrusting Dr Curtis *yourself* out the room. Forever out the room.

Yet—what *is* it?—somehow still here. His presence palpable. Lingering still in the room. Those wretched instruments possibly? There on the bedstand beside Vel. Arranged carefully in size-order cross the piece of green-coloured cloth. And getting up now—in a vaps— going round the bed to Vel's side. Lifting up the bedskirt and shoving the pile of rubbish beneath with the side of my foot (Vel's ruined dress, the pads of obeah-cursed rags, strips of blood-soaked bindings, scissors, the little pink disks of cotton and the wire-mesh mask there on top the pile where I myself had thrown it)—shoving it all under with the side of my foot, kicking it under the bed. Dropping the skirt. And quickly gathering up all those wretched instruments in their green pouch with the two cloth ties hanging from one side. Gathering them up in a bun- dle in my two hands and rushing in two strides to the window: pelting them through the gap of missing jalousies. Out the room. The last rem- nants of Dr Curtis. Hearing them land in the weeds below like a fist- ful of pelted gravel.

Taking a deep breath now, turning round, slowly realizing: not the instruments a-tall. His *smell*. His medical smell. That anesthetic (ether?), that, whatever it was he'd dripped every few minutes from the little metal tin into the wire-mesh mask over Vel's nose and mouth. Into the doubled-over piece of gauze stuffed inside. Returning to Vel again, get- ting down on my knees on the flooring beside her. Lifting the skirt again and reaching in under the bed. Groping about blindly among the pieces of damp, of bloodstained crusty cloth till I touch it with my fin- gertips: the hard, cold, wire-mesh mask. Turning it over and feeling blindly inside the cup for the wad of gauze. Pulling it out from beneath the bed. And sitting back on my heels raising it up to my nose: smell of rank pitch-oil. Of nail-polish remover. The medical smell of Dr Curtis.

Getting up from my knees and going into the WC, pelting the wad of gauze into the toilet, flushing it way. Standing above the swirling toiletbowl breathing deeply, raising my hand now to my nostrils: still on my fingers. Lingering still in the room. Opening the mirrored medicine cabinet above the washbasin and taking down the bottle of Limacol. Screwing out the cap and pouring the yellowish liquid over my fingertips. Passing them in two wet lines cross my forehead—a tingling crown. Touching my fingertips to either side of the back of my neck my head gently floating: the Limacol smell of stuffy old-age sickness. Of the neverending fevers of childhood malaria. A thoroughly West Indian smell: Guyanese toiletwater (an ancient Amerindian recipe?), familiar to us as memory itself.

Returning to Vel now with the open bottle of Limacol and sitting softly on the bed beside her. Opening the bedstand drawer and searching among the unused pairs of knickers, unused articles of underclothing—all moth-eaten shreds of silk and lace—some even belonging to mummy. Taking out a white linen kerchief and closing the bedstand drawer—and stopping suddenly; opening it again. Shoving aside the mound of undergarments and seeing it—unbelievably—there still at the bottom of the drawer together with my own discarded diary, my own expired passport: Vel's large brown tattered envelope. Untouched—like the diary, the passport, the knickers—in ten years. Its contents unexamined, unfingered not even *once* in these ten years (and scarcely even read through the *first* time). Taking the envelope out now with great care as though with exposure to the air it might even disintegrate. With the touch of my trembling fingers.

Softly pushing closed the bedstand drawer. Putting down the envelope and taking up the kerchief again from the floor where it's fallen. Smoothing the wrinkles out against the mattress. And folding the kerchief now as though it were a letter—in three, two creases—the bottom third folded between. Dousing it with Limacol and placing it carefully cross Vel's brow—like some kind of tribal headband—my fingers trembling still. Taking up the open bottle of Limacol, the envelope, and returning to my side of the bed. Lying down again on my back, my eyes closed for several minutes. Breathing in the familiar smell of Limacol, the large brown envelope pressed flat to my breast with my palms held flat, crossed, pressing against it. Several minutes. Breathing and rebreathing the smell of memory. Until I begin to feel the warm liquid seeping out the far corners of both my closed eyelids. Slowly. Running slowly in a continuous wet stream cross my temples back behind my ears. Soaking up in the soft mattress. Tears neither of sadness, nor joy, but simply exhaustion. Profound relief. Till there're no more tears left to pass.

Now pulling myself up to a sitting position with my back against the headboard. Opening the envelope flap as though I were turning back a clock. A calendar. Back to the very beginning: our introduction. Penciled in clear cursive between my trembling fingers, just visible beneath the evening's lingering light:

> *Velma Clarine Downs Bootman*
> *c/o Ansin Walker Bootman*
> *Basse Terre Trace*
> *Sherman*

Inside, together with the letter:

1) the recommendation, signed by Mrs Charles Pantin:

> *Velma has worked in my employ for two years. I have found her a responsible servant, honest and conscientious. She cleans well, and she could cook when I tell you, best float-and-accra I ever eat!*

2) the health certificate from A.B. Ballard, MD, Director of the Henly Mental Care Clinic:

> *I have treated Velma for depression and mild hysteria, culminating in an attempted suicide, and precipitated by the abandonment of her husband and the subsequent deaths of her two children. Velma has suffered a great deal in her short life, not the least of which has been extreme poverty, yet she has survived admirably well. At present she is in sound mental and physical health. I dare say, Mrs Grandsol, that she will not disappoint you.*

3) the police record, stamped by the District Chief, Alfred Alexander Wilchcomb, St John Parish and Environs:

Free of Charges.

3

Dear Mistress Grandsol, 28 April 1948

Please send for me to come as you servant. Di write to say you going be needing a next one to care for you, and that person could be me. Please let that person to be me, Mistress Grandsol! Di is my fourth cousin. Family sufficient to know, but not too much of family to tell a lie. Ask her about me. How hard I work. How much I need the job cause things terrible hard here in Sherman, Mistress Grandsol. Terrible hard. I know you would listen to Di cause she raise you up out the cradle, and work for you mummy since she was a young woman too. Ask her about me.

Di say whoever want the job must send 1) recommendation, 2) health certificate, 3) police record, and you could find them three in this same parcel. But Dr B, that is how I does call my trink-doctor in the psycob, Dr B say that I must write the letter too. He say Vel, write everything. He say that letter would be the best therapy for me, and good for you too to know just who is the person I am. How much I need the job. I tell Dr B that a young wealthy white-woman like youself would never take interest in a life that know only scourge and blight like my own, but he just answer as always in he English way, quite to the contrary. I say but Dr B, if I tell she everything, all about the suicide I try, and psycob, and trink-doctor and everything, I say Mistress Grandsol would take fright. She would startle to hear all that! Dr B say that is just the chance I would have to take. So I must write it Mistress Grandsol, everything, just as Dr B tell me, cause I does do whatever he say. He is a good good man, and if you ever have the fortune to meet he you would know too. Dr B give me back my life Mistress Grandsol, after I did already dead. He reach in the grave with he two hands and he pull me back out. Is Dr B teach me how to read my life. What it is to be a human being again.

So where to start? Start with this old house in this same parlourroom here where I sitting right now to write this letter. Granny Ansin big old house away up in the country, this same house where I did born and raise up in. Place call Sherman, I ain't know if you ever hear of a place call Sherman, Mistress Grandsol? And full! This old house did full-up with people when I first open my eyes, and it full-up with people still. Women and children and babies. Cause at that time there was Granny Ansin and Tantee Elvira and Tantee May, all they children and babies, my mother and me and my younger sister and brother. Wasn't no men. Not to say living in. Then nor now. Cause my Uncle Charpie, he was living to he own house in town, and Mr Bootman the Panama Man and he boy Arrows, they was living to town too. Never no men. They uses to come round mostly in the evenings, and only for two things. Eat and the other. And Mistress Grandsol, ain't no good reason to name the other.

My father, well I never know he, nor I didn't know my mother neither. To say _know_. Cause my mother get me when she did only fifteen–sixteen years of age, young like that. She, like she just hide-out in the bush and get me, and time as I grow little bit she did already pick up and gone. Left me there pon my Granny Ansin floor to raise up, me and my sister. Cause my mother carry my brother with she. He is a boychild, so she could carry my brother with she. Is Granny Ansin the only mother me and my sister know. Mother and father both.

We raise in this big old board-house, two bedrooms, with the parlourroom to front and kitchen behind. And this house did old then, so you could just think how it come now. Holes rotten through the roof, that galvanize, holes in the walls, holes in the floor with scorpion running beneath. You could just think Mistress Grandsol when the rain fall, how we did do! Both the bedrooms had in two beds, them coconut fiber beds, and still we had to sleep mostly pon the floor. We grow up sleeping mostly pon the floor. Cause Granny Ansin and Tantee Elvira, they did had a bed each to one bedroom, with four–five children sleeping together in the next two beds, so you could see how the most of we did end up sleeping pon the floor. So much of children. But didn't matter, cause in them days you didn't thinking nothing about that. You don't miss a bed till you grow accustom to sleeping in a bed.

Same as food. Cause in them days always had plenty food. Wasn't no starvation then. I could never remember no starvation then. All that come _after_. Cause in them days we had the pot! That was a big black belly-pot Mistress Grandsol, you never see a pot so big in you life. Granny Ansin cook that pot every evening. Cook that pot _regular_. You so accustom to that pot you don't miss it till it gone. Till it stand empty. Cause that's one thing you could depend is that pot. In them days.

When I did young I go at the government school they had for poor people. I did love that, reading and writing and arithmetic! But the bestest of them three is writing. I practice that so hard, drawing out the letters. Every chance I did get. I practice them letters till I draw them smooth like icecream! And you could see right here in this letter you holding, despite that I ain't practice a good long while. But then I had to leave school when I reach to twelve years. Only twelve years, and I had to leave already.

I ain't know what it is to be a girl Mistress Grandsol. I pass straight from child to woman without even a pause for girl between. _Girl_ is a privilege I never know. Joe was the boy hold me up. He just do how he know to do, how *he have to do. But me, poor me I didn't even know one thing. I didn't even know what sex was even. When he hold me down. And after, when I see all this blood pon my skirt. I didn't even know what it was. And I did so <u>scared</u>, and confuse, without nobody to explain me nothing. I just run from Joe, after that, I did so scared. I never give he chance to hold me again. Not after that! I never even give he chance to <u>know</u> me. And that Joe was a good boy, maybe the only good one I ever meet.*

I did had to leave school now. Cause don't be no schoolchildren in school pregnant. And after that only one time with Joe. Just one time. But I didn't know what it was to make a baby neither, never mind I raise with babies. I didn't know what it was to <u>make</u> a baby, <u>keep</u> a baby. And this baby so small. But he did pretty too. He was a boychild, and so <u>pretty</u>. You never see a baby so pretty in you life, Mistress Grandsol. My first boychild.

Now I got to think what I could do, I go at a lady name Mistress Bethel to learn the needleworks from she. Seamstress. I go with she a good time, and I did starting to learn them needleworks good too, and that's how I could sew good still up to now. Onliest thing is to go at Mistress Bethel house, I got to pass crossroads, and that's where a next boy, a next <u>beast</u> by name of Berry was living. This Berry hold me up when I coming home in the evening from Mistress Bethel. Hold me and carry me in the canes. He nastiness. So I can't go at needleworks no more, cause I know this Berry would hold me again. I ain't going by he. I get a job with my Uncle Arrows ironing out the seams for the nuniforms of those American soldiers off the ships. My Uncle Arrows daddy which is Mr Bootman the Panama Man, he collect the nuniforms off the ships from these soldiers, and he bring them back for Arrows and me to wash them iron out the seams. So now I ain't got to look for that Berry again, but is <u>he</u> coming in now by Granny Ansin house. He come looking for <u>me</u>. But still Berry couldn't hold me again. I too smart, and run too quick! But then one time he disguise up heself, that he could lure me in them canes just like that. Easy as that. But that's not the biggest trick, Mistress Grandsol. The <u>biggest</u> one that he did pull, the <u>worst</u>, is somehow he get me to like it. Una could suppose he did treating me more better this time, more gentle, and somehow he get me to like it. He get me to like it bad enough.

Now he coming in all the time by granny house, we going in them canes we sexing all the time like that. And Mistress Grandsol, once we start, like we just can't finish. <u>Whole</u> night! One morning I come in to iron out the seams, I so tired from going all the night long like that, I could scarce even pick up them heater-iron! You know, the big heavy heater-iron that heat with coals? Mistress Grandsol, that morning I must be scorch-up about the entire American Navy! Me <u>one</u>! And is not Uncle Arrows come that morning to find me a-scorching all them nuniform, is Mr Bootman the Panama Man come to find me! I just take off running and I don't look back.

37

Onliest work I could find to do now is go in the canes with my Granny Ansin. She didn't want me to go, but still I follow behind she. Cause that's hard work, <u>hard</u>, I could tell you, them canes. Not cutting. Planting and cleaning the fields. But that's hard work still! I grow accustom to that from early. All day long in them canes, then when night come I going back in the canes again with Berry. Mistress Grandsol, I did most <u>living</u> in them canes then. At that time.

4

That's when I make the first big mistake. When I find myself pregnant the second time, and Granny Ansin turn bad pon me and Berry both, and Berry father turn bad pon we too. Now that I pregnant the second time, I move out from my Granny Ansin house and I move in in a little shack side the canes with Berry. I did fall so bad for this man Berry now, he make me so I can't see straight. You know he get a job working in the fire service, hat and cape and everything, and so <u>handsome</u>! I couldn't even help myself to swoon behind he! And then I get Junie. My first girlchild. That child was so pretty, and good, and we living in we little shack-house with them canes right there beside whenever we want. Oh Mistress Grandsol, we did think we own the world! You know Berry start to come up in that fire service, they put he to drive the big truck that he did love so much, make me to feel so proud. We did meeting life so good then.

And wasn't only me he could charm. He charm the fire service too, cause next thing they put Berry in chief, firechief, and that's the <u>top</u> now. Now he got the works, badge pon he chest, everything. That badge like it go straight at he head. Make he to feel too big, and <u>boast</u>. He get in this habit now of going in town nights to beat up prostitutes. Prostitutes left over from the war. Girls that they put in prostitutes to go with the soldiers during the war. Cause now the war finish, and they got all these girls left over from the war. And now government put prostitution to illegal. Government always doing like that. So that put Berry in the right, cause you know here in a place like Sherman firechief is the same as policechief, so that put he in the right. Nobody couldn't tell he nothing. He get in this bad habit of beating up prostitutes. Course, he did going with them too, you know that, but that's only the smallest part. The worst is that beating, cause one time Berry beat a woman so bad he put she in hospital. Berry near <u>kill</u> this woman.

That's when everything blow up, cause the woman carry Berry before the Magis for that beating. You know they make plenty noise about that, cause Berry father was big-time people. They write up that case in the news with big headlines and everything. And wasn't nothing Berry father could do. Not even

38

for money self. Only pay out the fine, and they take way Berry badge in the fire service too.

That thing did knock Berry a blow, that incident. Bring he back to humble again. A time. Berry turn back to good a time. Well just as you would expect Mistress Grandsol, I like the fool that I born I go and take he back again. That's when he did start to drive the taxi. They put he to drive in taxi. And Berry did driving that taxicar so <u>proud</u>. Just now he making good money again, more even than the fire service. Now Berry say he want to move in in a two-bedroom house in town, leave that little shack side the canes that I did love so much. He say we can't be living in there no more, cause now I did find myself pregnant again, and he say we can't be living in there. But Mistress Grandsol, truth is I was thinking to <u>throw</u> this child. When I think of all the trouble this man put me through already. I did think to throw this child. But then Berry was so happy for this child, he did shout so much, he get me most to feeling happy too. I decide to bear the child. I say I would do it for he.

We move out from we little house, we move in in the two-bedroom house in town, and soon enough I get the next child. A girlchild again. I name she Joyce. I did think if I could put that name pon she, you know things might go back to good. We could go back to good again. But Mistress Grandsol, things don't go back to good at all. Things did go to more <u>worse</u> still. Cause now that woman that Berry put in hospital, that same prostitute woman that he did beat so bad, now she come behind he again. But not to carry he before the Magis. No Mistress Grandsol. This time she come behind he to carry he in she <u>bed</u>. Next thing I know Berry ain't coming home. He gone and living with this woman in she house.

5

Now come the scourge and blight, the worst, cause I got the children to feed, and not a thing to feed them with. That's the hardest thing in this life Mistress Grandsol. The hardest thing that I ever know. Harder even than death I think, cause that come like the <u>living</u>-death. To watch a child go hungry. To look at hunger in a child eyes. I pick up them children and I go back to Granny Ansin house in the country. I go back to working the canes, and things go back to good awhile. Well not good, but better still. Least them children could get little something to eat now. Most the time. Cause so much of children in that house to feed. So much! You know my younger sister she had about one–two already, and my children, and some my tan children was living still in the house too. And now granny getting old, she can't work so good as before, so is me one had to work to feed all these children. But I did cutting the canes now, not cleaning, cutting longside the mens, and you could make a good piece of money like that. Cutting the canes. Long as the strength last. And I <u>make</u> it last! I ain't got no choice Mistress

39

Grandsol, cause only other choice is go hungry. That starvation. I *make* the strength last. Work every day. Then all in a sudden the canes finish. Finish for good. Cause now the sugar industry gone bust. Wasn't no more canes left to cut.

Everybody suffer for that. Wealthy people and poor people too. Everybody. And you know when the wealthy people suffer, the poor ones suffer all the worst. Was the most Ansin and me could do to keep things together. Keep them children fed. That's when I did first start to work as servant, at that time, me and Ansin. Sometimes we catch a day-job with one the wealthy mistress in town. We could catch a few cents. But them jobs don't come too regular, not to *depend* on. Them jobs don't come too regular at all.

So that's when Berry start to coming in by the house again. Just when we reach the worst, Berry appear out from nowhere and he with food in he hands. Well I didn't even want to *see* he! Amount of hell that man put me through. But Mistress Grandsol, I *had* to let he in. I didn't have no choice. Cause that's the onliest way them children could catch little something to eat. The onliest way. Berry say he and the woman get a break-up, that prostitute woman that he beat, that he did living with. I tell he I don't *care*. I don't care cause I ain't *never* want to see he face again. Never!

But next thing he start to charm me again. Not only me, he charm Ansin, the children, everybody! He charm the bunch of we easy as rattles *off* a snake. Berry say how he did change. Say how he reading life different now. Then come the best one. Berry say how he want to *married* with me! Mistress Grandsol, I laugh straight in he face for that. I say I would *never* married with he. Not till hell catch fire! Then Berry explain how if we could married, then we could put in the claim for one them new houses government did offering then in the Family Plannings. *Concrete* houses, not board, and them houses have in pipes in the kitchen. *Pipes*! And I never see pipes before in no house but the whitepeople own.

I tell Berry we could married. We could married and move in in the Plannings, cause I can't live no more in that old house with scorpions running under the floor. But just as I say, never trust in government. Cause Mistress Grandsol, that Plannings wasn't no better than granny old house in the country, never mind it concrete. That concrete house wasn't no better at all. But still we fix up that house and them furnishings. We go back to living life good again. Berry behaving heself good again. Ok. Cause now he had to be driving that taxicar all the time, working all the time, now we had to pay every month pon house and furnishings both. *Seventeen* dollars! We had so much to pay, I take a day-job too, working at Mistress Pantin house. She didn't have no children, and I say she did miss that, cause is Mistress Pantin-self watch the children most the time whilst I work.

Next thing I find myself pregnant again, this the fourth time. I didn't want no more children. I make up my mind to throw this child. But just like the last time, I make the mistake to tell Berry. He shout so much and feeling so happy for that, he did get me most to feeling good too. Just like the last time, I say I would bear this child for Berry. I would do it for he. I say least now we living in concrete house, no scorpions under the boards, with plenty room, so I say I would bear the child. And I pray to God make this one a boychild for Berry sake, give he a boychild for he. Cause that's the best way to keep a man in the house. Keep he to behaving heself good. I pray to give Berry a son for he.

But Mistress Grandsol, I could never know what I did asking for when I ask for that. I could never know! Cause Berry did _already_ preparing heself to have a boychild then. At that same time, and with that same woman that he did beat. That same woman that he did living with. Is _she_ give Berry the boychild, he first son. And this child did _pretty_! Bright bright bright, and so pretty! This child come out near white. Cause I see this child. Everybody see he. This woman don't _finish_ from going round the place showing-off pon he. Boasting pon he. She use this child to get Berry back with she, the woman did. Next thing I know Berry ain't coming home again. He pick up and left me there with Junie, and my belly out to here with next one coming. Now I got to pay that house and them furnitures both, with only my day-job at Mistress Pantin.

Well I take that few cents that I catch, but I don't use that to pay-out the house. No Mistress Grandsol. That go to buy the quinine. Cause now I _got_ to throw this child. Ain't got no choice but try to throw this child. And I try everything. Everything that I could think. Obeah, bush-medicine, _everything_. But the most is quinine. I swallow down so much of that nasty thing! Till I did think that quinine would abort _me_! But don't do nothing for this child. Nothing. And have me feeling so weak, so dizzy, and working every day at Mistress Pantin to buy more quinine.

Next thing when I ain't looking little Junie gone and playing in the WC with all them toilets overflowing. The _public_ WC, of that Plannings, and Mistress Grandsol, that place so _nasty_. You never see nothing in you life so nasty as the WC of that Plannings! And when I ain't looking little Junie gone and playing in there. That toilet water and all that extrement. You know _extrement_, Mistress Grandsol? Little Junie did playing in all that extrement. That make she sick. Time as I take Junie to doctor she could scarce stand she was so weak, and fever burning a pitch. Doctor take one look and he say Junie suffering the cholera. Cholera that was going round that whole Plannings then. Doctor say I got to get she way from all that extrement, I got to carry she from that Plannings.

6

I take Junie up and I go straight in the country again at my Granny Ansin. I tell Ansin Junie sick, with cholera, say we got to stand the whole night tending pon she. But that was too late. That was already too late for that cholera. Cause Junie die before morning reach. The _shock_ Mistress Grandsol, mid say was the shock of Junie death send me straight in childbed. That same day that we bury Junie. Cause I went straight in childbed that same day. But that child born living, Mistress Grandsol. He did small, mid call it premature, but I _know_ he did living! I know cause I take he up in my own hands. I did _had_ to take up he.

But when I find that he did dead too, like Junie, when I _see_ he bury under the mango tree behind the house too, that thing did went at my nerve. Went straight at my nerve, Mistress Grandsol. I just didn't want to be living no more. Not with my babies dead like that! I just didn't want to live. I take up the big bottle of peroxide and I just drink it down. Straight down. I ain't stopping till that whole bottle drink. Onliest thing is they find me there, foaming at my mouth, they carry me in the hospital pump that peroxide out from my stomach. But Mistress Grandsol, you could never recover from that peroxide so easy. Not so quick. They had to keep me in the hospital after that. But I was in the psycob now, cause they say I gone crazy. I gone crazy and try to kill myself. They say I had to be in that psycob. I had to see the trink-doctor.

And that's when I come to know Dr B. Dr B is my trink-doctor. But he couldn't keep me in that psycob. Not much. I was only in there a week and he tell me I can't be in there. He say ain't nothing wrong with me. I can't be in there. That Dr B did talk to me so good. So _kind_. He say Vel, you need a change in you life. You need to get way from here. You need to travel. I say yes, Doctor! I would love that, I would love that very much! To travel someplace! But then when he leave I say, I say to myself, Vel, how you could travel any place? How you could _ever_ escape from here? Escape from you life?

That's just when we receive the letter too, same time as I reach home from that psycob. Cause that letter was there already waiting just like a wish for me. A wish for my life! Di letter saying how you going need a next servant. Well I say that person could be me. That person could only be me, Mistress Grandsol! I got a presentiment for that. That we going get along real good together. I most sure! And that's when Dr B tell me I must write this letter. This same letter. Dr B say I must write _everything_. That you could know just who is the person I am. That you could know just how bad I need the job. How bad I need to escape from this Sherman, be with you, Mistress Grandsol. I _need_ to be with you.

Well now the letter write. Everything. Only one last thing that I could tell you so you could know. One last thing. Di say in she letter how she must leave you now cause she pregnant. She haveen with child. She bound to leave even after all these years of working with you. Well one thing I could promise Mistress Grandsol, one thing that I could _swear_, sure as this pencil I holding, sure as these marks pon this page. I would _never_ do that. You needn't to worry about that, cause you would never see me pregnant again. Not in _this_ life! Not after watching them children dead pon my hands. Is _me_ would have to dead first, cause this breast could never hold that grief again. Never never never.

Cordial,
Vel

Sitting here with my back against the headboard, pressed uncomfortably against the knobby headboard, studying the dozen or so leaves of brittle, transparent onionskin held here in my hands. Lines upon lines of clearly penciled cursive. Words laid down as though upon water. Pages sinking through the depths like memories through the mind, ever-dissolving yet indelible, a woman's life, my still-trembling fingers. Wondering: *But how can I not have read this letter properly before? In ten years? How can I have lived for so long with someone and known her so well, so intimately, yet not have known her a-tall?* Wondering: *Though perhaps she had to teach me to read it first? To "read" as she says. In her way. And not simply her life: my own. Perhaps, till now, till this very moment, I'd been incapable? Perhaps this letter has remained there hidden in that bedstand drawer all these years waiting for me?*

Folding the pages carefully now along their own two memorized creases, the bottom third folded between, and gathering up the chits of the various certificates strewn cross my lap; fitting them all carefully back inside the tattered envelope. Placing it here on the bedstand beside me. Beside the open bottle of Limacol. The actual fragrance of memory, West Indian memory, washing through the room. Sitting here with my back pressed uncomfortably against the knobby headboard, thinking: *But how could Vel have let herself get pregnant again? How possibly, after all that? And not even how: by whom?*

Counting back the five months: *August.* But that was June, July? Early one Sunday morning, a peculiar woman knocking at the door: "*Hoo-hoo! Madam Grandsol, hoo-hoo!*" Not two minutes after Vel had left the house for her church service in town. I could see the top of this woman's hat through the window of the landing upstairs: an enormous white straw hat, red straw roses circling the brim. A *church* hat, I thought. She must be one of Vel's fellow parishioners, come to collect her for service, two minutes too late. But why was she calling out to *me*? Perhaps she was mad, I reconsidered, freshly escaped from the madhouse? (They come round occasionally Bolom, really the only visitors we ever get.) But this woman knew me by *name*? Certainly if I ignored her, I decided, she'd go away. She did not. Pounding her fist again and again against the door. Her awful, high-pitched, *screeching* voice:

"Hoo-hoo! Madam Grandsol, hoo-hoo!"

Eventually I descend the stairs, turn the key in the lock, creak the door open a crack.

She bursts in, shoving the door up against my chest, very nearly knocking me over backward. A *big* woman. Not wide: *tall*. Every bit of six feet. Now I'm quite afraid—alone in the house without Vel. Now I'm *certain* this woman is mad, mad as the stars. I've never seen such a hideous-looking creature in all my life. A curly platinum wig beneath the hat, the hat-tie arranged beneath her chin in a huge floppy bow. The skin of her face a peculiar copper-red, with a daintily freckled nose and smudges of rouge on her cheeks, bright red lipsticked lips. Loaded-down with jewelry, garish costume jewelry: earrings and necklaces and rings worn on the *outside* of her white cotton gloves. A glittering broach shaped like a sailing ship pinned to one point of her colossal bosom. With the sleeves of her peculiar gown inflated like two bal-loons, crepe ruffles running from her neckline right the way down to the hem—a foot too short, exposing thin ankles bunched in dusty hose, dusty high-heel shoes once coloured a fire-engine-red. There's a matching handbag dangling from one arm. And tucked under the other, a rather large tinned ham, which she now thrusts at me: a pres-ent for myself and Vel.

She introduces herself as Ansin, Vel's Granny Ansin, come quite from Sherman to visit her granddaughter. "But the bus break down a little ways past Couva," she informs me. "You know how them buses always breaking down? With me walking most the whole night to reach here this morning, and in them high-heel shoe!" She lifts a foot into the air, gesturing toward it.

"You must come rest yourself at once!" I say, flustered, quite aston-ished. I shift the tin to one hand and take her elbow with the other, leading her into the parlour. "Unfortunately," I say, "Vel's just gone to church, but she'll be back shortly."

Granny Ansin seats herself in one of the wicker chairs, blowing out an extended "*She-e-e-w!*" Suddenly I'm afraid the chair's going to crumble beneath her. She slips off her shoes, exposing a big toe pro-truding through a hole in one of her nylons.

"Could smell that callaloo cooking all the way from Couva," she says. "That girl could cook a callaloo, ain't so, Madam Grandsol?"

"You'll have to have some with us!" I say.

"Oh, that would be very nice, Madam Grandsol. And we could eat on that ham too." She nods at the tin in my hands, looking quite hungry indeed.

"Unless you'd like a cup now?" I say after a moment's silence, at a loss for anything else. "Tide you over a bit till Vel arrives? You must be *famished* after such a walk!"

"That would be very nice, Madam Grandsol. I would take just a little cup whilst we waiting. Just a little cup. And a glass of cool water, Madam Grandsol."

I'm happy to disappear for a few minutes into the kitchen. I ladle out a big bowl of the simmering callaloo, couple crabclaws, fill a tall glass with water, and I arrange everything with a linen napkin on the tarnished silver tray. Carry it out to Granny Ansin.

"Oh, thank you," she says. "I plenty famish in truth, Madam Grandsol. Just as you say."

I set the tray down on a side table, then excuse myself to return to the kitchen, realizing I've forgotten the soupspoon. Bolom, by the time I get back she's finished the entire bowl of soup, in addition to sucking the crabclaws *dry*—and without even removing her gloves! I stand there in a state of shock—holding the spoon in both hands like a microphone I'm about to sing into—watching her dab away the green moustache from her upper lip. Then she takes up the tall glass of water, drinking it down in three gulps, without even a pause between for a breath of air. She dabs at her mouth daintily again.

"Maybe a next little cup," she says. "I plenty famish in truth, Madam Grandsol. Just as you say."

Two more trips to the kitchen; two more bowls of callaloo. Eventually I carry the entire *jorum* out to the parlour. And now, Bolom, an extraordinary spectacle: Granny Ansin takes the huge pot from me in both her hands—clad in the white gloves with all the rings—tips it up to her mouth, and she drains the jorum down to the dregs! She hands it back to me, wipes the green residue from her lips, and she sends me back to the kitchen for another glass of water.

I fill up two, two tall glasses to the rims, but by the time I return to Granny Ansin she's fast asleep, snoring out loud. Only then do I realize she hasn't even removed her hat, its tie still arranged in the floppy bow beneath her chin. With her hands in the little white gloves she's not bothered to remove either, folded neatly on her lap, each fingertip stained a mossy-green.

I sit for a few minutes in the chair facing her, but I'm so disconcerted by the sight of this Granny Ansin snoring away—her mouth drooping wide open, smudged with lipstick—that I get up again to carry the tray into the kitchen. Then I set the table for lunch—which can only be the ham: we've nothing else to eat in the house. An *English* tinned ham. It's marked *FANCY, SPECIAL.* Bolom, I've not seen a tinned ham like this in years, perhaps not since before the war. It slices beneath the knife as smooth as *butter.* So appetizing, indeed, that I cannot *help* but try a piece. Just one little slice. Just two little slices. Three. *Four.* Bolom, it's as though Granny Ansin's ravenous appetite is contagious. Suddenly *I'm* the one who's plenty famished, stuffing the ham greedily into my mouth with *both* hands! Which is just how Vel finds me (in the confusion I've left the door wide open, swinging off its hinges): standing there in the kitchen like a wicked child, both my cheeks inflated with ham, fingers dripping, chewing and smiling ear-to-ear at the same time.

Vel, though, is not smiling *a-tall.* She examines the tin on the counter. "Where this come from?" she asks. "*England* tin ham? We ain't got no money for England tin ham!"

I'm still chewing, swallowing. "You've a surprise visitor," I say, catching my breath. "All the way from Sherman!"

"*Surprise visitor?* How I could have a *surprise visitor?*" She looks up from the tin. "You let he in here? You let that man come in in this house?"

"What *man,* Vel? It's your Granny Ansin!"

"*Ansin?* My *Granny Ansin?* And where my Granny Ansin is now?"

"In the parlour. Waiting for you in the parlour, Vel."

"And is my Granny Ansin big and tall? Is my Granny Ansin red-skin, a red-skin negro?" She chupses. "You ain't know that woman is Berry! That woman is Berry-*self,* dress-up in heself ganga! You let he to fool you like that?"

She takes off charging out the kitchen. With me suddenly so confused—suddenly so unnerved by all this—all I can think to do is to stuff another slice of ham. Bolom, I'm chewing the last piece fifteen minutes later when Vel returns. My jaw actually in pain. Dizzy from the lack of oxygen. Nauseous. Absolutely *bloated* having stuffed that *entire* tin of tinned ham!

"Mistress Grandsol," she says quietly, visibly disgusted. "Go and lock that front door proper. And don't you *never* let that man in this house again. Don't care if he come carrying a *cow!*"

8

By the time evening arrives I'm not feeling a-tall well. I lock myself into my room for the night earlier than usual. It's as though that ham is expanding inside my stomach. *Blowing-up*—a Christmas pudding plopped in boiling water. It's pressing against my lungs so I can scarcely breathe. I'm dizzy. Nauseous. (Though I will *not* permit myself to regurgitate the only meat Vel and I have seen in weeks, Bolom! Cannot *forgive* myself for gorging it all so monstrously!) I lie there bloated, groaning, seriously in pain. Holding my swollen belly with both hands. The only way I can stop the room from spinning is to let one leg hang over the side of the bed, my foot flat on the flooring. Bolom, I must have lain there like that half the night: feverish. Sweating. Absolutely delirious. The whole of that tinned ham inflating inside my stomach.

Suddenly, as if from a distance, I hear the creaking sound of splintering wood. I roll my head to the side, looking toward the window: climbing in through the gap between the jalousies is the most horrific, the most terrifyingly *beautiful* creature I've ever laid eyes upon. His skin the colour of terra-cotta—but shining like burnished metal, like the underside of a copper saucepan. His eyes and mouth and flaring nostrils a bright wet red. Hair positively *orange*. His chest and neck and arms glazed in sweat, glistening beneath the moonlight. *Rippling* with muscle beneath his glistening, glazed skin—the way strands of a ship's rope twist upon themselves wringing out water, stretched agonizingly tight. A demon dressed head-to-toe in burnished glazed glistening flaming skin!

In my state of delirium he's stark naked—he's actually bareback, wearing black trousers. In my state of delirium he's not even *human:* he's the phantom Bazil, the Jab-Jab, Satan himself climbing in through the jalousies into my room. He walks round to the end of the bed.

Turns slowly. Stands there staring down upon me with his chest heaving, nostrils flaring, his eyes flaming bright red. With me lying there before him not only stripped naked, but with my legs spread wide apart! Splayed wide open! And Bolom, I cannot move a *muscle!* The most I can manage is to shut my eyes. To lie there waiting with my heart pounding—a crazed little animal throwing itself up against the bars of my ribcage. Breathless. My stomach so painfully bloated only an instant before, suddenly the opposite: hollowed out, weightless, flying up over the summit of a sharp, steep hill. The bed suddenly dropping out from under me.

Nothing happens, Bolom. Nothing a-tall. Only the sensation of his hot breath for a moment against the side of my cheek, saturated with rank rum. A sharp tug against the back of my neck, and I feel his hot breath move away, withdraw. Now I open my eyes to see him bent over the lock of my bedroom door. In the moonlight, through the shimmering watery atmosphere of my delirium I watch him open the door and close it again behind him. And by the time I jump from the bed and run to throw myself up against the closed door, I can hear the key turning in the lock on the other side.

Locked into my own room, trapped! Unable even to go to Vel's aid below—locked now inside the house with this phantom Bazil, with this red Satan! This man she calls Berry—*her husband*—because now I know he's real enough. *Dangerously* real. Now I realize he's the same man who'd come to the house only a few hours before, hideously disguised as a woman.

Bolom, I cannot tell you how long I sat there on the flooring that night—dripping in sweat, my knees pulled up tight against my chest—back pressed flat against the door. Perhaps I waited an hour, perhaps three. Confused, desperate. Trying my best not to think of the horrors I could only imagine *must* be taking place below. Listening anxiously to the silent house: because in truth, I did not hear a sound the whole time.

The truth is that I cannot tell you what took place in Vel's bedroom that night. Between Vel and that man. That horrific, painfully beautiful Bazil. Because I did not ask her. That night or ever. And Vel chose never to tell me: not a *word*. When I finally heard the three soft taps of her knuckle that night on the door behind my back—an hour later or three—and I jumped to my feet and turned round for Vel to unlock the door and hand me back the key—my own golden skeleton key—she did not say a word. And before I could even look up into her face for an instant for some sign as to what had taken place—*rape or submission or seduction or nothing a-tall*—she'd already shut the door behind her. Leaving me standing there staring blankly at the closed door, summoning all the courage in me to raise my trembling hand only a little. To turn the key in the lock again.

9

Only she knows, Bolom. Only Vel can tell you who your father is: I cannot. Because the truth is that Vel never gave me the slightest indication. The truth is that I never even suspected Vel was pregnant. Not before a few hours ago. And why should I have, Bolom? How *could* I possibly have suspected that Vel was pregnant, when I've never seen her with a man? Never once heard her talk about a man. When there've been no men in this house. *A-tall.* Not for the whole of these ten years we've lived here together.

Only that night. That *once:* it can only have been him, Bolom. That painfully beautiful Bazil. Berry. Vel's *husband* (because so far as I know they're still legally married). It can only have been that terrifying night. That bizarre day: to have met him first disguised as a *woman*—as Vel's Granny Ansin! And to have been so completely taken in by him. That hideous hat, the wig of platinum ringlets, the hideous makeup. That peculiar frilly gown and all the jewelry, the pointy breasts. Raising the jorum of callaloo to his mouth in both hands, his white cotton gloves with the moss-stained fingertips! How can he have fooled me so utterly?

Returning that night transformed into the red devil. Breaking into the house the quickest, the simplest way possible; climbing up the drainpipe, in through the jalousies of my own bedroom window. Transformed now into *himself:* that terrifyingly beautiful Bazil. Horrific and beautiful both. Agonizingly beautiful. I can see, Bolom, how Vel might *swoon* behind such a man. I can understand well enough: your father.

Yet that was June? Late June or early July? And Vel distinctly said five months. Repeated it as though she were certain. As though she'd no doubts what-so-ever: *five months*. But that would've been *August?* Unless, perhaps, Vel miscounted? As she may well have? Miscalculated? Because Bolom, as I look down upon her now—as I study her dark figure lying here in the dark beside me—her belly does seem awfully enlarged for five months' gestation. Big and purple as a batchaks' nest! Lying here beside me with the pillows still stuffed beneath her buttocks, her breasts and belly rolling backward toward her shoulders. *Awfully* enlarged for five months' gestation. (And counting back again to triple-check—December, November, October, September, *August*— yes, five fingers; months; surely Vel miscounted.)

There's simply been no other men around. No other males. None, at least, that *I* know anything about. Here in *this* house. The little coolie-crabboy who comes by Sundays. Who sells us—or *gives* us more often than not, since we've not the money—the two blue monsters for our Sunday callaloo. The old bacra-johnny who comes round every few weeks, crawling under the gallery to sleep the night. Stumbling out the following morning with his bottle in one hand, his tattered cro- cusssack-blanket dragging behind him in the other—a cloud of yellow dust crossing the yard in the bright morning sun. With Vel and me standing there together at the kitchen sink, peering out through the window, giggling like two adolescent girls. Watching him cross the yard and stop—without fail—beneath the flamboyant tree. Letting go his blanket and putting down his bottle carefully for his ritual urination: a series of sharp, quick squirts, splashed against the base of the trunk— always exactly *fifteen* in number. With Vel and me standing there before the kitchen sink, arms wrapped round each other, peering through the window counting them out—*thirteen-fourteen-fifteen!*—and bursting into a fit of giggling like two adolescent girls.

No, Bolom. It could not possibly have been that old, stale-drunk bacra-johnny. Nor the little coolie-crabboy. Not possibly. It could only have been Berry. That painfully beautiful Berry. Your father. And is that so bad? Is that so awful, Bolom? After all, mightn't you have that same skin? That red burnished-copper skin? *Orange* hair? Those freckles on your nose. Mightn't you have those same dainty freckles on your nose!

10

Though, in truth, you've no father a-tall, Bolom. Because when you stop to consider it, does one hour or three—or three minutes or five of grunting darkness—does that constitute a *father?* You've really none a-tall. Perhaps though, rather than a father, you've a second mother? One black, one white; one African, one European. Two mothers and no father: somehow that strikes me as perfectly sensible. As perfectly *West Indian,* Bolom. (After all, between mummy and Di, I had two mothers and no father; and between the authentic Granny Ansin and Mrs Pantin, Vel, it seems to me, had two mothers and no father also.) Three of us, here together in this old, broken-down Colonial house. In this room with the rusty tin ceiling, the moss-eaten rotting rafters. That huge maidenhair-fern leafing out bold-faced above our heads. Three of us here together in this bed: somehow that strikes me as perfectly West Indian, Bolom.

Leaning forward and reaching out carefully now toward Vel. Placing my left palm flat against the downward curve of her round, taut belly. Between the deep indentation of her navel and her scrub of coarse pubic hair. Pressing softly. Carefully. And feeling that small yet unmistakable palpitation within: alive, still. Even against all the expertise of all the sciences. All the age-old wisdom. The forbidden female knowledge whispered mother-to-daughter and sister-to-sister across continents, seas, time. This child willing to defy its own fate. *Our* collective Caribbean fate. History. Faith.

Closing my eyes a moment in order to see it more clearly. To believe it more fervently. Pausing for a moment to feel more sensuously the breaths of cool seabreeze brushing over my naked skin. Listening to the water rolling up over the moss-carpeted rocks. Retreating again. That tiny palpitation. Spark of life. Large as the sea itself.

Sitting here with my eyes closed, my hand pressed softly against Vel's belly. Thinking, pronouncing the words aloud:

"My dear, dear Vel."

"*My* Bolom."

Balling up my right hand hard into a tight fist. Pulling sharply against the threadbare strip of black ribbon round my neck: burst.

Opening my eyes and sliding my left hand up over the curve of Vel's belly, over the indentation of her navel, up into the crevice between her backward-spilling breasts. My untrembling fingers searching there among the obeah shard of mirror, the small silver crucifix, and finding the strip of fishingtwine. My calm, untrembling fingers forming a small loop with the twine, barely visible in the dark. Passing the loop up through the ring of the key, down over the point, up along the key's length. Pulling it snug. A loop within a loop: intertwined inextricably. Locked together. My fingers letting go, after long last, letting go. The gift given. After long last.

first chaplet

d'Esperance Estate

*"That's her story. I don't believe it. A frivolous woman.
In your mother's place I'd resent her behaviour."
"None of you understand about us," I thought.*

Jean Rhys,
Wide Sargasso Sea

The Smell of Glass

1

Is that I remember, Bolom. Glasspane. For me it has a smell. Silvery and powdery and cool, even in strangulating heat. Smell of a moth's wings. From nine in the morning till four in the afternoon. Every day except Sunday, when I marched off with mummy to the first Mass. Perched as always on my pedestal of storybooks—still downstairs, I presume, still unread—Enid Blyton, and Hans Christian Andersen, and the Grimm brothers. The years of my childhood measured out in the number of volumes piled up to reach the window. Five: seven. Six: five. Seven: four. Standing there with my nose squinged-up flat against it, my weight leaning into the point of my chin, the twin-lobed cloud of vapor appearing and disappearing with each little breath. The silver moth pinned on its back between my lips and the glass, beating forever against my cheeks.

No one ever told me why Di, my nursemaid, called me in and fed me a slice of bake dribbled with golden syrup. Dressed me in my frock, and locked me into my little room every morning. Why Dulcianne,

Di's daughter and my only friend, was permitted to carry on running beneath the cocoa trees wearing nothing but her knickers. Scrambling through the tall canes behind my own beloved Daisy—a kind of straggly chicken we called a clean-neck-fowl—given to me by the overseer, Ramsingh. Somehow I sensed the mandate came from mummy. It was a look of glossy fear I sometimes caught on her face. I sensed it, too, in the way Di combed out my single braid—Cook said I had "bad" hair—always hurry hurry. Whereas she fussed over mummy's for hours. Then one day, curled up in the shadow of the tall green safe, I overheard Cook talking to Di in the kitchen: "Eh-eh, but you see how the blight does always fall pon the fourth generation? Blat-blanch, eh? White *koo-ca-roach!* Ain't no wonder madam wouldn't let she in the sun." She spoke in her chipped-up Dominican accent. Di chupsed as I took off running.

The sun, Bolom. I never saw it. For the whole of my childhood. So at seventeen when I went to England I actually caught sunstroke—actually pitched a faint! Standing atop one of those open-air, doubledecker buses for the tourists. Imagine: going to *England* to catch sunstroke. But it wasn't as though the sun could darken my skin in any case, not so a-tall. Simply turn it a bruised-up version of the same dusty grey. And by next morning the bruise'd be gone. Skin which never declared or disclaimed itself. Which never washed *clean.* One way or another.

But hidden away in my little room the sun could never reach me. Not my *bed*room, you understand; that was upstairs, on the first floor, cross from the kitchen. This was a basement room—*half*-basement, I suppose—so that my window looked out only a little above ground level. Its frame had been nailed shut for as long as I had known. Probably to keep out thieves, perhaps manicou—the monstrous, ratlike creatures which wandered in from the swamps at night, curried by the coolies and eaten with great relish. My window was covered with dust on the other side. Cobwebs with desiccated insects mummified at the corners. Before it there was yellowish dirt. A few dead-up weeds which'd surrendered to the lack of light. Above it stretched the wide, roofed-in gallery, running right round the house. In early morning gaps between the boards created a pattern on the dirt. Long slashes of yellow light, shifting slowly as the sun shifted positions. The glass of my window seemed itself to have yellowed, the picture of my childhood an old photograph even before I got to it.

In one corner there was a small graveyard of rubbish which'd been left rusting beneath the gallery: an old washtub, bicycle frame, a stack of sheets of corrugated zinc, an overturned plow with its rusted orange hooks clawing up blindly into the air. My window faced the back of the house, so I could see the block of concrete which I knew to be the back steps on the other side. And on my side, hidden from the rest of the world, a bunch of old crocusssacks spread out where I imagined a lagahoo—our version of a troll, but deer-footed—would crawl in under the gallery every night to sleep. For years Dulcianne kept me well geegeeree with her plan to crawl under ourselves after dark. Me holding up a bule-de-fay behind her, she a lasso to sling round his neck like a Yankee-cowboy.

From my window, between the graveyard and the concrete block of steps, I could see a long rectangle of bright light. A wall of bluegreen guineagrass sloping up behind it. (And if I closed my eyes tight tight to drown out the cicadas' sharp shrill, I could just hear the water beating against the rocks a hundred yards beyond; and I could almost see the brilliant glittering blue that is only the Caribbean Sea, wedge of a white sailingship shoving her way cross the horizon.) Within the illuminated rectangle, time to time, I watched the household coming and going. Mostly Di and Cook and Ramsingh, and on occasion mummy—her corseted eighteen-inch waist, of which she was so proud. Due to the pitch of the ground, the position of the gallery overhead, I could see only the middles of their bodies. From just above their knees to just below their ribcages. I became an expert on the swing of hips. Could tell whether Di was in a sweet or a sour mood, only by the bounce of her bamsee.

In the parlour there was an ancient grandfather's clock which chimed the hours. I could hear it too easily through the ceiling of my room. Every day I counted down fifty-two chimes! At precisely ten o'clock Miss Rupert arrived, and for two hours she'd give me lessons. In middle age, and on the wings of a horned engagement to marry, she'd been sent out from England to look after her widowed father. Mummy said she considered the tropics her own *purgatoire-privé*. I remember only her hands. They were perfectly shaped and ivory white, but what I remember best was the rubber thimble she wore on the index finger of her right hand. She used it to turn the pages of my books. It was pinkish-coloured and gummy-looking, the sort of thing bankclerks wore to count out stacks of money.

In my room I'd a miniature desk and chair, Miss Rupert an adult chair. She'd sit quietly at my side, leaning down a little to teach me the basic skills. Reading I found a boratious stunt. The stories so flothy and tamified, though I caught on effortlessly enough. The only pages I ever saw were the ones read under Miss Rupert's supervision, her gallanting rubber thimble pouncing on each poor word as I pronounced it aloud. I much preferred writing and sums, taking great pains in drawing out my letters and numbers. Particularly after I discovered that their character changed slightly depending upon which colour they were drawn in. A green 7 was not a yellow 7, which was somehow wantish. A red *A* was quite different from a strong blue *A*. This part of my lessons I quite enjoyed, as I enjoyed pleasing Miss Rupert. She was kind, and patient, though I sensed she considered me and all about me somewhat tragic. Somewhat at a loss for hope. She looked forward to the finish of our two hours together, almost as much as I did.

The highpoint of my day was when Di brought my breakfast. Soon after Miss Rupert left. (For some peculiar reason we always called lunch *breakfast*—breakfast *lunch*.) I sat in my chair and she in the adult one, facing each other. Di feeding me with a big silver tablespoon. I could feed myself easily enough, but I preferred Di to do it, only to have her there. Usually I'd have a piece of fried fish or fricassee chicken, a slice of steaming buttered christophine, always a pressed dome of white rice. Always there'd be a tall glass of coconut water, my dessert the sweet jelly remaining at the bottom once I'd drunk it down. Sometimes Di'd feed me the jelly using the same silver tablespoon. Or she'd leave me there with the tall glass upturned against my lips, my little hand reaching out to pat the bottom, till the jelly came sliding into my mouth.

Just as when she put me to sleep, Di would tell me stories while she fed me. Tales of the forest full of obeah and magic. Or she'd sing old calypsos in the patois I could not fully understand, though I thrilled at their slow, slanky rhythms. From the occasional wicked smile on her face, I knew her songs were well rude. The one about the lézard that got lost beneath the mademoiselle's froufrou! I'd tarry about my breakfast long as I could. Di, though, would often be in a flap. She'd have to get upstairs to set the table for mummy and daddy, frequently their guests too. To serve them their own breakfast.

Other than my miniature desk and chair, my books and coloured pencils and paper, I'd a huge chest in my room filled with all the toys and dolls sent by my English granny. None of these things interested me in the least, and I'd've happily traded them all away to have Daisy with me. To watch her scuttle back and forth with her ratty head bobbing. Feed her grains of rice one by one from between my lips, little kisses. With Daisy to play with, I might have even found my little room tolerable. I spent my time staring out the window. Mostly at nothing a-tall. Would wait two hours only to watch Cook's chuffy middle pass by for two seconds. On occasion an iridescent hummingbird would swoop beneath the gallery. A zandolee lizard'd zip past. On occasion I'd be entertained an hour at a stretch, a landcrab laboriously digging his hole.

2

I got into the habit of saying my chaplet. Not that I could've actually been praying, Bolom. Simply bored. Perhaps I only did it in imitation of mummy. Daddy—who pronounced Catholic *Cartholic,* and spoke of all things related with contempt—daddy called it "rolling beads." As though it were some sort of feminine neurosis mummy had inherited. His jokes (overheard through the crack of the parlour door, my parents with visitors on the gallery shaking-up sunset rum-cocktails), his jokes were always a bit sad, really. Always a betrayal of my father's own frustrations: "Jacqueline was so busy rolling beads she almost missed her honeymoon!" and, "We'd have a slew of stragglers by now, if Jacqueline weren't so busy rolling beads!" It was a sense of impotency I perceived in his voice even at my young age. The only mental picture I have of the two of them together, the way I saw them on evenings when Di sent me running upstairs to kiss them goodnight: daddy sitting up beneath the lamp with the big estate ledger in his lap, stub of a pencil in his oversized hand, his brow furrowed; mummy supine in the dark, her right hand extended from the mattress with her chaplet dangling, gold cross glinting at the end. But most evenings daddy wouldn't have even reached his bed as yet. He'd still be out in the boilinghouse lambasting the poor coolies. On such evenings I'd crawl up into the big bed beside mummy, and we'd say our beads together. Sometimes half the night, till daddy arrived.

Mummy's chaplet was pure gold. She'd had it blessed by the Pope himself on a pilgrimage to the Vatican. But my own was strung from tiny black pem-pem seeds—a local bush—with a silver crucifix at the end. I wore it like a necklace round my neck. It was a game I played with Dulcianne. That way, we told one another, a soukuyant could never suck our blood—the West Indian version of vampires, except soukuyants undressed their skins to become roving balls of fire, and in this shape they sucked their victims' necks. Dulcianne always brought a shaker of salt with her to the river, ready to sprinkle the soukuyants' curled-up skins, should we happen to find one. That became our defense against soukuyants: Dulcianne's shaker of salt, my own prayer-beads.

I always wore my chaplet round my neck, and after a time, quite by accident, I got in the habit of saying it. Standing there every morning with my nose squinged-up against the glass. It became a habit even before I realized. Sometimes I'd say the Holy Marys silently, sometimes I'd mumble them, sometimes I'd say them aloud. But I'm sure I never thought about the actual words—any more than I'd've stopped to study the lyrics of *God Save We Queen*. I scarcely even thought about what my lips and my fingers were doing. And when I bounced-up on the final Glory Be, I began again without realizing either.

There was a brief period though—perhaps it lasted a week—when I did pray my chaplet in earnest. I was eight years of age. First time, so far as I remember, that I actually became conscious of myself in my little room. Though I came to this awareness for very different reasons. My trouble started at Christmas Day Mass.

For the holidays we always received a chest from my English granny. It arrived weeks in advance, waiting beneath the staircase in the foyer for the actual day, the highlight of which was the ceremonious bursting of its metal bands. Always there was a wooden box of shiny red apples (each wrapped in tissue and packed in straw), a triple-tiered box of Swiss chocolates, bottles of Spanish sherry and French champagne, tins of tea and English biscuits. Perhaps a frock for mummy, a waistcoat or necktie for daddy. The balance of the chest contained presents for me: frocks and slips and hats, ribbons and bows, books, coloured pencils and paper, tins of Lyle's Golden Syrup, dolls with yellow hair and crystalline blue eyes which closed when I put them to sleep. The only gift which interested me, this particular Christmas, was a mauve-coloured glassbottle of Dr Magic's Bathsalts, *Guaranteed to turn any skin soft and pearly white.* The gift itself was absurd: not only did we have a sea full of salt just beyond the back door, what we did *not* have was a bathtub. I immediately thought to shake out the salts on a soukuyant's skin. And if it were a negro one—to watch it magically change colour.

I didn't have to report to Di for her to dress me for Christmas Mass till twelve o'clock (usually I had to wait till after Mass to go with Dulcianne to the river). So soon as I could I disappeared with my prodigious glassbottle. Di and Dulcianne did not live in the barracks with the coolie laborers. They had their own little mudhut with a thatched roof, not far from our house. I hurried there and showed Dulcianne the bathsalts. We took off running along the old trace, past the boilinghouse, the huge waterwheel where the canes were pressed before daddy brought the shining steam engine from America—coughing and belching and scaring the poor coolies half to death!—the two of us running full-pelt till we reached the river. When we caught our breaths we began searching in all the familiar caves, in the holes and crevices between the rocks, on the smooth boulderstones beneath the overhanging trees. We could not find a single soukuyant's skin. In our frustration we tried the salts on other victims: a pale-blue rivercrab, pinkish crayfish, lime-green iguana. Each time we were further scandalized. Finally Dulcianne chupsed, complaining, "These damn salts ain't worth a windball!" And she dumped the remainder of the bottle down a crevice where she said she'd found soukuyants' skins before. She corked it back and pelted it hard against a boulderstone. It only bounced off and splashed into the water, the two of us leaning over the cliff with our hands on our knees, watching Dr Magic disappear down the river.

Time as I reached church I was dead exhausted. It was all I could do to keep from booting-off asleep. My head felt like a giant balloon filled with water, like it weighed a thousand pounds. I could scarcely keep it balanced on my thin neck. It kept threatening to tumble backward or forward, and I kept catching it at the last moment, jerking myself awake. The church was full to bursting. For half of them it was the only day they came all year long. My father was one; it was the standard Christmas present asked of him by mummy, that he accompany her to the High Mass. Usually—to mummy's mortification—he remained outside, parked directly beneath Sir Walter Raleigh's upraised sword in the middle of the main square. From our pew I could see him through the corner of my eyes, beyond the propped-up jalousies: washing and drying and shining his silver Ford motorcar, pumping the tires one by one. Till Mass was finished.

But this Christmas Day I sat squeezed between them. Our Irish Monsignor—we called him Bumblebee—took advantage of his captive audience and unleashed a homily full of fire and brimstone. To our favor he was incomprehensible anyway. Particularly when excited, particularly when he spoke *English*. I was caught in one of those sweet, tingling moments between asleep and awake. All in a sudden my head snapped forward, and it was as though I were hearing his voice for the first time: *"Every one of you who has performed a mixed marriage has committed a mortal sin!"*

Daddy moved to get up—he wanted to bolt—but mummy reached cross me and put her hand firmly on his thigh. Held him down. Then he seemed to burst into flames. My father did, sitting there beside me. Like an instantaneous combustion. Like I'd moved up next to the big fire in the boilinghouse—that intense! Yet he did not sweat. (The English never did, Cook said, neither sweat nor smell.) I sweated for him. *Me:* I sweated like a man. Like Ramsingh when he chopped wood. Like the coolies when they cutlassed the canes. So by the time Mass was finished I was soaked through. My lace gown stuck to my back and arms, buckled shoes like pools of water, my knickers so wet and heavy between my legs as I genuflected and turned to leave, I was afraid they'd drop down round my ankles and trip me—send me flying on top my face!

Nobody said a word as daddy pelted the Ford home. Through the whole of Christmas dinner. The champagne bottle unopened in the center of the table, cold beads collecting into green droplets and sliding down the glass. I continued sweating like a grown man.

3

My father never said a word concerning our religion after that day. Not even in jest. Not about mummy's rolling beads, nor Monsignor's visits for afternoon tea, nor mummy's going to Sunday Mass. Because of course she continued to go, though now she had Ramsingh drive her in the old horsebuggy. And of course she continued to take me with her, the two of us dressed like brides in white lace, sitting on the bench behind Ramsingh, our long white veils trailing out in the buggy's wake behind us. My father could not have *prevented* my going, even if he'd cared enough about it to try. It was written into my parents' marriage contract—this, I found out later. Not a contract with God, or the Law, or even Monsignor. It was a contract with *gran'maman*—from infancy I called her MuMu, known to me only as the exquisite woman in the portrait at the top of the stairs, next to my goat-faced grandfather. Mummy's French-Creole mother: *The children will be raised Catholic.*

And so I was. Whether or not my father resented it.

But Bolom, for the moment I had my own trouble to contend with: if mummy and daddy had committed a mortal sin, where did that leave me? I *was* their mortal sin. The product of my parents' mixed marriage. Of course, I was too young at the time to know anything of the mechanics of sex. Of how such mechanics translated into racial inheritance, into skin colour. But certainly I knew enough to understand the implications of the word *mixed*. Particularly in connection with the word *sin*. Enough to see myself, even in my childhood imagination, as a still greater atrocity: I was the culmination of a long *series* of mortal sins. A *history* of mortal sins. Of mummy's and daddy's sin. Of MuMu's and my grandfather's sin—the horrid man I could only scarcely recall, lifting me every morning to kiss the portrait of my grandmother: "*Fais une bais à la MuMu, bébé!*" I was the end product of the original sin of my great-grandparents. The great-grandparents I knew nothing more about than what I'd overheard Cook say, curled up in the shadow of the tall green safe: that he was one them French *Comte,* true true. She, he own selfsame Yoruba slave.

It was a story I knew only the outline of at the time. Yet it weighed down heavily upon me like an entire history. And as I stood there on my stack of storybooks, nose and chin pressed against the glass—locked into my little room, a child eight years of age—I rolled my beads as seriously as if I could redeem the entire history myself. I rolled my beads for a whole week, over and over, *studying* every word. Until I had no voice remaining. No breath a-tall. Then I rolled my beads in silence. And the whole time I continued sweating bolts.

I had no idea what to ask Mother Mary *for*. Or Papa God. I knew only that I had to pray. Every time my thoughts drifted, Bumblebee's voice rose up out of yellow dirt to bring me back. Miss Rupert had gone to Barbados for the holidays, so she did not interrupt my prayers either. I fell into a kind of trance. I fell *basodee. Boobooloops. Bufutu.* As if I were sleeping with my eyes open. Though I wasn't tired a-tall: I felt like I could go on saying my beads forever. Caught up in the endless repetition. The cycles of repetitions. In truth, I'm sure I burnt a fever. (Maybe I'd even caught a freshcold playing on the river with Dulcianne that Christmas Day? some strange tropical virus?) Because this was a *physical* condition. My little body attempting to hold down its temperature with all the sweating. Actual streams running down my spinecord, backs of my arms, legs. My eyes unable to focus on things. To shift between foreground and background—as though I were stuck in some blurry, middle range. I became even less aware of myself in my little room. And when Di unbolted the door at four o'clock each afternoon, I didn't run first thing to Daisy's coop, then to find Dulcianne. I went upstairs to my bedroom. Drew the blinds and climbed in under the tent of mosquito netting. Lay on my back, eyes wide open, still rolling beads.

4

I was downstairs in my little room doing the same on New Year's Day. A week later. Only one remaining in the house. Di had come with my breakfast early, tried her best to get me to eat. But she'd given up and left the tray there. Gone with Cook to a fête in town. Mummy and daddy had not even returned yet from their own Old Year's Eve fête the night before. I stood as always on my stack of books, nose and chin leaning against the glass, chaplet dangling from my hand. And I'm sure Dulcianne must've crouched there before my window a long time before I actually saw her. She must have thought that I was ill and had come to find me; I'd not seen Dulcianne for the whole week. And perhaps from the dazed look on my face—even through the filthy glass—she realized there *was* something wrong with me.

As usual she wore only her knickers. Now she stood up straight to slip them off—either of us could have stood easily beneath the gallery without bouncing our heads. We'd seen each other naked countless times. Were quite used to pulling off our knickers and jumping into the river. On long hot summer afternoons we swam together naked for hours when Di took us to Huevos Beach. But there, hidden beneath the gallery, alone on that New Year's Day, for the first time I noticed Dulcianne's nakedness. Her beautiful skin—golden, rich like creamed coffee. In the yellow light it shone like molten metal. Because clearly Dulcianne was *mixed* too—the good mix, the happy mix—though Di never said anything about her father. Chupsed every time Dulcianne or I asked.

Now I felt faintly embarrassed. Suddenly faintly thrilled by Dulcianne's nakedness. Now my own skin tingled. The way it did when we first jumped in the river on a hot day. My chaplet slipped with a loud *clack* to the flooring, but I scarcely noticed. I continued staring up at Dulcianne. She knelt in front of my window, sat back on her heels, toes pigeoned, her bony knees almost touching the glass. Now she balled up her knickers. Used them to wipe a circle clean on the glass in front of my face; they were black by the time she'd finished. Now she looked at me for a second, closed her eyes, leaned slowly forward. Kissed my lips through the glass.

I closed my own eyes too. Pressed my own lips to glasspane too.

We remained like that for a full minute. An hour. For the whole of that long New Year's afternoon: it was an instant locked in time behind glass.

When it was over I found myself smiling. Dulcianne too. My skin tingling all over, crawling with invisible ants. We did not attempt to communicate with words. We simply smiled. Then Dulcianne took off running cross the dirt, a yellow stripe down each shin, her knickers a grey flag waving from her hand.

I remained with my nose and chin still pressed against the glass. Still smiling. After awhile I realized that for the first time in a week I'd stopped sweating. Instead of the perspiration running down my spinecord, there was still a trace of the ants streaming faintly *up* it. I actually felt calm. Cool now. And I could not remember what had tormented me so for the previous week. I said to myself: *You are eight years old. It is New Year's Day.*

Then I got down from my stack of books. Went to my desk and selected a yellow pencil from the metal box. I climbed back up. All the way cross the bottom of the white windowframe, with great precision, I wrote out:

LILLA GRANDSOL, 8 YEARS OLD, 1 JANUARY 1933

5

That evening, when I came in from feeding Daisy and putting her away in her coop, I found mummy on the back gallery. Di had just finished washing the holidays out of her hair, and now she was brushing it. The air smelling faintly of chamomile. Mummy was sitting in the old wicker rockingchair wearing her nightgown, head tilted back, her beautiful auburn hair almost touching the floorboards. The sun was just setting on a flat sea, and mummy's hair shone like flaming casuarina needles as Di pulled the brush down through it. It made a lovely sound, like walking barefoot over dry sand. I stood beside Di, watching and listening, still dreamy from the afternoon. And without even pausing to think about it, I asked:

"Mummy, what's wrong with me? Why am I a mortal sin? Cause I came out a blat-blanch?"

I saw the look of horror on Di's face before I saw it on my mother's.

She swung round and slapped me hard enough to send me backward sitting on the flooring. I was so stunned I jumped up again straight. She slapped me again, and I tumbled backward again. Then I realized my mother was crying.

"You have committed no sin," she said calmly. "How can a child commit a mortal sin? How possibly? It is *we* who have sinned because your father is a Protestant." She was silent a moment. Then the look flashed cross her face again.

"*Pas plus de blat-blanch!*" she screamed, and I was afraid she'd slap me a third time. I took off running.

As I lay on my bed that night, for the first time I could not wait to get downstairs into my little room. All of a sudden I could not be sure Dulcianne had come to visit me that afternoon. That it had happened for true. It all felt like a dream I'd conjured up—and then that confusing business with mummy! I wanted to be sure. To get downstairs before the circle on the glass disappeared. Before the dust covered it up. When I finally fell asleep I dreamt that I was writing on an old piece of yellowed paper with a white pencil. But the words were already there, already written out in white. They were my letters, just the way I would shape them. And as I moved the pencil cross the paper my words disappeared. When I awoke I was swimming in sweat.

The circle was there on the glass! I saw it the instant I entered my room. Shining brightly as a small oval mirror. Soon as Di turned the key I ran and climbed up on my stack of books. Verified that my writing was still there too. Then I got down and went to my desk. I selected a blue pencil this time. I climbed back up, distraught to discover that no space remained along the bottom frame of my window. Then I realized I'd no idea how to spell the words regardless. For a quick moment I could not even remember which language they belonged to. There was a small blank space before the first letter, the *L*. Another after the last digit, the *3*. Each large enough for me to squeeze in a letter. In each I carefully wrote a blue *B*.

6

Dulcianne had been strictly forbidden by her mother to play under the gallery, and it was nearly four months before she came to visit me again. I watched the circle on the glass disappearing slowly beneath a new layer of dust. Each morning I was further disheartened as Di closed the door, and I ran to climb up on my stack of books. Miss Rupert returned and my lessons continued, but now mummy lengthened them to three hours every morning. When I was not with her, or with Di eating my breakfast, I continued in my old habit of rolling beads. But my chaplet-saying became mindless again. A way to pass the time. Escape the boredom. Now, though, I rolled my beads with my eyes closed. I rolled my beads with my lips pressed against the glass. Center of my slowly disappearing circle.

At four o'clock when Di let me out of my room I ran as always to collect Daisy. Then to look for Dulcianne. On Sundays after Mass we went to the river as always to look for soukuyants' skins. When we grew hot we threw ourselves in the water. But now we swam with our knickers on. We hiked them up round our waists and let them dry on our bodies. We planned the usual monkeyshines, spoke of the usual things—duens and soukuyants and diablesses—even of the lagahoo sleeping in his bed of crocusssacks beneath the gallery. But we never mentioned that New Year's afternoon.

Still, though I told her nothing, I longed for Dulcianne to come and visit me again. As I watched the circle on the glass fade, I began to lose hope. I longed for that sensation on the surface of my skin. But when I closed my eyes and tried to imagine it—tried to see Dulcianne's golden skin—the feeling seemed very far away. Then one afternoon I made the obvious discovery. Or, perhaps, I only became aware of what my body all along had already known. I was standing on my stack of storybooks, triple points of chin-lips-nose squinged against glass. In my right hand I held a bead of my chaplet, rolling it slowly back and forth between my thumb and index finger. Eyes closed, words of the Holy Mary floating mindlessly through my head. Slowly I began to feel the ants crawling up my spine again. Pins-and-needles-prickling-earlobes. The tips of my elbows. Backs of my knees. Somewhere down deep at the bottom of my stomach. Tingling—below. It was my left hand, discovering the way on its own, pressing through my frock and my knickers beneath. Gently pressing. And I found that if I pressed in a certain way, the ants *streamed*.

7

I was nine years of age. I called it rolling beads too. Gave it the same name, in the secret, to myself. Or rather, I called the two activities by the same name. Because for me they became inseparable. Now, when I stood on my stack of books with my nose against the glass, eyes closed, chaplet dangling from my right hand, my left hand was busy also. The more I continued, the more pleasurable the sensation became. The more the ants streamed. (And it was years later, an adult, that I lay in my bed rolling beads in just this way, when a quote from the Bible flashed back at me: words of St Paul. And Bolom, I couldn't help but smile! *Let not thy right hand know what thy left hand doth.* So Bolom, I'd been quite right to confuse the two. To call the two activities by the same name.)

I'd almost forgotten about Dulcianne. Forgotten my longing for her to come and visit me again. Because when I opened my eyes and found her there crouched before my window, I was well embarrassed. But this time I was *not* also thrilled. This time I was *vex*. From the smile on her face—perhaps, again, from the smile on my own—I could tell she knew exactly what I'd been doing. (Dulcianne was a year older Bolom, had more than likely made these discoveries a year before I did.) Her smile was a new one—brazenly wicked. It made me vex. As though she'd done something to betray our friendship. But in a flash she stripped off her knickers again, not saying a word. Again she got down on her knees, sitting back with her legs tucked beneath her, and again she wiped a circle clean on the glass in front of my face. She leaned forward and pressed her lips against it, closed her eyes. This time I kept my own eyes open. Watched as best I could. In one hand she held the balled-up knickers. The other she placed below her belly—I could hardly see—but I knew well enough what *she* was doing also! The wicked smile printed on her face. Now I felt embarrassed for true. For both of us. I wanted to get down from my stack of books. I tried—I actually tried to pull my face away—but Bolom, now my lips were stuck like laglee to the glass! I shut my eyes quick quick. And I did not open them for a very long time. When I did, I was happy to see that she had gone.

But as I waited for Di to unbolt the door at four o'clock, slowly my anger faded. When she arrived to let me out, I went straight to look for Dulcianne. Didn't even remember to collect Daisy first. Of course, we mentioned nothing about her having come to see me that afternoon. Certainly nothing about rolling beads. (Bolom, to this day I've never told anyone but you that I call it that; and if Dulcianne had a special name for it herself, she never told me what it was either.) Though we played together every morning and every evening. It was as if we'd some unspoken rule between us; we never mentioned Dulcianne's afternoon visits. Nor what we did with our eyes closed. Lips pressed together on either side of the glass.

Because she came to visit me again the following afternoon. And then again two afternoons after that. Sometimes she came to visit me three afternoons in succession. We did not plan these visits, and I did not anticipate them in any way. At least not in the beginning. I did not worry that she would come this afternoon or the next. If she didn't come to see me beneath the gallery for a whole week, I wasn't much bothered. I waited patiently at my window, often rolling beads on my own. Time seemed not to matter then. As in a sweet dream, when the only worry is waking.

Bolom, it went on for nearly a year. When I think back, I'm still a bit astonished that it could've gone on so long. Dulcianne and I shared this secret life together. That we never spoke of these visits—never mentioned them to one another—made them all the more secret. All the more special. The longer our meetings continued, the more special they became. To the point I began to fear something would happen to prevent them. Still, I was not terribly worried. In my childlike sense of the world, I decided that Dulcianne and I were protected by a kind of magic. By a spell: nothing could possibly happen to separate us, so long as we did not speak of what we did together. So long as we did not say it to make it real.

How I wished I had some way to communicate this to Dulcianne! But in order to do so, I'd have to say it. And that would break the spell. Then I thought perhaps that I could write it in a letter. And I could leave it somewhere for her to find by chance. I began to compose the letter in my mind:

Dear Dulcianne,

I have to tell you this secret. We must never speak of what we do together. Not to each other or anyone else. To do so shall bring a great tragedy.

Cordially,
Lilla Grandsol

I thought about it so often I began to see the actual writing. Could imagine the letter in crooks of certain trees we climbed together. In crevices between certain boulderstones by the river. Then I realized

Dulcianne had not even learned to read yet. And I decided that in any case writing was far more dangerous than speaking. Because I'd overheard Cook talking about an obeah spell to give someone a fever, simply by writing their name on a piece of paper and passing a match beneath it. Or bruising them up by writing their name on the bottom of your shoe and treading upon it.

If I could just *think* the thought into Dulcianne's head! Dream it into *her* dream! In my frustration I began for the first time to hate words, language, which seemed suddenly such an awkward way to communicate. Which seemed suddenly to come *between* people, rather than bringing us together. My only consolation was that somehow Dulcianne realized how the magic worked. Somehow she understood.

8

Then one Sunday afternoon, as we lay on our backs on a smooth white boulderstone drying ourselves beneath the sun—we now wore bathing costumes beneath our frocks when we went to the river—Dulcianne rolled her head to the side to look at me.

"How it is you always praying chaplet *then?*" she asked.

My spine stiffened.

Dulcianne chupsed. "Me ain't talking to waste me breath, you know!"

My neck felt like an iron bar. Like a rusty standpipe. I stared up through the bright leaves. Through the green light.

Now Dulcianne rolled onto her side, holding her head up on her bent arm. "Eh?" she said. "How it is you always praying chaplet *then?*"

I swung onto my side and slapped Dulcianne so hard her head tumbled backward. Thudding against the rock. She was so stunned she sat up quickly and I slapped her again. Then I grabbed up my frock and took off running.

9

When I went to Daisy's coop the following afternoon and found her dead I was actually relieved. Even as I undid her stiff toes from the wire at the bottom—and raised her swollen little body to press against my breast, the tears already streaming down my face—I could only feel somewhat relieved: it was not the tragedy I'd come to expect.

"Scorpion bite she," said Ramsingh, "is for that she swell-up so." He promised another to replace her, a grey-and-white-spotted guineachick if I wished.

I told him I could not bear to have another fowl for a pet.

I went and found Dulcianne, and together we gave Daisy a proper burial. There beneath the flamboyant tree at the back of the house. We'd played with her beneath the same tree so many afternoons, Daisy fighting her way out of the mounds of red petals we piled on top her, her ratty head jerking this way and that. Ramsingh painted two short boards white and nailed them together into a cross. We mashed sea-grapes in a calabash to make a purple paste, and with a stick I wrote her name cross the crosspiece. Then I turned it over and on one arm of the back I wrote *MLO,* which I told Dulcianne stood for *mourned by loved ones.* On the other arm I wrote *D+L.*

Dulcianne came to visit me beneath the gallery the following afternoon. She stayed a long time. Long after the grandfather's clock in the parlour had chimed for two, then three o'clock. I began to worry that Di would come soon to let me out. I kept telling myself, *In just a moment you're going to open your eyes. In just a moment you're going to climb down from these books.* When I did open my eyes Di was there. But not in my room. She was outside, beneath the gallery, crouched down behind Dulcianne. I tried to scream but no sound came from my throat. Tried to get down from my books but my legs wouldn't work. She remained crouched behind Dulcianne for the longest time, and I stood paralyzed—eyes wide open, staring up at Di. At last she grabbed Dulcianne's arm and pulled her away from the window.

We had never seen Di so vex. "Nasty is nastiness you children could carry on with, oh *lors!*" she bawled. "And D-ann, how many times I *hot* tell you *stay out from under the whitepeople gallery! Papayo!*" She told Dulcianne that if she ever caught her there in future, she'd cut the skin of she backside so bad it would never again want to see chair.

By this time Dulcianne had pulled back on her knickers. She was twelve years old now and wore a frock. I was a little more than eleven, and I pulled my own knickers up from round my knees. Di grabbed Dulcianne's arm and pulled her out behind her, crouching low so as not to bounce her head. And on the way out Di did something peculiar: she shoved Dulcianne ahead into the light, and she grabbed up all the lagahoo's bed of crocusssacks. She disappeared with her bundle behind the cloud of dust, yellow light filtering through.

I cannot be sure whether Di told mummy what she'd seen us doing that afternoon. Bolom, I rather doubt it. Yet it was only a few days later when mummy announced that at the end of the summer, in September, I'd be going to live in the Ursuline Convent in Henly. All the way on the other side of the island. My father looked up quickly from his plate, but he remained silent. It was a Sunday evening. The one day of the week we ate dinner together. I stared at the pitcher of ice water in the center of the table, and soon I was sweating too.

My previous experience with nuns, when I'd made my First Communion, had been horrid enough. In catechism class they'd told me that I was *dull,* though in comparison to the five or six other children, I knew that I was not. When I arrived on the day dressed in a white muslin frock with tiny black polkadots—mummy'd had it made specially for the occasion—they made me take it off and go through the ceremony in my slip. "Not all the children," an older, harsh one said, "can afford a new dress to make their First Communion!" The other children laughed at me. A little negro boy said, "Look the blat-blanch! She making she Communion in she underdrawers!"

I knew nothing about the Ursuline Convent, except that this was where mummy had been sent to school herself as a child. She never spoke about it. One evening, when I found her sitting alone on the back gallery, I asked about the Ursuline sisters. "Oh," she said, "you'll find them very sweet, very simple. They're a semi-cloistered order. They do not get out much into the world." I was not sure what "semi-cloistered" meant, but to me the term suggested some slight physical deformity. A twisted hand or a clubbed foot. Which—I told myself—was certainly why they wore those long skirts in all the heat, why they always kept their hands tucked suspiciously inside their sleeves. Certainly why they seldom let them outside the spiked convent gates.

Now I began to dread leaving the safety of my little room. Every afternoon when Di came to let me out, I knew I was one day closer. I did not want to leave Di, but more than anything I did not want to leave Dulcianne. I could not imagine life without her. Could not imagine waking up in the morning without running first thing to the wash-stone to meet her. Dulcianne already there catching tadpoles in the little stream, or helping Di to beat out the clothes against the stone. And in three seconds my own skinny arms would be thick with suds to my elbows too, laughing and slinging a jersey against the washstone with all my might—*swatch-swatch-swatch!*—the bright morning air floating with bubbles. Drifting away between the tall cypress pines behind us.

But ever since Di had put a stop to Dulcianne's visits beneath the gallery, I felt almost as though we'd already been separated. Almost as though I'd already left. We did not talk much about my departure. Though Dulcianne made me promise that before I left, we'd crawl in under the gallery finally to catch the lagahoo—his bed had appeared again behind the back steps.

I managed to dissuade her until my final day. A Sunday, but we did not go to the river after Mass; instead we got Ramsingh to help us make the bule-de-fay, filling a rum bottle with pitch-oil and shoving a rag in the top. We told him we needed it to explore a cave by the river. Ramsingh even gave us a big box of kitchen matches. Dulcianne cut down a clothesline to make her lasso, and she practiced all day long, lassoing everything in sight: chairs and buckets and bushes, even the ham-bone from out the cauldron of splitpea soup cooling on the sill. This so confused Cook that she turned round and sat down on top the live coalpot! She jumped up bawling for Jesus' mercy, running for the pipe in the yard, her bamsee smoking behind her. Then she went after Dulcianne and me with her kitchenknife!

Though I wanted more than ever to listen to one of Di's stories on my last evening, I told her that I was too old for bedtime stories now. That I wanted to be left alone. And Bolom, it was as painful an untruth as ever I've told in my life. I waited a couple minutes after she'd closed the door behind her. Then I crawled out from under the tent of mosquito netting. I stepped out of my nightgown and pulled a frock over my head, buckled on my sandals. Then I eased the door open. I couldn't get out through the screen door at the back of the kitchen because Di would still be there, grinding the coffee and putting it to filter for the following morning. I slipped down the hall into the parlour. Climbed up over my father's desk to get out through the window. Out onto the gallery.

Dulcianne was there waiting for me by the washstone at the side of the house. My hand was trembling so badly I could not strike the match to light the bule-de-fay. There was probably still enough light to see without it, in addition to the porchlight above the kitchen door, but Dulcianne was insistent we do everything according to plan. She chupsed and lit it herself. Then she adjusted the burning rag, poking and pulling, her bare fingers working cautiously in the blue flame. She was all excited. I was scared to death.

Our plan was to circle round the flamboyant tree to the concrete block of steps, crouch down beside it, then to rush in and catch the lagahoo unaware. By the time we reached the steps I was breathing so hard I was sure I'd pitch a faint. We crouched beside the block of concrete—me panting, Dulcianne preparing her lasso. She looked at me and mouthed *one, two, three,* then she took off round the steps. It was all I could manage to grasp the back of her frock, close my eyes tight and let her practically pull me behind her, the bule-de-fay held carefully to the side. I'm sure I stood there a full minute before I dared open my eyes. When I did—and I raised up the torchlight to see better—I found the same thing I saw every day from the window of my room: a bunch of old crocusssacks spread out on the yellow dirt.

Dulcianne chupsed. "Must be we come too early. The lagahoo ain't reach as yet."

"I'm sure he's not coming!" I said.

Dulcianne chupsed again. "How you could say so easy?"

She decided the only thing for us to do was wait. She extinguished the bule-de-fay with a clap of her hands over the flaming rag, and we settled ourselves on the ground at the side of the steps, our backs leaning against the cool concrete. In no time a-tall we were both asleep.

10

I've no idea how long we'd been sleeping before Dulcianne shook me awake. Now it was pitch dark. I could hardly see her face, but I knew Dulcianne was excited again. There were growling sounds coming from beneath the gallery. From behind the steps: animal noises, *hurt* sounds. Dulcianne had already lit and adjusted the bule-de-fay, which she now handed to me. I was still half-asleep. The torchlight felt so heavy I could scarcely hold it up. Dulcianne readied her lasso, and again she mouthed *one, two, three.* Again I grabbed the back of her frock and shut my eyes. Let her pull me behind her. But this time the bule-defay slipped from my hand, outing itself when it hit the ground.

I stood beneath the gallery behind Dulcianne, eyes shut tight. When I opened them I could see nothing in the darkness. I blinked. Still nothing. I could hear the growling, *moving* sounds, a few feet in front of Dulcianne. Then I began to make out something—*appendages:* a human arm and a dog's tail and a deer's cloven foot. Then I felt Dulcianne grab my elbow and begin to pull me behind her. But now I was awake. Now I had to see! I pulled back. Dulcianne held tightly and dragged me out from under the gallery. All the way round to the side of the house, me struggling to free myself from her grasp.

"I want to *see!*" I bawled.

Dulcianne refused to release me. It was very dark. I could not see her face.

"Let me *go!*" I shouted.

Then she shoved me away hard. With the force of my own pulling I went sprawling against the washstone, bruising my forearm and the side of my face. A gritty taste in my mouth. I lay against the stone, crying now, Dulcianne standing above me in the dark. She still held the coil of rope. I could scarcely see, but I knew how vex she was, and I could not understand why. It was all happening terribly fast. Dulcianne held the coil of rope in both hands. She swung it with all her strength, lashing me cross the side of my face. Then she disappeared into the darkness.

I lay against the stone a long time. Crying, angry, very confused. Eventually I must have gotten up and gone to my bedroom. Because I awoke the following morning in my bed, a crust of dried blood between my lips. But surprisingly I found no mark on my face when I looked in the mirror. I washed out my mouth in the basin, and when I'd finished there was no sign remaining from the events of the previous night. I did not see Dulcianne that morning. No one seemed even aware that anything unusual had happened.

And it was not until we'd driven for several hours, mummy sitting beside daddy in front and me in the back seat, and we were climbing down from the mountains of the Northern Range with the air very cool, the Ford occasionally swallowed up whole by a misty cloud—the entire world *liquid,* and dripping, and smelling of wet earth—when all in a sudden my father coughed twice and made a peculiar sound to clear his throat: ha-*ham!* At that moment my eyes began to focus on what my imagination had concealed so well from me in the dark on the previous night. All those appendages. Suddenly they came clearly into focus, and I could make out the two figures entangled on the ground at Dulcianne's feet. I saw their wet, raw mouths moving, and I heard them emitting their animal noises. I saw that they were half-naked. That they were struggling—though as I watch the scene again and again, from the distance of a few hours or several years, still I cannot tell whether they are trying to clasp tighter together, or to shove each other brutally away. Suddenly I realized that it was *him* whom I had seen, and *her:* my father and Di. *They* were the lagahoo hidden beneath the gallery. They were the lagahoo crawling under each night, sleeping each night on the bed of old crocusssacks.

Rolling Beads

1

The convent was papery crimson bougainvillea splashed up against thick walls of coral blocks. Hot sun beating down on the playingfield. Smooth shadows beneath the banyan trees. The silver trickle of the fountain gurgling beneath moss-covered black stones in the grotto where the statue of Holy Mary hid. Where each morning on our way to chapel, still half-asleep, we paused to whisper together: "Blessed Mother pierce me through, in my heart each wound renew!" Sin and suffering, darkness and light, hell and heaven.

The girls, too, were of contrary types. The boarders—coming from as far as Guyana, Barbados, Trinidad—the boarders were little angels. Shy and sweet and very beautiful. Perfectly well-behaved. Most, like me, were French and English mixed. Otherwise they were Spanish and English. Most, like me, had families which went back generations in the West Indies—last remnants of what we'd once fondly called the Plantocracy. The day-students were little horrors. Perfect Warrahoons. They lived on estates in the country, nearby enough that they could be driven in in the mornings. Most were pure English. A few had even been born away. All very fair: springy blond locks and crystalline blue eyes, or carrot-coloured hair and freckle-peppered skin. They stared at me through squinged-up nostrils. Hesitant, for the moment, to pass a remark. I looked down at the flooring of polished coral blocks, studying the millions upon millions of crushed fossilized animals, thinking: *Whitee-pokee-penny-a-pound, if-you-don't-like-me-lick-me-down!* But Bolom, I didn't dare say it; I was the only girl in the convent with visible negro blood.

And there were two sorts of nuns. Different as the materials of their habits: heavy black serge—even in all the heat—from the veils on their heads to the hems of their skirts at their ankles, sleeves at their wrists; with bibs of bright white cotton, rising to form their wimples under their chins (we called them *turkey-wimples*), passing over their cheeks and circling their faces. There were the nuns, like Sister Frances, who were simple and generous. Softhearted. She slept behind the compartment of white screens in the younger girls' dormitory. Sister Frances was a chuff-chuff. Fat and happy. Her eyes big, and brown, and laughing like a cow's own. Every night before we fell asleep she read to us from a book of child-saints the size of a small tombstone. Pictures on the pasteboard pages: Bernadette of Lourdes, the children of Fatima. "Our Blessed Mother chose to reveal herself only to children," she would tell us, her accent a singsong Irish. "In heaven she surrounds herself only with children . . . like each of you. . . ." And we'd drift off to sleep.

Then there were the nuns like Mother Marie-Bernard, who taught catechism to all the grades and oversaw the older girls' dormitory. She told us about hell, as though from personal experience. Knew all of our secret, wicked thoughts, better than we knew them ourselves. Unlike the other sisters, Mother Marie-Bernard had been born and raised in Trinidad, yet she took care to speak with a proper English accent. But whenever she grew vex or excited, she spilled into rank Creole. This made us more geegeeree still. The idea that she was one of us, could have been any of our not-so-distant great-aunts. The older girls laughed, said she was going through the change. She couldn't *help* but be miserable. They called her Mother Marie-Bernard of the Burning Moustache Bush—BMB for short. And Bolom, her moustache was bushy for true; a furry caterpillar crawling cross her upper lip, coloured a fire-engine-red.

She wasted little time in getting round to her *second* favorite topic in catechism class. It was waiting for us one afternoon when we entered the classroom after recess—we'd scarcely been there at the convent a week—written cross the blackboard in tall capital letters: *SIXTH COMMANDMENT OF THE CHURCH: NOT TO MARRY A PERSON WHO IS NOT A CATHOLIC.* "Most of you," she said, "are the children of mixed marriages. For most of you, it is your foremost duty in life to pray for the conversion of your Protestant mother or father. Otherwise . . ." and here she lowered her voice, here she began flicking her long bony hand in the air—a peculiar West Indian gesture— her index finger smacking loudly against her thumb in a series of sharp quick *clacks,* "Otherwise," she told us, "they going burn-up sure-certain in everlasting hell!"

One of the little girls fled the classroom in tears. I was not upset a-tall. I could only sit feeling the heat of the pine bench striking up through my navy pleated skirt into my thighs. Striking up through my wrists just exposed below the cuffs of my starched white shirt (short sleeves were immodest), my hands folded against the edge of the hot pine tabletop. And I could only think that hell was too happy a place for my father. Now Mother Marie-Bernard would tell us to close our eyes, fold our hands now, meditate on the eternal flames, pray for the conversion of our loved ones. But Bolom, *I* could never pray. I could only close my eyes and push my little wrists still harder into the edge of the hot tabletop, and I could only whisper: *Please Dulcianne! Forgive me my father . . . OUR father, who will one day burn in hell!*

2

I used to dread waking up in the morning. Dread the sound of the chapel bell *ba-bong ba-bong ba-bong* already six o'clock. I'd squeeze my eyes shut and pretend I hadn't heard it. But the little girl on either side would already be sprinkling her face with water from the basin on the table between our beds. Already stepping out of her nightgown into her bloomers, the knickers devised for us by the convent—awful billowy things made of a stiff, tullelike material, bands of thick elastic cutting into each thigh and clamping round our waists. Already dressing in our uniforms and pinning our veils quickly by touch to our hair—no mirrors in the dormitory—hurrying to line up to walk in silence to chapel. We were not even permitted to brush our teeth for fear that a few drops of water would slip by accident down our throats. All fasting since the evening before in order to take Communion: no morsel of food or drink to have entered our little stomaches for twelve hours. Every morning of every day.

But even when we lined up again to walk to the cafeteria after Mass, we could bear neither the sight nor the smell of the hot porridge already waiting for us on the tables. Already smoking-up! (At least the cafeteria was cool, Bolom—it had no walls—only a piece of the same corrugated-zinc roofing, painted the same colour of sun-faded crimson, with the kitchen a separate building a short distance away.) And if our porridge had not already been served the steaming bowls were plonked down before us by languid, blue-skinned maids who never spoke to us or even looked in our faces. Who seemed to resent us, perhaps because their own children would be fortunate to eat a bowl of the same lumpy porridge the whole day. But hot porridge in the tropics! Bolom, I suppose it was the cheapest and most nourishing thing they could think to give us. Perhaps it was what they fed schoolchildren in England—the Ursuline Sisters were, after all, an English order. And the milk the maids sloshed from a pitcher into our bowls was just on the point of turning, if we were lucky. Most of the time it'd turned already—there was little refrigeration in those days, if there was any in the convent a-tall. We doctored it up with plenty sugar. Gave it a stir and swallowed it down quickly, even if we were already sweating. Because once it cooled it turned thick like laglee. And of course, we had to lick down every *scrap*.

One morning one of the maids put salt in the sugarbowl by accident (or perhaps not?). The sugarbowl which happened to end up in front of me. I sprinkled on a spoonful, stirred, tasted; sprinkled on a spoonful, stirred, tasted. Then I moved the sugarbowl closer. Shoveled on three heaping spoonfuls before I realized that it was salt. I didn't know what to do. The other girls were already lining up at the far side of the cafeteria, waiting to return to the dorms. But the older girl who was monitor at our table—a terribly shy girl from Martinique named

Justine—did not have the authority to let me go until I'd finished. And I suppose she was frightened of getting reprimanded herself. She offered an encouraging smile. I tried swallowing a few mouthfuls. Quickly as I could. By now I was already sweating—though the porridge had long since turned to cold glue—perhaps there were tears as well. Because I remember three big drops padding into my bowl. I looked up at Justine. There was strict silence during meals. I tried to whisper as quietly as possible: *"Salt!"*

She didn't understand.

By this time Sister Ellen had come over—one of the sisters of Mother Marie-Bernard's camp, of the same disposition. She gave Justine a sign and she got up; we were the only two girls left in the cafeteria. Sister Ellen walked round the table and stood behind me. I couldn't see her, only feel the heat of her presence. I continued sweating. Retching with every mouthful. But I continued swallowing. There was nothing in my stomach—only the porridge I had eaten and a yellowish bile—which I vomited into the same bowl. "Enough!" she said finally, and I listened to the quick claps of her leather shoes retreating cross the coral flooring. When I got back to the dormitory I collapsed in Sister Frances's arms, burying my face in her white bib. Until we heard the schoolbell clanging in the distance, and she smiled and I took off running for the classrooms.

3

I remained as solitary a child in the convent as I'd been at home. Perhaps more so. Because at least at home I'd had a companion in Dulcianne. Now I had no friends a-tall. Certainly not among the day-students, the whitee-pokees. They had me terrified. But I made no effort to make friends among the boarders either, though there were opportunities enough. Those girls seemed to me so perfect, so beautiful. I felt marred in their presence. Blighted. And as we walked along in silence to chapel, the cafeteria, the classrooms, I'd look before me at the line of silky heads of hair—jet, and auburn, and golden—glistening, floating in the early morning sun. And I'd tell myself: *That is what you are: a blat-blanch, a blighted child.*

I wanted no friends. None other than Dulcianne. In my eyes she was more beautiful than all the Creole girls in the convent. More beautiful and stronger. More alive. More *real*. Dulcianne was part of the tall cedar trees and the glittering river and the smoky, musty smell of the forest. She was connected to that life force, part of that world. How could I *ever* wish for another friend? And in my mind to have another would somehow be a betrayal of our friendship together. The *sacredness* of it— because that is what it became for me, Bolom. In my memory. I wanted no friends in the convent. Only to be alone, far off from all the rest. Alone with my memories of Dulcianne.

But there was scarce little chance of being alone. The nuns kept us busy every waking moment, moving in a line from one activity to the next. And as I sat squeezed between two girls in the hot chapel, on the hot classroom bench, I'd dream of my little room at home. Standing there on my stack of storybooks, my lips pressed against the glass, waiting for Dulcianne to appear. How I'd hated that little room all my life, how I longed for Di to lock me up in my little room now. To be by myself. Alone. With only the possibility that Dulcianne could come to see me. Could appear again from out the cloud of yellow dust.

I did discover one means of escape, almost right away; it was when we went each afternoon to the sea to swim. For the boarders this was the highlight of our existence, and we'd wait anxiously all day for the moment we could throw ourselves into the cool—*cold* in spots!—clear water. The Ursuline Sisters owned their own private beach, a small cove a mile or so away from the convent grounds. Every afternoon after tea we'd line up with our towels and bathing costumes rolled up under our arms. If one of the nuns went with us to supervise, we'd walk beneath the hot sun along the pitch road, through the center of Henly. But more often than not we were left under the charge of one of the older girls. Then we'd take the shortcut; an old trace which followed a dried-up stream, winding its way among clumps of creaking bamboo and thick bush.

For me to follow along that trace was to slowly shed the closed-in world of the convent. And when the trace opened up into a village of a dozen broken-down shanties, clutching for dear life to the side of the cliff overlooking the sea—the air smelling of rubbish, of salted careete drying like clothes on long lines, of cooking coalpots—I knew we'd entered into another world for true. Sometimes the little black children would stop their play and crouch naked in the dirt, a bicycle rim or an armless pink doll in their dusty hands, huge eyes as they watched us pass. Sometimes I caught a glimpse of a little girl my own age, her head a ball of plats with pieces of bright orange wool tied at the end of each one. Staring at us from the darkened window of her shanty. As I hurried along I'd wonder what separated me from that little girl. How it was that she ended up inside the shanty, dressed in nothing but a ragged men's marino, and me in the convent dressed in my starched, UC-monogrammed shirt. As I hurried along, studying the multitude of tiny, heart-shaped *kisses* stuck to my tall white socks, I'd wonder which of the two girls I'd rather be.

There was a cabana beside the beach where we changed into our modest, one-piece bathing costumes, made for us at the convent too, everything according to strict regulations. (Mother Marie-Bernard knew all about the new fashion rage: "This business they call the *bikini,*" she told us, "is not simply sinful, it is *lascivious!*") All we cared about was the cool water. There were swimming races which we could participate in if we wished. Games of water polo which we could play if we chose. But I always went off on my own, to the far end of the beach. There the furry casuarina pines spread out over the water, always shady and cool beneath them. The constant drone of the breeze through the pine needles was always for me somehow lonely, and nostalgic, and mournful. At the end of the cove the water was shallow and very calm. I'd duck beneath it and hold my breath, lying on my back on the powdery white sand, my nostrils pinched and my eyes open. Staring up at the mirrored, gently rippling surface. All the noise of the screaming girls disappeared the instant I ducked beneath the water, and I was alone! I'd stare up at my own distorted reflection on the inside surface of the water. And I'd imagine that that reflection was not me, it was Dulcianne—my opposite, my twin sister—floating facedown on the water. The bubbles slowly escaping my mouth would be swallowed up by her, one by one, in a silent, secret communication of slowly ascending pearls. The more I practiced the longer I was able to hold my breath. Until I could remain beneath the shallow water for as long as a minute at a stretch. And the longer I remained below with Dulcianne, the more I regretted ever having to return to the world of the screaming convent girls. As I lay on the white sand I'd dream that I would never have to breathe again. Never again have to leave the cool world of solitude and silence beneath the water. The world of my imagination and of Dulcianne.

There were other pleasant dreams. Recurring ones which I had in my little bed at night, not an arm's length from the girl asleep on either side. Dreams of Dulcianne and me living together. But strangely enough we did not live in the big estate house; we lived in Dulcianne's mudhut with the thatched roof, now deep in the forest. Though in my dreams Di was not there. It was only the two of us. And strangely enough, it was I who attended to Dulcianne. *I* who played the role of servant and she of mistress—a game we'd often played with the roles reversed in years previous—it was I who picked the guavas and sapodillas and pawpaws from trees growing wild from some abandoned estate. I who peeled the little, sour-sweet oranges with my penknife in a single curling peel—just as Dulcianne had always done for me when we'd gone on excursions in the forest. It was I in my dream who snapped the orange in half, sprinkled the pinch of soukuyant-salt from a mauve-coloured glassbottle. I who presented the orange with dripping fingers to Dulcianne. Sometimes I'd boil crayfish or crabs for her which I'd caught in the river. I'd boil green plantains for her in a rusted pitch-oil tin on the coalpot. And when the plantains were boiled I'd mash them in a calabash shell. Sugar them and feed Dulcianne mouthful by mouthful with my own silver tablespoon.

4

If Dulcianne still cared for me—if she still loved me! Because Bolom, now I dared pronounce the word. For the first time in my life. (I'd never used it with mummy and daddy; they'd certainly never used it with me.) A word more mystical, and compelling, and more powerful than all the rest put together: *God* and *grace* and even the newest addition to my vocabulary—that simplest of virtues which I'd always possessed without even knowing (or being told) to hold dear—my *virginity.*

I said it in the secret. To myself. At first geegeeree and quiet quiet. A whisper, a breath: *love!* Whispered with vague feelings of guilt, of

shame—which, at twelve years of age, I could scarcely begin to understand. But those feelings were mixed with a certain excitement too. A
certain tingling of ants crawling up my spinecord too. And soon the
excitement took charge over the other feelings. Soon I began to whisper the word with more confidence. With greater frequency. Until—
locked into one of the privy-stalls at the far side of the playingfield,
both hands busy rolling beads, my eyes closed—until I began to whisper the word again and again. Louder and louder. Until it became a
silent screaming inside my ears: *love! love! love!*

The WC was the only place I could find to escape them. The horrid
day-students. When the bell rang and we were excused for recess I hurried there straight. Locked myself into one of the privy-stalls and
remained until I heard the bell again. There were five such stalls. Each a
separate little cubicle the colour of faded crimson, a line of them at the
edge of the playingfield where it bordered the forest—just out of reach
on the other side of the spiked wroughtiron fence. Because in the convent, in those days, a toilet was nothing more than a bench with a hole
cut out, suspended over a deep pit. (The toilets in the dormitories were
newer and cleaner, far more sanitary—they flushed with water.) But the
ones in the schoolyard! The *stench,* the incessant cloud of mosquitoes
buzzing, the strangulating heat! At least the cubicles were roofless—so
some of the odour could escape and the rain could fall on occasion to
wash them down—not that that made much difference a-tall. Those
cubicles remained as vile-smelling before the rains as after.

Still, the WC became my place of refuge. My means of escape during the school day. I'd lock myself in and actually stand on the bench
with a foot on either side of the hole, my bloomers stretched between
my knees, hands busy, eyes closed. Because in no time a-tall I fell back
into my habit of rolling beads. My chaplet I continued to wear like a
necklace round my neck—the same chaplet strung from tiny black
pem-pem seeds—my own secret tribute to Dulcianne. It even pleased
the nuns. Eliciting comments on more than one occasion. They even
thought me pious! Which, of course, only served to increase the guilt,
the *pleasure* associated with my secret sin. Because certainly I knew that
my rolling beads *must* be a sin. How could it be otherwise, with *so* many
sins to be committed? And I knew that my rolling beads with my left
hand—my saying my chaplet simultaneously with my right—was not

merely a sin, it was a *sacrilege*. The stenching toilet seemed the appropriate place for my sinful pleasure. For me. (And Bolom, I know that in some perverse way I could never have admitted to then, never have begun to understand then, I know the vileness of the place even intensified my wicked pleasures—sent the ants up my spinecord *streaming*.)

But my hiding place was soon detected. One of the day-students—one of those awful, yellow-headed, blue-eyed whitee-pokees named Brett—was waiting for me at the far side of the playingfield after the bell rang. She held me up. Grasping hold of the fairy's loop between my shoulderblades at the back of my shirt:

"What you doing always hiding in the WC, eh? You *white cockroach!*"

I looked over my shoulder into her beady eyes—bits of milk-of-magnesia glassbottle pressed into clammy dough. "*Eh?*" she said again, and she shoved me forward. I closed my eyes and took off in a bolt, yanking through the loop of my shirt and freeing myself. She pursued me all the way back to the line of girls waiting to enter the classroom, bawling behind me: "*WC! WC! WC!*"

The following afternoon, locked again into one of the privy-stalls during recess, I heard a softish, *watery* noise. Somewhere above my head: *Shulsh!* (*A splash of water? whisper?*) My chaplet slipped with a loud *clop* to the wood flooring. I opened my eyes, raised my head, looking up: nothing. Only powder-blue sky above the hole of my roofless cubicle. Then I realized the noise had come from *behind* me. There was a ply wall practically bouncing me up at either shoulder, the hole in the bench between my brown oxfords. I couldn't turn round; all I could manage was to tilt my head backward, look upside-down behind me. What I found to my utter horror was Brett's face—her hands like claws gripping the ledge of the wall beside her clammy cheeks—beady glassbottle-eyes upside-down staring into mine—not a foot away!

I let loose a loud gasp yanked my bloomers by feel up round my waist. At that moment I heard a burst of giggling—shuffling sounds—through the back wall of my cubicle. And Brett's face disappeared, dropped behind the wall. My whole cubicle rocking slowly from side to side, touching one shoulder then the next. I guessed that two or three girls had been supporting Brett on their shoulders, hoisting her up so that she could peer down over the back wall.

If she'd seen! If she'd only realized!

There was a long minute of silence. No sound but the beating of my own heart—a crazed little animal throwing itself up against the bars of my ribcage. I held to the walls of my cubicle with both sweaty hands, my head still tilted backward, upside-down—spinning, ready to pitch a faint—waiting to see if Brett's wretched face would appear again.

Then they started. Quietly at first, then louder. Three, four—maybe a dozen of them—I couldn't see to know for sure. Because to me it sounded like a *hundred*. Surrounding my cubicle on all sides. Beating their fists against the ply walls. Beating in time to the rhythm of their own horrid chant:

> *White cockroach in the WC,*
> *WC! WC!*
> *Playing with sheself in the WC,*
> *WC! WC!*

They repeated it again and again, louder and louder. Because I'm sure other girls came running quickly to join them. To beat their fists too. Join in the chanting too. Bolom, it seemed to go on forever. In my mind it seemed an interminable nightmare. My whole cubicle shaking, *moving* under my feet! With me pressing both sweaty hands against the walls, ready to pitch a faint, breathing faster and faster. My little heart beating as loudly and violently as their fists forever—*bam! bam! bam!*—beating forever against the walls of my beating breast.

At last the bell rang. At last I heard it clanging faintly above the noise. But they didn't stop right away: their pounding and chanting must have gone on for another five minutes. Another *lifetime*. Slowly it began to fade, the girls leaving one by one to return to class. Then I heard a loud whistle. I heard a girl whisper, "*BMB!*" and another, "*Look: BMB!*" And I realized that Mother Marie-Bernard must have left the classroom to find out why it was half-empty, what was going on; she must've appeared *herself* at the other side of the playingfield—her two-fingered whistle was famous. Because now the beating and chanting stopped in one. Dropped to a dead silence.

And I breathed a sigh of relief. Got down and sat on the bench, not even bothering to raise my skirt and lower my bloomers, but sitting on my skirt over the hole just so. Plugging it up—the foul odour, the

88

stench rising in heatwaves from the pit beneath. I was dripping with sweat. My skirt and blouse both soaked through, clinging to my back and thighs. My feet in the tall white socks like standing in puddles of warm water. My little chest continued rising and falling with each panting breath, jumping with each beat of my crazed little heart. I let my head tumble backward to rest gently against the back wall. Closed my eyes. Willed myself to breathe slowly, slowly. My heart to soften its pounding.

Then I heard loud knocking on the door. My head snapped forward and I opened my eyes, my heart taking off again. Silence, more knocking. Then I heard Mother Marie-Bernard's voice: "Who's that in there? Get you little backside out here this *instant!*" She knocked again. I raised my legs and planted my little brown oxfords flat up against the door. Pushed my back against the back wall, ready to fend off *three* Mother Marie-Bernards! She knocked a last time. Then I heard an exasperated chups and she walked off, her long skirt swishing against her legs, leather shoes pounding softly on the hard dirt.

I let my head rest against the back wall again. Closed my eyes again: at least she didn't know that it was *me* locked-up inside the toilet! And in any case, I quickly realized, it wasn't Mother Marie-Bernard I feared. Not truly. Not *physically*. The most she would do should she suspect mischief was send me to detention-study—and that was a safety which, at that moment, I'd have welcomed only too gladly. My great fear was the day-students. The whitee-pokees! I decided to remain locked-up in my cubicle till I heard the final bell. Till they went home. Then I'd be safe. At least until the following morning, when I'd have to face them again. Now I willed my breathing to slow down once more, my pounding heart. Now I willed myself to drop asleep. Even in the stenching, boiling WC. If only for a little while. To enter into the world of my dreams. Put a temporary end to my waking nightmare.

And I actually managed to fall asleep for nearly an hour. Actually managed to dream my dream of Dulcianne again. Because it was the last bell at three o'clock which woke me. As I listened to the soft, distant clanging I even smiled: now I was safe! I waited for what I imagined was fifteen minutes. Maybe half-an-hour. Till I could no longer bear the stench and the clinging heat of my cubicle. I stood. Slowly slipped the metal bolt across—*click*.

The door burst inward—shoving me down on the bench again, the back of my head slamming against the back wall. Brett and another girl grabbed my arms, pulling me out the door. There were three or four others waiting outside. They all grabbed hold of me, laughing, taking up the chant again:

> *White cockroach in the WC,*
> *WC! WC!*
> *Playing with sheself in the WC,*
> *WC! WC!*

I struggled—kicking my legs and fighting to pull my arms away— powerless against so many. Most of them older, bigger than I was. They pinned me down on my back on the hard dirt, gritty against my wet shoulders, each girl holding onto an arm or a leg, Brett standing beside me. Something silver and shiny in her hands—and for a moment I was sure that it was a penknife! But it looked dome-shaped at the end, a shortish, silverish tube. Then I thought it might be a canister of lip-stick—any form of makeup was strictly forbidden in the convent, even body powder; and the only lipstick I'd ever seen before had belonged to mummy. Brett twisted the canister—a malevolent smile on her face, beady glint in her glassbottle-eyes—and I watched the bright red head slowly emerge. By now they'd simplified their chant, by now it'd grown louder: "*WC! WC! WC!*" Brett bent over and carefully drew a red line down the middle of the *U* monogrammed on my shirt. First I was con-fused, then I understood: she'd turned the *U* into a *W.* New initials on my breast-pocket: *WC.* The chant grew still louder.

She wasn't finished. The girls holding my ankles had them spread wide apart. Now Brett stepped round and up between my legs. I felt her shadow close down on top me, dark and suddenly cold. I shut my eyes. Felt my wet skirt flipped up, my bloomers yanked down round my thighs. Now I felt the sensation of falling—backward, falling through the air. As though I'd been thrown inside a deep, dark well. Falling and falling. Suddenly I felt the lipstick shoved up inside me, hard and ice-cold—opposite, somehow, to what I'd anticipated—a hollow stab. And I landed flat on my back, *thwack,* hard against the hard water at the bot-tom of the well. My entire body stung for a few seconds, seared. Then

I felt my arms and legs and neck surrender as if in exhaustion—relax, soften, turn to jelly—and I felt myself sinking, descending into the icecold water.

There was a last burst of laughter. I felt their hands like loosened ropes slip away from my wrists and ankles. I heard them walking off—their talking, laughter, the padding of their shoes on the hard dirt—but as if from a great distance. As if I were *overhearing* it in someone else's dream. I was shivering from the cold. Even beneath the hot sun. After a few minutes my trembling began to stop, and I opened my eyes: powder-blue sky, cloudless, silence. Without looking, I reached down and gently, carefully extracted the canister of lipstick. The metal now slightly warm to my touch, soft and slippery at the end. I flung it away. Heard it deflect *thwack* off the ply wall of my cubicle and land in the weeds beside it. Still without looking, I raised my hips off the dirt and pulled my bloomers up round my waist. Lowered my skirt.

I lay there for a long time. Eyes open. Staring up at the cloudless, empty sky. When I sat up and got slowly to my feet, I was so dizzy I could hardly walk. And it was not until nearly two hours later, when I went to remove my blouse in the cabana beside the beach, that I realized the fingers of my right hand were stained brown with blood to the last knuckles. I raised my skirt cautiously and dropped it again. I was still too stunned to be frightened, even worried. I simply waited for the other girls to dress quickly in their bathing costumes and hurry out. Then I pulled off my bloomers and hid them inside my rolled-up towel. When I got to the end of the beach, alone, I dug a deep hole and threw my bloomers in. Covered them up with sand suddenly so white I imagined that it was what snow must look like. Cold and stinging against my stained fingers.

5

That night I did not dream of Dulcianne. I dreamt that I was running through the forest, naked, being chased by a thin black mappapee snake. I would stop running and hide behind treetrunks and mossy boulderstones, catch my breath; but every time I raised my head there the mappapee would be again. Curled-up, his forked tongue flickering between sharp yellow eyes, his tail raised behind with the rattles shaking. I'd jump up and take off running again. As I ran the metal crucifix of my chaplet kept slapping against my chest and collarbone—hard, painfully sometimes—but I felt comforted to know that I was wearing it. Protected. I'd been running for so long in my dream that I felt exhausted. My skin slick with sweat, glistening.

Then I came to a small, pink cubicle—one of the convent privy-stalls—now deep in the forest. But I wasn't startled in the least to find it there. It was as though I'd been running toward it all along. I looked over my shoulder; the mappapee was still following. I entered the cubicle and slid the metal bolt across. Climbed up onto the bench—panting, my heart beating fast.

And when I looked down at the flooring there was the mappapee! Curled-up, his head poised ready to strike, forked tongue slithering between his yellow eyes. I reached quickly for my chaplet round my neck—groping—but couldn't find it. Looked down at my chest; it wasn't there! And when I looked at the mappapee again it was transformed into my black chaplet—alive! Curled up on the flooring with his tail raised behind now the silver crucifix shaking, rattling! He slithered up onto the bench—my living mappapee-chaplet—slithering up slowly along my glistening leg, slowly, curling round it, entering and disappearing inside me. Black bead by black bead his entire length until the rattling crucifix-tail at the end, which stuck at the crosspiece.

6

I awoke swimming in sweat. Reached for my chaplet round my neck; it wasn't there. For a moment I panicked. Then I realized I'd forgotten it on the floor of the WC. I took a few deep breaths, tried to calm myself. All the girls round me were sound asleep, peaceful. In all likelihood, I told myself, my chaplet was still there; no one used those toilets after school hours. I'd return first thing before class to retrieve it. And I realized something else, something so obvious I could scarcely believe I'd not seen it already: my chaplet would protect me against the day-students. That was why they'd been able to attack me, because I wasn't wearing it. I was sure! Now I tried to calm myself again. To time my breaths with those of the girls round me. All of them—something bizarre, something I'd never noticed before—*all* of them suddenly breathing together in slow, perfect rhythm. As though they were one being. Calm and quiet and peaceful. But *I* continued breathing fast. Sweating. The whole remainder of the night. My eyes open wide, staring up at the shadows on the corrugated-zinc roofing. Because now I wouldn't dare allow myself to drop asleep. Not for an instant. To chance facing the mappapee-chaplet of my nightmare again.

The following morning, as I sat on the bench squeezed between two girls during Mass, I continued sweating. I could feel it dripping slowly down my spinecord, vertebra by vertebra, a continuous stream beneath my sweat-soaked shirt—still with the red slash on my breast pocket. My skin felt like if it were boiling. Cooking from the inside. Even though I felt *naked!* Conscious for every instant that I wasn't wearing my bloomers—and sure that all the girls and the nuns somehow knew—could somehow see my nakedness beneath the navy pleats of my skirt.

Finally we returned to the dormitory after breakfast, and the maids were there as expected, waiting for us with the tall stacks of our laundry. Washed, starched, and pressed stiff like pasteboard—so that we had to *peel* our things apart. Not that I was bothered a-tall that morning; I only wanted to dispose of my lipstick-labeled shirt. Only *wanted* to pull on a pair of the torturous bloomers.

Laundry-day occurred twice a week. Clean sheets for our beds, towels, a fresh uniform for each of us—everything down to the individual socks labeled with our names—and of course, a clean pair of bloomers. We followed the line and dumped our dirty things into the middle of a sheet spread out on the floor, which one of the maids tied up into an enormous bundle and carried out on her head. Of course, next laundry day I'd turn up missing my bloomers. But Sister Frances would say they'd been lost in the wash, which happened on occasion; she'd send me to Sister Eustasia to be measured for another.

But despite my change of uniform, I continued sweating bolts. All day long. Because in the few minutes while the other girls stood lined up before the classroom, waiting to enter for our first lesson, I took off running for the playingfield. For my cubicle at the far end. My chaplet wasn't there! I got down on my knees in front of my cubicle, reaching in through the open door, searching over the flooring. Only then did I realize it consisted of wood slats—just like the flooring of the cocoa-house—narrow gaps between the boards so the rain could wash through: *my chaplet had fallen into the pit below!* I jumped up and looked down through the hole in the bench—the stenching, cockroach-scratching blackness—even considered reaching my hand in. But even if I dared—and who knew what creatures *besides* cockroaches lived below—I could never reach down far enough.

I hurried back to the classroom. Stunned. Stranded again in my waking nightmare. More frightened than ever to face the day-students. And Brett was in the same class! She shoved herself onto the bench on the other side of my table—directly opposite. My eyes stuck like laglee to the reading primer before me. I wouldn't raise them for the world! But I could *feel* Brett's eyes staring at me. Staring at my breast pocket where the embroidery no longer bore its red mark. I could feel the perspiration dripping beneath my shirt, down the backs of my arms, slowly down my spinecord.

During recess I hid in the shadows beneath the banyan trees. The ones nearest the school buildings, the safest ones, slipping from one tree to another each time a group of girls approached. Till I ran out of trees and had to pull off my oxfords, climb up into the banyan in order to escape them. During lunchbreak I went to detention-studyhall. Told ancient Sister Agnes that Mother Marie-Bernard had sent me because I'd not written my essay on presumption. But when I sat down in the empty classroom, took out my paper and pencil, I realized I hadn't the faintest clue what *presumption* meant.

I spent the hour writing a letter to Dulcianne. An *imaginary* letter, since I'd never post it; Dulcianne would not be able to read it. I told her my dream of the two of us living together in the forest. Of my feeding her the sugared foofoo with my silver tablespoon. On the last line I wrote: *In my dream you and I are married.* And I signed it quickly, *Love L.* I folded my letter and shoved it between my books. When I looked up Sister Agnes was snoring—snorting out loud. She chewed her toothless gums mechanically for a instant, then her jaw dropped wide open—a black hole. I couldn't help but remember my lost chaplet. Suddenly I thought of something: *Maybe I'd looked in the wrong cubicle?*

When the bell rang for afternoon recess I took off running for the playingfield again. I started with the farthest cubicle, checking them one by one. But I still couldn't find my chaplet. I started down the line a second time. In the fifth cubicle I found it! The very same one I'd checked that morning. It *had* slipped between the boards, hanging suspended over the stenching pit—but just as in my dream!—saved by the metal crucifix which stuck at the crosspiece.

I fished it out carefully and hung it round my neck. Inside my shirt, pressing the cold crucifix to my warm breast. Then I had an idea. I went to the weeds at the side of my cubicle and began searching among them. At the same moment, over my shoulder, I noticed a gang of ten or twelve girls approaching behind me—Brett the leader hurrying a few paces in front! Now I began searching frantically through the weeds, *feeling* them approaching behind me, the soft clopping of their feet like horses' hooves on the hard dirt. Louder and louder. Then I found it, the lipstick soft and squashed at the end, but still intact. I stood and drew the line carefully on my own breast. The *U* a *W* again: my own initials.

When I turned round they were standing there before me, Brett a pace in front. I could feel the cold metal crucifix against my beating breast. The cold metal lipstick canister clutched tightly in my hand. I took a deep breath. Held my head up and walked straight through them. Past Brett and straight through the middle of the group—as though they didn't even exist! And I continued walking at the same slow, steady pace. All the way back to the school buildings. I got into line with the rest of the girls, calm for the first time all day, waiting for the bell to ring. To enter for catechism class.

7

That afternoon Mother Marie-Bernard lectured us, for the first time, on the sin of masturbation. Touching ourselves with impious hands. With the devil's wicked fingers. Our sacred bodies which did not even belong to us, but to God. So how *dare* we profane them so? "Better"— she quoted Saint Paul—"far better to *cut-off* the left hand, if it doth offend the right!" But, as we quickly realized, there was something different about this sin. Some aspect of this sin which made it more immediately terrifying for us than all the rest combined. This sin, we quickly understood, had repercussions in the real world. In *this* world: *our* world.

Mother Marie-Bernard now revealed to us the forbidden secret. She now told us—and who could question it? who could doubt her knowledge on matters of *this* sort for an instant?—Mother Marie-Bernard now told us what our parents, and our nursemaids, and all the adults had kept carefully hidden from us throughout our childhoods. It had to do with *duens*. Where they *came* from. What caused these diab-children to be born so.

Of course, she didn't have to explain to us what duens were; we knew. As surely as we knew about soukuyants, and lagahoos, and diab-lesses. All of us—even the day-students who'd come from away—all of us had grown up hearing about them. Those stories were connected to our earliest memories. Part of our own language. We all knew that duens were children who'd never been baptized, but no one had ever told us *this* before. No one had ever suggested that duens came from any place in particular a-tall. We knew only that they existed—some of us had even seen them—living deep in the forest. When we chanced upon them we'd hidden quickly behind treetrunks and boulderstones, watching them catching crabs in the river, which we knew was their favorite food. Or we'd seen them collecting bushy dasheen leaves, chewing on tender tanya roots, their wicked faces half-hidden beneath their Chinee straw-hats. But no one had ever confided to us, as Mother Marie-Bernard did now, *why* these diab-children were born with their feet turned round backward, no genitals between their legs; *why* their mothers never baptized them, but disappeared first thing into darkest night, traveling deep as they dared into the forest to abandon their newborn infants; no one had ever told us there was some secret behind all this illicit business. Some hideous sin.

Neither had we ever seen Mother Marie-Bernard so animated. Pacing back and forth at the front of the classroom. Her back hunched-over, clenched fists withdrawn inside her black sleeves. Her red moustache-bush glistening with spittle, so now it looked as if it were flaming in truth. Suddenly she stopped her pacing. Suddenly she turned round at the top of *my* table—staring down at *me*, talking to *me*. "Continue touching-up yourself like that," she said—her voice lowered, bony index finger flicking *clack clack clack* against her thumb, just in front my face—"continue with this *nastiness,* young lady, and you going find youself pregnated with one of these duens! You hear? *Eh?* You going find youself haveen with a diab-*duen!*"

8

Bolom, I pitched a faint. Right there in the classroom. I pelted-down on the coral flooring in a dead faint. Because the next thing I remember was waking up in my bed in the dormitory, Sister Frances sitting beside me, pressing a cool Limacol-soaked kerchief to my hot forehead. When she saw that my eyes were open she smiled, soft and gentle, a relieved look on her face. I'd received a nasty blow on my forehead when I'd fainted, she told me. But that was not what worried her; she hoped I hadn't contacted some sort of virus, some sort of fever. I was burning a rather high temperature indeed. Sister Frances got me to drink some orange juice, holding the glass to my lips, then patting them dry with a white kerchief. She told me to try and rest myself, and before she got up she freshened the kerchief on my forehead with more Limacol.

Now I was alone in the dormitory for the first time ever. Silent, ten or twelve empty beds stretching away on either side. It was a peculiar feeling. I wondered how long I'd been there, and almost at the same moment I heard the soft clanging of the final schoolbell in the distance. Suddenly I began to recall catechism class, what Mother Marie-Bernard had told me. And after a few minutes I'd made up my mind that I was pregnant with a diab-duen. Though I knew the idea was *absurd.* That rolling beads could not possibly produce a child—even the devil's own. (That according to what I'd learned from Dulcianne, a woman could not get pregnant till she'd seen her menses—*even if she done been jooked by a man—or the devil-self—already.*) Still, I made up my mind I was pregnant with a diab-duen. How could it be otherwise, according to what Mother Marie-Bernard had said? And I had been rolling beads for longer than three years!

Bolom, I fell into a kind of stupor. A feverish trance. I fell *basodee.* *Boobooloops. Bufutu.* As though I were sleeping with my eyes open. Staring up at the shadows on the corrugated-zinc roofing. Because when Sister Frances returned an hour later to check my temperature, to freshen the Limacol-kerchief on my forehead, and she asked me how I felt, I could hardly work my lips to pronounce the words. When she came with a tray of food that evening, tried her best to get me to eat some dinner—*good* food, food which she'd toted all the way from the motherhouse kitchen—I choked on the tablespoon of splitpea soup which she put inside my mouth. I could not eat and I could not sleep. When the other girls arrived later I was aware of them changing into their nightgowns, climbing into their beds—I heard Sister Frances reading to us from the big book of saints—but only from a dreamlike, muffled distance.

It went on for five days. Bolom, sometimes I wonder if it went on for the entire five years I remained there in the convent. But it was five days later when I got the letter. Five days later when I was awakened from my stupor by reality again. A reality far more frightening, far more cruel, than my fiercest nightmare.

It was a letter from my mother. Sister Frances brought it to me on the same tray with the dinner I hardly touched. She said she hoped the letter would cheer me up. But when she left me alone again in the empty dormitory, and I opened the envelope, I could hardly focus my eyes in order to read it. Another of those long and terribly tedious letters which mummy wrote once a month. Another detailed description of the estate's financial problems, of the falling prices of sugar and cocoa and copra, of how my father had been forced to sell off another plot of land in order to stave off bankruptcy. The words floated before my eyes, blurred and meaningless. That is, until I got to the end of the letter. Until I reached the postscript. I sat up straight in my bed:

> *P.S. You will be saddened to hear that your foolish little friend Dulcianne has managed to find herself enfantement. She names the culprit as a boy no older or less foolish than she, living cross the valley on Woodford Estate. Fortunately John Rostrant has agreed to take her on as one of the servants of that household. Your father and I shall see to our share of the bargain: that the two scoundrels are married good and proper in the Church.*

9

When I slipped silently out of my bed in the middle of the night I was no longer sweating. No longer burning a fever. My head felt clear for the first time in five days and nights. Clear enough to see through Mother Marie-Bernard's absurd and *evil* delusions. Clear enough to realize I wasn't haveen a-tall. That in fact I'd have preferred to bear a devil-duen, than to have to acknowledge *this* reality. All the girls were sound asleep. Calm and quiet. Their breathing slow and synchronized as though they were one person. I did not dress or even put on my shoes. I slipped out of the dormitory just so—barefoot, wearing only my nightgown. Past the sleeping girls. Past Sister Frances's cubicle of white screens, which suddenly seemed aglow in the dark. I unbolted the door and slipped out into the night.

There was a full moon which lit up my nightgown as though it were glowing too. The sky seemed almost as bright as day. The shadows beneath the banyan trees almost as dark and distinct. Still, I could have found my way with my eyes closed. I crossed the grass of the school-yard, wet and cold with dew, the hem of my nightgown damp and dragging round my ankles. When I stepped onto the playingfield a layer of dirt stuck to the soles of my feet, feeling as though I were walking in sandals. I lifted the hem of my nightgown. The insects in the forest behind the playingfield were screeching with a deafening noise. Interrupted every few seconds by a hollow *toc-toc* sound. I went straight to the fifth cubicle. The one at the end. When I pushed the door open the stench seemed almost to physically shove me back. I did not pause for an instant. Found my chaplet by feel and raised it up over my head, the silver crucifix catching the light, flashing once. It splashed *thwack* in the thick darkness below.

10

Bolom, my remaining years in the convent passed as though they were months. Weeks really. At least I've scarcely any memories a-tall from that period of my life. No doubt I've blotted them out from my mind. The beginning of the war had coincided almost exactly with my beginning in the convent; and strangely enough, the finish of the war coincided almost precisely with my leaving it, six years later. But it was not until after I'd been at the convent a couple years, that we'd really begun to feel the effects of the war. The whole of Corpus Christi felt it. From the poorest to the wealthy wealthy. Of course, it was the poor who suffered. In the convent we were constantly reminded of just how lucky we were. And Bolom, I suppose we were lucky in truth. At least we *had* food to eat. But such food! The same stuck-up rice twice a day every day for lunch and dinner, which we called *pappy rice*. It arrived on our plates as cold clumps, with a distinct ammoniac smell which remained on our tongues for an hour after eating it. And just when we thought we'd managed to force down the last mouthful, dessert arrived in the form of pappy pudding. Whatever fruits or vegetables the convent managed to purchase from the villagers were usually spoiled by the time they reached us. During those years we ate hardly any meat whatsoever. Pork occasionally. Locally raised chickens once or twice a month, which we called *hard fowl*. We ate mostly fish. Fish which was salted and locally caught too, always stewed to death, always unquestionably *fish;* every day we smelled it cooking for two hours before we arrived in the cafeteria, all the way from the classrooms.

Every morning during Mass, every evening in the chapel again for vespers, we prayed that Great Britain and the Ally-forces would defeat Hitler. Little did the nuns know that Mother Marie-Bernard had been given a new nickname, MHM: Mother Marie-Bernard of the Meinkampf Hitler-Moustache. But we knew that even the Ally-forces could not defeat Mother Marie-Bernard. By that time I'd been moved to the older girls' dormitory, which she supervised. The morning I informed Sister Frances that I was seeing my first period, she smiled and held me to her breast, and after awhile I realized that she was crying. I could not understand why, and neither could I cry myself, though I sensed that I'd lost something irrevocably. Little did I realize that it was not simply my childhood, but Sister Frances too.

That afternoon I was moved to Mother Marie-Bernard's dorm, shocked and frightened to discover that all of us—*every* girl in the dormitory—all of us were seeing our menses at the same time. All our beds with a special plastic lining under the sheets. An awful crackling noise each time we moved a limb. And in MHM's dormitory, whether it was our time of the month or not, we were made to wear our bloomers beneath our nightgowns while we slept. In time I grew used to these changes. In time my body learned not only to sleep and eat and to mumble the same prayers in unison with the others, but to menstruate according to a single rhythm. And Bolom, though I've no way of knowing, I'm quite sure that each night while I slept my dreamless sleep, I breathed in perfect time with the other girls too.

Then the war ended. It was as though the entire world were suddenly awakened from the same endless, dreamless sleep. Even in the convent we celebrated with a dinner of mashed potatoes and gravy and *turkey*. Turkeys which arrived frozen from America on big grey battleships toting whole airports on their backs. Turkeys which were given out in the streets. Which went by the magical name of *butterballs*. Bolom, they melted on our tongues as though they were butter in truth. As though they were sacred flesh.

Each year the convent held a rather elaborate commencement program, marked by the annual visit of our Bishop from Trinidad, and coupled with a Confirmation ceremony for the younger girls who were ready. There was a procession in which the Virgin was removed from her grotto and pushed on a little cart through the streets of Henly. All of us singing the *Ave Maria,* two or three of the younger girls walking backward before the statue, shoeboxes strung round their necks, sprinkling the pitch with white oleander petals. Most of the graduating girls' parents came for the ceremony, some traveling from distant islands. But as I learned early that morning, mummy was ill and confined to bed again—on my previous visits home for summer and Christmas, she'd spent most of her time in bed stiff with jaundice, puffed-up with dropsy—so she and my father would not be able to attend. Instead, they'd sent a special parcel with the parents of one of the other girls: a new gown which mummy'd had made for my commencement ceremony—white linen with tiny black polkadots—the same material used to make the First Communion gown I'd never been able to wear years before. But I wouldn't be able to wear my new gown either. Mother Marie-Bernard and the war had changed things since mummy's days in the convent, and for the commencement we were made to wear our monogrammed school uniforms.

It was not until late that afternoon, while packing my last few things into my little grip, that I removed the gown from its pasteboard box and examined it for the first time. There was a letter of mummy's pinned to the breast pocket, sending prayers and regrets. Again, it was the postscript which caught my attention: *In the breast pocket of your gown you'll find a very special gift, passed on to you from your great-grandmother, given to me years ago upon my own commencement at the convent.*

I reached into the pocket and carefully removed my mother's gold chaplet. And I stood beside my little bed in the already nearly empty dormitory, already nearly silent, holding the chaplet by two golden beads between the thumbs and index fingers of both my trembling hands. I held it up to the late afternoon light, glittering, my heart beating fast. I closed my eyes. Raised my hands slowly up above my head. Felt it slip down gently round my neck.

Done-dey-boo

1

Mummy never allowed herself to love me till I was a grown woman. Till nearly too late. For her, it was like a child's discovery of water. The pure pleasure of reckless splashing. Of surrender to sapphire cool. Having stood on the shore for forty-seven years, beneath an unbiddable sun, looking away at the sea. For me, Bolom, it was perfecting a technique for drowning.

She I had always adored. Mummy was the most beautiful woman I had ever seen. Bar perhaps the portrait of the French-Creole woman at the top of the stairs, her mother—her mother who'd succumbed to cirrhosis as she would. But that grandmother I'd never known. Never watched her rustle cross the grass as a bell-shaped cloud of skirts and starched petticoats, tapering to her famous, eighteen-inch waist (*Crinoline* they had called her in her courting days). Or during one of my parents' fêtes, watching through the crack of the blinds as mummy danced a tango cross the gallery—not with my father, never with my father—and Bolom, if her partner were West Indian, now the whole fête would've stopped to watch too. Because now mummy would be teaching the scratchy gramophone music itself how to dance. Gliding in long steps forward and backward and forward, her left arm outstretched her fingers gently touching his wrist—becoming *his* pulse, discussing every movement of their bodies through that almost invisible touch of fingertips to pulsating wrist. Pausing now and turning just before the gallery railing. Leaning over his arm in a dip for a split second which lasted forever in the memory. Farther and farther back and farther still—till her auburn hair swept the floorboards—and rising effortlessly again into air which seemed different after she had moved through it—lighter, brighter—every watching breath upheld.

So imagine my distress the evening I returned from the convent, climbed the staircase in darkness and felt my way along the hall to my parents' bedroom. I entered to find her lying alone in the center of the big bed, visible only by moonlight. Lying on her back with the sheet tangled fiercely round one ankle. Her arms and legs and neck thin and hard and twisted as ficus banyans, protruding from her silk nightgown. Yet her belly was huge, bloated. Not taut like a pregnant woman's, a malnourished child's: it was soft. Misshapen. Dimpled through the silk. Spilling obscenely in the direction opposite to which her head was turned. The skin of her face yellow as the yellow of a hard-boiled egg's yolk. Her hair now completely grey, thin and matted. Most distressing of all, her smell—alcohol, yes—but when I looked closer, I saw that the front of her gown and the bed beneath her was soaked with urine.

I managed to change her nightgown and the bed linens, all without her regaining consciousness. Then I sat in the worn, navy-velvet, open-armed chair mummy always referred to as the fauteuil chair. Cross from the end of the bed. I kicked off my oxfords and threw my legs over one arm of the chair. Lay my head back against the other and closed my eyes. Listening to my mother's breathing. To the thin, drawn skin of her cheeks fluttering wetly at the end of each exhalation. Waiting for my father to arrive.

Already it was ten or eleven o'clock. Years ago, before I'd learned better, I'd've thought he was still out in the boilinghouse with Ramsingh and the coolie laborers. But the estate no longer produced any sugar—or copra, or cocoa—and according to the last of mummy's letters, father'd converted the few remaining fields to tonka beans. An experiment: he hoped to introduce the plant from French Guyana. Apparently, the beans flourished. Even in impoverished soil—as ours indeed was. But these beans would not be used to feed the equally impoverished local population. My father's brilliant scheme was to ship them abroad to America—as the French Guyanese did to France; history of the Caribbean—where they would be used for the production of perfume. I fell asleep in the armchair. Unsure in my exhaustion whether to laugh or cry over the absurd picture I conjured up; my father with Ramsingh and the laborers, picking beans by moonlight, the half-starved coolies pausing every now and again to sniff the beans for their ripeness.

After what seemed like only a moment, I awoke with the uneasy feeling that I was still dreaming. Transformed into my own mother. Lying alone in the center of the huge bed, changed somehow out of my convent uniform into a nightshirt I was sure *did* belong to her. And after a few minutes she entered the room so rejuvenated from the previous night, now I couldn't tell if I were awake or dreaming for true (I would grow used to these miraculous morning transformations Bolom, often gin-and-coconutwater induced, mummy's twenty-four-hour cycles of death and rebirth). Her face was freshly made-up. Fresh colour in her cheeks. At the back of her head her hair was tied with a bright scarf, and she wore an equally bright sundress which made her figure appear twenty years younger. Mummy sat on the bed beside me. I learned that it was actually two in the afternoon. That on waking that morning she'd found me fast asleep in the chair. Moved me to the bed and changed me into the nightshirt just as I had done for her.

I sat up against the headboard. "And daddy?" I asked.

"Your father . . ." mummy looked away, pausing such a long time I thought to ask my question again.

"Your father has taken to sleeping in a separate room. For the best, I dare say."

I was more startled to learn that this separate room was my own bedroom. Of the four or five bedrooms in the old house, mine was the only one downstairs. Quarters of the family wetnurse in generations past. I pictured my little room, my father in the little bed, his feet poking out the canopy of mosquito-netting, like an inverted funnel strung from the ceiling. Slowly my mind drifted back six years, to my last night before leaving for the convent. Suddenly I was vex. Hot-up with tired, old anger. I spoke out despite myself:

"*My* room? Convenient enough for himself and Di!"

Mummy looked at me as though she did not follow my meaning. Then she laughed out loud (uncharacteristically, I thought). And as she began to speak, I realized my mother was actually talking to me for the first time in my life.

"Oh," she said. "That. All that finished donkey's ages ago. Di won't have anything to do with him now. A-tall. They don't even speak to one another, haven't for years." She took a deep breath. "Of course, there're others. Your father hasn't changed, you may be sure. Now he's older, the girls are prettier and younger still—Lil, I shudder to think! Those children still in their granny's pic-o-plats, pieces of orange wool bowtied at the ends!" She shook her head. "But not Di . . . certainly not Di."

There was a terseness in my mother's voice I'd not heard before. I thought of all those rambling, tedious letters. The pages and pages of them. All those years while I was away at the convent; they'd amounted to nothing more than a cry for help. After another long silence, I said the only thing I could think of:

"How is she?"

"Di?—she's fine. Waiting to bring you your breakfast, I should think. She's had Cook do you fricassee chicken and steamed christophine. And she's had Ramsingh cut you water-nuts."

I asked instead for coffee and bake dribbled with golden syrup. And hardly had mummy disappeared downstairs when Di arrived with my request on the shining silver tray. We kissed, and she stayed while I drank my coffee—*real* coffee, thick and bitter and over-sweetened with condensed milk—two of us talking for an hour after I'd finished. She wanted to know all about Henly—her own village of Sherman was not far away; Di's mother had even done maidwork at the convent for a time. I told her how Henly had changed. About the American Base they'd built nearby with the wharf for their big battleships. And though I wanted desperately to ask about Dulcianne, I waited for Di to bring up her daughter's name herself. She never did. (Later I learned that Dulcianne was a sore subject, that three years earlier she'd taken up her child and "run foreign"—Canada, America, Di wasn't sure where; she'd not heard a word from Dulcianne since.) Di took away my breakfast things, but I did not get up from mummy's bed. I did not get up for the whole remainder of the day.

2

And I continued sleeping there with mummy, two of us together in the big bed, for nearly nine months. During that time I hardly saw my father—even when he was *not* away traveling—as though he did not even live in the same house. It was only the two of us, and Di, for nearly nine months. Till I left for foreign myself. For England. Because just like all young West Indian women, just like all young West Indian *white*women—particularly those referred to as the *highwhites*—which, despite any blood claims to the contrary, I most certainly *was;* just like all young West Indian whitewomen of my class and bearing and expectations, after my debut—pronounced *dey-boo*—but before my courtship and inevitable marriage, I had to go away to England for a year to get "polished."

This became mummy's obsession. My preparation and introduction to the social circles of Corpus Christi. Mummy's own particular obsession, because I gave little thought to the matter. *My* only thought was sleep. Or, more precisely, *half*-sleep; to exist in that delicious place between asleep and awake. At least for the unforeseeable future. Not to stir from that safe, cool place in the middle of mummy's bed. My eyes closed with the light swimming past a mottled red-orange-black on the other side of my eyelids. Naked with the sheet drawn up under my chin.

Because I forswore clothing. Forever. (And Bolom, I've actually managed in part, *half*-managed; because to this day, I've never put on a stitch of *under*clothing again—not a brassiere, not a slip, not a pair of knickers—*ever,* even through the worst of a wretched English winter.) Mummy had a healthy laugh at that one. At my pronouncement that I should become a nudist! At the very least, a nudist-Buddhist. That I should rise from my meditations in the middle of mummy's bed only on the rare occasion, togaing myself up in the bedsheet only then.

For the first month after my return from the convent, I very nearly managed to accomplish as much. I lay in mummy's bed all day long, eyes closed, perfectly content, listening to the sun buzzing on the corrugated-zinc roof above my head. Or sitting up against the headboard, listening to mummy planning away on the bed beside me (for the first month I think she hardly drank a-tall). Three times a day Di brought my meals, which Cook prepared as my fancy dictated, in addition to tea each afternoon. Di would sit in the fauteuil chair cross from the end of the bed, telling me stories, while I ate from the silver tray on my lap. Three or four times a week I'd tie up myself in a big square of batiked cloth we called a wrap—very much in vogue then, a method for rendering the formerly scandalous bathing costumes more discreet—except I didn't even wear a bikini beneath my own. And I swam in the river naked too. Dressed in nothing but my golden chaplet, strung like a necklace round my neck. I lay naked on my back on the smooth white boulderstones to dry myself. Still half-asleep. Till one afternoon I opened my eyes to discover half-a-dozen boys and a couple grown men too—all *highwhites,* of course—all hiding behind a clump of bamboo on the other side of the river, all staring at me crosseyed, their tongues dripping-down red and obscene from out their mouths.

Eventually mummy realized that if she didn't get me out of bed, there'd be no debut, or polishing, or anything of the sort. First destination was the beauty salon. But the poor hairdresser nearly bolted when she got my single braid untangled. At the sight of my mop of dirty-blond hair—enough for three heads at least—springing out in all directions, reaching down past my waist. Mummy was insistent on one of the new, short cuts. One of the new *bobs,* she said. (All the world was a bob then, Bolom—coquette bob, bohemian bob, French, Flemish, Romanesque bob, new-moon bob—even a drawing above my sink labeled *debutante bob.*) The hairdresser politely informed mummy that hair as coarse and crimped as mine, could scarcely be shaped into anything more appealing than a "sucked-mango-seed." In her frustration she closed her eyes and chopped off half-a-foot, perpendicular cross my spine, still a couple feet longer than most everyone else's. But after she shampooed it with henna and combed it out, my hair settled surprisingly (it'd never known any style other than the single braid). The result, Bolom, was a mild shock. For all three of us. But much more so for mummy and me, for a reason which could not possibly have occurred to the hairdresser; my hair looked almost as mummy's had years before. Almost as I remembered it. When our eyes met in the depths of the mirror, I knew mummy had seen the resemblance too.

Next stop was the dressmaker. A tiny, talkative, terribly top-heavy Englishwoman known as *Tweetybird-Tottots*. Mummy and I went through fashion book after fashion book. Bolt after bolt of creamy, crinkly material. Frocks to be selected for each stage of my social metamorphosis: 1) *flapper,* 2) *dey-boo,* 3) *done-dey-boo,* 4) *polishing,* and 5) *courting.* (That afternoon we only got as far as two done-dey-boos.) First we picked out outfits appropriate for tea parties. For the flapper dances held each Sunday afternoon at the British Club. The girls, I knew, had started wearing slacks. Some, I'd heard, even added to the impertinence with *washykongs!* Mummy was horrified; Tweetybird nearly pitched-down faint, salts retrieved from her handbag for a quick sniff. We settled for two sailorsuit-dresses, two teagowns, two simplish frocks. Next we selected my debut gown itself—mummy thought it essential that Tweetybird get started straight away. My gown was to be white lace, matching elbow-length lace gloves and widebrimmed lace hat, selected from another two catalogs, another two hours in the choosing. By the time we'd picked out a couple more frocks Tweetybird was so excited, talking at such a rate—her face purple as a governor's plum—now we were afraid she'd pitch a faint in truth. We decided to leave the rest for another day.

I was so exhausted by the ordeal myself that I spent the following three days in bed. Then my first frock arrived. A midcalf-length chiffon teagown. But mummy wouldn't let me put it on just yet. First she had Di wash my hair—*"endless henna!"* she ordered—and brush it out. Then, kneeling on the floorboards before me, my feet soaking in the zinc washtub, mummy snapped an aloe stem and painted my legs with yellow-green jelly. Scraped it away with father's razor. Then mummy rubbed my legs to glistening with coconut oil. She herself polished my toenails, painted them with clear lacquer. My fingernails. She herself painstakingly plucked my brows. Penciled them back in. Mummy powdered my face with Cashmere Bouquet. Carefully applied mascara, shadow, rouge—all for the first time in my life. Only when she went to paint on the lipstick did my neck stiffen for a moment. Then I relaxed. Allowed mummy the four little flourishes of her wrist with the red-tipped canister.

Finally I dressed in my gown and stood before her triple-glass-mirror. Bolom, I scarcely recognized my own reflection. Di dropped the hairbrush, whispering behind me: *"Papa-yo!"* she said. It was one of those silly stunts of nature. One of her happy blunders: the gangly, unseemly duckling changed to the graceful swan. I had, in fact, been transformed into a younger version of my own mother—to an extent. Because Bolom, I could never be so stunning as mummy once was. I did not have her classic features. Her magnificent hair. I did not have her rich Creole colouring. But I *did* have her height, and I had mummy's figure. Almost to a *T:* my own waist measured eighteen inches and-a-half. The trunk of mothballed frocks we found in the attic fit me almost as well as Tweetybird-Tottots's. More than that, suddenly there appeared some salient resemblance between our faces. More precisely, between the three faces reflected in the triple-glass-mirror, and the equally astonished face of the young woman looking over her shoulder in the white gown—her train so long it went cascading down the St Maggy Cathedral steps and out of the photograph—preserved behind glass in the milky-green, once-gilt frame on mummy's dressing table.

3

It was she who trilled at my transformation. Much more so than I did. Or differently: my own excitement was watching mummy's face light up. That same afternoon she rang Lady Tristleton and announced we were coming round for tea—momentarily, at Government House. But hardly had tea been served when Sir Eustace Tristleton himself—all fubsy-tubsy four-and-a-half feet of him, complete with curling waxed moustaches and silver goatee—roared onto the gallery pulling us together to our feet. We must all come with him at once to the Oval: "our boys" were about to finish off the Barbadian team in the finals of a three-day testmatch.

I'd never seen cricket before. Hadn't a clue how it was played. Sir Eustace's enthusiastic explications—he immediately linked his arm through mine and refused to *un*link it the whole afternoon—only confounded me further. It hardly mattered. I was fascinated by the man bowling. Couldn't take my eyes off him; I'd never seen such an awkward spectacle in my life. Thin as a candlestick. Seven feet tall (or so he seemed), even though he was utterly and profoundly *boseebacked*. Indeed, that was how the crowd cheered him on: *Bo-see! Bo-see!* His long, chicken-bone neck protruding from humped-over shoulders almost parallel to the ground. Bulging eyes upturned so only the whites showed. And more outlandish than his appearance was his technique for bowling: a run-up which seemed more like stumbling down a flight of stairs. Wind-up which called to mind an overturned tortoise trying to right itself.

Hardly had I taken it in when the match was finished. Bosee paraded off the field to the British Club, the rest of us following behind, me still linked to the arm of Sir Eustace Tristleton. I must be introduced all round, he was saying. But which young gentleman did I wish to meet first? Which cock-on-the-fence? I told him, of course, that I should like to be introduced to Bosee. "*Bosee!*" he said. "Why that boy was born so ghastly-looking, the midwife quit her profession!"

Nevertheless, we went off in search of Bosee.

Of course, there was such a crowd pressed round him at the British Club, that Bosee was the only cricketer on both teams I did *not* meet. In addition to every unmarried male younger than the age of ninety. By the time we found our way back to mummy and Lady Tristleton—sitting outside in near darkness on a bench beneath the arbor, a waiter poised at the ready behind them—they were both so thoroughly inebriated they could hardly stand. Sir Eustace had his chauffeur drive round to the back gate. When we got home Di helped me walk mummy up the stairs. Get her into her nightgown.

This time it was mummy who did not get out of bed for three days. Her skin yellowed with jaundice. Ankles puffed with dropsy. Twice she vomited blood. Dr Curtis—the little English doctor-in-residence whom I'd disliked on sight, ever since he'd treated me for childhood malaria—Dr Curtis came by the first morning and examined her, repeating what he'd already told her a dozen times. In the foyer he asked to have a word with father. I told him he was away on a trip—Venezuela or the Guyanas—I wasn't sure, hadn't a clue when he'd return. Then he took hold of my elbow. Staring up at me out of a set of watery, newt's eyes, pressed deep into the folds of his clammy, doughy face. He told me that if mummy did not restrain herself, she quite likely would not live out the year.

Dr Curtis frightened me so much that during those three days, while mummy recovered, Di and I dedicated ourselves to ridding the house of alcohol. Dozens upon dozens of bottles. Crates and cases of them. Even a barrel of rum in the cellar marked 1902. We began emptying them two-by-two down the washbasin. Then I had an idea: we filled up the entire trunk of daddy's Ford with bottles. Piled them high as the collapsible roof on the back seat. I'd never driven a motorcar before. Only narrowly missed a dozen coconut palms—a hundred-foot-drop into the river below—Di and me screaming with pleasure every moment of the way. First stop was the coolie-barracks. To the laborers we distributed a case of French champagne. Bottles of Spanish wine and sherry. To Ramsingh we gave three bottles of twelve-year-old Scotch. Then we drove to the center of town. I parked daddy's Ford in the main square, directly beneath Sir Walter Raleigh's upraised sword. Di reached cross me to toot the horn. And Bolom, not since emancipation was declared has St Maggy fêted itself so.

During those three days hardly an hour passed when some man or the other did not come calling at the house. Di'd hurry back to the kitchen where I stood waiting, and we'd laugh ourselves silly thinking up some new, outlandish excuse why I could not come to the door: "The young mistress seeing she womanlies today, Sir!" "The young mistress busy playing with she dollies just now, Sir!" "The young mistress wake with a nest of crabs biting-up she too-too-loo something *terrible* this morning, Sir! Poor child could scarce walk!"

When mummy heard what had been going on for three days straight (not the alcohol—at that discovery she seemed almost relieved), she had a conniption. Di was of course quite correct to send the young men packing. But she need only tell them—as they should know perfectly well themselves—that the young mistress could not *possibly* be seen in the company of a gentleman till she'd made her debut. Which, mummy said, would happen even sooner than she'd anticipated.

Of course, before I could make my debut, I had to learn to dance. So that Sunday afternoon mummy dressed me up in her own pearls and a cream-coloured silk frock, and we went to the first, and only, of my flapper dances at the British Club. It was not unusual for some of the mothers to go along. Most of the girls, though, went on their own. Riding their bicycles. (I, of course, had never owned a bicycle, hadn't a clue how to ride one.) Mummy thought the idea of grown women riding very unbecoming—though she quickly got over the bicycles—seeing them dismount in slacks and rubber washykongs! For me the whole scene called to mind the convent—most of the girls had even been there with me—and that was one place I did not want to remember a-tall. In any case, those girls were not going to teach me to dance: I'd already made up my mind not to stir from mummy's side, for reasons obvious enough—the bar, of course, was open for the chaperons. As it turned out, though, I didn't *have* to leave mummy's side. Because when the first record began to play, and all the flappers clasped hands and ran screaming to the center of the floor, they did not begin to dance exactly. Not in any way mummy or I recognized. They began doing something else. Something they called *twisting*.

And I was pleased not to have to return to future flapper dances. Because now began what may well have been the happiest period of my young life. It lasted nearly three weeks. Mummy woke me early one morning, all excited, took hold of both my hands and dragged me down the stairs. Out onto the back gallery. She and Di had lugged the old gramophone outside—I'd almost forgotten it—together with all the old records which hadn't been played in years. Mummy announced that she would teach me to dance herself. And Bolom, so she did!

From early morning till late into the night, the old gramophone crackling, mummy and I danced. First it was ballroom stuff: one-step and two, waltz and foxtrot. Then mummy taught me the Latin rhythms: rumba, and bolero, and pasodoble. She taught me to dance to calypso music—and now Di couldn't help but join us, winding up her waist and shaking her bamsee so—three of us splitting our sides with laughter. Till we collapsed all three together in a heap on the wicker couch.

Mummy taught me how to hold my head up, perfectly straight, without the stiffness. How I must avert my eyes—always, as though my only thoughts were the music. She taught me to lead a tango from the other side—secretly, deceptively, so *he'd* never even realize he was being led—and mummy taught me to do it as gracefully as she did. Till I could dip as effortlessly as she beside the gallery railing. Till my own hair swept the floorboards. Bolom, it lasted nearly three weeks. Like secret lovers in moonlight, mummy and I danced. Like ill-fated lovers, sure of our own destiny, we danced and danced and danced.

Finally the day arrived, not without disappointment on my part. Tweetybird brought my gown of white lace, the elbow-length gloves and hat, and together with mummy and Di they dressed me up. Mummy'd hired out the British Club for the occasion, as well as Boy Blue and his orchestra—the only negroes, other than the waiters and cooks, ever permitted to cross the threshold. Since father was away traveling, Sir Eustace happily agreed to dance the first dance with me as proxy; I was pleased myself. But Bolom, no amount of lessons could have made that first dance less awkward. Less devastating! Not that Sir Eustace was a poor dancer. Not even that the point of his nose reached precisely between my breasts. The problem was another matter entirely.

When mummy and I arrived at the decided hour, the orchestra was quieted and Sir Eustace took my arm to walk me slowly to the center of the dancefloor. Followed, to my great misfortune, by the stage spotlight. And in a moment of absolute silence—the precise instant in which Boy Blue and his orchestra drew in their breaths and prepared to strike up the first waltz—the little coolie-boy playing the tassa drums, quite beside himself with astonishment, burst out: "*But she ain't wearing no underdrawers!*"

It was of course true. And beneath the spotlight, my exquisite lace gown had gone *transparent*.

Someone gasped dramatically—followed by a loud *broops*—and when I looked round I saw that it was Tweetybird-Tottots, sprawled-out in a dead faint cross the flooring. A brief confusion followed—smellingsalts located and Tweetybird revived—but at least some of the attention shifted from my gown. Along with the stage spotlight, focused again on the face of Boy Blue. Eventually the orchestra started up. But too late; they'd all seen. Every *cock-on-the-fence* in that British Club. And Bolom, it seemed the idea of my not wearing underclothing—the very *concept* of it, together with the story circulating that I swam naked in the river regularly too—was enough to turn them all to wadjanks. Turn them all tabanca. Too-tool-bay. Tarangee-bangee. Send them all assassa-taps. I could feel them preparing to pounce. Could feel the heat pressing at me from all sides, tension mounting by the second.

And that was only the beginning of my problems. Because now, as I danced the first slow waltz with Sir Eustace, staring into the pool of light floating on the crown of his bald head—struggling in vain to concentrate my thoughts on the music—now, Bolom, I began to sweat. *Not a little.* So by the time that first waltz finished, my gown was soaked through. Nearly as transparent as it had been moments before beneath the spotlight. Sir Eustace—oblivious to the scandal transpiring before his own eyes—bowed gallantly before me, then turned round to announce:

"Right gentlemen, to your corners and come out boxing!"

They did. They came at me like wild Warrahoons. Like hungry Caribs after a quenk. And the more alcohol they consumed, the more unruly they became. Fighting-down each other to dance with me every time the orchestra paused. Till they began interrupting each other in the midst of individual dances. With me flung from one set of arms to the next. From ballroom, to Spanish, to calypso music. So that I hardly knew what I was dancing to myself. Unable to rest for a moment. Even to catch my breath. So confuffled that in the middle of one dance I pulled off my elbow-length gloves, sweat-soaked too, flung them to the flooring behind my partner's back. Finally I left three or four of them there quarreling, hurrying outside. They came following behind me.

In front the British Club there was an enormous samaan tree. Spread symmetrically in the center of the circular entrance. First I thought to hide myself in the shadows beneath it. But they came pursuing me even under the tree, leaving me no other choice; I pulled off my white pumps and shoved them under the joint of two exposed roots. Hiked up my gown and started climbing. Of course, I'd spent my childhood climbing trees with Dulcianne—and that wasn't so long before. In a few seconds I was out of reach. Out of sight. The wadjanks looked at each other as though I'd vanished into thin air, complaining drunkenly. They decided I'd given them the slip and returned to the club, hurrying back in themselves. I took a deep breath; now I was safe.

Then I realized there was someone up in the tree with me.

He was laughing quietly, screwing the zoot of his cigarette into the side of the samaan's trunk. Just above my head. First I thought maybe he was a youngboy who'd crashed the fête, climbed up into the tree to spy on the fancy people below; then I saw that he was wearing tails himself.

I was vex. Again. Aggravated anew by this man's mocking laughter. "I understand now why those outfits are called monkeysuits!" I said.

He didn't respond for a while. I watched the glowing zoot of his cigarette trail slowly down to the ground. Land with a splash of sparks on the hard dirt. "Miss Grandsol," he said finally, quietly, "in your place, I shouldn't be commenting on costumes."

I looked down at myself, almost having forgotten my gown. Now I couldn't help but smile. And after a moment I found myself laughing too, though I wasn't sure why—no doubt to release the tension which had been building for two hours straight. A long silence followed. Only the cool breeze in the samaan leaves. The distant buzz of the fête inside, a blast of brass each time the front door opened. Finally it was I who interrupted the quiet. "So tell me," I said, "what are *you* doing up here?"

He cleared his throat. "I needed to escape the crowd for a while, Miss Grandsol. Much as you did. This tree was the most convenient means I could find to do so."

"Well," I said, "so long as we're going to be stuck up here in the same tree, you may as well introduce yourself."

With that he swung down onto the limb beside me—on arms which seemed inordinately long—as easily and gracefully as any monkey might. I thought to comment on that too, but I restrained myself. Because Bolom, I knew him in an instant. Though not by the name he gave himself: Keith Woodward. I studied his lean face. His long, chickenbone neck. Even more hideous up close and in the half-light than he'd appeared from a distance. And after a moment I understood why he'd attracted me so from the start; he looked just like Daisy, my childhood pet! At that thought I must have smiled, because he asked me to please tell him what did I think was so funny.

"I've just realized," I said, "that you look exactly like my first love."

"And you find that comical?"

"Quite, if you consider that my first love affair occurred with a chicken!"

He let go the branch above his head, stuck his thumbs into his armpits, and began flapping his elbows. And Bolom, at the same time he did something extraordinary. Extraordinarily *ghastly:* he spit out the bridge containing his upper two front teeth, protruding out between his pursed lips! (I learned later that as a boy, he'd caught a cricket ball square in the mouth.) And at that moment—flapping his elbows with his front teeth protruding like a pointed beak—he really *did* look like Daisy! I laughed so hard I nearly fell out the tree.

Eventually Bosee flipped his bridge back into place with his tongue, and I wiped away the tears of laughter from my eyes. "She was a very special chicken," I said, swallowing to catch my breath. "What we call a clean-neck-fowl. For years we were quite inseparable."

"And what, may I ask, distinguishes your sort of chicken from all the others? Its cleanliness?"

"Of course not; its neck. Which is long and bony and bare of feathers." And after a pause I added, "Her name was Daisy. Just what I shall call you!"

"Agreed," he said. "Anything but *Bo-see.* I'm told it's some sort of island slang."

"It's what we call a humpback. Which, I might add, was one of my beloved Daisy's most memorable characteristics."

"Miss Grandsol," he said, "I quite appreciate your memories. Though I'd ask you to kindly savor them on your own."

"Agreed," I said. Then after a second, added, "*Daisy!*" And from that moment Daisy was the name I called him.

5

We sat up in the samaan the whole night. For the remainder of my debut, anyway—which, as it happened, was not much longer. Because it turned quickly to an out-and-out brawl. Two of the wadjanks who'd pursued me earlier appeared again beneath the tree, visibly drunker. Audibly too, their *proper* English slurred almost beyond comprehension. We strained to listen from our hidden perch. Each argued that the other had insulted me. Each claimed to take the insult personally himself. Each calling the other reprehensible, ungentlemanly, a scoundrel. Finally each claimed to have had his *tie* insulted. This left me quite bewildered, Daisy beside himself with laughter. He whispered that both were fellow cricketers, one a classmate at Cambridge; the other had been at Oxford. Their quarrel, then, had gone beyond chivalry and honor. It had ascended to *schools*. And that, I soon realized, was sufficient to bring them to blows. To bring *all* the proper young gentlemen running from inside the club, each ready to defend his tie.

Needless to say, things soon got out of hand. Eventually a police jitney arrived, its siren bellowing. Three policemen jumped out, bootoos raised, ready to restore order. By this time practically the entire fête had arrived beneath the samaan tree—all the men shouting, all the women in tears. Finally the little chief-of-police blew his whistle and ordered the badjohns, ironically enough, to go home and behave "*like you got education!*" Sent them packing like a gang of whatless schoolboys.

Daisy and I watched the last of the crowd disappear. Then we sat up in the samaan a little longer. Till the lights in front the British Club were outed, and the headwaiter came to lock the wroughtiron gates. Daisy called for him to hold on a second, and we scrambled down from our tree and out the gates—the waiter staring at us as if we were a couple of jumbies. Only then did I realize I'd left my shoes inside, and that that was probably for the best; I'd have a far easier time walking barefoot. What I did ask Daisy for was his jacket—not that I was cold, simply that my gown had caused enough problems for the night. I spread it over my shoulders like an immense black shawl. We walked through town, deserted at that hour of the morning, then down to the harbour and out to the end of King's Wharf. The tide and the moon were both full. Now Daisy removed his shoes also, rolled up his trousers, and we sat with our feet soaking in the cool water.

6

We hardly spoke. That evening or ever. And if I were pressed for one word to capture our friendship, it could only be that: quiet. But it was not an uncomfortable quiet. Nor was it an empty one. For me it was a luxurious, cooling kind of quiet. A quiet which reminded me, that evening and always, of the silence beneath the water. As I lay on my back on the white sand of that beach nearby the convent. Holding my breath with my eyes open, staring up at the mirrored inside surface of the water. Now—as we sat on the dock with our feet soaking in the cool water, watching the sky slowly catch fire beyond the open mouth of the harbor—now I closed my eyes to imagine Daisy's face reflected there. On the rippling, silvery inside surface of my imagination. Unseemly. Hideous. To me somehow beautiful.

Moored alongside the wharf was the launch which transported passengers out to the big ships when they came calling. The launch which would transport me also, in a couple months' time, to the ship which would carry me away to England. Away from Corpus Christi for the first time in my life. I mentioned this to Daisy, with a half-hearted attempt to feign excitement. The truth was that I'd no desire to go to England a-tall. Especially since my *polishing,* after spending the last part of the summer with my grandmother in London, was to take place at another Ursuline Convent—the Ursuline Motherhouse in Kent. That very thought filled me with dread. (Though, as it turned out, it needn't have; because I'd be called back home before the first session could finish.)

Daisy told me he had little desire to return to England. He'd come to the island for a two-week visit, and so far, he'd remained for two years. Actually, though, it was not the first time he'd set foot here; though he'd left before his first birthday, Daisy had actually been *born* in Corpus Christi. His birth, he explained, had come at the end of a five-year assignment, during which Daisy's father had been transferred to the island as the branch manager of Barclays. His parents had filled him with their utter horror of the West Indies all his life. What Daisy discovered here, thirty years later, was quite the opposite. *England* was the place to which he felt no desire to return. Ever. Either for love or cricket, he told me. And no amount of money in the world—though the West Indians had long ago reached world-class level—could equal a cricket match in Lancashire on a brisk, dewy-cold English morning.

In any case, he continued, it seemed his meager fortune was to be made right here in Corpus Christi. The government was at that moment considering him as the principal architect for an extensive project to be known as the Family Planning. Low-cost housing for the poor. Daisy spoke of the proposal as though it were some sort of humanitarian calling. As though it were fate keeping him from returning to England. Little did I realize the same *fate* would involve me too, though it wouldn't save me the trip to England for my polishing. Wouldn't save me confronting a second set of Ursuline nuns.

But the real reason *I* did not want to go to England, of course, was my fear of leaving mummy. I was terrified of what would become of her without me. Only then did I realize I hadn't seen her since we'd arrived in the British Club that evening, nearly nine hours before—it was already five o'clock! Suddenly I felt concerned, though I told myself that surely the Tristletons would've looked after her—and at that thought I truly became worried.

Our only means of getting home at that hour was on foot. A walk I'd never made before in my life. A walk which'd always seemed—at least in my childhood imagination—to have been impossible. The property of the estate *alone* always seemed such a vast expanse separating us from town. But as I now realized—with more than a mild shock—in the years since my childhood St Maggy had grown. Frightfully. Almost to the point of swallowing up d'Esperance Estate. What surrounded it now was not endless canefields, not impenetrable forest, but little wood houses. Most of them actually shanties: broken-down constructions of stolen rubbish. Or roucou-scrubbed mudhuts—the inevitable red-and-white Hindu prayer-flags planted in front—tattered, tired-looking, drooping dustily at the end of their long bamboo poles.

Before I knew it we were walking up the broken stone drive to the house. I looked down at my filthy feet, at the blackened hem of my gown, breathing a sigh of relief. But as we paused in the middle of the drive before the old estate house—as we squinted up through the hard morning sun—it was as though I were seeing the house, also, for the first time in six years. The leafy ferns growing out between crooks in the gallery railing. Paint-chipped walls. All the moss-eaten filigree and rotting rafters. Castoroil bushes big as *trees* growing out of the roof—out of huge holes rusted through the layers of corrugated zinc. And at that moment I realized, for the first time, that St Maggy's despair had begun swallowing us up too.

Suddenly I remembered mummy. Without a word I tossed off Daisy's jacket, letting it fall to the ground behind me. Took off running through the front door and up the stairs. Di was sitting on the bed beside her, holding her hand. Mummy so still in the center of the big bed she seemed not to be breathing. And when I pressed the back of my hand to her cheek it was so cold, for a terrifying instant I thought she'd stopped breathing in truth. I sat on the bed beside Di, and after a few minutes she let go mummy's hand and put her arms round me. I pressed my face into Di's bare shoulder, allowing her to rock me gently back and forth, back and forth. And after a time Di began making a peculiar, *clicking* sound with her tongue against the roof of her mouth: calming, soothing. A sound I knew well from my childhood, remembered from the many occasions I rushed crying into Di's waiting arms. We remained like that for several minutes. Eventually I told her to go home and get some rest herself. At the door to mummy's room I stopped her, reached behind my back and unzipped my gown, letting it fall to the flooring. I stepped back and picked it up, handing the gown in a ball to Di.

"*Burn it!*" I whispered. "Or keep it yourself. Only make sure I never see it again!"

I closed the door and slid into bed beside mummy, too exhausted even to worry about washing my feet. Anxious only to close my eyes. To put an end to that nightmare of my debut.

7

Mummy was not long recovering this time. Still, I did not leave the house for several days. Though hardly an hour passed that Di did not go to the door to turn some young gentleman away. After what I'd witnessed at my debut, I wanted nothing more to do with those *gentlemen*. I felt different about Daisy, though he did not come to the house; it was I who went calling on him. The following Sunday afternoon at the Oval. When practice was finished we spent the evening together. Though I made sure to bring him home—that way I could look out for mummy.

And soon Daisy was coming for dinner three or four times a week, for those few weeks which remained before I left for England. This suited Daisy fine. Not only did he love walking through the old house (he said it was one of the few buildings of the true Colonial style still standing), but he found the impeccably English dining at Chancellors Boarding House impeccably tasteless. Whereas at home—with mummy and Di and Cook to fuss over him—he was sure to sample some new, exquisite West Indian dish: pepperpot, or pasteles, or Creole chip-chip

121

stew. Or curried mutton, not English style but East Indian. Mummy, of course, dedicated her entire days to the planning of these meals. Which pleased me thoroughly; not only to share mummy's enthusiasm, but at least I was not the focus of her attention for a change.

She was just as fascinated by Daisy as I was. In just the same way. "He's so *atrocious*-looking," I heard mummy say one morning, even before I'd opened my eyes, "that after a time he begins to appear beautiful." She gave him her own nickname: *Yeux-de-poisson-beau!* Each time he spit out his front teeth and did his Daisy imitation, mummy'd laugh like a young girl. Di'd drop whatever she was holding and bawl out, "*Oui fute, Papayo!*" And she'd take off running for the kitchen, laughing too. Best of all about Daisy—at least so far as I was concerned—as a professional athlete he did not touch a drop of alcohol. Not even wine at dinner. This, I knew, secretly pleased mummy too.

When I come to think of it, that was my official *courting,* if I had any: those quiet suppers at home with mummy and Daisy. Because soon as word got out that we were a couple, etiquette dictated that the other gentlemen stop calling at the house. With great relief on my part. Besides the fact that Di and I had gone beyond the limits of our imaginations in thinking up excuses: "The young mistress belly bad this morning, Sir!" "The young mistress busy on the toilet making ricewater-stools all day long, Sir!" "The young mistress ain't wipe sheself proper and catch a terrible bitty-bambam in she bumbum today, Sir! Poor child could scarce walk!"

I was happy not to see them again. Or the young women who kept them company. Fortunately for me, Daisy was not one for fêtes. Weekend excursions down the islands with the other young people. Even Sunday picnics at Huevos Beach. This, I soon realized, had to do with the fact that he did not drink. That inescapable West Indian pastime. The one aspect of island life which cut cross *all* social and racial barriers; not even a walk round the savannah was possible without stopping at a parlour to fire a rum-cocktail. Daisy and I spent our evenings sitting on the back gallery after supper. Listening to the wind in the tall flamboyant. To the water rolling up over the rocks and receding again. Looking out over the calm, moon-glittering sea. Often an hour at a stretch without a word spoken between us.

Finally the day of my departure for England arrived. Actually, I left earlier than I was supposed to, because I insisted on going on one of the British Petroleum tankers. Mummy could hardly scrape enough money together to send me on the cruise ship; and even if he'd had it, father was not around to ask for more. Whereas on the BP tanker, the crossing from Corpus Christi cost only thirteen or fourteen pounds; a pound a day, meals in the ship's galley with the sailors included.

Only because mummy seemed so set on it, could I possibly consider leaving. But in truth, her health during those last weeks was better than it had been in years. And now I could leave her under Daisy's charge. I implored him to continue his suppers with her at the house, by then seven nights a week. He assured me it would be his pleasure. Implored *me* again and again not to worry. Of course, I knew better. And early that morning, as I looked back over the foamy wake of the launch, two of them standing alone at the end of King's Wharf, I could only wonder if I'd ever see my mother again. Daisy, I suspect, saw the fear in my face (I never asked him). Because at that moment he spit out his teeth and did his clean-neck-fowl imitation. It *was* the last time I saw my mother. And even over the roar of the boat's engine, I can still hear her laughing like a young girl.

8

I was seasick practically the entire voyage. Hardly left the confines of my tiny cabin—which, fortunately enough, had a kind of toilet built-in under my mattress. A few mornings I managed to make my way to the galley for a late breakfast, which I ate alone. Di and Cook had packed up a hamper of food for me—so big it occupied practically the entire upper bunk—so I didn't even *have* to venture into the galley. When I did go for my first dinner (on the evening of the ninth day, the tanker anchored in calm water off the Azores Islands), I realized that I was the only female on board ship. All the sailors' eyes stuck to me like laglee. Every instant I ate my supper! So did the eyes of the other passengers—five or six older Englishmen. As soon as I finished I hurried back to my cabin. Bolted the door shut.

Only a few minutes later came the first knocking; the first-mate wanting to know did I wish to take some air on deck. I spoke through the closed door. Told him thank you very much, but no. After awhile I began to hear them carousing in the galley on the level above my cabin—their sailor songs, laughter, an occasional muffled shout or whistle. Soon I heard pounding on my door again, the drunken voices of three or four sailors outside. When I did not answer, they began shouting obscenities. I turned sideways sitting on my little bunk, my back against the metal wall, bare feet pressed-up against the cold metal door. The vibrations of their every blow traveling up my legs. Every blow sending the back of my head butting against the wall. They came pounding several more times, shouting more obscenities, on and off the whole night.

When I eventually fell asleep—my feet still pressed-up against the door—I dreamt my dream of running naked through the forest, chased by the thin black mappapee snake. Only now my dream seemed to go on interminably. For the remaining three days and two nights till the tanker arrived in London. Because each time I came upon the same tiny, crimson-coloured cubicle in the forest. Each time I looked back over my shoulder to verify that the mappapee was still following—no matter how exhausted I felt—I continued running in my dream without daring to open the door.

9

I was so relieved to see my grandmother that I wanted to throw my arms round her. Only the look on her face prevented me from doing so. First I thought she didn't recognize me (I'd only seen her three times in my life, on her three visits from England, and the previous visit had actually been seven years before). I was wrong: she knew me straight off. Reached to shake my hand limply. "You're absolutely as stunning as your mother," she said. "I should hope you didn't inherit *all* her qualities!" With that she turned her back to me, and I followed behind, toting my two grips.

She knew more about mummy and daddy than I did. At least she seemed to have spent more time contemplating their relationship— which from a young age, I had very happily ignored: mummy's alcoholism, father's adultery. I could hardly remember a time when it had been any other way. And during my previous months at home, my father'd not even been there to remind me that they *had* marital problems. Bolom, in my mind it had never even been a marriage. More a sort of *agreement*—and very *English* at that. (In the West Indies couples fought like dogs and made love like cats, between the two screeching into the night all night long. To my knowledge—but perhaps all children think of their parents in this way?—mummy and daddy had never done either.) In any case, it was clear from the first time I looked at my grandmother that whichever version she'd gotten of mummy and daddy's situation, had come from my father. Clear, too, that she held my mother accountable. That she'd grown to despise her and *her* West Indies. Clear from the first time I looked in my grandmother's face that somehow she held *me* accountable too. If only because I now looked so much like mummy.

My grandmother wasn't always openly hostile. Too frequently, though, she couldn't restrain herself. Some comment concerning my backwardness, my lack of exposure. She was flabbergasted that I walked about her tiny flat slipperless. That once I wandered absentmindedly out into the *street* barefoot! Though the weather during those first weeks in London was glorious—just like Christmas weather at home. I left the flat first thing in the morning; returned an hour after sunset. I'd walk the streets till I felt ready to drop. Then I'd collapse on a park bench, or hop on one of the bright doubledecker busses.

Then—within the space of a couple hours one morning—I watched the sky turn dark and cold and dreary. After that I never saw the sun. The temperature suddenly so cold I couldn't *think* of leaving the tiny flat. Though the alternative was my grandmother's condescending face. I'd lock myself up in the WC—the warmest room in the house—sometimes two hours at a stretch. Until my grandmother began her innuendos concerning what I *was* doing inside!

I actually began to look forward to the convent in Kent; it could never be worse than my grandmother's tiny, freezing flat. It was in fact better. Much better. For starters it was warmer—with *electric* heaters in each of the dormitory bedrooms—and only two girls to a room. I'd sit on the rug before the heater till my whole body glowed. Till I felt radiant. My little roommate from Bristol thought me the funniest thing. Between my obsession with the heater and my island speech, she never stopped giggling. And those Ursuline nuns were much more modern than the ones I'd known at home; I'm sure Mother Marie-Bernard would have thought *those* nuns scandalous—one of them even smoked cigarettes! But I'd hardly been there eight weeks when Daisy's wire arrived. Together with funds sufficient to take the cruise ship (which actually made the crossing in half the time).

From the look on Daisy's face I knew I'd arrived too late. We took a taxi from the harbour straight to the Queen's Park savannah. Then we walked cross the tall grass to the tiny Pechet Cemetery in the middle— reserved only for blood relations of that founding French family— Daisy walking beside me toting my grips. On the way across I'd thought to pick a handful of flowers: oleander, poui, poinsettia. Whatever I could find. But all I could come up with was a kayakeet bush—actually a kind of weed—tiny red and orange flowers, together with clusters of bright purplish berries. I broke off a branch bursting with both. The cemetery gate was locked. Daisy had to help me climb up over it. Then he had to show me the plot, because even though I knew where the rest of the family was buried, it would be up to me to arrange for mummy's headstone. A small white cross marked the grave. I lay the kayakeet branch beside it. But as we stood there before mother's plot, listening to the silence of the little cemetery, suddenly I couldn't pray. Couldn't even remember the words—despite all my years in the convent. I could only think of the small wooden cross Ramsingh had made and painted white for my pet fowl Daisy, so many years before. That was the first death I had known; this was only the second. And though I felt silly mentioning it, I told Daisy the story. It turned out Ramsingh had made mummy's cross too.

That, I quickly decided, was too much of a coincidence. I got down on my knees in the moist dirt before the cross. Mashed the kayakeet berries in my palm until I had a handful of purple paste. With my index finger I carefully painted one of mummy's initials on each arm of the cross: first a *J* and then a *G*. Then I mashed more berries. Got up and kneeled again behind the cross. On the back of the crosspiece I painted the initials of her two mourners: *D+L*. When I was finished, I looked up from my kayakeet-stained hands at Daisy standing above me. He gave me a look as if I'd lost my head.

We climbed back over the cemetery fence and crossed the savannah again. On the road we flagged down a taxi. But after we got in I decided I wanted to walk home. Paid the driver to drop off my two grips, and we climbed back out.

10

It was late afternoon when we finally walked up the stone drive to the house. For some reason—though I hadn't had any communication from him the whole time I was in England—I assumed my father would be waiting inside. I'd actually spent the entire crossing thinking about him. More time than I'd even spent thinking about mummy; and I still wasn't ready to face him. At the front door I turned and led Daisy along the gallery round to the back of the house. We sat on the stoop, watching the last of the sun vanish behind the dark purple wall of the sea. Eventually it was I who interrupted the quiet: "In all your letters, you never mentioned the Family Planning project. Whatever became of it?"

"Still in government negotiation," he said. "And you know about that. But I'm still hopeful."

There was another silence. Again I interrupted it, this time with enough courage to say what was truly on my mind: "I presume you've had the pleasure of meeting father."

"Actually, I haven't yet." And after a moment, he added, "I don't expect to anytime soon, either."

I turned to look at the side of his face, his chin still pointing away at the sea. "I'm afraid," he said, "that your father won't be setting foot on this island for a good long while. The moment he does, the bankers will have him taken off to jail." Now Daisy turned to look at me. "Lil, they're ready to foreclose on whatever remains of your family estate. Which, as it turns out, is not much more than this house."

I sat there speechless. Daisy continued looking at me.

"Your mother," he went on, "had little idea how bad things had gotten, fortunately enough. Di and I were at her bedside when she died, upstairs, as peacefully as could be hoped."

Now Daisy turned to look away at the sea. I was afraid to do so myself, somehow finding comfort in the outline of his face, silhouetted against the sunset; I'd spent even less time contemplating the estate's finances than mummy had. The sudden thought of losing it, I found devastating.

"I've looked into the situation," Daisy said after a time. "And though it's more money than I have at present, I'd like to put in the application to purchase it back from the bank." Now Daisy turned again to look at me. Suddenly smiling. "I'd like to do a little family planning of my own, so to speak. That is, of course, with your consent, Lil."

I smiled too—straight off. And though I wanted to give him my answer immediately also, I forced myself to wait awhile. Looking Daisy straight in the eye. Studying his face against the backdrop of crimson sky. Forcing myself to listen for a moment to the breeze in the flamboyant tree. To the gentle waves rolling up over the rocks. Until I could no longer hear them for the beating of my own breast.

Then I answered: "Make the application," I said. And after a moment, added, "*Daisy!*"

d'Esperance Estate

1

Daisy wanted a church-wedding. Not even his own church: mine. Actually, it was a promise he'd made mummy. That should I agree to marry, we'd have the ceremony in the Catholic Church. For Daisy, Protestant or Catholic, one was as good as another. Or as bad. I felt indifferent myself. In truth, I'd spent little time thinking about it, despite mummy's endless planning. Now that I did, a Catholic ceremony seemed inevitable enough. Though Daisy agreed that it would be a quiet one, following so closely on mummy's death.

And a quick one, due to the arrangements Daisy had made to purchase the estate back from Barclays Bank. As I understood it, mummy—who'd inherited the estate from her own mother—mummy'd passed it on to me by way of a Deed of Gift. Common practice in the British West Indies. This, I suppose, avoided death duties. More importantly, it avoided the probation of a will (mummy's attempt to save me from father's clutches). Unwittingly, though, all she'd made me heir to were his debts. But by a second Deed of Gift I would make

Daisy joint-proprietor—joint-pauper. The estate could then be bought back from Barclays under both our names, this way dodging the stamp taxes—which, in 1946, only amounted to 2½%—but Bolom, we could scarcely scrape enough money together as it was. Actually, the only thing that was clear to me was that all this commess had to be completed *posthaste.* The wedding quicker still. So if Daisy'd promised mummy a Catholic ceremony, I found little reason to disagree. And in any case, so far as my relationship with the Church was concerned, the convent had long exhausted me of all my youthful anger. Left me feeling numb inside. Dead-up myself. Or so I thought.

It was the ancient Irish priest, Bumblebee, who met us at the rectory door. Immediately I felt a warm stickiness in the palms of my hands. He recognized me too. Straight-off. Though I'd not been to Mass at the St Maggy church for years—and for that matter, neither had mummy. But as Daisy informed me with a whisper (while Bumblebee disappeared into his bedroom for a moment), mummy'd asked for the priest in her final hours; it was Daisy who fetched him to the house to administer the last rites. Bumblebee who performed the interment—while I hurried toward Corpus Christi on my ship from England.

He returned wearing his pasteboard collar, charged-up to speak to us in an official capacity. Changing the subject in one from our marriage to Daisy's conversion. In a single breath. "You'll be swearing to raise the children in the Catholic Church regardless," he said, wattles warbling above his stiff collar. "Even if you *insist* on a mixed marriage. And the proper way to raise spiritually healthy children, Mr Woodward, is to heal *yourself* properly first."

Daisy gave me a look like he hadn't understood a word. For me, only one word was necessary: *children.* (A word which in my mind, Bolom—despite all illogic—was synonymous with *duens.*) Suddenly my skin felt as if it were cooking from the inside. Suddenly sweating bolts. When I grabbed Daisy's hand to pull him out the rectory, my palm was so wet it slipped out. Sent me bounding up against the back of the door, bruising the side of my face against a little window covered with a rusty screen—a gritty, metallic taste in my mouth. I flung the door wide open. Grabbed hold of Daisy's elbow with both my hands. Dragged him out the rectory all the way out into the middle of the street.

We hardly spoke during the taxi drive home. When we arrived it was still well before noon. I told Daisy I needed a cool seabath at Huevos Beach. Led him along the trace to the dilapidated shed which had once been the boilinghouse, but which now housed father's old Ford. Hidden away beneath a dust-covered black tarpaulin. Surprisingly the bank had never come to claim it. More surprising still, it started with the first try. Daisy had an English driver's license, though he'd hardly used it since he'd arrived on the island. I had no license a-tall. Even so, *I'd* already made up my mind to drive—for the second time in my life. Of this I hardly needed to warn Daisy; I nearly knocked-down a dozen coconut palms before we reached the main road—nearly pitched-down over the cliff into the river below—Daisy's face white as a ripe cocoplum.

First stop was Government House. I hadn't seen the Tristletons since I'd returned from England. They offered sincere condolences. I told them to hurry and get on their bathing costumes, because we were all going for a picnic at Huevos Beach. Quite possibly they were trying to humor me—Daisy included—thinking I was suffering a shock due to mummy's death. Because in two minutes flat we piled back into the Ford ready for the beach. All pretending my driving was absolutely normal, though I nearly met with an accident at every turn! The other cars screeching off the pitch left and right, blasting their horns—not a single word that I was driving in the opposite direction.

Because instead of the beach, I drove to the courthouse. It was a Saturday morning. Of course the magistrate was not there. Luckily, though, he was still asleep in his house cross the street. His wife answered the door, apologizing for her husband who she said was suffering a wretched case of "monkey-knee-syndrome." Sir Eustace laughed aloud and marched straight past her, pulled the magistrate out of bed. Got him to fire-down a quick rum. A rolypoly, brown-skinned negro with a shiny bald head and thick, tortoise-shell eyeglasses—which he scrubbed earnestly with his shirttail the whole time he spoke, holding the glasses only an inch in front of his nose—his bulging brown belly exposed, jiggling-way, deep purplish navelhole staring up at us out of the middle.

In the space of fifteen minutes Daisy and I were married. The Tristletons standing as witnesses, standing there in their matching hibiscus-flowered cabana suits. The little magistrate scrubbing away at his glasses, mumbling inaudibly behind them. At last he dropped his shirt-tail. Carefully fixed the wire curves of his eyeglasses behind his ears. He turned to Daisy: "You could now please kiss the bride!"

An awkward silence followed. Because as Daisy and I suddenly realized, we'd never kissed. Not once. Not in a romantic way. (As though our courtship had proceeded at such a rate Bolom, we'd never had time; skipped straight to practical matters, and never given that part a thought.) To my knowledge, we'd never even held hands. And in that awkward moment of my wedding—the moment *most* women dream of their entire youths—Daisy did just what I feared most he might: he spit out his front teeth and began flapping his elbows, doing his clean-neck-fowl imitation. The Tristletons looked at each other as though he'd gone vie-kee-vie. As though he'd lost his head. The magistrate so incredulous he took off his glasses again to examine the lenses. Daisy flipped his bridge back into place. Put his arms round me and waited for me to close my eyes, kissed me as earnestly as the little magistrate scrubbed his glasses. A few minutes later we were all piling back into the old Ford. This time joined by the magistrate and his wife—now dressed in their own matching hibiscus-printed cabana suits—and I drove off ceremoniously tipping the horn—*be-be-beep-be-beep-beep!*—this time in the proper direction for Huevos Beach.

2

As slow as Daisy and I were in getting round to the rituals of courtship, we were prompt in confronting the proprieties of marriage. Because we consummated it that same night. Here, in mummy's own bed. This same bed in which I, and mummy, and mummy's mummy before her had been conceived, and born, and had consummated their own marriages too. Actually, it was as much my doing as Daisy's. Perhaps more so. Because when he emerged from the WC wearing his long-sleeved sleeping costume, dressing gown, and burgundy bedroom slippers (some of the "necessairs" we'd stopped to pick up at Chancellors Boarding House on the way home), he found me in the bed waiting. Already stripped-down naked naked. Dressed in nothing but the gold chaplet strung round my neck. I told him the truth: that I didn't *own* a nightgown. Hadn't worn one since I'd left the convent. Daisy, I'm sure, was startled and a bit embarrassed by the ease with which I regarded my own body. *His* too. Because when he stripped off his nightclothes—when he stumbled nervously on a pajama pantleg, tumbling backward into the fauteuil chair, knees agape—Bolom, when I caught a *glimpse,* I suddenly lost my wits to my curiosity. And I committed the indignity of sitting up in bed, of crawling on all fours to the end of the mattress for a better look!

I'd never seen anything so peculiar in all my life. I was fascinated: *there* was the clean-neck-fowl. There was my longlost Daisy—her skinny, gangly neck drooping down from her little fuzzy body—there nestled between Daisy's legs. I even let loose a childlike peal of delight! Poor Daisy looked *horrified.* Like he wanted to bolt. Like suddenly he didn't know *what* he'd gotten himself into with this marriage. Bolom, I did the only thing I could think of. Only way I could hope to save the situation. I lay back quickly and reached over to out the light, sending the room into pitch darkness.

Of course, now my hands couldn't restrain themselves from examining in the dark what I'd just seen in the light. And, of course, with my touch the clean-neck-fowl began a series of transformations. Almost immediately. Assuming increasingly alarming textures, and temperatures, and *proportions.* Bolom, I pulled my hand away like I'd reached into a live coalpot. Now *I* didn't know what I'd gotten myself into with this marriage. Because to me, in my vivid imagination—in the thickness of that inksquid slippery darkness—to me that sweet banty clean-neck-fowl suddenly felt enormous. Monstrous. How possibly was *she* ever going to fit up inside little *me?* The very idea seemed absurd. It seemed impossible—and even if it were possible, I did not want to find out how. A-tall a-tall a-tall! Now *I* wanted to bolt. To take off running like a dog from he own big-stick. Literally.

Somehow Daisy sensed my fear. Somehow he perceived it. Because now Daisy took charge. Tenderly, patiently, and—something a little surprising—confidently too. Led me through those alarmingly impossible mechanics. And what had at first seemed to me so *strange,* the *physicality* of it—because I had the distinct notion that he was turning me inside-out, peeling my moist skin backward like an overripe mango, stopping-up my every orifice—so utterly peculiar, I remember thinking, *He's inventing this, surely! This can't be right!* What had at first seemed to me so strange, soon began to feel fairly natural. Which is not, of course, to say that I experienced any pleasure. Not that first time— indeed, not for a while, and that discovery would be my *own* doing— but Bolom, neither was the experience much painful. Not much. Not as I'd anticipated so geegeeree only minutes before. In truth, the whole business was over with almost before I realized. Almost, I think, before *Daisy* realized—the *Oh!* escaping his mouth at the culminant moment sounding more surprised than anything else. And a few minutes later Daisy was already sleeping peacefully. I lay there at his side, listening to his calm, quiet breathing. Comforted for the first time since I'd lain beside mummy in the same bed, many months before. Relieved to surrender myself up to sleep too.

3

Only one problem arose in the purchase of d'Esperance Estate back from Barclays. It suddenly became clear that father'd peddled-off the land on which stood Di's little house. (Actually, mummy'd signed away almost *all* the estate's property at his urging, most likely clueless as to what she herself was doing.) Di had lived in that little house since the age of fifteen. Since mummy and daddy were married and she'd come from her village to work on the estate. Though *I* seemed to feel more sentimental about the little house than she did. After all, that was the place I'd run to every afternoon of my childhood to collect Di's daughter, Dulcianne. The place—before we took off running again for the river, the cocoafields—the place where Dulcianne and I had ourselves played "house." She the servant serving and me the mistress mistressing, sometimes with the roles reversed.

Because when I informed Di of the situation she only chupsed: "Dou-dou," she said, "is praise like *peas* the last night I sleep beneath that caratroof!" And when I went with her a couple afternoons later to see it for the last time, I understood why: my childhood memories had greatly romanticized that little mudhut, its hardpacked clay walls and thatched roof. It was—I realized now with a shock—not much larger than a large closet. Its floor—had it always been so?—nothing but earth, pressed hard and smooth by generations of feet. No electricity and of course no running water, no kitchen. The cooking done outside on a coalpot beneath an enormous chenet tree, a table and chairs beneath the tree also. The mudhut's furnishings consisting of little more than a bed with a coconut-fiber mattress, a press for clothes, rockingchair, and a narrow cloth-draped table pressed against the wall—Di's *chapelle,* her altar—now bare.

That chapelle had fascinated me as a child. With its flickering candles, bowls of sweetoil, its slow-rising curlicues of Creole incense. Behind it, on the wall, a glossy lithograph of the Sacred Heart—the heart itself in flames, pierced by a blood-dripping dagger. And beside the lithograph a picture-prayercard given to Di by mummy years before, preserved behind glass in a little gilt frame: La Divina Pastora, the Black Virgin of Maraval. But the main feature of that chapelle had always been Di's three statues, simultaneously Catholic saints and Obeah powers. Di spoke of them as though they were alive, as though they were close relatives: St John the Baptist-*Shango,* St Michael-*Ogun,* St Anne-*Oshun.* And alongside each statue, that power's particular tool: a two-edged wooden sword, bullpistle whip, and a rusted penknife which, according to Dulcianne, Di utilized to write messages from the dead in the dirt. Not in English writing, but in Yoruba. Now all that remained of that chapelle was an old saltfish-crate, toppled onto its side. All Di's years of belongings reduced to a bundle tied up in the bedsheet, which she hoisted onto her head.

But Di was thrilled with her new living arrangements; she'd move into my own former bedroom, downstairs in the big house. That bedroom was perfectly suited as servant's quarters, with its own WC and its own entrance from the back gallery, so Di could come and go as she pleased. It was also nicely located cross from the kitchen, since now Di did most of the cooking (assisted, in the best-intentioned bumbling manner, by me). Cook had disappeared soon after mummy's death. She was never heard from again—we all assumed she'd returned to Dominica—probably because she'd "disappeared" the family's silver teaservice with her, sent out from France a hundred-and-fifty years before. But I would as easily give up that teaservice as have to tolerate Cook. I'd never gotten along with her, and for that matter, neither had mummy or Di. And in any case, even if we could have afforded it— which we decidedly couldn't—Daisy and I did not need two servants.

Not like mummy and daddy, who in the old days had done so much entertaining. There was also the old French custom of traveling on weekends to visit neighboring estates—sometimes two hours to get from one to another, though their properties actually adjoined—so guests often overnighted at the house as well. In those days, in addition to the two servants, there'd also been a washerwoman, a groom, and a butler for fêtes. But Daisy and I were hardly interested in fêtes. Neither our own, nor the ones we were constantly invited to. We were not much interested in company a-tall.

Daisy and I kept our own quiet company. For us, that was the newly discovered pleasure of marriage; the feeling of another's gentle presence, always near. Even if I were alone upstairs in the bedroom, Daisy below in the parlour reading his cricket news, there was still the sensation of his presence nearby. Bolom, for me it became a palpable thing. A kind of cooling comfort. Every evening after supper, two of us sitting together on the gallery looking out over a moon-glittering sea. Every morning, waiting with my eyes closed to hear Di's knuckle tapping on the bedroom door. And Daisy rising to twist the blinds open a slash. To collect the tray clattering with our cups of coffee, the small bake buttered and quartered, tins of Lyle's Golden Syrup and Carnation sweetmilk. Smelling the coffee then and sitting up with my back against the headboard, eyes still closed, listening to the sun already buzzing on the corrugated-zinc roof, to the water washing over the rocks down below, the kiskadee with her nest in the flamboyant calling, *Qu'est-que-ce? Qu'est-que-ce?* and me answering silently, *Nothing, nothing a-tall and all the world!* And opening my eyes then to that quiet confirmation: Daisy juggling a golden thread of syrup between two quarters of bake.

Other than the Tristletons—who'd arrive occasionally unannounced, Sir Eustace sounding the horn of his Austin Healy sportscar *a-hooga! a-hooga!* till we walked to the end of the drive to open the gates—other than the Tristletons, no one came to the house. The very thought of locking those ancient wroughtiron gates was one no estate owners would have tolerated, except when *not* in residence. Daisy and I were quite content to be left alone. No one came to visit, and for those first months of our marriage, Daisy and I scarcely left the house either. Once a week Di and I made an extravagant excursion of our trip in father's Ford to market in town. I still hadn't learned to drive it properly, but neither was I much interested, nor had I any intentions of obtaining my license; so far as I was concerned, that would spoil the pleasure. Once a week Daisy went to the Oval for cricket practice, sometimes returning by midday. Until the season started there'd be no three-day-tests, no traveling to family islands for matches, no other obligations of any sort. Daisy was still unemployed. But for those first months of our marriage, neither was he much worried. In time he'd be hired as architectural consultant for the Family Planning project, just as he'd always hoped—though that would not occur for another six months.

Meantime Daisy dedicated himself to repairing the old house. But the building was in such poor shape—all rust-bubbling tin and rotting rafters—Daisy so slow and meticulous, it seemed the project could go on forever. I was convinced it would. What did it matter? Daisy was thoroughly pleased with himself—he always said it was the old house he'd fallen in love with first—and I could very happily watch him all afternoon long, replacing a single stanchion of moss-eaten railing. Most days he labored alone. Though occasionally, when the sea was rough, Ramsingh would come to assist him. Since the estate's failure Ramsingh had become a fisherman. But I was appalled to hear he still hadn't learned to swim—informed him we'd start lessons immediately. What if he should fall overboard? The boat capsize? "Mistress Grandsol," he said, "the day I fall in the sea is the day I learn to walk pon water. All the way back to Calcutta!"

Ramsingh was an expert carpenter—it was he who'd kept the estate house from tumbling-down over the years—but he was slower and even more meticulous than Daisy. Again, I wasn't bothered in the least. Now I had the double pleasure of watching the two together. And Bolom, only to see them cross the gallery carrying a sheet of lattice-work or corrugated zinc was like watching a comedy routine. Gangly Daisy in front nearly seven feet tall, all humped-over, boseebacked; little Ramsingh behind well under five feet, standing so erect he seemed to be tilted backward, trying his best to see in front of him without stumbling. Often I'd burst out laughing at the sight of them! The two turning together to give me a look like I'd gone vie-kee-vie, tripping over each other, the sheet of latticework flexing and flipping *wha-whalp* to the gallery flooring. Even so they made progress. At their own slow pace. Daisy more pleased with himself and the old house every day.

Then one morning I awoke late, startled and frightened for the moment to find myself alone. I jumped out of bed and hurried down the stairs, and not before I put my hand on the cold knob to throw open the front doors, did I pause to realize that it was Sunday morning. Daisy had gone to the Oval since early for cricket practice, Di to church-service in town; I was alone in the house. But I did not *feel* alone. That was the strangeness of it. And as I stood there, stark naked on the silk Persian rug before the big double doors, beneath the French chandelier glittering with morning sunlight, looking round me at the walls of that enormous entrance hall—at the portraits of the goatfaced Frenchman at the top of the stairs, my exquisite great-grandmother there beside him, all silence except her eyes—as I stood there on the rug with my hand on the cold doorknob, I had the distinct notion that there was someone there with me. A presence—not a jumbie or a spirit, because I'd given up believing all that nonsense since childhood—but a *living* presence. And not a thief or a badjohn either: a kindly, comforting kind of presence.

Bolom, I was so convinced of it that I began walking room to room. As though I'd expected to find someone waiting quietly for me in one of them. Through the livingroom, the dining hall, kitchen. Out the back door now along the gallery. Right the way round the house and down the front steps. And not before I turned round in the middle of the drive to squint up at the old house looming above me—standing there like a madwoman, stark naked in the bright morning sun—did I realize who it was. Now I recalled standing there in that same spot nearly a year before, on the morning after my horrid, horrid debut, squinting up at the old house in just the same way: as though I were seeing it for the first time. On that morning I'd been shocked at how decrepit the house had become. Now I was shocked to see it transformed again, almost to the original splendor of my earliest memories. Slowly but surely Daisy'd succeeded in rebuilding it. In the process he'd managed to saturate every board and piece of zinc with his own gentle presence. His trace was everywhere, inside and out. Shining cross the surface of every floorboard and rubbed deep into the grain. That was what I'd perceived even on the surface of my naked skin. That cooling breath of air. What I was sure of now as I entered the house once more, as I climbed the stairs to return to my solitary bed.

4

That year Sir Eustace did get us out of the house on one occasion; he bullied us into joining his carnival band. Actually, he had no trouble persuading us a-tall. Daisy'd taken part in carnival the year before—the *finish-of-the-war* carnival—and he'd thoroughly enjoyed himself. He was terribly eager. I, on the other hand—though I'd heard of carnival all my life—had never participated; even if mummy and daddy *would* have allowed it, by the time I was old enough I was already away at convent. But the truth was that most whites did not take part—certainly not the *high*whites—certainly not in those days. They considered carnival something vulgar. Something for blacks and East Indians, for poor people—at best for foreigners, who knew no better. The priests considered it *scandalous*—all curious in the least, since the festival had its start with the French aristocracy—still, in fact, tied to the Church calendar. For most whites the extent of their carnival involvement was the fancy-dress masquerade at the British Club, where no blacks or East Indians were allowed entrance. All of which made *me* the more eager to take part too.

And since all the talk that year was American Airlines, that was the band we would play with. Indeed, it'd been due to Sir Eustace's influence that the Airlines decided to make St Maggy one of its six Caribbean stops, in addition to Havana, Port-au-Prince, Port of Spain, Kingston and Bridgetown. In addition to American Airlines, Sir Eustace was the band's primary spokesman and sponsor. Of course, to play in a carnival band did not actually mean to play a musical instrument; it meant to dress in a costume—to play a *mas*. The only actual musicians belonging to the calypso-orchestras which led each of the bands, traveling slowly before the masqueraders on the beds of open jitneys: musicians playing steeldrums, African congas and East Indian tassas, horns, trombones, quatros. With all the masmen following behind on foot, perhaps beating together a pair of tok-tok sticks, a bottle-and-spoon, or shaking up a pair of shack-shacks. This, while singing out a calypso at the tops of their voices, winding their waists and jumping-up behind the music-blasting jitney—far more accurate descriptions of those gyrations and saltatory-spasms than *dancing*. This went on for half of carnival Monday and all of carnival Tuesday, ending at midnight for the onset of Ash Wednesday.

Daisy happily volunteered to construct our two costumes. In accordance with the band's theme, we were to play Uncle Sam and the Statue of Liberty. For days Daisy thought of nothing else. First he ransacked our wardrobes for the appropriate clothing: a pair of his own white cricket trousers, blue-and-white-striped shirt, red bowtie; my own multitiered, cream-coloured chiffon evening gown, white pumps, elbow-length white gloves, brassiere, hose (the last few, of course, belonging to mummy—which should have made me suspicious from the start). Daisy used pasteboard to construct a towering, wide-brimmed tophat, painstakingly painted in stars-and-stripes. Then he cut out a tall crown, glittered it silver, and inset red plastic lighthouse windows. Finally Daisy dedicated himself to the huge torch, glued together from a piece of driftwood and a dozen twisty-knotty coconut stems— each glittered to a roaring red. *So* big and obzockee, I wondered how possibly he meant for me to tote it.

And it was with more than a mild shock, early that carnival Monday morning, that I discovered he didn't; *he* planned to play the Statue of Liberty, and *I* was to play the costume of Uncle Sam. Bolom, I was so astonished I tumbled my cup of coffee over the bedsheet! "Certainly," he said. "I'm the architect. Isn't appropriate I costume myself as the edifice?" He seemed astonished that I could've gotten it the other way round. And after his last sip of coffee, he added, "Besides, what sport is there in our dressing ourselves up in our own clothes?"

Bolom, as reluctant as I was to admit it, he had a point. And soon as I gave myself over to the idea, I began to enjoy myself too. *Nearly* as much as Daisy, who insisted straight away that I apply my own makeup to his face. Powder it with Cashmere Bouquet. Paint it with shadow, rouge and lipstick. Bolom, he was absolutely the most *hideous*-looking transvestite I'd ever seen in my life! Peering over his shoulder and pursing his ruby-bright lips in the mirror, winking, speaking in a high, *lithpy* voice: "*Hurry up thweetheart, let's make a thcandal this morning!*" I laughed till I choked. Till tears filled my eyes. Then I sat at the dressing table and set myself to equaling Daisy: with the eyebrow pencil I drew a thin moustache on my upper lip, curling exquisitely at each end. Thick, bell-bottomed sideburns. Bushy eyebrows. Then I tied my hair back. Used a great glob of Daisy's Butch to plaster it down on top.

Our clothes fit each other surprisingly well. Daisy's cricket trousers, of course, a foot-and-a-half too long, cuffed round my ankles; my own evening gown a foot-and-a-half too short—especially after Daisy'd finished stuffing mummy's brassiere with ample cottonwool. Finally we went downstairs, arm in arm, and presented ourselves to Di. She let loose a scream and took off running out the kitchen. But in a second she returned, laughing—blowing deep breaths at the same time, *sheeeu! sheeeu!*—and fanning her face with her kerchief like she was about to pelt a faint. "*Jesan-ages!*" she said. "Ugly is ugly me never see ganga-man so *ugly* in all me days! Oui *fute* papayo!" Then she turned to study me: "But the madam handsome, you know. Handsome too bad!" I, of course, was convinced I looked a sight—but certainly far less hideous than Daisy. He offered Di a dainty curtsy, took my arm again to walk out to the motorcar, and we drove off with Di looking behind us from the front door, still fanning herself with her kerchief, still faint with laughter.

5

Even *jumping-up* could not, with any accuracy, describe the epileptic spasms which I witnessed from Daisy when we joined the band and the calypsos started up. Of course, I'd never seen him attempt to dance. But as awkward as I thought his cricket bowling was that first afternoon I laid eyes on him—the same moment, I'm quite sure, when I fell instantly in love—*this* was worse, and in *that* costume! I followed behind him spellbound. Absolutely as captivated as I was horrified. And in some way I would not want to try to explain—even if I could—never had I felt so attracted to him. Never so much in love. Of course, it wasn't long before the other masmen discovered Daisy's extravagant dancing techniques. Not long before they formed a circle round him. Screaming with laughter! Particularly little Sir Eustace—himself playing the Empire State Building, in a costume that stood nearly ten feet tall—laughing so hard he toppled over backward onto the pitch, requiring half the band to stand him on his feet again.

But all that commotion was only a prelude to the later discovery of Daisy beneath his costume by his fellow cricketers. Reggie, our local star-batsman, was the first to pick him out: "Oh *lors!*" he bawled. "Is *me* to liberate Miss Liberty this afternoon!" Bolom, that bunch truly *did* get on scandalously—in ways to shame more than the Church Fathers. Poor Daisy trying his best to keep their hands out of mummy's over-stuffed brassiere, his overstuffed bamsee, fending them off as best he could with his torch.

It was well after midnight when we returned to the Ford, only to find it blocked in on all sides by other motorcars—perhaps till Wednesday morning; we had no choice but to walk home. This, after following the band all day long. After walking every street in St Maggy at least twice. By the time we arrived home we were so thoroughly exhausted, all we wanted was to throw ourselves in the bed. Which was precisely what we did—filthy as we were, pausing only long enough to toss off our crown and tophat—*promising* each other that in just a minute we'd get up to remove the rest of our costumes. To shower and scrub off the makeup smudged on our faces.

Of course, we never managed to get up again that night. Neither did we manage to join the band again on that carnival Tuesday morning. Because by the time we *did* finally get up out of bed, the band had already been in the streets half the day. But we did not spend the morning sleeping. Quite the contrary. That morning I awoke to the sensation of Daisy's lips, pressed passionately to mine. It was several minutes before I opened my eyes. Several minutes, indeed, before the thought even crossed my mind that I was still costumed as a man—dressed head-to-toe in Daisy's clothes—he still costumed in mine, his face still smudged with my own makeup.

Never had we made love so fervently as we did that morning. Never so passionately. Still half-dressed—to be sure, removing our clothes only so far as necessary—not because our passion did not allow us time, but because, as we quickly discovered, we did not *want* to remove our costumes. To return to our proper genders. Bolom, it wasn't the idea of making love to a person of the same sex, not really—oh, I'm sure it was that too—but it was more the idea, somehow, of making love to ourselves. Of embracing our own *self.* Our own selfsame *other—* own inverted mirror-image, separated from us by the pane of glass—

even as peculiar as that notion may sound. At least that was what the experience was for me, as closely as I can come to understanding it. Because the truth is that I cannot speak for Daisy. The truth is that we never did discuss the emotional chemistry of whatever took place on that Tuesday morning. Never spoke of such matters a-tall, *ever.* Understand, Bolom: ours was a complicity of silence. A silence never to be intruded upon or in any way defiled by words; an unspoken understanding between us—all the more clear and binding *because* it was never given voice. And Bolom, whatever happened on that Tuesday morning never happened again.

Which is not, however, to say that the pleasure I experienced for the first time during sex that morning was not repeated. Not in the least! That pleasure was simply a trick of my own body, which I learned by accident. (Just as I had learned it quite by accident years before, standing there on my stack of storybooks with my lips pressed against the glass, rolling beads.) That morning my left hand discovered that even as I lay on my back beneath Daisy, my eyes again closed, I could touch myself. There, in the same place. Just as I did when I was alone. My right hand mechanically finding a gold bead of my chaplet strung round my neck; I discovered that I could continue my habit of rolling beads, even during sex. Even as difficult or awkward as the possibility may sound physically. Because it was not awkward a-tall. (Indeed, since then I've often wondered whether or not the female organ is shaped the way it is for just this reason? To allow a woman the possibility of making love to herself, even while she makes love to a man? Whether or not *this* is its uniqueness and superiority over the male's?) I discovered now that I could accomplish it with the least of effort. Easily enough. So by the time Daisy'd reached the peak of his own pleasure that morning, I had already taught myself to achieve the same—at precisely the same moment.

6

The return to my habit of rolling beads, which I'd discontinued since our marriage, did wonders for our sexual relationship. At least to begin with. Till then sex had been something I'd put up with more for Daisy's sake. Neither pleasant nor unpleasant—but certainly not pleasurable.

Of course, Daisy realized this too, with not a little alarm. *He* was as happy with my newly discovered pleasure as I was. Indeed, I'm sure my own ardour added to his. No doubt he found all that chaplet business peculiar, perhaps even frightful. Especially when—as happened on more than one occasion—I burst out reciting the Holy Mary at the top of my lungs, at the most inopportune of moments! But I dare say that after a time Daisy grew used to my *peculiarities.* After a time he came to accept them (perhaps to the point of finding a perverse kind of pleasure in my own perversions). All I can say is that what began with our marriage as a once-a-week activity at best, soon became a nightly event. Often a morning one as well.

But now this became more my own doing. To the point where sex became something Daisy put up with more for *my* sake. *Daisy* lying beneath me now in the supine position, me the rider perched above—but the rider somehow also *ridden*—sitting tall above him now with my head thrown back, my eyes closed, knees bent kneeling beside his hips, my feet tucked tight beneath his thighs, both my hands busy rolling beads! Understand, Bolom: after those first months of our marriage—those first months of abstinence from rolling beads—rolling beads soon became my obsession again. My repressed desires resurfacing with such urgency, now I could scarcely restrain them. Till one night I got up and hurried into the WC—almost before Daisy'd finished—*so* much in a hurry I felt my chaplet slap against my chest with every step. I locked the door behind me, took my seat on the toilet, and I continued rolling beads. Till I felt limp with exhaustion, spent—my entire body shining with a film of slippery perspiration. Till I had only enough strength remaining to drag myself back to bed.

7

That night I did not dream of running naked through the forest, pursued by the thin black mappapee snake. In this dream I waited patiently for him. Sitting there naked on the bench, locked into my toiletstall again at the far side of the convent playingfield. But I was no longer a child; in this dream I was a grown woman. It seemed as though I'd been waiting there on the bench the longest time. Still the mappapee had not appeared. Eventually I closed my eyes, let my head fall gently backward against the back wall of my cubicle, willing myself to drop asleep even within the confines of my own dream.

When I awoke the first thing I did was to feel in the dark for the chaplet strung round my neck. Of course I wasn't wearing it. But for the first time I wasn't worried either. I peered down at the slatted flooring of my toilet chamber, for the first time actually *relieved* to find the mappapee coiled-up there. Tantalizingly attracted by those sharp yellow eyes, by his horrid forked tongue flickering between them—his tail raised behind rattling in ominous, enticing spasms! In an instant the mappapee transformed himself into my little black chaplet of pem-pem seeds—as if at my own bidding. I stretched my left leg out toward him; watched my mappapee-chaplet slither up onto my foot, slowly up along my naked shining shin, felt him winding himself wetly round my thigh, slowly entering inside me. I watched perfectly calm. Unafraid. Bead by bead by bead.

But when he reached the last little black bead, the little silver crucifix rattling at the end of his tail—and I prepared myself to awaken now from my dream—now I did not wake up; now the little crucifix twisted quickly halfway round, disappearing instantly inside me. *Gone!* The last trace of him! I stared incredulously. Blinking as though I were seeing things. As though my *eyes* had made the fatal mistake. Now I shoved my fingers inside—frantic, desperate—feeling up as far as I could reach—as though I could grab hold and pull him back out! But already I could feel him moving deep inside me. Now with a kind of hollow rattling—muted, resonant, throbbing—twisting his way through the slithering channels of my dark insides. Now I could feel the perspiration dripping from my skin. The stench rising in heatwaves from the pit beneath.

Now I heard pounding on the door, my whole cubicle shaking. Silence: I looked up. Pressed my bare feet against the metal door, my bare back against the cold metal wall. Pounding again. Now I heard Mother Marie-Bernard's voice. But not bawling: in this dream I heard her calling out to me with a kind of demonic laughter. My own demonic annunciation: "*Lilla Grandsol, I told you to get out from inside there! Now you find youself haveen with a diab-duen! Pregnated with a devil-duen!*"

145

8

I awoke screaming, swimming in sweat, lashing my head side-to-side on the sweat-soaked feather pillow. Scaring Daisy as much as I myself was frightened. He reached cross me to light the lamp on my bedside table. My legs were all tied-up in the bedsheet. Twisted round and round itself and round my ankles—like thick, white rope. Gently Daisy untied them. Twisted out the sheet and pressed the wrinkles smooth against the mattress. Then he balled up a corner and began wiping the perspiration away from my skin. From the crevices between my toes, along my legs and torso, all the way up to the beads of sweat strung cross my forehead. When he'd finished I was still trembling. My heart still pounding against my chest like a small crazed animal. My right fist clutched so tightly round the crucifix of my chaplet that when Daisy slowly undid my fingers, we saw that it had cut into the surface of my skin; that I held a bright drop of blood in the center of my palm. Daisy raised my hand to his mouth and gently licked it away. Finally he put his arms round me, and after a while Daisy began making a soft, clicking sound with his tongue against the roof of his mouth. Soothing, comforting. A sound somehow rescued from my earliest childhood—because it was so familiar—though I felt far too shaken at the moment to search my memories for it.

Eventually I stopped trembling. Eventually Daisy dropped off to sleep again. Breathing peacefully, his arms still wrapped loosely round me. I reached over to out the lamp, but I did not dare close my eyes. Did not dare allow myself to drop asleep, to chance facing the mappa-pee-chaplet of my nightmares again. I lay there studying the shadows on the ruffled zinc ceiling. *Not* thinking. Because it wasn't until several hours later, at almost the precise moment I heard Di's knuckle tapping with our coffees on the bedroom door—as though that gentle tapping were my *second* summons for the night—that I made the connection between what Mother Marie-Bernard had told me in my dream, and my own reality. At that moment it dawned on me that, in fact, I'd not seen my menses for as long as two-and-a-half months.

At first the thought struck me as absurd, impossible—how could I not have realized? for so long?—but it *was* possible. Because now I recalled that my last menses had coincided almost exactly with Daisy's trip to Jamaica for a cricket match, and that was the first week in April. This was already the middle of June! Somehow the fact that my menses were late hadn't even entered my mind. Not simply because I seldom worried about it (ever since I'd left the convent my menses frequently *did* come late, or early—and occasionally I skipped a month altogether), but simply because the possibility of pregnancy was one I never contemplated a-tall. For me that idea was *so* undesirable—so impossible even to consider—that I never allowed myself to think about it.

To such extremes that I never even considered precautions to prevent my becoming pregnant. Of course, in those days there was no sort of contraception anyway. At least none readily available to us—not on an island ruled over as much by the Catholic Church as its own colonial government. Though I suppose there must have been ways. Oldtime folk methods passed mother-to-daughter for generations. But even if she knew of them, *my* mother had not been around to teach me such things. I suppose, also, that the blacks and East Indians must have had their own recipes and bush-medicines—more ancient and secret still—but I'd never thought to investigate those till it was too late too.

Di tapped on the door again. Again I did not get up to collect our coffees. I lay there listening as Di chupsed softly and set the tray on the flooring beside the door, turned and retreated down the stairs. But even as I listened to Di quietly descending the stairs, I'd already made up my mind to go to her, soon as Daisy left the house: there was no one else. Certainly I couldn't go to Dr Curtis—mummy's former physician and Daisy's great admirer—even if he *would* stoop to such a thing; and in no way did I feel comfortable enough to question Lady Tristleton how to go about aborting a child. Because there was no doubt in my mind that I was, in fact, pregnant. No doubt, either, that Daisy *wanted* this child; since his first mention of marriage he'd spoken of "family planning." But I could not possibly bear a child. Not possibly. It was beyond my emotional capabilities. And I knew then as clearly as I know it now, that I was being directed by a paranoia instilled in me years before I could have begun to recognize it, and which now, years later, I could scarcely begin to articulate even to myself. In my own mind bearing a child was beyond my *physical* capabilities, despite all illogic.

I had to find some way to abort it, and I had to find some way to do it secretly. Di was the only person I could go to for help. Soon as Daisy left the house. Because fate—or Providence, chance, whatever you choose to call it, as if to confirm or mock my wretched predicament further still—fate had seen to it that the first of those Family Planning housing projects was to break ground on that very morning. And not even in St Maggy: *fate* had gone so far as to determine that this first Family Planning was to be built on the other side of the island, in the coastal village of Henly—on a construction site located, in fact, not far from the Convent's front gates!

9

Di turned away from the coalpot she'd been fanning vigorously with a piece of ripped pasteboard: "Mean you want to *throw* the child? But darling, what you want to do that for? Young and fresh-marry and everything?"

The look of despair on my face was answer enough. Di chupsed. Dropped the piece of pasteboard she was holding into the coals. After a few seconds it exhaled a puff of white smoke, then burst into bright red flames. "Dou-dou," she said, "you give me a *difficult* work to do there. Make the man to *give* you the child, that one easy. That one no problem. But throw the child once it make? That not so easy a-tall!"

Nevertheless, Di assured me that of course there were ways, plenty of ways, though no one of them was certain. Despite the fact that each of the methods she referred to fell under a different category of *science:* bush-science, obeah-science, medical-science. No one of them was foolproof. Still, Di took me in her arms and tried her best to console me: "Never you mind, Dou-dou. We going fix-up! One of them science bound and blidge to fix-up!"

That same morning she took me thiefing pawpaws at an old Chineeman's house located not far from the front gates. Of course, those trees had once grown on the estate's property, but that was long ago. Now they were so tall we could not possibly reach the fruit. And judging from the amount that had fallen to the ground, neither could the oldman. But in two seconds Di'd hiked up her skirt and tucked it in at her waist, shimmying up one of the tall, skinny trunks. Thirty feet into the air. She picked only the young pawpaws—small and hard and milky-green—which she let fall to me waiting below. There with my skirt held out before me like a net to catch them. By the time the old-man came out to curse us Di had ascended a couple more trees, and we'd collected a couple dozen young pawpaws. Piled then in the center of Di's head-kerchief, which she'd taken off and spread on the ground. Now she grabbed up its four corners into a bundle and we took off running—the Chineeman cursing and pelting us with a shower of rotten pawpaws. On our way home we wandered through the forest along the river—the only bit of forest not built up by little board houses—and Di collected the other ingredients for her bush-medicine: a mound of castoroil leaves, several pimply-skinned, cucumber-shaped fruit I knew to be caraili (but which Di called *womb-fruit*), as well as the leaves of a vine she referred to simply as *scientific bush*.

When we got home Di sliced the fruit, putting it with the other ingredients in a big basin of water to boil for several hours. This she strained through cheesecloth and put on the sill to cool. That afternoon Di made me drink down a tumbler full—bitter like mauby without the sugar—followed by a tall glass of water. An hour later another big tumbler. Another tall glass of water. But when the time came for the next dose I was already sitting on the toilet, suffering stomach cramps and chronic diarrhea. This Di took as a *good* sign! Soon as I got out of the WC she made me fire-down another tumbler. By the time Daisy arrived home that evening my condition had worsened. He offered straight away to go for Dr Curtis. I told him *no!*—perhaps a little too vehemently. Tried my best to convince him that I was fine. This went on for three days and nights. Till I was so weak Di had to walk me from the bed to the WC. Still, I continued taking her bush-medicine. Till I'd swallowed down the last tumbler.

I remained in bed recovering for another three days. Meantime Di'd begun communicating with her saints on my behalf. Shango and Ogun, she said, were playing the fools—holding up their tongues. But Oshun, Mistress of the Waters, was willing to speak; *she* would be the one to help me. As soon as I felt strong enough Di brought me downstairs into her own bedroom, for the first time since she'd moved into the house. In the corner stood her chapelle—just as I remembered it from childhood, when I'd gone to the little mudhut to play with Dulcianne. The air of Di's bedroom was already clouded with Creole

149

incense. She had me light five candles of a skyblue-coloured wax, place them on the chapelle round the statue of St Anne. Next she took up a tiny brass bowl containing a wafer of glowing sweetoil, there also before the statue, and she poured out a single drop into the palm of my right hand. Closed my fingers round it. She told me to squeeze the drop of sweetoil with all my strength—tight tight tight.

Meantime Di showed me a little pouch she'd sewn together from silk of the same skyblue colour, which she called a "monstrance." Into it Di deposited a branch of Ti Mari and a lock of my hair. She used the same scissors to snip-off a fragment of cloth from the sleeve of my housedress. Next Di carefully undid the fingers of the hand I still held squeezed tight—the same hand, I suddenly realized, in which Daisy'd found the drop of blood a week before. And when Di finished opening my fingers—with an eerie feeling of déjà-vu—there the drop of blood was again. Shining just the same in the center of my palm. Di dabbed it up with the fragment of cloth she'd snipped away from my sleeve, pressing it also into the pouch. Finally Di dropped in a smooth, round stone—"for gravity," she said, "so the monstrance could pelt proper and sink." The open end of the pouch she tied together with a piece of transparent fishingtwine, tying on a loop large enough that the pouch could hang round my neck, where she now placed it. I would wear this monstrance for five days and nights. Then, on the fifth night, I'd pitch it into the sea. Five nights later—beneath a full moon, with a full tide—I would wade out into the water up to my waist, "so Oshun could call the child back to sheself."

Four sleepless nights followed. On the fifth, as planned, I slipped out of bed and met Di downstairs on the back gallery. The moon over the water was not quite full, but the night was bright as day, the shadow beneath the flamboyant tree every bit as dark and distinct. This we carefully circumvented: "Never cross the night shadow of a tree," Di whispered, "there Brazil waits." I followed Di down to the sea. Reached my arm far back. Pelted my stone-weighted monstrance at the lopsided moon. As far out over the water as I could manage.

Another four sleepless nights. On the fifth, again, I slipped out of bed. Met Di downstairs. She'd promised a full moon; the moon was full. Promised a high tide; the tide was in. Di and I waded hand-in-hand out over the rocky bottom, till it reached our waists. The water so clear, and calm, and bright we could see the undulating spines of every black urchin. The pulsating inner organs of every transparent minnow. Each of our toes against the moss-covered rocks. There we waited till daybreak, hand-in-hand, both of us shivering in the cool water. Waiting for what, I wasn't quite sure. Perhaps for my menstrual fluid to cloud the crystal water? Nothing happened. Nothing, at least, that either Di or I was aware of. Finally she chupsed. We waded out again.

By now I was sure that I could feel this child growing larger and larger inside me. By now I felt desperate. More exhausted though, than hysterical; because in truth, I'd hardly slept a-tall in two weeks. Hardly more than a few catnaps during the day, my wicker chair pulled out beside the gallery railing, beneath the bright sun. Not only was I too afraid to sleep at night—hour after hour staring up at the shadows shifting cross the corrugated-tin ceiling—I was too preoccupied. Lying there with my eyes open wide, listening to Daisy's quiet breathing beside me. Fortunately, for both of us, the building project kept him busy all day. Practically every day. Mostly driving back and forth between St Maggy and Henly, a two-and-a-half-hour trip each way. And when the Family Planning did not demand Daisy's time, cricket did, because now the season was in full swing. Daisy had gone from spending practically all his time with me at the house to spending prac-tically none. Which, as I say, was fortunate. And by the time he got home late each evening, he was too tired to do much other than eat his dinner and drop asleep. Too tired and preoccupied himself to worry much about my condition. Especially when I insisted over and over again that I was fine. Because of course, Daisy noticed. Noticed the dark rings round my eyes, my ragged expression. Asking again and again did I go see Dr Curtis. Again and again I gave an excuse.

Finally, though, I did go to see Dr Curtis. But not at Daisy's bid-ding—at Di's. She'd heard of still another method for throwing a child, this one making use of *medical*-science; it involved the taking of quinine tablets.

"Quinine?" I asked. "But that's used to treat *malaria?*"

She repeated: "*Quinine.* Me ain't know nothing about no malaria. But *plenty* women does take that to throw they child. Pharmacist know it too. That's the problem: pharmacist would never sell you them pills without the prescription!"

But—again, as my faithful accomplice or contender *fate* would have it—I had indeed suffered malaria as a child. An awful strain they said came from the Maracaibo Swamps of Venezuela. Carried cross the Gulf not by mosquitoes, but by oilmen returning to the island for their Christmas holidays. For years, also, I'd suffered relapses; and each time I'd been given quinine. A complete history of which—I realized straight away—was most likely contained in my medical records in Dr Curtis's office. Indeed, it had been Dr Curtis himself who'd prescribed those tablets for me as a child. And when I told him that I'd been suffering the bouts of chills and fevers and sweats again, it was Dr Curtis who prescribed the pills for me now, however reluctant he was to do so. Because of course, he wanted to run tests. Saying that I did not look a-tall well; that, in addition, quinine was no longer the treatment of choice for malaria. I got up from the waitingroom bench and stood staring into his shiny red face. Into his watery, colourless eyes.

"Dr Curtis," I said. "*I* know well enough what I need. *You* just write out the prescription for quinine tablets." He did. Without a further word.

That afternoon Di and I drove round to each of St Maggy's three pharmacies. At each I told the pharmacist to please treble the prescription. Each of the three complied. Bolom, as awful as my childhood memories were of those tiny white tablets, this was worse. Far worse! No doubt because now I took the pills in such heavy doses. *Such* doses that initially I couldn't keep them down. But as fast as I vomited them up I swallowed more again. First those pills had me feeling terribly nervous, jittery, fidgeting day and night. Then I began to feel *dizzy*. So dizzy that one afternoon I slipped on the ceramic tile in the bathroom, fell and hit my head against the pipe beneath the sink. Di heard the thump below in the kitchen and came running up the stairs; she found me facedown in a pool of blood.

Still I kept swallowing the tablets, till I was sure those pills were going to abort *me!* I no longer felt nervous, dizzy. Now I felt simply lethargic. Tired. That was the rhythm of those quinine tablets: nervous, then dizzy, then simply tired. So tired I did not want to get up out of bed, even if I could. Now I slept all the time. Deep, dreamless, *bottomless* sleep. Falling and falling through an ink-dark void. No hard, ice-cold water at the bottom of the well to catch me. I told Daisy the same thing I'd told Dr Curtis; that I was suffering a relapse of my childhood malaria. Begged him not to worry. I was going to get better. Soon enough. I was going to be fine.

I did not get better. Not for two, perhaps three weeks—because I lost all track of time then. Time reduced to tiny white tablets. Till I'd swallowed down the last one.

10

Again I remained in bed recovering for several days. The child in my womb still unaffected by the bush-medicine and all the quinine tablets. Then one morning, just as soon as Daisy left the house, Di burst into my bedroom, all excited, all out of breath. I made a space for her to sit on the bed beside me. Told her to calm herself. It seemed she'd been speaking with Oshun again (she said it as though she'd just put down the telephone). And it seemed that there was someone on the other side who wanted to help me. But—as I understood now—Oshun could only speak for herself; she could not speak for this soul on the other side. The soul, however, could speak *through* Oshun. Could communicate with us in writing through Oshun's "tool," the rusted penknife.

"Is a *white*woman," Di said. "*Must* be a whitewoman, cause this woman only want to write *English*. And no soul never speak to me before in that."

Di was convinced this woman on the other side was mummy, though she couldn't be sure. In any case, Di said, the woman was going to have to speak to *me;* Di could never write in that English crabfoot writing.

That night I slipped out of bed and met Di downstairs on the back gallery. For the third time. I felt reluctant to do so; by this time I'd had enough of Di and all her *sciences.* Nevertheless, she managed to persuade me for the third time. Now the night was very dark. No moon a-tall. Di'd made a bule-de-fay from a bottle of pitch-oil with a rag stuffed in the top, which she now struck a match to ignite. She led me cross the guineagrass to a patch of yellow dirt beneath the flamboyant tree. There we sat Indian-style, facing one another, the smoking bule-de-fay placed off to the side. Di held the rusty penknife in her hands.

She threw her head back and began mumbling in her own language—French-Creole, or Yoruba, or a combination of both, because I couldn't be sure—looking up as though she were talking to the tree. Then she opened the penknife. Leaned forward and used the blade to wipe a square clean in the yellow dirt—as if it were a blank page of writing paper—the bangles on her wrist rattling with her every movement. Then she gave me the penknife.

"Write," Di said.

I looked up: already her eyes were shut tight. I reached out and pressed the point of the penknife into the middle of the page, shut my own eyes too. Tried to feel whatever it was I was meant to feel; of course, I felt nothing. Nothing more than silly. But I kept my eyes closed regardless. For two, perhaps three minutes. So long that I actually began to boot-off asleep. But suddenly I shook myself awake; someone had moved my hand. For no longer than a split second—but I'd felt it! First I was sure that it'd been Di. But when I looked at her Di's eyes were still shut tight, her hands still folded loosely on her lap. Then I thought perhaps I'd imagined it. But when I looked down there was a mark on the page. *Two* marks—like two tadpoles pressed head-to-tail together. I pulled the knife away. They did not seem to be letters, not even *a* letter—just two indecipherable scribbles—which, peculiarly enough, I found comforting. Suddenly I didn't *want* those marks to be writing. Suddenly all this obeah business had gotten a little too geegeeree!

Di took up the bule-de-fay and held it above the square of dirt. "What it says?" she questioned.

I studied the two tadpoles. "Nothing. It says nothing. Not so far as *I* can tell."

Di chupsed. "Bound to say *something.*"

"Nothing! At best a *d* and a *p*—but Di, that's an *awful* stretch. And it doesn't even amount to a *word.*" With the flat of the blade I wiped the page clean. Snapped the penknife shut with a little cloud of orange rust. Gave it back to Di.

"Come!" I said, already starting to rise.

"Don't you know nobody with initials of *d* and *p?*"

I shook my head.

"Certain?"

154

"No!"

But even before we reached the back steps, I'd thought of something; of someone whose initials *were d* and *p.* Someone, in fact, whom mummy used to speak of all the time. But this someone was not even a person. She was a *statue:* a little madonna called La Divina Pastora, kept in the small church in Suparee, an East Indian village beside the Maraval Swamp. Despite all mummy's talk, I knew little or nothing about her. Only that this madonna depicted a young girl some claimed was East Indian, others African, still others Amerindian. She'd inspired this sort of collective following; even the Catholics claimed she was a negro incarnation of the Virgin Mary. They called her the Black Virgin. But her Spanish name—part of a tradition brought to the island from the Venezuelan mainland, because I knew that too—her Spanish name was the one mummy'd always used: *La Divina Pastora,* the Divine Shepherdess.

But I quickly rejected my idea, even before we'd reached the back steps. This would mean that the writing I'd written in was *Spanish.* And *I* could neither read nor write Spanish. *Neither* could mummy.

Nevertheless, I told Di.

She climbed the three steps up onto the gallery, turned round to look down at me with the bule-de-fay lighting up her face from below—like some sort of ancestral sorceress in truth. She announced: "Tomorrow morning first thing we making the pilgrimage to Maraval!"

Maraval, in fact, was ten miles away. Di knew the walk and the madonna well; she'd made several such pilgrimages to the little church before. But it was a cool morning—even beneath the bright sun— and, in truth, I felt stronger that morning than I had in weeks. The sun-softened pitch upon which we walked soon became a hard gravel road, then a dirt trace—two dirt tracks with a column of weeds pressing up between them. The trace passed through village after village of mudhuts and little board houses. Half-naked children playing in the dusty front yards, screaming and running behind their half-starved animals. Occasionally the trace passed through fields once planted with cane, now overgrown with bush. Fields of coconut palms, most already dead from neglect and disease, their headless trunks piercing the blue sky. Or fields laid out in grids of cocoa—once the property of estates now abandoned—the trees dripping with moss. All gone to bush. A primeval forest of scarcely a century before, now reduced to scrub.

Eventually we passed through the village of Suparee. Just like all the others before it, perhaps with a greater number of dusty prayer-flags flapping at the ends of their tall bamboo poles. Posted in the same dusty front yards before the same mudhuts and little board houses. I knew we'd reached Suparee village, because already I smelled the swamp.

The little block church was painted a dingy grey, perched—incredibly enough—just on the edge of that stenching morass. It was empty, dark and cool inside. Di touched her finger to the basin of holy water beside the door, crossed herself; I did the same. At the front of the church there was a small, dome-toped niche pressed into the wall beside the altar—a dark hole, with a quantity of tiny red flames flickering before it. I assumed the madonna was kept there, though I couldn't see her a-tall for the darkness within. Only the bright flames of the votive candles. Di led me up toward the niche, toward an increasing pungency of Creole incense. We climbed three little steps lined with bowls of sweetoil, knelt at the little wroughtiron railing.

Slowly my eyes adjusted, and the madonna began to take shape out of the darkness behind the candles, each flame cupped in red glass: she was scarcely more than three feet tall, with tiny dark eyes and nose and mouth, her skin a charcoal black. The only visible part of the statue was her face; her head was covered by a long veil, her body by a gown trailing down behind her—both more yellow than white with age. In her arms the little bride-child seemed to be holding an infant, though it was impossible to tell for the mound of offerings piled up there: coins and rings and silver Indian bracelets, tonsures of hair, plastic flowers, trinkets, crude wooden crosses, the tiny skyblue shoe of an infant.

I knew Di was waiting—waiting for me to do *something*. What, I wasn't quite sure. I stared up at the statue as though *she* might give me the answer. All that came to mind was another little Virgin, the one in the convent, half-hidden behind the rocks of her little grotto. The sad trickle of water gurgling-up below. Now I saw myself as a child again, in the early morning, still half-asleep, dressed in my convent uniform. I heard myself whisper again: "*Blessed Mother pierce me through, in my heart each wound renew!*"

Suddenly I wanted to run from that chapel. To run from my past, and all my history, and from this little black madonna. I stood to do so. But before I could turn my back, something caught my eye—there, hanging round the madonna's neck: a chaplet, gold like my own, though tarnished now to a milky-green. Suddenly, despite my anxiety, I *couldn't* turn to leave. Couldn't move my feet or even turn my head. Suddenly, despite my anguish, I knew why I'd come on this pilgrimage.

Now I lifted my own chaplet up over my head. Dragged it out through my mound of thick, coarse hair. I reached out with my chaplet suspended between the thumbs and index fingers of both my trembling hands. Suspended by two golden beads. Swinging slowly back and forth, its little crucifix flickering red with reflected candlelight: I let go. As though I were letting go not of any life within my womb, but of my own. Watched it slip down gently round her neck.

A Golden Skeleton Key

1

Di was convinced she'd been given the child, *my* child. As it turned out, though, she wouldn't actually find herself pregnant till nearly a year later. Yet from the time we left the little sad madonna—from the time we turned our backs to the stench of that Maraval Swamp, and began our long journey back home—Di believed that my child had been taken away and given to her. That had been her petition. Made just as soon as I'd finished making my own. Just as soon as I'd offered up my own golden chaplet. Di removed one of the bangles rattling like old bones on her wrist—East Indian bracelets pounded out from the silver of indentureship shillings, now fashionable for African Creoles—and placed it atop the mound of offerings heaped up in the little madonna's arms. Begging her for the very child I myself had begged her to take away.

Apparently, Di'd been trying to get herself "haveen" for several years. With a *slew* of men. A slew of men subjected, most without their consent, to a *series* of scientific doctorings. Nothing had worked. (For Di that is: since she'd begun her experiments no fewer than half a dozen women had come personally to thank Di—not simply for sending their men home once she'd finished—for sending them in such *good* condition they performed better than they had in donkey's ages, most for the first time in donkey's ages.) Di did not want a man to humbug her life. A-tall. What she wanted was a child to care for in her later years; she wanted to raise another child. In the little house which she would build with her savings for the two of them. The little *concrete* house—first of its kind in her village of Sherman. Ever since Dulcianne had disappeared to America, Di'd longed for another child. She knew there was little likelihood of seeing her daughter, or any grandchildren her daughter may have given her, ever again. But Di was at least as old as mummy would have been. Over *fifty*. So you can well imagine my reaction, that afternoon as we followed along the dusty trace back to St Maggy, when Di informed me of her petition to the little madonna: that she give her a child, *my* child.

Though five days later, when I *did* see my menses, I began to wonder. Began—for a period of five or six weeks *after*—I began to actually believe Di. Maybe a miracle *had* taken place. Maybe Di *had* been given the child—even as impossible and preposterous as I knew the whole business to be. Because Bolom, there was one thing about which I could be certain. One event, of all those questionable others, about which I could be sure: I did not miscarry. I did not lose a child. At least not in that way. When my menses did come, five days after the pilgrimage to Maraval, they came very light. Extraordinarily light. Even for me. *Not* as though I were losing a child, but simply as though my system were starting up again after a temporary lapse. Starting up again freshly. Slowly. After a temporary lapse—as accurately as I could calculate it—of *three* months. So what happened to the child? Di was sure she knew, ecstatic for those five or six weeks, begging me again and again to start crocheting her a bonnet and baby-booties, the tedious art of which I'd learned from Sister Frances in the convent. With me actually ready to take out my needles, actually beginning to believe Di. Because I was certain I did not miscarry.

Di did. Di miscarried *my* child—the same child she'd begged the sad little madonna to give to her—five or six weeks after I'd seen my own extraordinarily light menses. Because ever since the onset of her menopause several years before, Di's menses had been sporadic. Heavier than normal when they did come, sometimes three months in sucession, sometimes not for three months together. The menses Di saw five or six weeks after mine were so extraordinarily *heavy*—even for Di— she could only conclude *she'd* miscarried. That was the only explanation she could come up with: she'd lost the child. And now Di was more convinced than ever that this child had belonged to me. The very child she herself had thrown with her own obeah-sciences!

Now, of course, Di was disconsolate. I, on the other hand, was secretly very pleased. Secretly very happy. Because during those five or six weeks, when I began to wonder whether Di could actually be pregnant at her age—*wherever* the child had come from—I began to worry about the inevitability of losing her. Began to worry, for the first time, about the vulnerability of my world. It lasted only those several weeks. Now, happily, I could forget the whole thing. Because of course, there was still another explanation. Another *logical* explanation: that neither I, nor Di—neither one of us—was ever "haveen" a-tall. That all that pregnancy business was just another fiction of our hysterical, overactive, female imaginations. Bolom, that was what *I* chose to believe. And now I could write it off. I could dismiss it all. Easily enough. As though all that haveen nonsense had never even happened.

Our lives could return to normal. Mine, Di's, and Daisy's too. *Daisy!* It was as though I'd not seen him in months. As though during those months we'd made a clandestine contract to meet only in deep sleep— between nightmares. But now I felt as though I were slowly awakening. Slowly coming back to life. Now, at least, our marriage could return to normal. Could return to *quiet*—because normalcy, sanity, whatever was that? For any of us? Bolom, our marriage did return to its former quiet. To its former cooling comfort. In a way. For a time. There was even a phase, toward end, which almost convinced us we'd gone full circle. Back to the very beginning. But in truth, our marriage never returned to what it was that first year.

2

Now the first of those Family Plannings was completed. The first of those housing projects built all the way on the other side of the island,

160

in the village of Henly. Now, at least, Daisy no longer had to make those two two-and-a-half-hour drives every day. Yet he was not a-tall pleased. Though all the talk in Corpus Christi then was the success of the new housing project. A success, for the most part, attributed to *Daisy*. His name appearing almost daily in the newspapers, beneath bold headlines: *FAMILY PLANNINGS*. Three more such projects had already broken ground. Two in the outskirts of St Maggy, one in a nearby village. Several others were under government consideration. Yet Daisy was not a-tall happy.

He was convinced they were building not low-cost housing for the impoverished, but ready-made tenements. Unsound and unsafe. Built according to no kind of construction standards Daisy had witnessed before. Certainly not in England. The truth of the matter, though, was that these buildings were not *built* here; they were assembled. That was the problem. Daisy had little control over the actual construction, if he had any influence whatsoever. Any say in the design, or the quality of materials used, or how they were used. It soon became clear to Daisy that he was not the "architect" for this housing project a-tall. Though that was the title he'd been given. Though his salary was handsome indeed. (Indeed, I think he'd have been happier paid the half.) It soon became clear to Daisy that he was nothing more than a front for the project's legitimacy. A name. One which could conveniently be attached to newspaper headlines—a name conveniently already familiar to most from cricket headlines. A man's name. Not the title of a conglomerate, or a company, or a sub-company: Lucayan Cement, New World Steel, Hispano-American Constructions. A success which could be claimed not only for Corpus Christi, but, in a sense, for the entire Caribbean: the largest manifestations of *FAMILY PLAN-NINGS*. And if, for some unforeseen reason, difficulties arose—if, due to improbable circumstances, the project failed—the blame could be placed on a foreigner: an architect certified in England, at Cambridge University. A realization which caused Daisy no small amount of personal concern. No small amount of personal pain.

They were pre-fabricated constructions. Constructions of limestone cement originating at one end of the curved backbone of islands, in Freeport, Bahamas; meshed steel fabricated at the other end in Port of Spain, Trinidad; molded and poured smack in the middle of the

Caribbean, in Havana, Cuba—utilizing the full fruits of American ingenuity with American dollars under American supervision—constructions of concrete slabs numbered, and labeled, and strapped down to the decks of open barges like colossal packs of playing-cards. Pieces of God's own jigsaw-puzzle. Shipped up and down the backbone of Caribbean islands. The prototypes here to Corpus Christi.

Daisy was abject. "They were far better off in their villages in their little board houses," he told me one morning, both of us sitting up in bed drinking our coffees. "We've packed them up in little plaster boxes . . . nothing but half-cooked tenements . . . just add on a little tropical heat. Instant slums I call them, Lilla. Give them a year. Two at best."

We went together to the inauguration ceremony of that first apartment complex. I at Sir Eustace's urging, because I'd no desire a-tall to return to Henly. First time since I'd been in the convent four or five years before. But even in that short time Henly had changed to the extent I hardly recognized it. What I remembered as a little village on the coast—one one-lane pitch road fingering off into countless dirt traces—was now nearly a full-grown city. Choked with motorcars, and jitneys, and trucks. All smoking on the sun-softened pitch in the waves of heat. Blowing their horns and weaving their way among donkey-carts and buffalo-drawn tractors left over from another age. My heart skipping a beat as we drove past the convent, though that hardly seemed the same either. The nuns, I knew, had been replaced for the most part by lay teachers—not even spinsters sent out from England—but by local, island, Creole women. The girls themselves—I could see them now playing beneath the banyan trees, their uniforms of navy pleated skirts and UC-monogrammed white blouses—every race and skin colour. Every conceivable mix. But what startled me most as we drove past was something else; in my childhood memory that convent had seemed so *isolated*—even from Henly—separated from the rest of the world by its spiked wroughtiron fence. The gates and the fence were still there, changed only from crimson to the slightly darker colour of rust. But all the surrounding forest was now consumed by tenements. Not a tree in the dusty yards before them. Each compartment of each unpainted, grey-white cement box spilling out an endless stream of ragged, screaming children. The grounds of the convent itself—which in my childhood memory had seemed so immense, a world all its own—I saw now hardly occupied a single city block.

What shocked me further still was the location of Daisy's building; so far as I could tell (because we approached from the other side), this Family Planning was built back-to-back with the convent playingfield. So that if I were to walk round to the other side of the long building, I would confront the line-up of little, crimson-coloured toiletstalls. I was almost sure! And when Sir Eustace took Daisy and me on an enthusiastic *tour* of one of the apartments—as though Daisy'd never seen them—walking room to room rapping our knuckles on the white concrete walls—*see how solid, eh!*—one by one turning the tap above the little sink in the kitchen to witness the magic of flowing rusty water; in the midst of that tour an awful, sinister idea occurred to me: perhaps this Family Planning had been placed in that position precisely to take *advantage* of the convent's toilets? Perhaps that line-up of crimson-coloured toiletstalls was meant to be shared in common? Because so far as I could tell—unless I could have missed it? unless in his excitement Sir Eustace could have forgotten to point it out?—so far as I could tell, the little apartment through which we toured contained no WC.

Bolom, I didn't ask. I didn't want to know. I wanted to go home. To get away from that Family Planning, and that convent, and Henly as fast as father's old Ford could carry us. Which was precisely what we did. Soon as Sir Eustace finished snapping the red ribbon stretched cross one of the apartment doors with a golden scissors.

3

Daisy released all his frustrations in his cricket. He attacked it with full concentration. With a commitment both physical and spiritual. For three days before every match I could feel his slow withdrawal from all else round him, then his slow resurfacing again for three days after. As discouraging as his work had become, as quickly as his dedication to it had flagged, his devotion to sport (never quite the same, he always said, since he'd left England) became that much more, and more again. Cricket now consumed Daisy. With a quiet intensity, a controlled passion as clean and sharp and palpable in the air round him as static electricity. And that year the St Maggy Cricket Club, and Daisy in particular, was playing better than ever. So much so that Daisy was convinced that next year, next season, they would travel to England to represent the West Indies. He was certain.

For me—other than the pleasure I took in watching Daisy bowl, which was considerable—for me cricket was a boring stunt. Frank tedium. Quite possibly I'd never understood it properly. Despite the hours of explanation Sir Eustace had given me when we'd first gone to watch Daisy play. Though I'm sure I never expended much effort. Because I believe my dislike for cricket—my *disdain,* if I'm to be truthful—derived from something else: cricket seemed to me so terribly *English.* Everything about it was English: the sparkling white white uniforms was English, the slowness and orderliness of it was English, the breaks for tea English, the exaggerated *gentlemanliness* of it—which did not convince me for an instant—was so so English. Everything, it seemed to me, that was *not* West Indian. Everything, it seemed to me, that I wanted to escape and negate. And Bolom, for the life of me I'll never understand how West Indians can be so obsessed with cricket. Though Daisy assured me again and again that West Indian cricket— *West Indian* cricket!—was like no other in the world.

It was about this same time, at the height of his newly discovered devotion, that there came from Daisy a rather peculiar request; he wanted me to attend his matches. Peculiar, it seemed to me, because he'd always been so indifferent about my going before. When I'd first met Daisy I'd gone with the Tristletons, usually mummy as well—for her and Lady Tristleton it was strictly a social outing; they hardly even glanced over their shoulders down at the pitch—I'd gone to the matches because it thrilled me to watch Daisy bowl. It thrilled me still. But the hours and hours of waiting for Daisy's sessions of bowling, often finished in fifteen minutes, hardly seemed worthwhile. Especially since the better Daisy bowled the sooner his sessions ended, which always displeased me. When I stopped attending the matches Daisy did not seem bothered in the least. And I'm quite certain he wasn't. Daisy played for the camaraderie of the game, not the admiration—much less the adoration—of his supporters. Any such adoration on my part I'm sure he'd have found repugnant. Now, though, for some reason or another, he wanted me there. My presence there in the Oval. Perhaps for no better reason than he thought it would do me good to get out of the house. But whatever the reason, I was certainly happy to comply. More than happy; it was one of the few requests of me Daisy ever made.

And it did do me good to get out of the house. And I did enjoy myself, did rekindle my thrill in watching Daisy bowl. Most afternoons I'd ring Lady Tristleton and we'd go together. "An outing for the girls," I'd say, making sure Sir Eustace went on his own. Of Sir Eustace I was slowly becoming suspect, on several counts. More than any, of course, over all the Family Planning business. Though Daisy assured me Sir Eustace was as much the strawman as he was. Perhaps even more so: all decisions, he said, financial and otherwise, were made by the cabinet of ministers—local men—who usually did the opposite of whatever Sir Eustace recommended. In any case, I didn't even want to *hear* about Family Planning, a topic Sir Eustace seemed hardly able to leave untouched for the stretch of an hour.

I went with Lady Tristleton. Mostly we talked about mummy. At that time too, for whatever reason, I seemed to miss her more than ever. I missed her terribly. Lady Tristleton, I knew, missed her nearly as much; she and mummy had been friends since before my birth. Since before she'd married Sir Eustace. And I could very happily listen to stories of those old days all afternoon. Some of them even scandalous. Precisely the ones Lady Tristleton liked best to tell.

Then one afternoon, as we sat together in the Oval beneath our usual, overly-large straw hats, after a lull in the conversation—and without my even pausing for a moment to contemplate what I was about to say—I asked:

"How *ever* does one avoid pregnancy?"

Lady Tristleton turned so quickly the brim of her hat collided with mine, knocking them both completely off our heads. She burst-out laughing. "My dear," she said, "I assure you, at my age, that's no longer a major concern." And after fixing her hat properly on her head, quite encouraged, she continued: "Not that it ever was, really. . . . Quick little visit to Dr Curtis. Always my solution, the few times little Sir Eustace did manage to get me in trouble."

Lady Tristleton read the shock in my face—she seemed to enjoy it—and in an attempt to scandalize me further still, she added, smiling, "Of course, quite often I couldn't be entirely sure little Sir Eustace was the source of my trouble."

Suddenly I was too taken aback to even respond. Instead I looked down at the hat I held in my lap, studying the flowers stitched round the rim in red-and-green-coloured straw. Lady Tristleton continued, but now in a different tone. As though she'd realized, after a moment, that I'd actually asked my question in earnest. Asked it of her as though *she* were my own mother. That, perhaps too, beneath the risked intimacy of my question, there lay a certain urgency.

"I have, come to think of it, heard of one preventative measure. Though it sounds to me awfully astringent. Awfully messy."

Lady Tristleton knew of several women who swore by what was commonly called *la douche violent. Violent,* she explained, was a play on *violet*—the bright purple crystals of potassium permanganate, which I was already familiar with as an antiseptic, readily available in the pharmacy. *Violent,* said Lady Tristleton, because the douche made quick work not only of a man's seed, but any *other* wretchedness he happened to be offering along with it!

She went on: "As I say, though, I've no personal experience with *la douche violent.* Dr Curtis was always my solution. To be candid, on no fewer than *four* separate occasions. I certainly wasn't interested in childbearing. Nor child-*rearing.* Let his mistresses suffer that!" She paused. Adjusted her tone once more. "Coming from your French-Catholic upbringing, I'm sure all that sounds terrible enough. Don't misjudge me, Lilla. Worse still, don't misguide yourself: Dr Curtis has performed such *services* for the women of Corpus Christi—the wealthy women of Corpus Christi—for years. And, my dear, it's as quick and painless a remedy as can be imagined. In and out in time for afternoon tea."

Lady Tristleton paused again. And it struck me, at that moment, how matronly she sounded. How much, in fact, she sounded like *mummy*—speaking to me out of my own memory—though for the life of me I could never imagine *those* words coming from mummy's mouth. But then, as suddenly as I'd felt drawn to Lady Tristleton—as suddenly as I'd felt comforted by the easy familiarity of her voice—she said something to drag not only the pitchpine bench upon which I sat out from under me, but the entire cricket stadium:

"Lilla, I suppose it would be no breach of your mother's confidence, now, to tell you that she made one such visit to Dr Curtis herself. During, if I'm not mistaken, your second year at the Ursuline Convent.

In any case, you must realize that I tell you this about your mother only as a devoted friend. As a friend who loved her dearly. I tell you because I think you've a right to know."

4

I was shocked, certainly. But I was *not* scandalized. Other than by my own naïveté. After a few days though, I got over my shock. After a few days I began to appreciate Lady Tristleton's having confided in me as she had. I certainly did not think less of her. Or of mummy. On the contrary, I began to admire them both in a new way. As women willing to take their lives into their own hands. And believe me—in *this* place, at *that* time—it would have been something unusual. It would have been something extraordinary. I began to admire them for their strength. Especially mummy. I could never have imagined her capable. One thing for certain: scarcely three months before, I'd have done the same. Had I truly *needed* Dr Curtis (for more reason than to tell me that I did not need him). Of Dr Curtis himself, of his willingness to perform those illegal operations—and at that time in this place they were highly illegal—I wasn't quite sure what my feelings were. Only that I did not like him. Only that I could not admire him: he seemed to me simply spineless and self-serving. And for some reason both illogical and unfounded, if not unduly unkind, I knew that somehow I'd always held him accountable for mummy's death. Always felt that had he been *firmer* with her—had he admitted her to hospital perhaps? at least until I returned?—she may not have died. Nevertheless, only the thought of those stubby, red, hairy fingers reaching up inside me made me cringe, no matter how quick and painless! I hoped terribly *not* to need him again. And Bolom, it hardly seemed as though I would.

Now Daisy and I scarcely made love. Once weekly at best. If even that. For a time—during those months of my ostensible "malaria" relapses—we did not make love a-tall. For me it would have been impossible. Of course, during that period Daisy was himself preoccupied. With both his job and his cricket. Though that was hardly the reason. Then or now.

Ever since I'd offered up my golden chaplet, ever since I'd given up my habit of rolling beads, I'd given up any pleasure I may have had during sex. But whereas before I'd taught myself that pleasure—and sex was something I'd put up with for Daisy's sake, neither pleasant nor unpleasant—now it became a frustration. A frustration which, for Daisy's sake, I did my best to hide; but a frustration which, despite my efforts, I could not keep hidden. A-tall. Bolom, it was like asking someone to scratch an itch for you. It never quite satisfied. Left you feeling simply raw and anxious. Or, perhaps more accurately, it was like having an itch you *refused,* resolutely, to scratch yourself. An itch you spent the whole time thinking about, yet spent the whole time trying to ignore. Daisy, of course, noticed. He noticed acutely. Perhaps even painfully. To the extent that it made pleasure for *him* almost as impossible. But even that was not entirely the reason we seldom made love.

It was because when we did, perhaps once a week, our lovemaking was now followed directly by *la douche violent.* Almost before poor Daisy had a chance to roll off me. I rushed into the WC, locked the door and stood crouching over the spouting bidet, a leg on either side, douching myself down with a caustic, concentrated solution of potassium permanganate crystals. *Violet/violent.* The dark wretched liquid bubbling-up deep inside me. More than *astringent:* it was like washing my insides out with pitch-oil. It *smelled* like pitch-oil! Bubbled-up inside me like the dirty froth round the rim of the pitch-oil tin. *Boiling-up* inside me, burning like an open wound doctored with lime-juice. Dark violet bubbling splashed over the pale skin of my abdomen, pale skin of my inner thighs. Dark violet bubbling streaming down the insides of both my pale, trembling legs. Over the lip of the white porcelain bidet like a bashed-in cow's head—dripping down violet blood. Bubbling out over the white porcelain tiles.

Daisy could not have known exactly what I was doing. So frantically, secretly locking myself up inside the WC with the tap—*shower? bidet?*—running, spouting hysterically. Certainly he saw those stains like violent bruises on my inner thighs—as though we *had* participated in violent sex, as though he *had* violated me brutally—dark stains like bruises running down the insides of both my legs. My violet knobs of ankles. Because it took three days of scrubbing my skin each time to remove the stains completely. Certainly Daisy saw the stains the following morning on the white porcelain bidet. Between the tiles—a grouted violet grid which never again scrubbed clean. Yet Daisy did not ask. I did not tell him. Soon as I poured out the last violet crystals from the last little cork-stopped glass vial, I made the rounds of St Maggy's three pharmacies and purchased three more.

5

Eventually we no longer made love a-tall. With the most curious result; we fell in love. All over again. Bolom, it was as though some weight, some unlooked-for pressure were lifted slowly from our relationship. From our marriage. And our marriage seemed to return to what it had been in the very beginning. There was, Daisy and I both knew, a certain artificiality to all this. (As if time *could* be turned back? As if memory *could* be washed away clean?) That artificiality we very easily ignored. Very happily ignored. Because it was as though this new phase had come to us after an extended period of fatigue. After a seemingly endless exhaustion. Bolom, it was so easy to go back! Back to cooling comfort. Back to quiet.

We'd been married longer than two years. In a sense, what we returned to now was not even the first days of our marriage; we returned to the time before. To the days of our courtship. To a time when sex *would* have been impossible. Literally impossible. Something we could not even contemplate because it could not yet exist. For Daisy and me, it meant returning to an easier time. A far less cluttered period of our lives. And just as in those early days of our courtship, just as in those first days of our marriage, we returned to our habit of sitting each evening after dinner on the back gallery. Looking out over a flat, moon-glittering sea. Not talking. Not thinking. Floating in the coolness of each other's quiet presence.

Now cricket season was over. Now Daisy spent less and less time at the various sites of the various Family Plannings. He knew perfectly well he could almost cease from going altogether. That the various local contractors, in fact, would've been only too happy had he left them alone. Left them to cut more corners. To do an irresponsible job more irresponsibly. This, for the most part, kept him from giving up his own job. For Daisy it became a duty not only to himself, but to whoever were going to be the future families living in those buildings, investing their lives' savings in those Plannings. At least he could make sure some standards were met. (He'd created quite a controversy by demanding that one building be disassembled and reassembled entirely; it'd been planted down, for all practical purposes, on pure *sand*—fewer than half the foundation pilings Daisy's blueprints required had been driven a-tall.) At least—though he suffered no illusions as to the amount of good he was capable of doing, though to accomplish that little bit of good called for an unending uphill battle, unwavering frustrations—at least it was something. Something more, perhaps, than whoever might replace him in the job might be willing to do.

Then there was his salary. His—by his own admission—overly handsome salary; that was *not* so easy to give up. Daisy calculated that in less than a year's time, with any luck a-tall, he'd have paid off his entire mortgage on the estate house. Settled our debts completely. Even if the government contracted no further buildings. And I know Daisy seriously hoped they wouldn't. Bolom, in less than a year's time Daisy *would* complete those mortgage payments. He *would* pay off all our debts on the house. But Bolom, what I could never have begun to suspect then—what, I'm quite sure, Daisy himself could not have suspected—was that in less than a year's time, when Daisy would complete the last of our payments on the old estate house, he would do so only in time to leave it forever.

Just as during those first days of our marriage, Daisy again dedicated his free hours to whatever repairs the old house required. Just as in those days, when the wind blew and the fishingboats could not go to sea, Ramsingh again came round and the two of them laboured together. But the old house needed few repairs now. Now Daisy and Ramsingh worked on new projects. Created new things: they built a shed for the garden tools. A proper garage for father's old Ford. They converted my own little basement room into an office for Daisy— erected bookshelves, a cabinet with dozens of cubbyholes for Daisy's rolled-up blueprints, a tilted drafting table (though *I* didn't want to see this new office a-tall, told Daisy I refused to stir-up all those childhood memories by descending into my little room). And there were still more projects: Ramsingh and Daisy cleaned out and enlarged the cistern which collected rainwater from the roof. And even after all that digging they dug out a duckpond, there beside the little stream where Dulcianne and I had caught tadpoles as children, where every morning—our bony arms thick with suds to our elbows, screaming with laughter—we'd helped Di to beat out the clothes against the wash-stone, work done for years now by a Maytag machine.

But the project Daisy was most enthusiastic about, the one to which he dedicated all his free time for months, was a series of special cages in which he kept and trained homing pigeons. The birds had been a passionate hobby of his as a boy—a boy growing up in the outskirts of sprawling London—kept in a line of cages balanced atop the wall sur-rounding his family's eighteen-square-feet of perfectly manicured backyard. It was one of the few stories of his childhood Daisy ever told me. How for years he'd exchanged messages with a woman in her nineties, Anastasia Cancampkins-Camps, whom he'd never met. How they'd shared all their secrets, everything about each other except one thing: their addresses. And when the same message returned unread for several weeks, Daisy packed up his knapsack with provisions and water sufficient for three days. As agreed, he set off following the bird. Anastasia, he discovered, lived on the same street, three houses away—her own eighteen-square-feet of backyard a profusion of stacked-up, feather-lined cages and cooing pigeons. He questioned a man replac-ing some tiles on the roof: the old dame, the roofer said, had piped-off the week before. That morning Daisy set free all Anastasia Cancampkins-Camps' pigeons. He returned home, dripping down tears, and did the same for his own.

Ready to start dripping down tears myself, I asked him how he could *bear* to raise those birds again? (In addition to the fact—one I never shared with Daisy—that those terribly pedigreed pigeons looked no different from the ones happily making caca on Sir Walter Raleigh's head in St Maggy's main square!) These new birds, Daisy explained, would never carry messages. They'd be trained to fly around free for a few days when he let them go, after which time they'd return to their cages to be watered and fed. And on Christmas morning that year, with a small celebration, Daisy let loose his birds for the first time. They flew in a group, circling the house several times as they gained altitude, wings clapping together as if in their own feathery applause, then they tilted off in formation toward the horizon. An inverted V of seven white dots against the cobalt sky. Within the week they'd all returned, each to their respective cages.

And it was shortly after the Christmas season that year, in the weeks approaching carnival—as if to confirm any vague sense we may have had that our lives were traveling backward, that our marriage had indeed turned full circle—there came from Daisy another peculiar request: he wanted to go on a *honeymoon*. I tumbled my cup of coffee over the bedsheet. Daisy was serious; he wanted to give me a honeymoon in Barbados. Not our second honeymoon, Daisy specified, our first, because in truth we'd never had one. What with our purchasing the estate house directly following our marriage, we'd never been able to afford a honeymoon. What I found peculiar—after swallowing my initial shock at the request itself—was Daisy's timing; not that his honeymoon idea had come two-and-a-half years late, but that he wanted to take it precisely during those five days of carnival—the standard holiday of three festival days, plus the Saturday before, plus the Ash Wednesday after. I found it peculiar, because we'd both so enjoyed carnival the year before. And in truth, we could have gone on this honeymoon anytime we wanted. In addition, that year Sir Eustace was sponsoring a band dedicated specifically to the St Maggy Cricket Club—more than any other reason, we both knew, due to his admiration for *Daisy:* the band was to be called *Commonwealth Cup.* All Daisy's fellow cricketers would be playing mas together. All, in addition to Sir Eustace, anxious for Daisy to take part too.

And in any case, *I* did not like this honeymoon idea a-tall. Though my objections had nothing to do with playing mas—or not playing mas. I did not want to go to Barbados during those five days of carnival, because that was precisely what all the highwhites in Corpus Christi *did.* Practically every one of them; they escaped in throngs to Barbados. Leaving the hooligans at home to carry on with their vulgar displays. And Bolom, I could think of no nightmare more horrific than to be shipwrecked in Barbados with them! Nevertheless, Daisy was insistent. Eventually I gave in to his request. How could I not? Daisy so seldom asked me to do anything.

It was the first time I'd traveled in an aeroplane. The second time—I'd spent those months in England—that I'd left the island of my birth. To my surprise—and slight embarrassment—Daisy'd booked us in the honeymooners' suite at the Crown Point Hotel. A bungalow perched high on a cliff overlooking a turquoise sea. There were steps cut out of the rocks which descended between two coral-white bluffs to the private honeymooners' beach. Not even boats could float cross the reefs to gain access to it. We spent our days soaking in the cool water. Our meals left waiting for us by a maître d' we scarcely saw, the plates of food kept warm beneath their pewter canister-covers. Those meals we ate in the deep seagrape shade of our gallery, where tiny birds came with a great rush of beating wings, snatching grains of rice from our outstretched palms. Other than that maître d', and the maid who arrived once or twice while we were there in the bungalow—apologizing profusely to the "young *mharsters*" in her loose-jawed, open-voweled Bajan accent—other than the maid and the maître d', we saw no one for five days. For Daisy and me it was a perfect honeymoon. Perfect for the very reason which, for most couples, it would have been a perfect failure. Because it was not really until we'd disembarked from the aeroplane in St Maggy at the end of those five days, among the throngs of highwhites we'd so happily avoided, that it fully dawned on me that during the whole of our honeymoon we'd not made love. Not once. We'd not even tried.

6

The following morning, soon as Daisy left the house, Di burst into my bedroom: "*Haveen!*" she cried. "*Haveen-haveen-haveen!* Divina Pastora done give me back the child. *You* child!"

It had been nearly a year since we'd made our pilgrimage to the little madonna. Nearly a year since we'd been through, and gotten over—or so I'd hoped—all that "haveen" business. Now Di stood beside my bed, breathing hard—*sheeew! sheeew!*—telling me she was pregnant again. With *my* child. Just as she'd begged the sad little madonna nearly a year before.

Between each extended exhalation Di fanned her face with a flowered kerchief. Actually, she pelted the kerchief against the side of her neck, caught it, and pelted it again: a series of soft, flowered cuffs. The silver bangles on her wrist rattling with each one. I made a space for her to sit on the bed beside me, our backs pressed against the headboard. After a minute Di seemed to have caught her breath. Though she continued pelting herself with the kerchief.

"Di," I said, "at your age, even the possibility of pregnancy is practically nil. You know as well as I."

She chupsed. "Is for that me could know the child come from La Divina. How else? And me ain't see menses not a *once* since then? Since that time?"

"Then how," I questioned, "can you be so certain you're pregnant?" As always, Di was skinny as a standpipe.

"You pregnant you does know," she said. "You does *feel* that! Same way you did feel it too!"

Now I lost my patience: "Nothing of the sort! I don't believe we were ever pregnant a-tall, either one of us!"

Di chupsed again. "All that amount of problems we go through, and you going tell me now you wasn't pregnant? Nor me?" Di tossed the kerchief against her neck one last time, caught it, and spread it out on her lap, carefully smoothing the wrinkles. After a moment she said quietly: "Whitepeople foolish in truth!"

I smiled. "Now that's the first reasonable thing you've told me all morning." And in an attempt to humor her, but in a voice which came out sounding only condescending (those same words would return to mock *me* soon enough Bolom, would become the silent refrain of my *own* sleepless nights soon enough); in my foolish, condescending, horridly singsong voice, I told her:

"What*ever* shall become of me without you!"

Di did not notice my condescension. She went on to explain, in all earnestness, what we were going to have to do. We were going to have to write a letter to her family in Sherman, and ask them to send a servant to replace her—"family" for Di seemed to mean the entire village. The young people, Di said, the nieces and nephews and grands and them, they had learning; they could read the letter and write back too. Di had a great-aunt by the name of Ansin. Ansin had two granddaughters. Both had done servant's work. But one, Di explained, was a *wabeen*, a *wassa-wassa*, a *whatless want-a-wallop*. After a quarrel with her grandmother, she'd pelted a big stone and hit her cross the head. Ansin had taken her to court and the magistrate had fined the granddaughter and given her a "charge." The problem, Di said, was that she couldn't remember which granddaughter was which. That was why, in the letter—*our* letter, the letter we'd compose together—we'd be sure to specify, among the other requirements, that the applicant for the job had to send a *police record*. That way we could be sure to get the right granddaughter (not, I assumed, the *want-a-wallop*).

"Cause you don't want nobody living in you house that got a charge with police and like to pelt stones!"

"I should think not!" I answered, smiling. Because in truth I wasn't taking on Di and this letter a-tall; I simply refused to believe that she was pregnant.

7

Daisy always met me at home after his cricket matches. I'd agreed to go to the Oval—happily agreed—but I refused flatly to go to the British Club afterward. Not that Daisy'd ever asked me; it was Lady Tristleton each time who tried to coax me into following along. I always had her chauffeur drop me at the house. In truth, I'd not returned to that British Club since the awful night of my debut. Not once. Daisy himself had never much liked it; and though he seldom said anything, I knew he found the club's unabashed racism inexcusable— the rest of us were so accustomed to such attitudes we could not even see them. Normally Daisy did his best to escape the mob which rushed to the club to celebrate their cricket victories. And that year there were only victories to celebrate.

So as I waited into the evening for Daisy to return home after the Kingston match, I was becoming concerned. Eventually, at about ten o'clock, Sir Eustace pulled into the drive, the horn of his Austin Healey bellowing: *a-hooga! a-hooga!* I hurried outside to meet him. Sir Eustace was all excited, his face red as roukou, telling me again and again not to worry—*so* many times that, indeed, I was becoming quite terrified! Apparently Daisy'd been involved in some sort of row. At the British Club, of all places. Immediately my mind flipped back to scenes of my debut. Sir Eustace's story was beginning to sound just the same: all the crowd had become involved in the argument, the headwaiter had called in the chief-of-police, the chief-of-police had shut down the club and sent everyone packing. But at this point the stories veered off. At this point Sir Eustace's voice began to falter. Unfortunately, he said, the chief-of-police had arrested two men. And in a voice lowered further still, he informed me who they were: Reginald, St Maggy's famous batsman, and *Daisy*.

In any case, of course, I mustn't worry. I mustn't worry. He was on his way to the jail at that very moment to talk some sense into that chief-of-police. "The man's mad!" he said. "You just can't go locking-up our star bowler and batsman! What's this wretched island coming to?" And with that he sped off.

Of course, other than the news of where Daisy was, Sir Eustace's explanation did little to settle my confusion about what had actually happened—what had actually *caused* the row—never mind settling my nerves! The whole business seemed so unlike the Daisy I knew—always so calm, never raising his voice—that I really did not know what to think a-tall. I remained none the wiser that night either, sitting in the wicker chair downstairs in the parlour, in the dark, waiting for Daisy to arrive home. Because he did not return till the following evening. But a few hours before dawn Sir Eustace returned in his place, his face even redder than the first time. He informed me that the matter still hadn't been cleared up, but the good news (*good news?*) was that an emergency session of the court had been called for the following afternoon. Unfortunately, though, Daisy wouldn't be released till then. Sir Eustace was in such a state that it did not occur to him he *still* hadn't explained to me what had brought on the argument, why Daisy'd been locked up in the first place. But rather than press him for more overexcited, incoherent information, I sent him home to bed.

And a couple hours later, soon as Di awoke that morning, we walked together to town—Daisy'd driven the car to the Oval on the previous afternoon, where, of course, it remained parked; I wanted to buy a newspaper. That seemed to me the quickest, most logical way to find out what had happened and begin to make some sense of it. As expected, the front page contained a large photograph of Daisy and Reginald De Bassier, both crouched on one knee side by side on the brown clay of the pitch—Daisy holding the ball, Reginald brandishing his bat. There were two feature stories that morning, and, interestingly enough, the photo served *both* stories. Suspended in a sea of print between the two sets of headlines: *ST MAGGY TAKES KINGSTON IN VICTORIA PARK OVAL; CRICKETERS ARRESTED IN BRITISH CLUB SCANDAL.* In addition to the two stories, the remainder of the paper consisted almost entirely of *letters* relating to the "scandal": from the chief-of-police, from the headwaiter at the British Club, the owner of the club, from the president of St Maggy's Cricket Association, from concerned citizens—including a peanutvendor at the Oval—and a baffling letter from Sir Eustace himself. Apparently, I wasn't the only one who'd had a sleepless night; it seemed the whole of St Maggy had been up all night writing letters.

But the story of the "scandal," as best as I could assemble it—reading *between* the official version and all the letters—was this. As always, the cricket spectators had rushed to the British Club following the match, Daisy among them; and, this time, also Reggie. (One letter— the peanutvendor's—suggested Reggie and Daisy'd *borne* the vexed mob to the gates of the club like the old slave rebellions, every man-jack bearing his bootoo and bule-de-fay!) But the headwaiter had stopped Reggie at the door, barring his entrance. Reggie, he claimed, was not a member. Reggie informed him that he'd come as Daisy's *guest*. The headwaiter countered with the club's regulation: *locals could not qualify as guests*. (Everyone, needless to say, knew Reggie—at least everyone associated with cricket; they'd all watched him from the time he was a boy with a homemade bat defending a sweetdrink-crate wicket, a prodigy rising up out of the poverty-stricken streets of St Maggy. A modern-day fairy tale. Or as close to one as we in the West Indies ever managed to get.) But "*guest mean guest*"—this phrase lifted from the headwaiter's letter—which meant *foreigner,* a foreign passport: English, French, American.

At this point in the fray, apparently, Reggie'd produced a document to silence not only the headwaiter, but—said Sir Eustace's letter—"the complete concomitant cantankerous crowd": he showed them his English passport. His *new* English passport. So new it did not yet contain a single stamp. It seemed Reggie had been planning to emigrate to England for some time, his parents and three older brothers having done so years before. Only his alliance to West Indian cricket had kept Reggie at home. But now that he was going to England to play cricket—as we all hoped!—he was going to stay. Reggie was so sure of himself—and of the St Maggy Cricket Club—that he'd gone so far as to have his family process his passport: Reginald De Bassier was an English citizen.

Nevertheless, the headwaiter refused to let him into the club, calling the passport a "boldface-fakery." ("Tomorrow the boy coming with a next one from Japan!") He'd called in the chief-of-police. And now the comic twist to the story: the chief-of-police *refused* to arrest them. But Reggie and Daisy *insisted*. But the not-so-comic twist, the point which the newspaper story and every single letter failed to mention—the thing which everybody, apparently, seemed incapable of *seeing*—was that both Reggie and that headwaiter were black men.

Daisy did not arrive home till late that evening, still dressed in his whites from the previous afternoon. He said that all charges had been dismissed; the court hearing had never even happened. I could not be sure how much this displeased Daisy. And I did not ask him. Not that evening or ever. (I did not even read the follow-up story and letters in the newspaper the following afternoon when Daisy brought it home.) He looked exhausted. We ate our supper and went afterward, at his suggestion, to sit on the back gallery. And when I looked over at Daisy after a few minutes, he was already asleep in his chair.

8

For weeks Di continued pestering me about the letter. Every morning as soon as Daisy left the house. For weeks—*months* in fact—I paid her no mind. Treated both the letter and her professed pregnancy as though they were something comical. On a few occasions I even laughed outright. Then one morning, standing beside my bed, Di lost her patience: she lifted her dress up high above her waist.

"*Look!*" she demanded.

Her belly was big and round as a football. When I touched it with my trembling fingers, the skin stretched cross it felt as tight.

We composed the letter that same morning. That very instant. But Bolom, I was in such a state of shock, so completely taken aback by the sudden realization that Di was, in fact, *very* pregnant—that, in fact, she'd be leaving me forever in only a few weeks' time—I couldn't begin to contemplate the words which I wrote out with my own hand. Could hardly even see them appearing behind the pen as I dragged it cross the page. I could only transcribe mechanically whatever Di dictated:

Dear Ansin and all the family,

The wealthy mistress where I working all these years going need a next servant to care for she. Cause now I haveen praise God and the Lady bound to get a replacement. Whomsoever want the job must send 1) police record 2) health certificate 3) recommendation. Send all. Send quick. The mistress is a good woman, and she going treat you good, never mind she white. In truth, I does call she me white daughter. Hope all is well in Sherman and them.

Cordial,
Dalila Bootman Walker

That same afternoon (fate again: advocating coincidences, advocating soft conspiracies), that very afternoon the St Maggy Club was to play the finals of a five-day-testmatch with the Port of Spain Club. The victors would go to England to represent the West Indies. On the four previous afternoons I'd gone with Lady Tristleton to watch Daisy bowl. He'd bowled well. They'd all played better than ever; there was little doubt as to who'd be traveling to England. Yet that was not the reason I rang Lady Tristleton, at the last moment, and told her not to have her chauffeur pass for me. I simply could not get over my shock at losing Di. Could not possibly face that Oval full of bawling, jubilant spectators.

I'd listen in on the wireless. Father's old wireless. But as I sat alone in the parlour that afternoon, all alone in the house (where Di'd disappeared to I did not know—perhaps she'd gone to the match herself?), as I sat there in the parlour I could not concentrate on the announcer's flat voice. So distraught was I over Di. I simply could not *hear* what he was saying. Though every fifteen minutes I clicked the finger-worn, brown volume knob a notch higher. Till the old wireless *boomed.* Sending vibrations down the arms of my wicker chair. My bare feet practically bouncing on the twitching floorboards.

This went on for several hours: the wireless blasting, my *not* hearing it. Daisy's name—I was aware of at least that much—had been mentioned a few times. But for the life of me I wasn't sure if it was anything more than announcer's flap, or if he'd actually gone in to bat or to bowl. I wasn't even sure which side was leading! In my state of distress it hardly seemed to matter. *Nothing* in the world mattered so much as my loss of Di. I could think of nothing else; of all those years she had cared for me. My entire life! Di'd even nursed me together with my own mother, nursed me together with her own daughter.

She was part of my earliest memories, which I saw now with my eyes closed like old, yellowed photos in a family album: me perched on the kitchen counter while Di fed me a piece of bake dribbled with golden syrup, Di dressing me in my first frocks, platting my rope-thick single braid. Soon the photos began to flick past so quickly they became a moving-picture, then one with sound: two of us downstairs in my little room in the basement, Di feeding me breakfast with the big silver tablespoon. And after I'd swallowed down the last of my dessert of coconut jelly, Di would tell me stories. Tales of the forest full of obeah and magic. Tales of diablesses, and soukuyants, and lagahoos. Or she'd sing old calypsos to me in the patois I couldn't completely understand, but couldn't have minded in the least. Simply to have Di there with me was enough! Two of us alone together in my little basement room. And if the rest of the world were suddenly wiped away above us, if it disappeared completely, Di, I always believed, would still be there with me.

Suddenly I caught a vaps: suddenly I felt the inexplicable desire to return to my little basement room. I'd not been down there since before I'd left for the convent—in nearly ten *years*. Somehow I felt that there, in my little room, I might find Di. Might recover her for one last instant—even in my childhood memory—before I was forced to relinquish her forever.

I flipped off the wireless. All the furnishings bouncing round the room thumped into place. I hurried down the narrow stairs. Flipped on the light: Bolom, for an instant I thought I'd entered the wrong room. I would have been sure I *had,* had I not recognized the line of children's books tucked in along one of the shelves. Nothing else seemed to have survived from my childhood years. Not even my little window; it'd been replaced by two larger louvered ones! The very walls of my room seemed to have expanded to accommodate Daisy's furnishings. Somehow, as I looked round me, it seemed to have *grown!* Much larger than I remembered it to be.

In the very center of the room stood a tall, tilted drafting table. A mound of huge drawings spread out on top it, each curling successively off the edges like the ripples of a pebble pelted into water. And at just about the spot where the pebble would have fallen, I now noticed a tiny typewriter; *tiny*—that typewriter *did* seem to belong to a child—with its little black keys and shiny gold letters. But that typewriter had not belonged to me. I'd never seen it before.

I stared at it for a long minute—perhaps simply because it occupied the centermost point of the room, perhaps because I could not imagine Daisy's huge hands on those little keys—but only after a long minute did I realize that it contained a sheet of paper. Back-rolled on the type-writer's tiny carriage so that in order to read it, line by line as the print rose up out of darkness, I had to roll the carriage slowly forward:

Dear R—

You have asked me to give you my answer. Despite my deliberation, I cannot give it. But Fate shall answer for me (though, at this moment, and by our own doing, Fate indeed seems heavily weighed in your favor). Tomorrow we play the finals of the Port of Spain match. You have warned me that irregardless of the outcome you are fast on going to England. You shall not return for a very long time. (How you can say this having never set foot there, having never seen the place, I do not know!) Your plans, you say, are set. A new life: another world. It is up to me now to choose my place in it. This is what I will tell you; that should we win tomorrow, should we go to England together, then I shall not return either. Then this letter shall be mailed to you in due course.

Lilla knows nothing of any of this. How can I tell her of a change so great I cannot fathom it? in but a few short months? How possibly can I explain to her what I, myself, cannot understand? Even though I can admit freely now that I have fought these desires all my life. That they were precisely these desires which came between Lilla and myself, long before you broke the surface of my own resistance. But how can I possibly articulate to her any of this? More still, how can I pronounce the words that will shatter an affinity gained in measured silence? In quiet complicity? If, indeed, I must speak. Fate shall be the first. Know then that if these words pass before your eyes, we shall have celebrated an uncertain victory together; Lilla and I, who care for each other in our own particular way, who care for each other a great deal, shall have to suffer a certain loss.

—K

Bolom, I cannot say how long I stood staring at those words, reading them again and again. Perhaps only a minute. Perhaps a lifetime. All I know is that when I finally back-rolled the letter into the darkness of that tiny typewriter, and turned round, Daisy was standing there before me. Dressed again in his cricket whites. Again he looked thoroughly exhausted, bent-over; perhaps I also saw his lower lip tremble slightly. I could only think of one thing to say. One question to ask. Because just then it occurred to me that, in truth, I was not sure:

"Who won the match?"

Bolom, I know now that in the moment of crisis between two people, one is chosen to be strong, the other allowed the luxury of weakness. Perhaps that choice is made at random, in the instant of the moment. Perhaps it is written in stone from the very first moment those two people meet, stranded together at the top of a samaan tree. Bolom, I cannot tell you. All I can say is that what happened then was just the opposite of anything I would have imagined, even up to a moment before; it was Daisy who broke down now. Daisy who wept now like a giant, bent-over and broken child. And it was I who consoled him. I who took him in my arms and held him tightly. And after a minute—as though it were some sort of bodily reflex, involuntary, primal, matronly—after a minute I began making a soft, clicking sound with my tongue against the roof of my mouth. Soothing Daisy as though he were my own child.

9

I awoke on the other side of sleep. Not the dreamer caught in her dream, but the dreamer who has lost her sleeping self. That other self which the dreamer, down deep in the depths of her dream vaguely knows, recollects, only vaguely, but sufficiently well to provide the ballast so that her dream itself does not explode up out of water. Where there is no sleeping self remaining to return to.

The following morning I got up out of bed and went directly outside to the line of cages where Daisy kept his homing pigeons. Cooing softly and doing their silly, thick-necked dance in the hard morning sun. These were not Anastasia Cancampkins-Camps's pigeons. I did not set them free. Without malice, without anger, without haste, but with a compassion I knew as genuine, I removed them one by one from their cages and carefully wrung their necks. Just as I'd seen Di do with the fowls in the yard countless afternoons sitting beside her on the back stoop. Only my operation was far easier. These birds were so gentle they did not even struggle, but pecked tenderly at the purple veins in my transparent palms. Easy as sliding a ring off the index finger. One by one. Seven times. Till I had a little mound of white feathers at my feet. I took them up all together, a warm pillow held in both arms against my breast, and carried them over beneath the flamboyant tree. With a spade I dug out a small hole in the dirt, but sufficiently large to swallow them all.

Then I retrieved the letter from the basement and drove father's Ford to town. Addressed the envelope and posted it myself: *Reginald De Bassier, c/o St Maggy Cricket Association.*

When I returned home I made the coffee—it was past ten o'clock but the house was absolutely silent, still asleep, both Di and Daisy! I carried the coffee upstairs and woke him. We drank in silence. Daisy went off to work.

A few days later the letter arrived from Vel, Di's cousin, Ansin's granddaughter, saying that she wanted the job very much. At least that was the gist of the letter, because it sprawled on and on over so many pages, I could not bear to read it through. The large brown envelope also contained her health certificate, reference and police record. There were no charges; she was not the want-a-wallop. I tucked the letter and the various certificates back into the envelope, hid it with my diary and passport beneath the mound of unused knickers in the bedstand drawer. Then I drove to town and I purchased a bus ticket from Henly to St Maggy (Henly was closest to Velma's village of Sherman). But Bolom, I could not answer Velma's letter. What would I write? That I was pleased she was coming to replace Di? That I looked forward to meeting her? None of that was true. I counted up the days and wrote May 7 in large figures on the back of the red pasteboard bus ticket. Slipped it quickly into an envelope and addressed it in care of Ansin, my own address across the back flap, licked the gum and plastered it down. Posted it off.

May 7 would be the day, according to my calculations, on which Daisy's ship would sail. It seemed appropriate that Vel should arrive and Di depart on that same day. As it happened, though, I'd miscounted; and

Daisy'd already been gone for a day on the evening Vel knocked timidly at the front door. Di, I can only assume, knew nothing of the circumstances of Daisy's leaving, other than the fact that he was going to England to play cricket. I, at least, did not tell her; and I'm quite sure Daisy didn't either. Nevertheless, when I informed Di of the date set for Velma's arrival, she told me she wanted to stay on with me as long as she comfortably could. A few weeks, possibly another month. "However long it take for the girl settle in proper!" It was my one consolation as I waited for Daisy to leave.

Bolom, though it was only a matter of weeks, eventually I even grew weary of waiting. Grew weary, I suppose, of my role as the stronger one. A role—I realized at the same moment I'd assumed it—which I would have to play out till the bitter end. Now I began to feel anxious. Now I wanted the end to come and be done with. To be over. *Then,* I told myself, *then at last you can die in peace.*

But in the final days, quite to my own surprise, I entered a period of calm. That was the rhythm of Daisy's departure for me, of those last weeks, the way my *body* responded: from strength, to anxiety, to a kind of calm. Perhaps it was the calm of acceptance? I could not understand it myself. Was not prepared for it when it came; that calm took me completely by surprise.

And it was during this last period of calm that I came up with the idea of the key. The gesture of the key. Actually, it was a gift which Daisy had given me years before, soon after our marriage. In those days we'd inherited, along with the old estate house, a tremendous iron ring completely encircled by keys. Big iron skeleton keys. One for each door, and Bolom, you cannot imagine the number of doors there are in this old house. That ring was so heavy I could scarcely pick it up. But during those first days of restoration, Daisy, in his patient, methodical way, had gone from door to door and fitted all the locks to the same key: the big double front doors, our bedroom door, the door at the back of the kitchen—all of them. (As a boy Daisy'd been fascinated with clocks, with time-pieces; and the mechanism of a lock, he told me, functioned in much the same way.) Slowly but surely Daisy reduced the entire iron ring to a single master skeleton key, which one evening before supper he presented to me as a gift. Bolom, I did not have the heart to tell him we never bothered to lock the doors! Not even the big double front doors; not *once* could I remember locking them. No door other than the one to my little basement room.

Only a week before Daisy's departure, I took the key to the Royal Crown Jewelers in town. To the dodgy little shop on Abercromby Road, the dodgy little monocled Englishman inside. Counting karats. I'd decided to have a copy made in solid gold. A golden skeleton key. Key to the house Daisy'd loved so much. Where, should he ever decide to return, I would be waiting for him. That would be my final, silent gesture to Daisy.

10

He would leave by ship. In those days they'd not yet developed the aeroplanes with sufficient range to cross the sea to England. In those days, England was still far away. There was likely to be a big celebration at the docks to send off the cricketers. I could not bear to be among that crowd. Told Daisy I wished to say good-bye to him at the house.

On that morning, as on every morning which we'd spent together for the previous three years, we drank our coffees sitting up in bed. Then Daisy got up and showered and dressed. He was just packing his sleeping costume into the suitcase when we heard Sir Eustace's horn. He closed the suitcase gently, but it gave out a very loud *snap*. I threw a robe round myself and followed him down the stairs. At the front door Daisy put down his suitcase beside the other one already there waiting. Cleared his throat and told me that he was going into the kitchen to bid farewell to Di.

I stood waiting before the front door, my bare feet on the worn Persian rug. Looking up at the chandelier suspended above my head, at the portraits hanging on the wall; and for a moment I felt sure the silence of that house which I had always so treasured, was going to crush me. The feeling passed by the time Daisy got back, and when I turned to him I became the strong one again. Pressing the key blunt-pointed, point-first into the center of my transparent palm—as though I were trying to pierce my way through it. I looked up at Daisy. Bent-over and broken, perhaps I saw his lower lip tremble slightly.

Bolom, at that moment I knew I would not give him the key. Knew that he would not see it, or even hear of its existence. That my gesture, indeed, was far far from silent. That in fact that key only attempted to negate a reality I did not want to accept. A reality which had taken Daisy all these years and our marriage too to come to accept himself. That to give him that key, now, would be the final act of weakness. And I would not allow myself such weakness. That that gift, perhaps all gifts since the beginning of time—every gift a woman has given a man or he to her—that gift amounted to little more than the self-indulgence of the giver, and at that moment I could not permit myself such a luxury. I could only take Daisy in my arms, trying to pierce the key through my transparent palm even behind his back.

Daisy opened the door and took up his suitcases. From the open door I watched him walk to Sir Eustace's sportscar, tuck one suitcase behind the seats and the other into the trunk. Watched him close the trunk softly with a *snap* which again came out far too loud. Watched Daisy turn round and look up at the old house one last time, watched his eyes travel slowly down and settle, for one last instant, on me. He got in, bent-over and broken, and Sir Eustace gave one last horrid bellow of his horn as he drove off.

I took a step backward and shut the door. Turned the key in the lock.

Sleep

If cycles of REM sleep are to be regarded as
signs of "dreaming," their occurrence in the fetus . . .
raise[s] yet other obscure questions.

John Bishop,
Book of the Dark

1

one karat two karats three karats four karats five karats six karats seven
one carrot two carrot three carrot four carrot five carrot six carrot seven

karats eight karats nine karats ten karats eleven karats twelve karats thirteen
carrot eight carrot nine carrot ten carrot eleven carrot twelve carrot thirteen

karats fourteen karats fifteen karats sixteen karats seventeen karats eighteen
carrot fourteen carrot fifteen carrot sixteen carrot seventeen carrot eighteen

karats seventeen karats sixteen karats fifteen karats fourteen karats thirteen
carrot nineteen carrot twenty carrot twenty-one carrot twenty-two carrot twenty-

karats twelve karats eleven karats ten karats nine karats eight karats seven
three carrot twenty-four carrot twenty-five carrot twenty-six carrot twenty-

karats six karats five karats four karats three karats two karats one karat two
seven carrot twenty-eight carrot twenty-nine carrot thirty carrot thirty-one

karats three karats four karats five karats six karats seven karats eight karats
carrot thirty-two carrot thirty-three carrot thirty-four carrot thirty-five car-

nine karats ten karats eleven karats twelve karats thirteen karats fourteen kar-
rot thirty-six carrot thirty-seven carrot thirty-eight carrot thirty-nine car-

ats fifteen karats sixteen karats seventeen karats eighteen karats seventeen
rot forty carrot forty-one carrot forty-two carrot forty-three carrot forty-

karats sixteen karats fifteen karats fourteen karats thirteen karats twelve
four carrot forty-five carrot forty-six carrot forty-seven carrot forty-eight

karats eleven karats ten karats nine eight seven six five four three two and one
carrot forty-nine carrot fifty carrot and then fifty again up to hundred carrot

again and again and again calling **D-a-i-s-y! D-a-i-s-y!** and not knowing a-tall
again and again and again calling **S-u-u-e! S-u-u-e!** and not finding her no-

if I am searching for my husband or my pet clean-neck-fowl not knowing a-tall in
where searching by that river where I uses to take she to drink all confuse now in

your dream Bolom which is which not understanding where I am to look in her coop
you dream Bolom which is which if is Joyce-Junie where am I to look how a child

behind the kitchen in his office downstairs in the basement with this skeleton
could dig out that big hole in a concrete wall but that concrete it did rotting

key in my hand fingering twitching incessantly but you know he was so gentle
I could remember boiling bubbling off the wall but you know she was so tame

gentle he could just take my happiness and go away with me alone forever calling
tame anybody could just hold the rope and go-long quick with she so easy calling

D-a-i-s-y! D-a-i-s-y! up the stairs in this bedroom-sanctuary-cell for ten years now
J-u-n-i-e! J-o-y-c-e! in the living we Family-Government-Plannings running quick

the key in my hand in the lock on the other side of the door turning to lie here
pulling she in through the hole on the next side of that big big circle they did

again in this bed on my back this golden skeleton key fingering fingering night
put for those people to dance in this crop-over everybody firing firing the waters

after night alone in this little room downstairs in the basement standing here
they making one set of noise for this fête they had the big fire beating cooking

on the stack of my storybooks my eyes closed my lips pressed hard against the
and I see like my sister boyfriend beside bareback and shining in the flames of

glass with my chaplet in my hand fingering fingering and now opening my eyes at
sweat my Uncle Charpie there only whispering whispering and me pushing through

last to find him gone forever now that I could know that it was him quiet beside
the people closer now to the fire that I could know that it was she burning in a

me all this time the presence of another alive hurrying that afternoon soon as
fever in my arms cake in mud up to my knees all the dress soak through with

190

Di lets me out running quickly her coop stiff stiff at the bottom now he was
mud this child all in a sudden feeling so cold cold in my arms silent she was

dead my sweet Daisy Daisy dead my hands trembling little Daisy Daisy dead in
dead my sweet Junie-Joyce dead in my arms trembling little Joyce-Junie dead in

my hands and I just press her tight to my breast with the tears wet on my cheeks
my arms that I just press she tight to my breast with the tears wet pon my cheek

to tell Ramsingh never again will I have another clean-neck-husband for my pet
and I just fall to my knees there in middle that dance-music-circle for my child

pressed tight to my breast running to call Dulcianne two of us to bury her there
my legs all scrape-up smear with blood from them bramble and I just cry for my

beneath the flamboyant tree behind the house that her soul might be lifted up
Sue I just cry for she and send Arrows to bring the little box white in he daddy

when it flowers so they say because everybody longs for that in this life at last
Mr Bootman motorcar that we could bury she too beneath the mango tree be-

to be dead and buried so quiet and peaceful happy forever
hind the house my four sweet babies dead and bury forever

2

so I say yes we will marry if you wish now that mummy is dead and we will
so I say yes we will marry if you want now that Junie-Joyce is dead but not

have the ceremony in the Catholic Church as you had promised her we can purchase
no fancy ceremony in the pappyshow church as you say with me in such a bad state

d'Esperance Estate straight away free of death-duties purchase-tax whatever it
of despair grieving so much to make style-up wedding with gloves I say let's we

was with Bumblebee only insistent that Daisy convert Catholicism-Protestantism
just go before the Magis and finish you know all them compartment houses in the

*one as good or as bad as the next but I say **no in no uncertain terms** instead*
*Plannings going give way just now that I say **not even for money-self** that we*

of the picnic now at Huevos Beach with Sir Eustace Lady Tristleton in the Ford
ain't got nor time to waste before all them Family Plannings finish quick to go

straight to the Magistrate's house and Sir Eustace pulling him out of bed to fire
straight at the Magis to pronounce pon we and Berry friend Lewey to stand as

a quick one fast as parragrass **you could now please kiss the bride** in the Ford
witness too fast as parragrass **you could please now kiss the bride** with we own

again the six of us for the picnic finally at Huevos Beach that when we arrived
marriage-certificate and them birth-papers for Junie-Joyce that we did need too

home and Daisy appeared out the WC dressed in his slippered nightgown of silk
me and Berry straight at the Health make the application now that little brown

pajamas and me waiting in the bed stark naked as always embarrassed now to strip
Father Christmas and I say Sweet Jesus that we get the last of them compartment

down too with me suddenly so intrigued actually getting up onto my knees and
houses in the Plannings I say let's we move in in that concrete house tonight-

crawling to the end of the bed a closer look at those things hanging **O-o-o-o!**
self three toads-in-a-bucket climbing them stairs little Junie-Joyce **H-o-o-o!**

O-o-o-o! because here is my clean-neck-fowl at last my long-lost dear Daisy her
H-o-o-o! loud to hear the echoes off them concrete walls of we spook-manchant

skinny gangly neck drooping down from her little fuzzy body here nestled between
and who ever hear of spooks living in a concrete house with we pipe in the kitchen

Daisy's legs with poor Daisy so taken aback by my enthusiasm all I can think to
that I can scarce even help myself from opening again and again to see coke-cola

do is out the light but of course my hands can **never** restrain themselves from
flowing in we own kitchen in we own sink I can **never** restrain myself to turn

examining in the dark what I had seen so suddenly **monstrous monstrous**
in my sleep on the floor that night with all that **shrew-honk shrew-honk**

that how possibly can **she** fit up whole inside little **me** suddenly feeling so soft
again I only want to **feel** that concrete against my **skin** I want feel that so cold

soft inside-outside moist skin backward like an overripe mango outside-inside
cold in the morning so wet against my cheek that I jump up quick say we sleep

suddenly so strange that he's inventing this surely this can't be right those
in toilet water last night that water is toilet water you ain't know it stand

192

impossible mechanics alarmingly so strange over before either could know it
for **White Colonial** but Father Christmas couldn't change we compartment

sleeping peacefully breathing quietly at last comforted now for the first time
for we to sleep in toilet water flooding through the place cause we own was

since I'd lain beside mummy this same bed only months before and Daisy can
the last to give way so we just mop it out sprinkle with lye we just get used to

start to refurbish the old house patiently board by board and trellis by trellis
living with that toilet water cause least now we living in concrete house ain't

with that big iron ring and so many keys each one to a different door and so
no scorpions running under the floor and we fix that compartment house so

heavy I can scarcely pick it up painstakingly one lock then the other fitted to
nice we get all the furnishings one time with little bed for Junie-Joyce and we

the same master skeleton key for a present to me one night before supper I could
own big bed in we room that mattress was foam mattress I say we would have to

only smile since we'd never once before long as I could remember locked a single
get gun and shoot it first and he say just as always let's we hot-up them sheets

door now that it was carnival season with Sir Eustace so terribly anxious to
right now but I say how I ain't got no long-dress nor no highheel shoe that

have us join the band **American Airlines** was all the talk that year but of course
I could go now at this **Firemen Ball** but then Berry say this one is costume party

Daisy needed no coaxing a-tall setting himself straight away to the construction
you know disguise we could disguise-up weself however we want you don't needing

of our costumes Uncle Sam and the Statue of Liberty a big pasteboard tophat
for no long-dress nor highheel shoe and I say well what you going as how you

painted in stars-and-stripes Daisy's white cricket trousers a blue-and-white-
disguising yourself he say I going do just how I do in the canes I disguising

striped shirt suspenders an enormous pasteboard crown with red plastic windows
as woman and I say no you wouldn't not before the people like that I be so shame

glittered silver at last the big torch from a piece of driftwood glittered flaming too
you to dress up ganga like that but he don't pay me no mind he go at he granny

193

and my own gown pumps and mummy's brassiere too which should have alerted me
house thief she pump-sleeve long-dress she wig too with all the ringlets and she big

from the start he would play the Statue of Liberty certainly painting his nails
broad-hat with my own brassiere stuff to here with toiletpaper he disguising-up

with my bright red nailpolish and painting on lipstick on his lips my own rouge
with my bright red nailpolish and he paint on lipstick pon he lips my Cashmere

on his cheeks that man looked so funny well I never a transvestite so very ugly in
pon he cheeks that man did look so ugly well I never see ganga-man so funny in

all my life I laughed so that morning so certain my belly would burst with the
all my life we did laugh so hard for that I did sure my belly going burst them

tears in my eyes and he speaking in that silly voice now with a big wink of his
tears in my eyes and he talking in he ganga-man voice now he say blinking he

eye **hurry up thweetheart let's make a thcandal this morning** I say Dear Jesus
eye **I going find me thweetman make me thome breads tonight** I say Sweet Jesus

look at this man what will you do with him stuffing up mummy's brassiere out to
look at this man now what you going do with he ask then you ain't disguising-up

here with tissue-paper mummy's hose and my pumps too leaving me no choice other
youself what you disguising as so I say if you going as woman I could go as man

than to disguise myself now in his clothing penciling a curly mustache with my
that's all it is so I dress now as he I put on he long-cape dragging from the fire

eyebrow-pencil big big tall tophat painted in stars-and-stripes now and Daisy's
service and he big boots big red fireman hat and we go-long just so we mount

own cricket trousers rolled-up his striped shirt suspenders the two of us hurrying
pon he bicycle to go in this fancy whitepeople fête and we style-up with them too

to join the band all Daisy's fellow cricketers discovering him at once dancing
we eating cakes drinking cokes and waters for the men and dance is dance we

hideously this Miss disguised such a scene so scandalous with Reginald the star
dance at that Firemen Ball till we did most ready to drop such a good good time

batsman **is me to liberate Miss Liberty this morning** but how could I even begin
that night **you keeping me from my foxtromp rhythm** there front we little shack-

to suspect then or Daisy himself jumping-up dancing ourselves to exhaustion and
house side the canes without even no music dancing we little two-step right there

then to walk all the way home arm in arm **oh we were so terribly happy then**
in the silent holding tight he strong arms **oh we did meeting life so good then**

3

with that coalpot cooking and Di already in the kitchen my little bake I
with that big pot black and had on two handles to carry out in the yard I

can remember so well buttered and quartered and dribbled golden syrup mornings
could remember a-bubbling with all the people when they reach home pon evening

first thing the only ones awake in the house and Di lifting me onto the counter
throwing in what food they got hand of green-figs cassava pumpkin peas potato

feeding me mouthful by mouthful the two of us alone here together in my little
eddoes chicken fishhead from the docks like my Tantee May she bring home big

room in the basement the highlight of my day sitting before me the tray on her
fishhead throwing inside that pot cooking with the wood fire beneath of electric

lap feeding me mouthful by mouthful with the silver tablespoon my breakfast of
poles they did cut down for poor people cause we didn't have no electricity then in

fricassee chicken beside the little dome of white rice and the piece of buttered
the country but we did had them poles to make fire with and it kicking that

christophine with the tall glass of coconut-water held in both hands tipped up
thing did kicking and when that pot come off the fire to carry out in the yard

sliding into my mouth my dessert of sweet coconut jelly till I finished eating
like a big stew with dumplings and granny dipping the ladle and we all eating

all my breakfast Di would tell me a story of the forest full of obeah and magic
all the people in the yard neighbors from the street we all eating from that one

lagahoos and soukuyants but the thing I so liked the **most** the **best** was when now
pot everybody together so but the thing I did like the **most** the **best** was when now

Di would sing to me the patois I could scarcely understand the smile wicked
Uncle Charpie kill a pig butcher a pig that nobody tell me to do that I just

on her face like the lézard that got lost beneath the mademoiselle's froufrou but
look I just say well that thing must be good I just collect it up in my tot when

then she would always be in a flap to hurry hurry upstairs to set the table for
Uncle Charpie stick that siphon come I just run with my tot to cook it right

mummy and daddy and often their guests too to serve them their own breakfast
there beside the fire stirring and it come just like scramble egg to put in pepper

leaving me there alone again in my room hours and hours waiting standing there
thyme shado-beni all chip-up in my tot I eat that blood I did love that blood of

on my stack of storybooks my lips pressed against the silver moth rolling beads
Uncle Charpie so much I could eat all the blood and ain't giving nobody none

locking myself inside the WC the line of little cubicles there the far side of the
cause in them days I uses to bathe beside the pipe nights cause so far to carry

playingfield soon as the bell rang for recess standing there on the bench with
that water bucket most a mile to that spicket standpipe we uses to call it with

my knickers pulled down stretched between my knees when I hear a watery plashing
my panties pull off quick shove between the joint of one them tall bananas growing

behind and I look over my shoulder quickly I dropped my skirt so quickly now
behind and I look over my shoulder careful I raise up my skirt slow my piece of

with my chaplet slipping out my hand dropping to the flooring of the sweathouse
soap and my rag and I fill my bucket with water begin to scrub but then all in a

for the cocoa slotted too saved by the crucifix between the two boards dangling
sudden when I look down my bucket gone and I couldn't find it no place I say

suspended over that boiling stinking pit retrieved carefully calm again I forgot
what the hell going on here but then I look again my bucket right back there

that noise I didn't pay it any mind I raise my skirt and I start to rub again
again that I don't pay it no mind I raise my skirt and I start to scrub again

when suddenly now the watery noise **again** I drop my skirt so **quickly** again looking
when I look down my bucket gone **again** I drop that skirt so **quick** again I say who

upside-down behind my back finding Brett's clammy doughy face beady milk-of-
the hell gone with my bucket and he say I going mash it up I say what you you

magnesia glassbottle-eyes staring down at me an instant disappearing with my
going mash my bucket I ain't even know who Joe is what you want mash-up my

whole cubicle rocking side-to-side now thinking oh if she had **seen** oh if she had **only**
bucket for Joe he say you know what I want I say I ain't **know** what he did **want**

realized what when a second later their fists beating pounding **white cockroach**
my hand in this lock-grip that all I could do is follow thinking **this man going**

in the WC screaming and beating their fists again and again now playing with
murder you now in them canes that I couldn't see he running behind now and not

sheself in the **WC** in the **WC** in the **WC** at last hearing that recess bell ringing now
seeing knowing **nothing nothing nothing** my feet ain't even touching he man-voice

one by one slowly leaving me there locked up inside my little cubicle sweating all
swirling round my head with them canes lashing cross my face loud and then all

the stench rising now in heatwaves up from the bottom of that pit but I wouldn't
in a sudden silent in some place he carry me now a cave or a hole or a shack or

dare open that door not again till that final bell at last **ringing ringing** and all of
what I could never say all I know is one moment we did **running running** and next

them shoving in the door and pulling me out holding me down Brett standing above
moment we stop and I feel he shove me down he holding me down pon the ground pon

me penknife-lipstick red her fist flipping up my skirt flipped up falling through
my back and I falling falling now through the dark empty silent falling through

the air of that deep well when all in a sudden thwack the hard hollow stab of
the air of that deep well when all in a sudden whacks this pain come searing

that lipstick thrust inside me **thwack** flat on my back against the hard ice-cold
through my middle sudden **whacks** flat pon my back against the hard ice-cold

water at the bottom of that well sinking slowly inside that pain and now their
water at the bottom of that well sinking slow slow in that pain so harsh I ain't

hands holding me down slip away I could only lie there squeezing my eyes shut
know if we lie there a time or what all I know is we lying now we walking I did

awhile after I open them to see the pale-blue sky reaching down slowly feeling
walking behind he in the dark of them canes he lock-grip all in a sudden just

removing the warm metal canister soft red lipstick at the end I pelt it away to
slip and when I look up there was that spicket there was my bucket beneath like

get up walking so *dazed* in that bungalow beside the beach I reach I see all this
nothing ain't even **happen** I take it up I go home but when I reach I see all this

blood my fingers stained with **blood** dark brown **blood** when I lift my skirt to see
blood my skirt did stain with **blood** thick brown **blood** when I see this I did think

my knickers were stained with blood too I pull them off roll them up the towel
he did kill me I think I going kill he I didn't know but then I remember that

hidden till I reach the cove at the end of the beach and I dig out a deep hole there
menses that I did had that one and only maybe it was the same thing my skirt I

throw them in with my stained brown fingers numb in the white snow I could only
throw it down in the toilet I had to throw it way that amount of blood it couldn't

imagine cold and white against my fingers covering it up forever and I carry
never wash like that so I throw it down in the toilet but then I couldn't carry

myself down to the cool water submerge myself in that cool clear water my breath
myself up in the bed that night I just couldn't sleep in that bed now with all them

upheld with my eyes open I had to be by myself quiet alone in the world of my
children sleeping beside I had to be by myself sleep alone that night so I just

imagination staring up at my own reflection floating facedown on the surface of
throw myself pon some sacks of peas Ansin pigeonpeas granny had there drying I

the gently-rippling clear water I just dream I dream I **dream**
throw myself pon them sacks and I just sleep I sleep I **sleep**

4

when he rolls off for me to jump up quickly rushing into the WC with poor
when he roll over for he to just take a swing of he long arm of he fist that

Daisy lying there confused frustrated no doubt as to what I might possibly be
Berry lying there he just swing like that he didn't even sit up that blow knock

doing with the door locked and that bidet spouting like a bashed-in cow's head
me over backward like big seawave I there lying pon the ground all the blood

198

the purple crystals **la douche violent** violet splashing over that white porcelain
spilling my mouth **bust clean across** and poor Junie-Joyce that she could scarce

cracks between the tiles in a grid of bright purple shoving the crystals up inside
even walk then pulling pon my dress pon my sleeve she trying to raise me up off

me burning a raw wound scrubbed with salt that astringent **vile/violent/violate**
the floor I go in the kitchen under the pipe so much of **blood/bleeding/bled-up**

stains on my abdomen running down my legs as though we had had violent brutal
pon my mouth my dress soak I just take and bury beneath the washbasin outside I

sex in truth Daisy always so gentle such soft caring and understanding with me
dig the hole and put the two cement blocks on top beneath the basin them police

so desperate obsessed with my own fears so many horrors I gave that poor man but
could never find that shirt like that so much of things I do for that vagabond but

I was so **terrified now** to find myself pregnant ever since I was a younggirl in that
I was so **glaze now** with he this time I say never again I take-up carry Junie-Joyce

convent Mother Marie-Bernard told me my child would be born a **duen** imagine that
at crossroads catch the bus go straight to Sherman straight at **Ansin** house to my

woman was so **malevolent malevolent** she was **malevolent** to the core **malevolent** to
granny I say **extrement extrement** you know is **extrement** we living in **extrement** in

her very bones with me too young to realize too young before I could understand
that place did make Joyce-Junie so sick with cholera we got to tend pon she the

not simply believing but knowing as though it had happened already pregnant now
whole night running at she stools so weak them pills the doctor give to she and me

with this diab-duen inside me that day in catechism class when she broached her
too to boil the water to take them with that they couldn't do nothing it already

favorite topic of masturbation touching-up yourself with the devil wicked fingers
too late for that cholera so we stand the whole night tending pon this child next

bony flicking **clack clack clack** against her thumb in front of my face continue with
morning she was **dead dead dead** my sweet baby Junie-Joyce was dead in my arms I

this **nastiness** younglady you going find youself pregnated you hear haveen haveen
did so **startle** by this thing mid say it was the shock send me straight in childbed

with a *diab-duen* with me already rolling beads now for five **years** pitching a faint

I did **traumatize** by that she say even though now I couldn't **feel** that grief yet it

right there in the classroom me pelting down on the flooring a moment later in the

send me in childbed that same night we did bury Joyce-Junie but I know I certain

dormitory alone **basodee boobooloops bufutu** as though I were sleeping with my

that child did **living** he **breathing** he **alive** I sure about that cause I take he up

eyes open the feverish trance pregnant with this diab-duen from all that rolling

I had to take he up hold in my arms but I was naked then that was the mostest

beads according to this Mother Marie-Bernard of the Burning Mustache Bush like a

thing I could think to wrap the sheet round and I go stumbling out behind the mango

fiery caterpillar crawling cross her upper lip oh I was so so terrified knowing now sure

tree behind the house and when I see the mid and Granny Ansin that they did bury

that I was pregnant without a doubt even though I hadn't yet **seen** my menses even

he too I just didn't want to be living after my four babies now **gone** dead and I just

and that diablesse the mother-of-Satan herself the greatest fear in my life to

go beneath the house in that shower-stall that we did had there I take up that

find myself pregnant again years later a grown woman suddenly a child again

bottle of peroxide and I just drink it down straight all that peroxide and I out

haunted by those same terrors instilled engraved on my unconscious my overactive

but when I wake to find myself haveen again Berry say make this one a manchild

female imagination childhood-trauma repressed returning an adult a child again

for me he so happy the next thing I know he gone again my belly ready to bust

hysterical female imagination with no choice but abort to throw this child now

with next one coming no money food in that house to feed Junie-Joyce I didn't

swallowing the little white quinine it wouldn't do **anything** for this monster in

have no choice but try to throw that quinine don't **nothing** do for this child in

my belly I was certain demanding from Dr Curtis the prescription for feigning

my belly out to here I just bind it up to go at the pharmacist say I suffering

malaria spells in order to purchase the quinine tablets I just swallowed down

malaria spells I got to get more of that quinine powder I just drink it down

little white pills and so **dizzy** after so **weak** and finally so **tired** I can recall
that thing did had me so **dizzy** I feeling **weak** now feeling **tired** I remember

that was the rhythm of those quinine pills I swallowed down so many I went into
that was the rhythm of that quinine powder I swallowing down so much I went at

the WC that afternoon I was alone in my bedroom Di down in the kitchen cooking
Mistress Pantin house to catch a few cents so that afternoon in the kitchen cooking

suddenly so weak the room spinning round I slipped on the porcelain tiles I fell
suddenly so weak the room spinning round I slip pon them porcelain tiles I fall

and hit my head on the pipe beneath the sink I was out **cold** from that blow for
bounce my head pon the pipe beneath the sink I did out **cold** from that blow for

Di to hear my fall the kitchen downstairs and come pelting up the stairs to find
Mistress Pantin to hear the fall upstairs and come pelting down the stairs find

me lying there my head in a pool of **blood** he says **Lil you must be more careful**
me lying there my head in a pool of **blood** she say **Vel you must be more careful**

when he arrived home Daisy was **mortified** and me saying I'll be better quick as
Mistress Pantin she say you going **lose** that child you must take the vitamins

A and **B** and **C** only a relapse my childhood fantasies nothing a-tall but he none-
B and **D** and **C** and she take out she billfold she press three dollars crisp in my

theless calling Dr Curtis to make the appointment Daisy he was so very good kind
hand just like that say you need money Vel you must tell me she was so good kind

to me that man was like the father I never had
to me that woman was the mummy I never had

5

on our way home we always stopped at the Prime Minister's house to steal
on we way home we uses to stop front that Prime Minsiser house and thief

two **colossal** eden-mangoes from the big tree growing in front running back to
two **big big** eden-mango out from the tree growing side the gate pelting back in

the car with the coolie yardboy running behind us his cutlass raised above his
the car with the little yardboy pelting behind we he cutlash raise up above he

head bawling behind **get from this yard crazy thiefing whitewomen you think**
head bawling behind **get from this yard crazy thiefing blackwomen you think**

cause is the PM own them fruits be public property *jumping in quickly now she*
cause is the PM own them fruits be public property *jumping in quick with she*

in the side-seat and me in the driver's the engine started quickly to take-off
in the driver-seat and me in the side that motor fire so quick now to take-off

bat-out-of-hell hurrying straight to Huevos Beach because the only way to eat
bat-out-of-hell pelting straight to that Huevo Beach cause onliest way to eat

those *mangoes properly is sitting in waist-deep water two of us stripped down*
them *mango proper is seat youself in waist-deep water two of we stripping down*

in one she to her bodice beneath her dress and me of course stark naked without
in one me in the shift beneath me dress and she naked naked as she born with no

underclothing the beach vacant as always on Wednesday at midday giggling like
underclothes the beach empty like always on Wednesday midday laughing same as

two adolescent girls doing something illicit ripping off long chamois-strips
two younggirls carrying on wicked misbehaving peeling off in long soft strip

of skin with our teeth the juice running sticky sweet down our chins necks our
of skin in we teeth all the juice running sticky sweet down we chin we neck we

tottots dripping with that juice sticky sweet sweet so **lovely** *bright orange flesh*
tottot dripping with that juice sticky sweet sweet so **eatable** *bright orange flesh*

texture of **human** *flesh a baby's* **backside** *Bolom sucking those big hairy seeds our*
feeling like **human** *flesh a baby* **bamsee** *Bolom sucking pon them big hairy stone we*

cheeks puffed-up sucking with all the life left in us exhausted now and so sleepy
cheeks fat blow-out sucking with all we strength remaining dead-up now sleepy

climbing out of the water slowly up onto the shore dripping all caked in sand
climbing up out the water slow up pon the shore still dripping cake-up in sand

white up to our knees dressing back in our dresses clinging our skin wet still
white high as we knee throwing on we dress again sticking to we skin wet still

dripping in the Ford driving ever-so-slowly with the other motorcars pomping at
dripping that motorcar she driving slow slow with them other motorcar tipping at

202

us now to hurry up back at the house again she with the basket on top her head
we now to hurry up back at the house again me with the basket top my head with

toting all the food behind me opening the door unlocked with this golden key
all the food toting behind she opening up the door unlock with that gold key

hanging round my neck extracted and turning again in the lock on the other side
hanging round she neck out and in straight again in the keyhole on the next side

the two of us locked-up again for another week but then that night earlier than
the two of we lock-up again for the next week but then that night I see he as

usual in my room with the door locked lying there feeling all bloated sick my color
usual only dignify again now through the kitchen window beckoning with money

green I'm sure thinking dear Vel dear Vel how can I have stuffed so monstrously
green he hand not calling Dulcianne Dulcianne I say don't do it Vel then I think

what's she going to do with me letting him in like that tall and strong so easy
what we going do only thirty-three dollars left that sack beneath the floorboard

for him to climb up the drainpipe through the gap in the jalousies the easiest
last time I climb up the drainpipe through the gap in the jalousie the easiest

way inside the house swiftly before I couldn't do anything a-tall so delirious
way inside she room secret before she wouldn't know nothing I got to do it now

that I couldn't move before I could realize and I could think of some way to stop
that I got to do it before she could realize and I could think of some way better

*him come to rob rape molest a rich whitewoman or something **something** but then he*
*get a day-job with some other rich whitewoman or something **something** but now I*

*didn't even **touch** me climbing in through my bedroom window me lying there*
*ain't got no **choice** I climb out through the kitchen window I follow behind he*

silent beneath him stark naked at the end of the bed chest heaving smelling rank
silent beneath the house he had the blanket dirty crocusssack not smelling stiff

with rum lying there on my back with my eyes shut tight tight waiting but he
with waters I lie pon my back I close my eyes tight tight cause I did sure he

*wouldn't do **anything** only feeling his rank breath against the side of my neck*
*couldn't do **nothing** only feel me up little bit he nastiness and then that money*

203

hot in his hand the key on the ribbon round my neck my eyes open quickly to jump
hot in my hand but that night I ain't know maybe he take tonic to make he stand

up before I could think what he could do that key was turning in the lock on
up before I could know what he was doing that night he hold me down before I

*the other side sitting there listening to nothing but **silence** the whole entire time in*
*could push he off shove he out where he find that **strength** but somehow he manage*

*truth and yet I **know** I know it was that night because when else ever has there*
*before I could **know** I know was he that night then after sometime I uses to think*

*been a man in the house it could only have been **him** it must be **him** and now **you***
*well I could be a prostitute then I could do it for **she** I do it for **she** but now **you***

Bolom to come between us that age-old fear of all mistresses who come to care so
Bolom to come between we same old-age fright of all servant who come to care so

for their servants surely as I have come to care for her more than I could never
for they mistress as sure as I have come to care for she more than I could never

*have understood before say the word **love** more than any husband's-wife before all*
*have understand before say the word **love** more than any wife-husband before all*

*this and now you child come to separate us one from another unless possibly **you***
*this and now you child come to separate we one from the other less someways **you***

are the very thing to bring us together because why not why on earth not simply
is that very being to bring we together since who say no who ever say no only

because society says two women together black-white with a child of their own
cause the people say two womens together white-black with a child of they own

in the same house and happy also let us not forget this happiness also more than
in the same house and happy too that we can never forget happiness too more than

***ever** before in my life I say let us dream now of our two races black and white*
***ever** before in this life I say let we dream now of two peoples white and black*

***together** in one child let's dream of birth shattering this invincible glass pane*
***together** in one child let we dream of birth swallowing this invisible glass pain*

be-
be-

tween we forever **you** *Bolom melt from out we mouth in broken glassbottle of words*
tween us forever **you** *Bolom smash it now to hell and let us kiss one another at last*

let we wake from this old-age nightmare and live side by side happy here in this
let us awaken from this age-old nightmare and live happily together here in this

big old board-house two peoples two language two race to cleave together in one
old colonial house two people of two languages two races brought together in one

child one hope for all the world unite up here under this galvanize-tin roof the
child one hope for all the world united here under this corrugated-zinc roof the

three of we in this big bed better than any husband-wife and child a family for
three of us in this big bed more than any wife's-husband with child a family for

the Caribbean in this room that she does think without no questions so positive
the New World in this room which has been my self-imposed prison-sanctuary

for ten years now that I ain't never once come inside to step cross that doorsill
for ten years now that I have never once allowed Vel to step cross the threshold

of this room with she gold key hanging round she neck turning the lock morning
of that door this golden key hanging round my neck turning in the lock morning

noon and night I could never understand but she is the madam and me the servant
noon and night I could never understand myself this obsession with this golden key

but even if was the other way I don't judge nobody I got to respect she privacy
but even so Vel understood refused to judge me she always respected my privacy

but then I begin to question about all that money we living pon she had to hide
but then I began to question myself why all this nonsense and what I had to hide

in she room lock-up secret secret she **think** *cause one day I say now well that*
in my room locked-up again secret I **believed** *it was the psychological response*

money she give me every month that 15 dollars of my salary it going finish **soon**
to Daisy's leaving me all this uncalculated unconscious rolling beads I'd **always**

cause she could never have **that** *much money hide way it going pon five years now*
done it I could never blame **that** *on poor Daisy I recall calculating five years now*

I figure 15 dollar/1 month × 12 month × 5 year = 900 of dollar or 9,000 cents
figuring 15 decades/rosary × 12 months × 5 years = 900 decades or 9,000 HMs

*madam did pay me out **already** I get **such** a **fright** I did say I **got** to go look in*
*or masturbations I **should** say I got **such** a **shock** I thought **such** foul perversity*

she room how much money she got remaining I trying to thief she key weeks and
such self-indulgence for a person to be so very sealed-up within herself so cut off

weeks and can't thief it one night all in a sudden she just hand it over for me
from other human beings independent or in spite of sex or sexuality unable to

to bust in every night for five weeks waylaid cleaning and reading she diary
respond to another man or woman to give of oneself pleasure offered sexual

every night at last the same brownpaper-sack under she bed and I count out 300
or otherwise simply human affection life itself a gift unable to give innumerable

*dollars remaining such a drain of my preoccupation cause that's **plenty** money*
*possibilities and yet so so locked-up within herself to know nothing **other** than*

plus I had some money stash every month I taking out 3 dollars out my 15 and
that solitary pleasure when you stop to consider that 3 chaplets make 1 rosary

send the remainder to Granny Ansin cause she got all them children to feed so
every night and day too without exception once I even stopped to count it out

I figure 3 dollar/month × 12 month × 5 years = 180 of dollar + 300 dollar that
figuring 3 chapts./ros. × 12 months × 5 years = 180 chapts. × 50 HMs/1 chapt.

she had left add to mine = 480 dollars together = 4,800 cents cause very next day
with 1 ros. per 3 chapt. = 5 decades multiplied = 9,000 Holy Marys/masturbations

I take my money and put it there in she secret place beneath the floorboard of
in actual point of fact without the slightest exaggeration manipulation of the

*she room and every month she give me the salary I climb up and put it back **right***
*female genitalia is so pleasurable perhaps even healthy too perhaps not to **those***

where it come from cause that same money gots to go to pay for food for both of
extremes but who is to say what is normal normality's whatever is normal to me

we living together off that cash that I didn't even worry my head to count it
or you so long as it doesn't infringe or impinge upon the rights or pleasures

208

out no more cause that's plenty plenty money we had stash beneath she bed but
of fellow human beings but that is precisely the problem since pleasuring one-

then one time I say I better count it 33 dollars left I did so fraid two nights
self alone is pleasure withheld from one another maybe the solution then is give

later he appear again before the kitchen window money green in he white hand I
and take but still the problem of solitary activities like rolling beads and then

say don't do it Vel you don't need to do it but then I was climbing up already
there are others also reading also writing every time I lose myself inevitably

out follow he beneath the gallery he dirty crocusssack how I could never know
as if it had a mind of its own my left hand especially when I'm here so alone

must be tonic he take or something **something** the **lack** of drink I think well you
locked in my room so very isolated **insulated** from **human** affection but no longer

could be prostitute now you could do it for **she** you could do it for she and **you**
never again with her lying here beside you **all** pain and pleasure leading to **her**

both I could remember good one night must be five year back I hear now like this
that I can recall so well one night must have been five years ago she heard that

brams of something pon the ceiling above my head and I jump up quick out the bed
thubb me falling onto the flooring above her head to jump up quickly out of her bed

in the middle the night I did think **thief** I think **thief in the house** I grab up
in the middle of the night thinking **thief** thinking **thief in the house** grabbing

my big scissors from under my bed a dagger raise high above my head I step out
her big scissors from under her bed a dagger glinting above her head to step out

slow now watching for this thief I so fraid for mistress all in a sudden I hear
slowly now looking for this thief so frightened for me when suddenly she hears

she crying moaning now soft at the top the stair that I raise up that scissors
me crying moaning now softly at the top of the stairs and raising her scissors

more higher in the air I mounting slow I ready to strike-out starting to make
still higher in the air climbing slowly ready to strike-out beginning to make

she out sitting there pon the floor she back press up flat against the door of
me out sitting there on the flooring my back pressed flat against the door of

she bedroom naked naked she feet dirty she legs cover in slime scrape-up smear
my bedroom stark naked my feet filthy my legs covered in slime scraped smeared

with blood from them bramble with she arms wrap round she knees pull up tight
with blood from the brambles with my arms wrapped round my knees pulled tight

against she chest trembling crying and now she look she see me standing there in
against my breast trembling crying and now I look hard to make her out there in

the dark with this scissors raise up high above my head that I put it down slow
the dark with that scissors raised up high above her head putting it down slowly

pon the ground with she reaching out at the same time she hand reaching up to me
on the flooring and me reaching out at the same time my hand reaching up to her

now with that white envelope bawling take it post it right now immediately and
now with this white envelope bawling take it post it right now immediately and

me saying soft soft never you mind mummy I going post it mummy never you mind
she ever-so-softly never you mind mummy I going post it mummy never you mind

reaching down and taking way this envelope with the key inside and she bedroom
reaching down and taking away that envelope with the key inside and my bedroom

door lock and the front door too tuck inside the bosom of my nightgown and then
door locked the front door too tucked inside the bosom of her nightgown and then

reaching to take she up in my arms hold tight tight and walk she slow down the
reaching to take me up in her strong arms ever-so-tightly walking me down the

stairs inside my own room my own little bed both of we here together and she
stairs into her own room her own little bed two of us here together with me

bawling still take it post it now and me shush shush mummy never you mind the
bawling still take it post it now and her shush shush mummy never you mind the

next morning climbing out the window making pretend to post it way both we two
next morning climbing out the window above the sink to post it away both of us

climbing out the window laughing like two younggirls doing something wicked
climbing out the window giggling like two adolescents doing something illicit

misbehaving and **she** dressing now in **my** clothes with she own lock-up inside she
misbehaving and **me** dressing now in **her** clothes with my own locked-up inside my

210

*room and I say please Mistress let me take a tuck them tottot out to **here** and*
*room she saying please Mistress let me take a tuck my tottots out to **here** and*

*she stuffing them up with cottonwool more bigger **still** and my little minidress*
*me stuffing them up with more cottonwool further **still** in her little miniskirt*

so short with them long legs too and no panties neither she winding up she waist
so scandalously short not wearing any knickers either hips swinging like a bell

*with all she bamsee **expose** and me **please mummy not in public like that front***
*with all my bamsee **exposed** and she **please mummy not in public like that front***

the people I be so shame *with she laughing still we two like husband and wife*
the people I be so shame *with me giggling still two of us like husband and wife*

sleeping together tipping upstairs in she room reading every night for five weeks
sleeping together in her little room in her little bed every night five weeks

she diary oh we was so happy happy then I could remember
together oh we were so terribly happy then I can remember

7

when granny she had the picnic we uses to call it mission day and now this time
when mummy decided that morning she'd teach me to dance herself she and Di

was Ansin turn to cook she make so much of sandwich cakes and cokes fruits she
lugging the big gramophone all the old records which hadn't been played in years

did buy for this picnic me and Berry planning we know we could spend the whole
out onto the back gallery mummy took me in her arms teaching me first the ball-

day together in them canes she wouldn't be there and then I see granny with the
room stuff one-step and two waltz and foxtrot then she taught me to dance the

big basket all that food I say well look that basket very big for you to carry by
Latin rhythms rumba and bolero pasodoble old crackly calypso records Kitch

youself up the hill she say I got a presentiment of bad something going happen
Atilla and Roaring Lion the Lords Executor and Pretender and Protector and

with you today I say you just go-long and catch and I would hurry carry the basket it
Melody and Boy Blue and the then young Sparrow which hadn't been played in years

211

so heavy and I bigger than you and just so I following behind she up the hill but this
when mummy and daddy had their fêtes with me hiding in my room peeking through

time I throwing out so much of sandwich two–three cokes them cakes I must be
the blinds father never asked her to dance a-tall but if her partner were West

throw out about five piece of vanilla cake and chocolate too hand of bananas so
Indian leaning over his arm in a dip her auburn hair sweeping those floorboards

much of food I throwing out that basket he following behind but keeping to the
teaching the music itself how and now me with Di unable to hold herself back

canes collect-up all the things I throwing out that hamper I so shame when the
either winding her waist and shaking her bamsee so the three of us collapsing

*bus reach and I hand granny back she basket near **empty** now but she ain't notice*
*together a heap on that wicker couch absolutely **splitting** our sides with laughter*

she climb up and she go-long in the bus and Berry come now with all that food we
and mummy taught me how I must hold my head up without the stiffness to lead

could scarce even carry we hurrying in them canes to make we picnic now we
him so deceptively he'd never even realize how he was being led so effortlessly

do little something we eat a sandwich then we do little something more we eat
ill-fated secret lovers afraid of our own destinies we danced and danced and

piece of cake like chocolate or vanilla cake then we do little something again
danced till the very moment of my dey-boo at the British Club for Sir Eustace

drink a coke off and on and off and on we doing like that all morning long ain't
to dance the first dance with me as proxy taking my arm to walk me to the center

stopping not for nothing we could never hold weself back we eating till all that
of the dancefloor in a moment of silence but she ain't wearing no underdrawers

*food finish we ain't leaving **nothing** in that picnic was picnic we did make that*
*beneath the stage spotlight **nothing** under my gown stark naked Tweetybird-Tottots*

morning then he say he going home and shower and change and I say I going home
pitching a faint sprawled-out smellingsalts dancing my gown suddenly transparent

and shower and change too that we could meet back later that evening the canes
again with all the perspiration of every cock-on-the-fence staring preparing to

again but I did so **thirsty** from that picnic so **much** of **food** we **eat** and so **early**
pounce on top me did **hungry** all suddenly so **tabanca too-tool-bay tarangee-bangee**

too I say I going at a girlfriend of mine house this girlfriend she had plenty water-
out of their corners boxing wild Warrahoons hungry Caribs after a quenk running

coconut them trees so tall them coconut stand and get so big cause them people
behind me I could only think to take-off climbing up the tall samaan tree more

fraid to climb so **high** but this day I feeling like I is **boss** I say aloud how I is **boss**
afraid now to climb **any** higher all of a sudden this **cock** one of those same **cocks**

I going climb-up in them tree I get a big long ladder and I start to climb you
waiting for me there at the top of the same samaan tree so frightened but still

know this ladder get a belly a belly of **sinking** but I don't stop I continue on to
climbing higher now to escape all those **cocks** waiting for me there at the bottom

climb and just when I reach in the middle of that belly in the middle of that
complaining drunkenly climbing up toward him perched there only to discover

ladder all I hear is **placks** cause that ladder break and all I know is I **flying** I
suddenly this cock is a **hen** there at the top waiting for me my beloved **Daisy** my

flying through the air **placks** I land pon my back that hard ground below next
childhood pet clean-neck-**hen** that I loved so my dear Daisy and Dulcianne too

thing I hear my girlfriend she call for my Uncle Arrows to come in he car he
soon as Di lets me out of my room to take off running collect her up and call

daddy Mr Bootman the Panama Man had car my uncle say she always playing man
Dulcianne two of us wearing nothing but our knickers saying how it is you always

playing like she **be** always hop pon trucks and all them kind of man-thing but I
praying chaplet **then** me ain't talking to waste me breath eh you know but now I

couldn't even **hear** he talking my Uncle Arrows cause I did **flashing** and then when
couldn't even **hear** her talking so frightened now to hear the **words** written aloud

I want to talk all them waters come I did **foaming** at my mouth from that fall but
secretly in a letter somehow to dream to **think** that forbidden word into her head

thing I remember good is them waters had in colours **bright bright bright** colours
locked in my little cubicle screaming silently aloud **love love love** now for the very

213

like piece of colour glassbottle that thing did keep me from talking I couldn't
first time ever in my life of that sacred secret forbidden life we lived together

communicate with nobody my **needs** that glassbottle did come between me and my
our two worlds separated by **only** the pane of glass between us kneeling my your

words like I want say I and it come out a green glassbottle I saying **you** and it
skin golden glistening I dream without that glasspane my lips to **yours** pressed

come out red glassbottle say **he** say **Berry** and it come out yellow glassbottle
so softly the glass vanished **you** and **me** no longer on either side separated not

all them colors green and red and yellow and purple glassbottle that was the
even by invisible barriers of words so difficult so necessary to dissolve with

onliest language silent foaming out in my mouth ever
only the silent language of our lips speaking forever

8

and ever since that night I uses to go with my Granny Ansin she had the choir
and ever since that day Daisy announced he wanted to give me the honeymoon

practice that she would go pon she boyfriend Lambert bicycle with he driving pon them
in Barbados though we'd been married two-and-a-half years already I had the sense I

pedals and Ansin sitting pon the crossbar I could just hold on that fender and
was sure our lives were turning traveling backward then indeed had turned full

go-long running behind and I could visit with my cousin whilst they in church
circle with this sudden request though in truth what with that purchasing of

this night it getting late past ten now I hear **glerring glerring** Lambert pon he
d'Esperance we'd never been able to afford a **honeymoon honeymoon** I burst out

bell my grandmother call say time to go home I bawl out I coming I run out to
so startled now spilling my cup of coffee over the bedsheet after swallowing first

catch the fender and running behind onliest thing is they moving a speed tonight
my initial shock what I found so peculiar was not the request itself but Daisy's

but I could run fast too I hold that fender and running behind all in a sudden
timing not the fact that it had come two-and-a-half years after the fact but the

Lambert shift quick in the dark like that I say this very strange now that he
fact that Daisy wanted to take this honeymoon in Barbados precisely during

shifting in the canes like that but then una could suppose my granny want use
the five days of carnival three of the standard festival plus the Saturday before

the toilet or something so in them canes I ain't thinking nothing particular but
jouvert Sunday dimanch gras plus the Ash Wednesday after I thought peculiar

then I notice I say well my grandmother looking very big and tall tonight all in
since we'd so enjoyed carnival the previous year and this year especially so with

a sudden Lambert stop and my granny hold my hand tight tight in this lock-grip
Sir Eustace sponsoring the band Daisy and all the cricketers Commonwealth Cup

and I look in my granny face see this **vagabond** it was Berry dress up ganga just
was all the talk in St Maggy though how **possibly** could Daisy have even suspected

like my Granny Ansin and driving the bike is he friend Lewey I say wait is you
himself then though possibly come to think now perhaps Reggie was indeed on his

again that Berry he did had on he grandmother big broad-hat she wig with all the
mind even unconsciously Daisy may have known or suspected or vaguely feared the

ringlets she pump-sleeve long-dress and she earring big tall redman dress up in
confrontation himself with himself sexually-emotionally and so his insistence

he granny clothes ganga I say to Lewey why you drive this man bike for me to
on our taking that honeymoon precisely then when actually we could've taken it

hold the fender like that he say you **know** with money anything goes you **know** that
at any time a-tall so I said absolutely **not** was my answer to his request in **no** un-

and just so Berry jump-off the crossbar for Lewey to go long driving the bicycle
certain terms will I consider shipwrecking myself in Barbados then regardless

leave me there in the canes with this **brute beast** I say I ain't talking with you no
of mas or not playing mas with those **highwhites** all running escaping in throngs

matter what he say wait I go through all this to get to you dress up myself in
to Barbados leaving the hooligans at home to carry on with our vulgar displays

ganga and you ain't going talk with me you think that I could let you go so easy
I could think of no nightmare more frightening devastating to me than I could

215

I say well talk then talk then what **you** want cause I could **never** fight he big so
only remember now in the clarity of **your** dream Bolom it **never** would surface so

tall redman talking talking talking but then I ain't answering he only I say why you
clearly my dreaming dreaming dreaming only to hear what I would never even allow

does have to bully this is **bullying** this ain't no love he say well I feel something
myself to hear see Reginald **bawling** is me to liberate Miss Liberty this morning

for you I say well I don't feel nothing for you I just feel when I look up in you
but Daisy was so insistent on escaping for this honeymoon then that finally I

face hatred like I want to kill you or you going kill me he say you could just shut
agreed and how could I not Daisy asked so little of me really that honeymooners'

or let me cuff you up in you mouth I say I know you going cuff that's all you
suite was so exquisite looking over the turquoise sea glittering sitting in the

could do is cuff he say why you keep telling me things make me mad why you
lush seagrape shade of our gallery tiny birds with a great rush of beating wings

keep running from me I say well just do it quick and let me go cause onliest
snatching grains of rice from our outstretched palms that not till we arrived

thing I want is get way from you but then I start to think I say well look you
home amidst the throngs of sun-bruised pickled highwhites did I realize that

could just give up cause he so tall and so strong and plus I say well if he could
not once during that entire honeymoon not a single time could we even possibly

put heself so low to dress as woman dress up heself in ganga only to get through
wait to get home so exhausted able only to throw off our crown tophat throwing

to you maybe something there in that and then he lie me down some dead canes
ourselves into bed just so glittered filthy still in our filthy costumes our makeup

he find some place soft for we to lie and now he start to feeling me up but not so
smeared on our faces to drop instantly asleep and wake the next morning to that

rough this time he did feeling he fingers more slow more gentle now the onliest
sensation of Daisy's lips pressed softly passionately to mine not even realizing

thing is he did look so funny in that wig that makeup lipstick pon he lips and
for several minutes that indeed we'd exchanged genders in our sleep each dressed

216

long pump-sleeve dress with he brassiere stuff to here I couldn't even help
in the clothing of the other looking into a mirror without the glasspain to

myself to smiling little bit I didn't fraid for he now not dress like that and I
divide each from our own other self like making love to ourselves now and I

just close my eyes I did kind of relaxing into he fingers did moving so gentle now
just closed my eyes I let my body relax mechanical fingers of both hands finding

I just go soft inside I go all to waters them deep blue and purple and warm wistful
a bead of my chaplet round my neck touching myself gently there even during sex

waters and he raise up he go warm deep inside and I just melt down soft into it
easily enough so by the time Daisy reached the peak of his own pleasure I had

like that floating oh I did liking it so so good that time he did know it too
already taught myself to achieve the same at precisely the same moment

9

and so then one time I see he walking with a woman beside all in a sudden I feel
and so that one Sunday I didn't have to wait till after Mass to go with Dulcianne

jealous jealous jealous and ain't know why I just couldn't see he with she and I
running running running to the river carrying Dr Magic mauve-colored glass-

strike-out two big stones I pelt at he I break he fingers but then after he hold
bottle with those bathsalts guaranteed to turn any skin to pearly white the two

me up say why you I walking with a woman beside you pelt that stone to break my
of us searching desperately for a soukuyant's skin to pour them on and watch it

fingers I got to tell my mother the truth I got to hit you so back she could know
magically change colours looking in holes under rocks in crevices between those

I say well if you got to please you mother hit me back but please don't cuff me
boulderstones beneath the overhanging trees and not finding a single soukuyant's

too hard next thing I just take off running he could never hit me then he hit me
skin in our frustration trying our salts now on other victims a pale-blue rockcrab

a time I went at Sunday school I did sitting there and ain't see he coming only
pinkish crayfish lime-green iguana with Dulcianne chupsing pelting the bottle

217

thing I know is **whacks** he cuff me hard front everybody now my granny she start up

hard as she could **thwack** against the boulderstone these damn salts ain't worth a

say alright Mister I going carry you front the Magis for my child he say woman

windball that bottle unbroken splashing into the water with both of us leaning

when she break my fingers you ain't tell she nothing my granny say I ain't see

over the cliff watching Dr Magic disappear down the river feeling so very tired

she break none of you finger but I see this one and next thing police come they

by the time we arrived in that church bursting with people for this Christmas

did write up this and that and the next and so went in court only me and my granny

High Mass and my father too his gift to mummy with me squeezed between them so

nobody but my granny with me she say girl keep on I say wha she say girl keep

exhausted it was all I could do to keep from booting-off asleep my head like a

them shoes on but I couldn't stand for my feet in them shoes cause Joe look down

giant balloon filled with water weighing a thousand pounds that I could scarcely

pon me from that box you know he got all he friends with he they ca-hooting and

keep balanced on my thin neck threatening to tumble backward or forward I kept

thing but not Joe he just looking down pon me out from he eyes this gaze that he

catching at the last moment jerking myself awake Bumblebee droning particularly

call up make me **stupid** make me so I can't think can't breathe proper that Joe he

when he spoke **English** incomprehensibly on and on with me now caught in one of

was so handsome with he dark skin and he did quiet he was the onliest good one that

those warm tingling moments between awake and asleep suddenly my head snapping

I did ever meet he just make my head to swirling everything did swirling so round

forward as though I were hearing his voice for the first time every one of you who

my head in that court when Magis ask Joe you hit she Joe say yes Magis ask what

has performed a mixed marriage has committed a mortal sin my father jumping up

you hit she for Joe say she break my finger so I knock she now Magis ask me you

to bolt mummy holding him down an instantaneous combustion beside me suddenly

break he finger and I say yes and all them youngboys laugh at that Magis say for

so hot as if I'd moved up next to the big fire in that boilinghouse still he could not

why he say then why you break he finger well I just strike-out now say I see he
sweat Cook said the English never do nor smell neither but I sweated for him

with a woman and I just didn't want to see he with nobody but me and they all
I sweated like a man like Ramsingh when he chopped wood thinking how mummy

laughing now ca-hooting and thing but I just didn't care I didn't care if they want
and daddy had committed a mortal sin where did that leave me I was the product

laugh at me Magis say you does go with he and I say no I don't does go with he
of their sinful mixed marriage a blat-blanch sitting there on the bench sweating

well more laughing now at that ca-hooting all but Joe he don't be laughing he just
bolts like a man by the time Mass was finished my lace gown was soaked through

sitting there looking pon me he eyes that gaze he call up to send that court all
stuck to my back my arms buckled shoes like pools of water my knickers so wet

them people swirling round my head cause I crying now I did start to crying I
and heavy between my legs as I genuflected I was afraid they'd drop round my

just kick off them shoes and I take off running running I run from that court
ankles to send me sprawling on top my face before I could escape that church

1 0

into the bush side granny house I uses to hide my little white shoebox with
into my little room at nine every morning I had a flat metal pencilbox with

all my things I had a lipstick and nailpolish and sometimes Mistress Pantin she
all my colored pencils my English granny sent gifts in the Christmas chest she

would give me few them big brown English penny I buy little Cashmere some Pons
would send me paper and books dolls and ribbons and once the Dr Magic bathsalts

I could remember them two good that was the bestest thing that Pons Cashmere
I can remember but the present I enjoyed the most was that flat little tin metal

Bouquet and I had a little compact too with little mirror for me to paint on my
pencilbox with a hundred different coloured pencils I discovered how numbers and

lipstick my nailpolish that I wrap everything neat in white tissue paper in my
letters changed slightly depending upon which colour they were drawn in when

box hide beneath a bush side the house and once I could remember I was eight
I wasn't standing on my stack of storybooks before my window rolling beads I

years old I get pencil I write out my name careful as I could cause I could read
practiced drawing my letters and numbers and once I even wrote my name there

and write both from early I uses to love that so much drawing out the letters I
beneath my window labeling my childhood world with a yellow pencil carefully I

draw VELMA CLARINE DOWNS BOOTMAN, BASSE TERRE TRACE
wrote out B LILLA GRANDSOL, 8 YEARS OLD, 1 JANUARY 1933 B

clear cross the top of my little shoebox clean as I could I uses to lie there in that
clearly cross the bottom of that white sill of my window with a strong blue pencil I

bed sometimes with all them girls sleeping beside sometimes mostly pon the floor
climbed down again to put it away in the little metal box only to climb up again

and I could close my eyes and imagine my box there hid beneath the bush secret
on my pedestal of storybooks Enid Blyton and Hans Christian Andersen and the

with my name and all my things I could see them all there so perfect and I take
Grimm brothers all still unread standing there always hours and hours with my

them out one by one and wrap out the tissue and wrap it back so neat in my
lips pressed against the silver moth pinned on its back between my lips and the

little white shoebox I had some penny too Tantee May and Mistress Pantin
glass beating forever against my cheeks my little fingers rolling a bead of my

they would make me a present time to time penny or two that I could save them
chaplet round my neck without even realizing my eyes closed my lips pressed to

secret I uses to dream I had a whole English pound a hundred penny in my box and
the center of the circle wiped so clean on the other side with my little fingers rolling

I could count them out one hundred Happy Penny ninety-nine Happy Penny ninety-
I would count them out one Holy Mary two Holy Marys three Holy Marys four Holy

eight Happy Penny ninety-seven Happy Penny ninety-six Happy Penny ninety-five
Marys five Holy Marys six Holy Marys seven Holy Marys eight Holy Marys nine

Happy Penny ninety-four Happy Penny ninety-three Happy Penny ninety-two Happy
Holy Marys ten Holy Marys one Holy Mary two Holy Marys three Holy Marys four

Penny ninety-one Happy Penny ninety Happy Penny eighty-nine Happy Penny eighty-
Holy Marys five Holy Marys six Holy Marys seven Marys eight Holy Marys nine

eight Happy Penny eighty-seven Happy Penny eighty-six Happy Penny eighty-five
Holy Marys ten Holy Marys one Holy Mary two Holy Marys three Holy Marys four

Happy Penny eighty-four Happy Penny eighty-three Happy Penny eighty-two Happy
Holy Marys five Holy Marys six Holy Marys seven Holy Marys eight Holy Marys

Penny eighty-one Happy Penny eighty Happy Penny seventy-nine Happy Penny sev-
nine Holy Marys ten Holy Marys one Holy Mary two Holy Marys three Holy Marys

enty-eight Happy Penny seventy-seven Happy Penny seventy-six Happy Penny sev-
four Holy Marys five Holy Marys six Holy Marys seven Holy Marys eight Holy

enty-five Happy Penny seventy-four Happy Penny seventy-three Happy Penny sev-
Marys nine Holy Marys ten Holy Marys one Holy Mary two Holy Marys three Holy

enty-two Happy Penny seventy-one Happy Penny seventy Happy Penny sixty-nine
Marys four Holy Marys five Holy Marys six Holy Marys seven Holy Marys eight

Happy Penny sixty-eight Happy Penny sixty-seven Happy Penny sixty-six Happy
Holy Marys nine Holy Marys ten Holy Marys one Holy Mary two Holy Marys three

Penny sixty-five Happy Penny sixty-four Happy Penny sixty-three Happy Penny
Holy Marys four Holy Marys five Holy Marys six Holy Marys seven Holy Marys

sixty-two Happy Penny sixty-one Happy Penny sixty Happy Penny fifty-nine Happy
eight Holy Marys nine Holy Marys ten Holy Marys one Holy Mary two Holy Marys

Penny fifty-eight Happy Penny fifty-seven Happy Penny fifty-six Happy Penny
three Holy Marys four Holy Marys five Holy Marys six Holy Marys seven Holy

fifty-five Happy Penny fifty-four Happy Penny fifty-three Happy Penny fifty-two
eight Holy Marys nine Holy Marys ten Holy Marys one Holy Mary two Holy Marys

Happy Penny fifty-one Happy Penny fifty Happy Penny and fifty again all the way
three Holy Marys four Holy Marys five Holy Marys six seven eight nine ten and

down till I reach the end three two one Happy Penny
up again to reach the beginning again one Holy Mary

A World of Canes

"A voice is heard in Rā'mah,
    lamentation and bitter weeping.
Rachel is weeping for her children;
    she refuses to be comforted for her children,
    because they are not."

Jeremiah 31.15
Matthew 2.18

A Nice White Little Box

1

That big pot, dream of that pot. Big black belly-pot, and had on two handles. Dream it there in the middle the kitchen. Dream it *a-bubbling.* With fire kicking below and smoke rising to top. That was in Granny Ansin house away up in the country, big old board-house where I did born and raise up in. That house was standing pon posts, we did call them groundsels, with the underneath part open and the kitchen to the back. And the kitchen, I could remember the kitchen was dirt floor, earth. The bedrooms and the parlourroom they was board floor, but the kitchen earth, and it had in fire. So you cook to the fire with wood. Good hard big-wood, like old electric poles government did cut down to sell to poor people in the country. Cause wasn't no electricity in the country, not at that time, but we did had them poles to make the fire with. And that kitchen so rotten you didn't need for no chimney. Smoke just go through the holes. You know, roof build with galvanize, and that galvanize so rusty and rotten, smoke just go through the holes. Or go anyplace, cause at that time you just couldn't care less. So that fire kicking, it *kicking.* And when that big black pot come off and carry out in the yard, like a big pork-stew with green-fig, cassava, carrot, dumplings. Bolom, feed everybody. That one pot. All the family and all the neighbors standing round the circle, with that big belly-pot to middle and the plates in we hands holding, and steam rising and pot bubbling and food smelling so *good,* and granny dipping out the ladle and we all eating. We *eating.* Everybody! Dream of food, dream of that pot!

Food, plenty food, in them days. Cause in them days everybody would add little something to the pot. Everybody in the house, living pon the street, you know everybody throw in little something inside the pot. Like my grandmother, she working estate, one day she bring home big sack of potatoes. Next day yams, pigeonpeas. My aunt, she working in town, she bring home piece of meat from town. Or buy big fishhead at the docks. Fishhead to make soup. You know, everybody add little something. Like you cleaning you field today you got onions, throw in some onions. Tomorrow might be eddoes, cassava. You hear of somebody picking green-figs, you go and they give you hand of green-figs, or plantains. Everybody add what little they got, and we could *all* get food like that. Cause that pot cook regular. Cook *every* night. That's one thing you could depend is that pot. In them days.

But the thing I did love the most, the best, well my tan husband, he uses to raise about five-six pigs in the yard. That was my Uncle Charpie. Nasty old Uncle Charpie. He just build a shack-fen, little fen, to keep the pigs in, so when things get hard up, we just kill a pig. Sell a pig. Keep some the pork for weself and sell out the rest. Kill the pig early morning, that way the pork could sell quick. Sell fresh. That's when I did catch the blood too! Ain't nobody tell me to do that. I just feel, I just say, *Well that thing bound to be good.* I did only reach about six-seven years then, no more. But I could remember watching up at Charpie, and that blood coming out like that, like a siphon, and spilling out pon the ground, and I could remember saying to myself, *Well that thing bound to be good.* One day I just catch it up and I cook it. You know, when Charpie stick the pig, I just run and hold my tot beneath. We did call it a tot cause it ain't got no handle, like a sweetmilk tin, or cornbeef, we did call it a tot at home at that time. So I run quick and I hold my tot beneath the pig neck, where the hole is, where he get stick. You know, they would got that pig holding, and that blood just do like a siphon, *pssst!* out from he neck. I just collect it up and I carry and I season. Put in blackpepper, put in basil, shado-beni, things growing in the yard, thyme and basil and shado-beni and different things, and fresh like that. Just snatch off some, and you know, chip it up in the same tot. I stir with a fork and I hold it right there above the fire, cause they would got that big fire build outside in the yard, with the barrel that cut to hot the water to scald the pig. I hold my tot right there, cook my blood right there. When that blood cook it get hard, but I keep stirring stirring and it come just like scramble egg. Now I sit down and I eat. I sit down and I eat and I ain't giving nobody none. Cause that thing did taste so *good.*

Then one time I remember I did get scared. You know, they did had that pig holding, and when he stick, when Charpie stick the pig, that pig kick. Bolom, he *kick!* One time I say, *Well what now if that pig kick you up in you head? What if they ain't got he hold proper, and he foot loose, kick you up in you head?* I say, *That pig would kill you like that! Kill you dead dead, just like that!* I did scared now. My Tantee May tell me, she say, "Vel, you ain't going for you blood?" I say, "No." She say, "You going let you blood waste out pon the ground? Waste out pon the ground like that?" I say, "Let Charpie collect it up." My tan say, "You know he ain't going. You know he ain't going collect it up. You know that. He going let it waste out pon the ground is all."

I didn't answer she nothing, I just say, *Well it would have to waste-out then. Cause I ain't going by that pig to get kick in my head.* We was all standing round the big fire then, in the dark, cause still early morning. We was all standing there waiting for Charpie to stick the pig. But when I see he stick, and Charpie stand up with he face sweating and reflecting in that fire, when I see that blood coming out and wasting pon the ground like that, Bolom, I just couldn't keep way. Just couldn't keep the feet way. I *had* to run with my tot and collect up. Every *drop* was left in that pig!

2

That was in Granny Ansin house away up in the country. And in that big old house was living my granny, my Tantee Elvira, she six girls, me, and my sister. Wasn't no men. Not to say living *in.* Cause my Tantee

May she was living to she little house by the side, but she husband wasn't living with she neither, old Charpie. He just uses to come home visit pon evenings, some the time. Only Clive was living with my tan, she boychild, but sometimes I uses to sleep over by my Tantee May too. My other uncle he wasn't living with we neither, Mr Bootman the Panama Man. He was living with he son Arrows to town. So that was twelve people living between the two houses. Three women, nine girls, and one boy. Wasn't no men.

Nor my mother wasn't living with we neither. She uses to visit, she uses to come home must be about every two weeks, just to see how things going, catch little something to eat. She, you know it look like she just hide out and get me, before she know anything. What is what. She did had about fourteen–fifteen years when she get me, still young. So she never tell me nothing about my father. I only get to know he when I grow older, when I reach about seven years. That was when I hear somebody saying how this man such-and-such is my father, and I just go at the house and I knock the door. I say, I look up in he face and I say, "You is my father?" He say, "Yes. I is you father."

So we just get introduce like that. And from that day we just keep in contact, but not, you know he could never claim me for he own, put me under he name. He done married and have he children and he house proper. He could never claim no hands pon me. But I did like he still. I did feel that I could *call* he for my father. I could say that, to myself, in the secret like. Say, *That man living there in that house is you father, you is he child.* I could say it like that, even though I didn't have no father in truth. My father could never claim no hands pon me. He was a joiner, uses to make furnitures. But my father wasn't my mother kind of man, and that's the reason why my mother did never like me. Cause I look just like my father. I dark like he, I make with he features. And I carry on like he too. I know. Looks and ways, and that's why my mother did never like me neither.

My mother didn't like me nor my sister. My sister she for somebody else, she never even find out who. My mother did only like my brother of we three. He living by she, so he could get he food and he clothes, my mother uses to fix up my brother food and he clothes for he. But me and my sister, we got to scramble for weself. Eat what we could eat, you know, survive how we could. I uses to say, *Why my mother don't like me? What wrong with me?* I go cross to my Tantee May, I ask her, I say, "What happen that my mother don't like me? Cause I ain't got no father or what?" She say, "Child, you ain't to worry you head with that." She say, "You mother going regret the day she ain't know una. You, nor you sister." But still I couldn't stop my head from thinking about that, how the family make and everything. How it *come*. I just couldn't stop from studying my head about what it is to make the family.

3

Then one time my Tantee May went in childbed to have she baby. She did went to have the baby home, as people uses to do in them days, all we gather round the bed with the mid, some standing to the parlour front-room. Granny Ansin was there, Mistress Pantin was there, Tantee Elvira, Dorine, Ellis. Mr Bootman the Panama Man was there with he son Arrows, Uncle Arrows. And mummy was there with she boyfriend, that Andrel Bay Brown, with me there and my sister and my brother. And Tantee boychild Clive was there in the house with she husband, that nasty old Charpie. So the mens they was mostly in the parlour-room firing waters, and we was in the bedroom waiting for the birthing and eating cakes and drinking cokes. I could tell you that little house did so full up with family, it was most ready to *burst*. And sometimes one the neighbors from the street would drop in too, like Mistress Bethel the needleworks woman, she bring a nice vanilla cake and everybody take piece. All we talking and eating and laughing and having weself a good good time for that birthing.

But then now soon as things start in, in the last minute, up and say the mid that something wrong, something *wrong*, and tantee got to carry to the big hospital in town. So Mr Bootman up and gone for he big motorcar, and he was moving slow and rickety already with the waters. Tan gone in the backseat stretch out with Ansin and Mistress Pantin and Tantee Elvira, and the mid she must of go too, with all the mens most in the front seat what could fit. Mr Bootman tip the horn and drop a gear and that big car let loose a chups of white smoke, and everybody bawl *w-e-e-e!* with dust raising and all the children running screaming behind.

Quick so the house quiet quiet. Dead quiet. Me one inside, so it seem, only me. All up and gone and left me there like if they ain't notice, forget. Left me there sitting pon the bench in the parlourroom eating a piece of cake and crying. I was crying for my tan, cause I was so *fraid* for she in that hospital! I did love my tan so much, so much. Cause my Tantee May give me dress, slip, hat for church, everything she give me when my *own* mother ain't give me, my tan, and I was crying for she. I was crying cause I did think people only go in hospital when they dying, near dying, and I was fraid so bad for she in that place. I say, *Them people, you know most of them there people in hospital does dead in childbed you know? Dead straight way like that! Cause mid ain't know what to do, and she carrying tan in hospital and thing, you know she can't born the child and wait to the last minute, that child kill she like that. Kill my tan just like that!*

I was there sitting pon the bench in the front room, parlourroom, and crying, now I hear somebody like Uncle Charpie, my tan husband, hear now like Charpie calling to me from out the bedroom. But he calling very quiet. Call like a whisper like, say, "*Vel! Vel!*" Like that. But I ain't move. I say, *Wait! He ain't gone? All up and gone and he ain't gone?* Then Charpie call again, quiet, "*Vel! Vel!*" Still in a whisper. But still I ain't move. Now he come out in the parlourroom, he there in he baggy old drawers, he dirty old vestshirt. And he sit down pon the bench and he pull me cross to sit pon he. *Sweet Jesus!* I there pon this bench sitting, and he pull me cross, you know, on top, and he foist me down pon he. *Hard.* He foist me down hard pon he and he start up. *Doing* pon me! Bolom, I could remember that there like now. Just like now. I eating this cake, and crying, and he, this vanilla cake in my hand turning to sticky now, like wet, and running down my arm sticky pon my wrist.

But he couldn't get nowhere. Too *small*. Eight years old. So then, so then I just get fed up. I just get fed up with he. I wasn't scared, no, not then. I didn't even *know* what I did had to frighten for. I was more *confuse.* Just get fed up. I say, *Wait! You tan sick, and what he trying to do? What he playing with you like that for?* I say, *That ain't the right way. That ain't the right way, when people crying to stop a person from crying.* Bolom, I did want to run, get way, but he, then he foist me down *harder* pon he. He pull up pon my dress, pon my slip that I was wearing for that birthing. You know what he was trying? To do? You know what he was trying to do to me? *Intending?* And me only eight years. Eight years old with nobody else in the house. And all I doing is crying. Crying for my tan. The most is crying. And cake in my hand wet.

Last he let me go and I take off. Bolom, I *run!* I hide out in the canes. Cause you know all behind tan house was them canes, estate, and I hide out in there the whole night. Most the next day too. I hide out till I see the others come back, come back in Mr Bootman big car with he. Cause Bolom, I ain't going back inside that house. Not with Charpie in there! Nor I ain't going inside granny house neither. Not by myself. I wait till I see the others come back. They come back with Tantee May, but they don't bring the baby, cause that baby dead in hospital. But my tan didn't dead, and I was so happy for that! I did feel sad for that little baby, true, but not too much. Cause they say when a baby dead like that it just go straight in heaven. Straight. And I did think heaven must be full-up with little babies, *full,* amount of babies dead like that. But that's the onliest thing I did know about babies, at that time, that most of them up in heaven. The biggest part of them little babies up in heaven. I didn't make no connection, with Charpie, he nastiness, nor I didn't even *want* to know nothing about he neither. Just keep-way from he. He and all the rest. Best as I could.

4

But then in them days all the mens uses to cut canes in crop-season. All the mens. Cause in them days everywhere was canes canes and more canes, and all the mens got to cut canes in crop-season. So the children got to ask for break from school, cause we got to carry the breakfast for them working out in the field. And Bolom, them fields far. Must be about ten–twelve miles from where the school was. *Far,* real far. I ask for break, I come out at ten o'clock from school, you know when two o'clock reach I only now going back in school. I just do it for favor for my mother. And she wasn't even living with we. But she ask me to do it, so I tell she I would do that for she. Granny pack the breakfast pon morning, and I carry it for my mother boyfriend. This Andrel Bay Brown. Cause I get to thinking, I did think that if maybe I could get to *know* he, little bit, and we could get to like one another, he could be more like my father. Maybe my mother would come back home, and we could all be more like family then. So I tell my mother I would carry the breakfast for he, tell she I would do that, I glad to do that. I did reach about ten years then, una could suppose. Ten going on eleven.

So when I arrive in this field, I find Andrel sitting down beneath the big tamarind tree, shade tree. He there catching the cool, waiting for me to bring he the breakfast. So I give he the basket and he take out, was a metal bowl with stew chicken, and rice, pigeonpeas, all cook together and still hot. We did call that cook-up, or pelau. We did call that cook-up at home then. He had some fruits too, was a pawpaw, and hand of sicreyea figs, the little sweet bananas. And he had a bottle full with soursop drink, and wrap in a damp towel that it could stay fresh like that. Cool like that. So he spread out the breakfast pon he shirt there beneath the tree. You know he was sitting there bareback, relaxing in the breeze. He say, "Why you don't sit down little bit catch youself a cool? Cause you know that sun going be *beating* up the road to walk back now." He say, "You could keep me in company whilst I eat."

So I sit down, sit down near he in the shade of that tamarind tree. He was there sitting by heself beneath the tree, and that tree was a good distance from where the other mens was. They taking they breakfast now too. And he did seem kind of, he did seem little bit lonely sitting there like that, there by heself. I did feel little bit sorry for he. So I sit down, he commence to eating he breakfast, I watching, he eating he cook-up. Then he ask me if I want some. I say, "Yes. I would take some." Cause you know that food was still warm from when granny cook it. But he tell me I must move closer. So I ain't thinking nothing, I push over sitting little closer by he. But before he give me the bowl to eat, he take up a spoonful and push inside my mouth. I say, *Wait! What this man feeding you like that for? You ain't no baby that got to get feed*. But then when I swallow, *next* spoonful, quick again he push inside my mouth. I say, I talk up to he now, I say, "You don't bound to feed me like that already. I's a *grown* person. I could eat for myself." He say, "That's how I does like to eat." I say, "Well that's not how *I* like to eat! I like to eat food for myself, I don't like nobody to feed me!"

He put down the metal bowl now, and he take up the bottle with soursop drink. He wrap out the towel and he screw out the lid, say, "I got a special way I does like to drink too." And now he take up my hand, cause I was sitting there just beside he, he take up my hand and pour out some the soursop over, and some going pon the ground. Then he start to licking licking pon my hand, that white pulpy thing, he sucking pon my fingers.

Bolom, I pull my hand way! I pull it back straight. I say, "Wait! You's a child? You's a child that you got to play games like that with you food?" He say, "That ain't children games, that's *adult* games," and he smiling he teeth big like that. He say, "You wait till I start in pon them figs!" You know he was lying there beneath the tree, and bareback, half-sitting up and half-lying down, he back resting against the tamarind. Now he pour out some the soursop drink pon he bare chest, that white pulpy thing, and smiling big, he pour it down he chest down the front of he pants. He say, "This adult games and you could lick from my chest. You could drink from my navelhole too."

I jump up. I say, "You's a *stupid* person, throwing-way good food like that." I say, "You's a *fool!* Cause that's one thing you don't play with is food, one thing you got to respect is food! One thing!" I say, "You's a stupid person, you's *uneducated.*" And I run. Bolom, I take-off. Leave he there laughing behind.

Next day when I give he the basket, he give me this letter that he did write. Cause I was ready to leave, take-off. I was ready to run again. But he give me this letter, say, "Read it. This a letter that you could read it." Cause I could read good from early. So I go-long reading this letter, pon my way coming from carrying the breakfast, walking back from the field. When I reach home I give it to my granny, this letter that he write. Cause I did had enough with this man. I did had enough of he. And I know that if I show this letter to my mother, I know that she would say just what it was she *do* say, say how *I* write it. Cause I could write good from early too. And she couldn't write nor read neither, my mother. So when she came to visit at the house my granny tell my mother how he did give me this letter. Write it just so, that he did want to *frig* with me. Write:

Dear Miss Velma,

I want to frig with you. You mother wouldn't know nothing. And I would give you money every weekend that you could spend. Buy what you want.

Cordial,
Mr Andrel Bay Brown

Bolom, I could see that writing there just like now. That *crab-foot* writing. I did reach only about ten years, ten years is the most. Bolom, everything happen so fast, so *fast!* My life. This woman thing and this bad luck thing.

So when granny tell my mother, course she say, "That ain't true, she making up that. He ain't ask, he would *never* ask she that." But then my grandmother present she the letter, and my mother couldn't answer one word. My granny say, "You think that she, you think that she could make up that? This girl left school, left Sherman and gone all out in the fields to carry the breakfast for he, and this the thanks! this the thanks! that he did want! this is what he did want to do to she! And you got the nerve to say she *lying!*" My granny tell my mother, "You never did like these children anyway. Least the two girls. You got one child and that's you boy." My grandmother say, "Well I ain't got much, but I going keep them in here. Least the two girls. You go-long!" She tell my mother just like that. *"Go-long!"* And my mother went long *shameface.* So that finish with that. Finish. Cause I did never see my mother again. Never again. After that day.

5

Time soon come I approaching a woman now. Getting pretty, real pretty. I walking with my little minidress Tantee May give me to make the style then. I walking with my little bag, my clasp and thing. Mistress Pantin, she give me little Pons, you know in them days didn't had much of cream, just Pons. Pons Cold Cream, I could remember, and powder, like Cashmere Bouquet. I could remember them two good. Mistress Pantin give me little Pons, and I catch a few cents from somewhere, I buy little powder, little Cashmere. And nailpolish. I hide them away secret in a little box. I had my little white shoebox, all my things wrap nice in tissue, that I uses to keep hid under a bush side the house. It was my secret, but even so once I get a pencil and I write my name cross the lid, tall clean capital letters, *VELMA CLARINE DOWNS BOOT-MAN, BASSE TERRE TRACE.* And that writing did make my secret more special still. I had my little white shoebox, but I didn't know what it was to be a woman yet. I did had my first menstruation, yes, but didn't see nothing after. Just one. And I didn't even know what it was even. I say, *Well maybe that come again? Maybe that's just something that come again?* I didn't know, nor didn't had nobody to explain me nothing neither. My Granny Ansin, she never tell me nothing, nor my Tantee May. And I didn't talk to Tantee Elvira too much, nor my mother wasn't there no more neither. And I's the oldest girl, I didn't have no older sisters in the house, nor cousins could tell me nothing. Explain me nothing. So when I see this menstruation, I did worried, I did worried *plenty,* but then I say, *Well maybe that's just something got to happen?* I didn't make no connection, with baby, nor nothing so. I just know babies come when they come, and I did fraid for that so bad since my tan went in hospital. Since that baby near *kill* my tantee in hospital!

So then in them days I uses to bathe in the night, go at the pipe, standpipe, we did call it a standpipe at home at that time. That pipe must of been about half-mile from where the house was, to the pitch road where the pipe was. Government put that pipe there for poor people to draw water. Cause in them days the houses didn't have in pipes, for shower, not the poor people. But we had a place build under the chenet tree that you could bathe private, little stall, shower-stall. Shower-stall and toiletstall build together, beneath the big chenet tree side the house. Onliest thing is it ain't got no roof, that shower-stall, and them boys from the street, you know they like to climb up in the tree and peer down. Them boys always doing that. Ogle you whilst you catching you bath. So I uses to go for my water at night, bathe in the night when it good and dark. When them boys wouldn't be watching. But you know it tiring to go all the way to that standpipe for water. That bucket *heavy.* One night I was feeling tired, I just say, *Chups!* Say, *I going bathe right here.* Cause ain't nobody does go to the pipe at that hour in the night, and even if they do, you could see them coming. You could hear them coming a long way off. Didn't make no sense to carry that water all the way home. I say, *Chups! I going keep a watch over my shoulder, and I going bathe right here.* And from that night I just get in the habit of bathing there side the pipe.

So it night now, good and dark, *dark,* and I carry my bucket to catch a bath. I rest it down beneath the pipe, open the water, and I full up my bucket about half-full. My rag and my piece of soap right there keeping in a joint of one them banana trees behind the pipe. So I reach

235

it down, and I start to soap out my rag inside the bucket. Now I look over my shoulder, I listen a minute, make good and sure ain't nobody coming, then I slip out my panties and push them in a joint of that banana tree. I raise up my skirt, my little minidress, and I start to soap. But when I turn round to wash out my rag, ain't find the bucket. I say, *What the?* Say, *You bucket gone!* I feeling in the dark now, feeling for my bucket, and I look up peering in them bushes. Cause you know behind that pipe had a lot of thick bushes and bananas that you could scarce see inside. But when I look down again my bucket back there again. So I ain't pay it no mind, I wash out my rag tranquil, look over my shoulder again, raise up my skirt and commence to wash. When I look down my bucket gone again! I say, *What the hell! What the hell happen with you bucket?* But when I look down again I find the bucket back there again! Same place, and still half-full. I say, *Wait! Something wrong with you eyes? You eyes playing fool with you?* So I wash out my rag in the bucket, look over my shoulder again, raise up and commence to wash again. Bolom, when I look again, my bucket gone *again!* I say, and I speaking aloud now, say, "What the *hell* going on here? Where my bucket gone?"

Now I hear a voice, I hear a man-voice say, "I gots it." Bolom, I drop that skirt quick quick! Cause I did *startle.* I say, "*You* gots it? *You* gots my bucket? *Who* you is?" The man-voice say, "I is Joe." He there standing behind them banana trees where the pipe is, but that place *dark.* I can't see he. I can't see nothing. I say, "I ain't *know* who Joe is. What you gone with my bucket for, Joe?" He say, "I going mash it up." I say, "Mash it up? *Mash* my bucket?" I say, "What you want mash-up my bucket for? I ain't do you nothing. You best give me back my bucket!" He say, "I going mash it up." I say, "Best give me back my bucket, or I would call police!" Course I did know wasn't no police nor *nobody* else there round that pipe for me to call. Not at that hour. He did know too. He say, "Come for it. Come for you bucket." I say, "I ain't *know* where you is." He say, "You know where I is cause you could hear my voice. You could hear me talking. Come for it."

So I gone now, must be about five–six steps where he is, where I hear the voice, but you know that place *dark.* Behind the spicket where the canes start. Just behind. You can't see nothing inside them canes. Nothing nothing nothing. I say, "I can't see *nothing!*" He say, "I here." So

I gone five more steps deeper inside the canes, and still nothing. I say, "I *can't! I* can't *see!*" He say, "I here." So now I gone more deeper inside the canes about five–six more steps, and now I feeling, well not fraid, more *spooky* like, the silent. And you know, ain't seeing nothing, and ain't understanding why this man want thief my bucket. What he did want.

I say, "You there? Joe? You there?" Now I hear he voice *behind* me, and more a whisper like, say, "I here." Like that. I say, "What you? What you *want* with me?" He say, "You know what I want." I say, "I ain't know what you want. What you want with me, Joe?" Now like he voice in *front* now, he voice in front me again, onliest thing is, I ain't *hear* he move in front. Spooky, real spooky. Like he voice did swirling round my head. In them canes. I standing there in the silent, breathing heavy, all in a sudden I feel he hand grab on my hand. My same hand that still did holding that piece of soap. Soap squeeze out pon the ground and he grab on tight, and I ain't know *how* he could hold so tight with my hand all soapy-up like that. He grab on with this lock-grip, hard, real hard, and he start to pulling now, pulling me now and running through the canes. So I running too, running close behind he, running in the blind, cause them canes *black*. I can't see! But *he* could see, somehow he could *see*, so I only running behind. Like he did cut-lash heself a trail through them canes, or something, for he to know. But I ain't know nothing, nor can't pull way out from he lock-grip neither. Onliest thing for me to do is run. Run behind he fast as I could, *run*, like when you running down a steep steep hill and you feet can't scarce keep up. Can't scarce keep the momentum up. Like you feet ain't even touching ground, ain't carrying no weight. Like if somebody throw you inside a well, deep dark water-well, black, and you falling. You falling and you can't stop you can't fight you can't do *nothing*. Onliest thing that you could do is fall. *Fall.*

When we reach, now we reach inside a clearing where he done cut-lash the canes, una could suppose, cause una doesn't know if it's a clearing or a cave or a shack or what. Onliest thing I know is ain't no more canes in my face, lashing pon my face. So we stop, we stop now, and now he hold me down pon the ground pon some dead canes, dead grass. One moment I did breathing fast fast, next moment like I stop. Like I *stop* breathing now. One moment them canes lashing pon my face, screeching in my ears, like a sharp shrill screeching sound, *loud,* and next moment everything quiet, dead quiet. I still falling, yes, but now like I falling in slow-motion, in empty space. Now I falling inside the silent. Feeling far away, far far away falling inside the dark empty silent. All in a sudden *whaks!* this pain come searing through my middle. Down there. I feel this pain searing through my middle. And I, like I hit the ground *whaks!* like I hit the hard water down at the bottom of that well. Flat pon my back. And now I sinking. Now I sinking slow inside that icecold freezing water. Inside that pain.

That thing did hurt so bad! So *harsh!* Like a fire did come searing through my middle, hot, or cold-cold. Like when you touch a block of ice and you hand stick, burn. You can't pull it way, all you could feel is that pain searing. Bolom, I ain't know what he do, what it is he do to me. All I could know is that hurt, that pain. I ain't even know if we did lie there a time after or what. All I could know is he still holding my hand, that lock-grip, we lying, we lying and now we standing, we walking again. He leading me walking through them canes again. Leading me someplace else again. He ain't saying nothing now, nor me neither. Just walking behind he in the black. And still I ain't even see he face proper. Ain't even see he face good! All in a sudden he grip slip, slip out like a rope that knot and just slip, and I, like the weight, like that momentum was carrying me forward. I take about five more steps through the canes, and when I look up, there is that standpipe again. There is my bucket below. My bucket again like nothing, like nothing ain't even *happen.* Onliest thing is that pain, to remember by. That pain that I still was feeling. Cause that pain like it leave the mark pon my body, the *impression* of that pain, that I still was feeling. So I take up the bucket, ain't even remember my panties, I take up my bucket still half-full with water, and I raise it up pon my head. I say, *Leastest thing you could do when you reach home is bathe. Try and bathe.*

But when I reach home and I see the *blood,* all this blood pon my skirt, all that mess, I could of *kill* he! I did think maybe he did kill *me!* Then I remember that menstruation, that first and only that I did had and not know, and didn't see nothing after. I say, *Well maybe that's the same thing?* I did think maybe it was the same thing. I say, *That's the first time I know he too. Know a man.* And I, I was *confuse.* I had to throw down my skirt inside the toilet. I *had* to throw it way, cause that blood could never wash. That mess! I throw-down my skirt down inside the toilet, and I bathe. I scrub. But that impression pon my body wouldn't go way, wouldn't *dissolve*. Scrub out from my skin. Time as I finish I so tired I can't scarce drag myself up in bed. And I didn't even feel to sleep in that bed neither, not with them other girls, four–five of we sleeping to the same bed. I did feel to sleep by myself, that night. I sleep right there under the house, pon some sacks of peas granny had there drying. I fall down pon them sacks of pigeonpeas and I just sleep. Onliest thing is sleep. Sleep.

6

Next day, or maybe about two–three days later, I going at crossroads to catch the bus, I see he again. See this Joe. Cause I *know* it was he, even though I did never see he face proper. This Joe come walking behind me. I turn and he turn too, walk behind me too. Bolom, I take-off. I *run!* Every time I see he, must be about a week, two weeks after that, after them canes, I take off and I running. And I could run *fast*. He couldn't catch me then. I ain't going at that standpipe no more neither, not in the *night*, not for he to hold me again. I go in the day. Bathe at home in the day. Or save water till night come to bathe. When he, when this Joe hold me up the second time, about two weeks later, walking to catch the bus, crossroads, when I couldn't run from he no more. When I *tired* running from he. He hold me up my hand in that lock-grip again, and he say, "I see you sporting that skirt. I watch at you with them bright nails. I take you for woman. You ain't no woman. You's still a little girl!" That's when I see he the second time, when he hold me up the second time. He say, "And plus you keep running from me. Why you keep running from me for?"

Bolom, I was vex. I did had enough, enough of he. I say, "I ain't got no hands to do with you! No *hands* to do with you! I got to put in, got to throw my clothes down in the toilet, all them kind of things." I say, "I ain't in *business* with you. You does mash-up people!" He say, "That got to happen." I say, "That don't got to happen! That don't got to happen! Not like that!" I say, "Why people don't, why people does *do* like that? Why you? You sick or something? You sick?" He say, "Girl, you been lying." He tell me that. I tell he he sick or something, he say you been lying.

That was the second time, when I couldn't run from he no more. I get to feel, you know, *confuse*. I did had to tell somebody. I did had to talk with somebody. Explain, get explain. But ain't nobody. I didn't had nobody to tell me nothing. Nobody but Joe, this Joe. I did think, I did feel maybe be could answer me some things, explain me some things. I could feel that he was a nice boy too, deep down. I say, "Joe, you's a nice boy. I could feel that you's a nice boy. Why you *do* like that? Why you?" He say, "That got to happen." I say, "That don't got to happen! *That* don't! Not like that! You does mash-up people!" I say, "To *hell* with you!" After, you know after I start to talking, I feel he dirty. He *dirty*, and I dirty too. So we got to keep way. We got to keep from one another. I say to hell with you.

Never follow he up, nor go behind, nor talk, nothing. Just leave he to heself, do what he want, and I go by myself. But in truth I did feel he was a nice boy. A nice boy, cause this Joe wasn't no man, he was a *boy*, sixteen-seventeen years of age, nothing more. But he was tall and good looking. Very strong and very dark, quiet. He didn't talk too much, not like them other boys. Running off with they mouth and talking big. He did different. When he speak you could feel he voice quiet, calm. I did kind of, I did start to like he. Little bit, maybe little bit. But I ain't know that till *after*. I see he with another girl, walking. I just get jealous. I just get jealous jealous jealous, and ain't even know why. After what he do to me? After all that? But I just get jealous. I strike out! I throw one big rock. One *big* rock I throw at he break *two* of he fingers.

Next day he ask me, say, "What you hit me for?" I say, "I ain't know." He say, "I got to hit you back." I say, "Oh my sweet Jesus don't kill me! Don't hit me too hard!" He say, "What I going tell my mother?" I say, "Tell she you fall or something." He say, "Can't tell she that. You hit me with a woman next. I walking with a woman and you throw two big rocks at me and you break my finger." He say, "I can't tell my mother that I fall down, not with this woman walking there. She *glad* to tell she. She glad to tell my mother that. I got to tell my mother the *truth*." He say, "And I got to hit you back. I got to hit you back that she could *know*."

I say, "Well if you got to please you mother please her then, hit me back. But don't hit me too hard. Please don't hit me too hard!" I standing there, and waiting for it, waiting for he to cuff, but then I feel my feet couldn't keep still. Just couldn't keep still. I take off. I *run*. He could never hit me then. He could never run so fast as me. Bolom, I uses to be athlete at school you know. Uses to run at school, long distant. About two miles, three miles. Round Keslins-Noble and back, about two laps, three laps, *fast*. But not in no shoes. I could never run in no shoes. I did feel like them shoes *weighing* me down. And I uses to take off like a jet. He could never hit me then.

7

He hit me a Sunday morning I went at school, Sunday school. He was sitting by the side, and I ain't see he when I pass, or I would of run. It was a Pentecost, not Pen, like Baptist, the jump-up stuff. I love that. *Testifying!* I did love that. He was sitting right there, and I pass and ain't see he sitting there. He just jump up and *whaks!* cuff me hard, front everybody, side my head. That thing knock me off balance. Knock me over backwards, that cuff, cause I wasn't looking for it, and I fall.

My grandmother stand up and she see, and now my grandmother say, "Alright Mister. Alright Mister, I going lock you up for my child! I going carry you in the court for that!" Joe say, "Woman, I don't care one damn where you carry me." And now he start to get on, you know, say, "When she break my fingers, you ain't tell she nothing." Granny say, "I ain't *see* that. Ain't see she break none of you fingers. But I see *this* one!"

Well my granny, you know, she call police, police come and they write-up, this and that and the next. So, went to court. Joe, and he friends, he had some boyfriends with he, you know how youngboys got they friends? Full up that court full full. And you know how them getting on? *Ca-hooting* and thing? And poor me! Me one with my grannny. Nobody but my granny with me. She say, "Girl, keep on!" I say, "*Wha?*" She say, "Keep them shoes on!" Cause I did kick them off. I just couldn't stand for my feet in them shoes. I kick them off. I did want to run from that court too. Then Joe, Joe look down pon me from that box. He look down pon me out from he eyes, this gaze that he call up. He call up this gaze make me *stupid*. Make me so I can't think, can't breathe proper. Like everything did moving, swirling round my head.

So now Magis, Magis ask Joe, "You hit she?" Joe say, "Yes." Magis say, "What you hit she for?" Joe say, "She break my finger, so I *knock* she!" Now Magis ask me, "You break he finger?" I say, "Yes," and everybody laugh now. Magis say, "For why?" I say, "I see he with a woman! I see he with a woman and I just didn't want to see he with nobody but me!" And everybody laugh more at that. Them boys, more laughing. But I just couldn't care! I just couldn't care if they want laugh at me. Magis say to me now, "You does go with he?" I say, "No. I don't does go with he." With more laughing, ca-hooting and thing. Everybody but Joe. He ain't laughing. Joe just there looking pon me out from he eyes, this gaze that he call up. I run from that court! Cause I was crying, I did start to crying now. I run. Granny Ansin, she was so vex. She was so vex with me. Cause *she* had to take up them shoes and carry them home.

8

So, charge dismiss. Magis dismiss the charge. I did feel so bad, so *shame!* I did want to look for he, for Joe. Cause I could feel that maybe he did, you know, that maybe he did want. But I did had to make the next move. Me. After all that, court and Magis and everything. But I couldn't. I did feel too shame. When I see he again, I just run. I run.

But then now about two months after that, about four months, four months after the canes, I feeling, sleepy. Feel, just *sleepy*. All in the day was sleep. All in the night was sleep. Just can't keep the eyes open. If I go at school, I just rest my head pon that desk and I sleep. Onliest thing was sleep. Just one menstruation. Just one, and then not again. And then that one time in the canes with Joe. Just that one time. I ain't know my mother, nor my mother ain't know me. She could never tell me nothing, about baby, nor men. Nor she didn't even uses to be at home. Nor my granny, nor my Tantee May, they never tell me nothing. And you know I was just twelve years old, I did embarrass to ask about them things. I feel like them things *dirty*. And you know I's the oldest child, my sister, she could never know more than me, nor my cousins.

Now my granny and my tantee turn bad pon me. They turn bad pon me, *mean*. Give me hard looks, words. They give me hard words. They never speak like that to me before. Never! Not my Granny Ansin. Not my Tantee May. I did feel so bad. And *dirty.* I did feel I's a dirty old piece of dirty rag. I feel I's the dirtiest thing that living. I didn't want to go at school no more, I did feel too shame. I *couldn't* go at school. You pregnant you can't go at school. Don't be no schoolchildren at school pregnant. I just look for place in the canes and I just sleep. Whole day. I didn't want to eat nothing. Just trying to keep off. Far from everybody. I just trying to keep far off by myself.

I ain't know what happen to the baby. Cause I ain't *see* no baby. I just know I was in the hospital, the maternity. Still first. Still first I could remember a man come at Granny house, doctorman, brown-skin doctor. I ain't know who call he. I ain't know why he did come. All I know is he talking with Ansin in the front-room, he talking and then more mens come, was two black mens, two black mens dress all in white. They hold me down. Cause I did want to run! They hold me down and they give me injection. My arm. Then I was in the ambulance driving to someplace, to the big hospital in town. I know that for sure, cause I was moving. But that injection had me so *drowsy,* and so. But I know I was driving to someplace then. When I get at the hospital, *next* injection. Then they put this gown pon me. Doctor gown, and tie at the side. But I couldn't tie that thing! I couldn't even lift up my arm! I just watch at the nurse tying at my side like in a dream. That gown was white, and had on pink elephants. Lot of little pink elephants. And that did make me feel more like a dream still, them elephants. Cause I never see no elephant before. Don't be no elephants in Sherman, Bolom. But I know they could never be pink, that rosy pink. I sure about that. So then. That's all. That's all I could remember. And falling. Falling again in that water-well. And black. Onliest thing is there ain't no bottom to that well now, ain't no water to reach, hit. That icecold water. Onliest thing is falling.

Then I wake up. I wake up and I was in the doctor bed, and still wearing that gown tie to the side. I ain't know what happen to the baby. Cause I ain't see no baby. I only know that it was gone from out my belly. I know that, cause I could *feel* it gone. You carrying a baby all these months and it gone you does know, you does feel that. But I ain't know what happen to the baby. I was in that hospital about a week, ten days. Cause I didn't even know what was the time in that place, when was day and when night. I ain't talking to nobody, them other womens

243

in the ward, round me, different beds. They all dress in that same gown tie to the side, same pink elephants. They all talking to one another, they laughing, they caring for they babies when the nurse bring them. They feeding they babies. But I ain't got no baby to feed! I didn't even know why I was in there, with them other womens. I ain't talking to them. I ain't talking and I ain't sleeping neither. Now I *can't* sleep. I can't sleep and I can't eat. Not much. Nurse come and she bring rice, bring fish, flyingfish. But all was tasting in my mouth like cottonwool. Onliest thing that I could do is lie there with my eyes open and not think. Try and not think.

Nobody never visit me but one person, Mistress Pantin, lady by name of Mistress Pantin, tan of mine. She come the day before I leave the hospital. She tell me they wouldn't let she in before, before then, cause I was very sick. But they tell she I better now, I most ready to go home now. Mistress Pantin come and she bring clothes for me, new clothes that she did buy. Was a blouse and skirt and new shoes, and white socks, a panties. She give them to the nurse and nurse give them to me the next morning. Nurse tell me I ready to go home.

That morning Mistress Pantin come again, but with Mr Bootman the Panama Man this time. She come with he in he car. They say they going carry me back in the country, back to my grandmother. Cause that hospital was in town, and Mistress Pantin and Mr Bootman was living to town. So I get up from the bed to go now. I was dress and everything, dress in my new clothes that Mistress Pantin give the nurse for me, but I was lying in the bed still. I get up ready to go now, slip on my shoes, and nurse say, "Wait." She say, "Wait here." Now nurse gone and she come back with this baby. Nurse come back with this baby wrap in little blanket. Little pink blanket, and *swaddling!* Nurse give me he to hold! Give me this little baby to hold up in my own hands!

9

My sweet Jesus that was a little doll! A little *doll,* and so *pretty!* I just couldn't left that baby to sleep. Just couldn't left he out from my hands. I couldn't left he hardly to sleep. Cause he so pretty, and pink, all I want to do is hold he all the time. Everybody who see he say how pretty. Well it wasn't much of people. Mistress Pantin, Mr Bootman, but they say how pretty he was still. Granny Ansin say how pretty too, the first, but then she ain't pay me much of mind again. Nor the child neither. Like she was vex with me still, and my Tantee May. Like them two was vex with me still. But I don't care! I don't care about nothing but my baby, my little baby. And them others, my sister and my cousins, them other girls in the house, they only fighting down each other to see who is the first to hold he. I strike out! I say, "Don't you even *think* about that! Cause onliest person going hold this doll-baby is *me!*"

Onliest thing I couldn't understand is the milk. Cause every time I try to feed he, he would, that milk would come back out. Come back down through he nose. Come back in white bubblings, like white froth. I hold my teat inside he mouth but he don't take it, suck, he don't *suck* at it. I hold and I try to, you know, squeeze out some, milk out some, but that milk just wouldn't go inside. Wouldn't *take*. Or come back down through he nose. But he never cry. He never *once* cry. I say, *Well if he don't cry then he can't be hungry. Cause if he was hungry he would cry.* So I wasn't worried. I say, *This child so good! He so good, and so pretty!*

But then one evening my grandmother, my Granny Ansin, she look cross and she say to me, "Why you don't *leave* that child? Why you don't *put* he down? Night I can't sleep. You, and that child! Always *taking* he up." She say, "That child got to go. Got to *go!*" She say, "When you pick up that child you don't feel strange? You don't feel *funny?*" I say, "Yes. I does feel funny. I does feel my head getting *swirly.*" I tell she that. You know, head swirly like, *scary*. But still you try, you try and you hold on, and favoring. I ain't know.

1 0

Next morning I look, I call quick to Ansin. You know my grandmother wasn't lying down far from me. She bed wasn't far from mine. I look and I call to Ansin quick, I say, "Ansin, look what happen! To the child!" She say, "What happen?" I say, "This child never cry. This child never once cry. And look, look where he mouth full with ants!" She say, "That child ain't *come* to stay. And you always *taking* he up. Ain't come to stay. Come to go. That child *dead!* You can't *see?* That child dead long time!"

I throw he out from my hands. Throw he pon the ground. All the ants! You know, *ants!* Was in that child mouth. Them ants was *eating* he. Eating that child. All where he was lying circle, circle with ants. *Circle.*

He was ten days when I carry he out the hospital. So, fifteen. Ten plus five is fifteen. He ain't even went out the house. But that child did breathing. He did breathing good enough, and pink, and pretty. I ain't know what happen. Maybe I do something? But when she, when Ansin tell me he dead, I did already know something happen. The wrong. Cause if ants bite you, you does *feel* it. But how, how them ants could be eating up he? When I look them ants was boiling out from he mouth, he nose, *boiling.*

Like he was dead already a day, maybe two days. Cause that previous morning he was living. I *know* he was living. And you know sometimes you look at a baby and he smile, and you could smile too? You look at a baby and you know he yours, he yours, and you could smile too? Sometimes he eyes open, and sometimes they don't be open. And still always he sleeping. I ain't know if I was too young to notice. I ain't know what went wrong. But my grandmother, she tell me, "He ain't come to stay. That's why he ain't cry. He ain't sin. He ain't do nothing. Just here for little time."

So we bury he. Dorine sister which is Ellis, Dorine is my cousin. Dorine got a sister does make clothes, needleworks. She make and bring the dress for he. Cause we uses to put boys in long-dress too. You know, to Christen them in, carry them out in. Onliest thing is, my baby never Christen. My baby never even leave the house. Only to bury. That was the onliest time my baby leave the house. Granny and me dress he up in the little dress, we put he inside the box. Arrows bring the box for he, wood, and cover with white. A nice white little box. Didn't even get chance to name he nor nothing. Nor Christen nor nothing. Nothing nothing nothing nothing.

A World of Canes

We begin with love? Bolom, I ain't know what we begin with. What you call that? *Bullying.* You call that bullying. We begin with bullying, meet up with little love. Maybe little bit. Una could suppose.

I could remember the first time. I did going back at the elementary now, this after all that confusion with hospital, and baby, everything, I did going back at the elementary school, Sherman-St John. I did had thirteen years then, and Berry, he did had about sixteen. Thirteen and sixteen, two children, nothing more. We wasn't nothing more than two children then. Well, my little cousin, he was going at the elementary too, which is Clive, my tan son. So the elementary was close to the private school, high school. Berry going at the high school. This bigshot Berry, badjohn, vagabond, he want beat up all the poor little children. Big tall redman. He with he bamboo stick. You know, long big stick of bamboo stick? Pon afternoons you passing the high school, going home, he going at the high school, he want say, "Get!" Beating you, "Get home!" All the little children.

Well one day somebody lose a pen. Was a ink-pen somebody lose at the high school, one of them ink-pens with the ink inside that you could write just like that. Word get out that somebody lose a pen. The elementary children now, you know, they all gone running looking for this thing. My cousin was one. So when I come out from school, I hear this lot of combruction going on. When I look, my cousin *bleeding*. All pon he head bleeding. I say, "Clive, man, what happen with you?" He say, "Berry hit me." I say, "For what?" He say, "Ain't know. Berry just hit me and cut me, he bamboo." I say, "You find the pen?" Cause I ain't know, I say, *Well maybe if you find a man pen, man want take it back, you want keep it for youself, man want beat you for it?* I say, "You find the pen?" Clive say, "Ain't find no pen. I did *looking* for it, long with everybody else, and Berry just beat me like that!" I say, "Beat you just for beating sake?" He say, "Must be." Well that one hot me up too bad. I did vex too bad for that. I go and I start up pon this Berry now. I say, "You only want beat he cause he poor. Cause he ain't got nothing. But if he didn't poor if he had money he would *deal* with you!" This Berry tell me, he say, "You going deal with me now. *You* is." I say, "I going deal with you now I know exactly what you is. You ain't know what *I* is, but I know exactly what you is, and I going home tell my grandmother and we going carry you in the court. We going carry you before the Magis for beating this child!"

So. Gone home. Clive, the children, you know all the gang behind we. I tell Granny Ansin what happen, we fix up Clive head with a plaster, and my grandmother gone up the hill now at he grandmother. Cause Clive was living with we now, in Granny Ansin house. He mummy, which was my Tantee May, she gone and living with some new man in town. So Clive move in living with we, about six–eight of we living together with Granny Ansin in she house. And Berry mother, she wasn't living at home neither. Berry was living with he grandmother too. So my grandmother gone up the hill now at *he* grandmother. But Berry grandmother only want say, "Una see? Una *watch* at Berry beat the child? Una got witness?" Whole lot of cadovement like that cause she ain't want *tell* the boy he wrong. I say to this Berry now, "Alright boy, you could run till night catch you, but one of these days you going find out from me." He say, "You can't do me nothing, I going

248

kick you." I say, "Yes, that's all you could know about is kicks, and brute, but one of these days I going give you some kicks too!"

So from that time I did hate this Berry. All the children at school, just couldn't stand he. Cause he unfair. Cause he big and tall and red. And show-off. You know, he drive he father bus down the hill and show-off. He living to he big block-house up crossroads, top the hill, he grandmother and he father living with he. He father got the bus park in front, little minibus, carry people in town, church service, thing like that. They got money. *Every*body know what they got. Berry, everybody know about he.

2

I was going back at the elementary school now, finishing up at the elementary school now. Cause after that confusion with baby, and hospital, I go back again that I could finish up with my schooling, my learning. Whatever amount of learning could be allowed for poor people living in a place like Sherman. Well not straight-way. I couldn't go back in school straight-way, cause I still did stun from that experience I had in the hospital, death of my baby. That thing did leave me *stun,* like sleepwalking, walking in my sleep, maybe a good two–three months after that experience. I did awake, yes, but like I did sleeping too, same time, pon my feet. Maybe two–three months after.

Then one day Ansin bring a old obeahwoman at the house that she could look to me, see about me. How come I sleeping pon my feet like that. Well obeahwoman take only one glance and she say I suffering the maljoe, how she call it, that evil-eye that I did had pon me, that somebody put pon me. Obeahwoman say that same maljoe kill the child too, my little baby that dead. Well I ain't know what it is she do, what it is she do to me, but time as this obeahwoman leave the house I was awake again. I was back to myself again. She wake me up first, and then she give me the mirror to wear. Little piece of mirror, shard of mirror, with the tiny hole punch to top that I could pass the fishingtwine through, and wear from my neck hanging. That same length of fishingtwine that I had already with the little silver cross Ansin give me when I make the baptism. So now I could wear them both, Ansin lit-

249

tle cross and this shard of obeah-mirror, both hanging pon the length of fishingtwine tie round my neck. Obeahwoman say I *got* to wear it. Cause that mirror would protect me that I couldn't catch that maljoe never again. Long as I could wear that mirror. Well I didn't know, I didn't sure, cause I did never put too much stock in the sciences, them old-time obeah-sciences, and Ansin neither. But then I start to think, I say, *Well in truth Joe is the body put that baby pon me. He did name Joe, so maybe that maljoe was something he put pon me too, long with the baby?* I didn't sure, cause I did like Joe. He was a good boy and I did like he too. I didn't think that he could put no evil pon me, and kill a innocent little baby like that. Not Joe. He could *never* do that. Onliest thing I could think is maybe he do it without intending. Maybe that maljoe was just something he had pon *he,* like a feature like, and he didn't even aware of that for heself. Maybe *all* the mens got something of that maljoe pon them. I just didn't know, I wasn't sure, but I wear my obeah-mirror still. Oh, yes. I did never take that thing off. Not even to bathe! Cause I say least now I wouldn't have no more babies to dead pon my hands again. Never again.

So I start back in the elementary school, and time soon come when I finish too. Cause I didn't have so long to go to finish again. I got to look for work now. I can't go at high school, ain't got nobody to send me at high school. Buy me books and different things. I got to look for work. So my grandmother, she arrange for me to go by a woman does do needleworks. I go by this woman to learn the needleworks from she, Mistress Bethel. But to get from Sherman to Mistress Bethel house now, I got to pass crossroads, you know, got to pass *he* house, where he living, this Berry. Well that ain't nothing. Ain't nothing in that. I ain't fraid for the man, I ain't thinking nothing about the man. I just keeping to myself, go long about my business. My grandmother, she buy couple dresses for me, you know, to go at needleworks, I press them and I make them neat and thing. So I walking, my little bag, my clasp and my earring. Looking pretty, real pretty now, and I pass this Berry sitting relaxing pon he gallery. Big wide porch in front the house. Well this Berry stand up and he watch at me, you know, ogle me every time whilst I pass. I say, *What this man watching at you for? What he watching at you for like that?* But he ain't tell me nothing, and I ain't saying nothing to he neither. I did had it pon my mind still from what he do Clive. And from that time I just couldn't *stand* he.

Then one time I had to go up crossroads in the night, there where he was living. I had to go up with a cousin of mine to meet with she friend. She friend uses to work at this shop, grocery shop, selling groceries. This shop close at seven o'clock, you know seven o'clock *dark*. This girl *fraid* to walk home by sheself come seven o'clock. So we gone to meet with she, you know, keep she with company. We leave home about six, six o'clock come already you can't *see* you hand in front you face. So we gone over. We making plenty noise, bunch of we walking together must be about five–six, we going over to bring my cousin friend. You know must be two–three miles from Sherman to crossroads, but all is canes. Canes canes and more canes. That place. And so dark. So we got to pass by this man house, coming *and* going.

When we get there now, when we approaching this Berry house, you know he got a lot of little pups. Lot of little pups. Like he had a slut–dog or something, uses to got pups all the time. And he just keep the pups, raise up the pups. But anyway, he must be had about a dozen pups. We did frighten enough for them dogs, yes, but long as he there, you say, *Well he would call them back. If he there he would call them back, them dogs ain't going be out in the road.* Well anyway you more scared of he than the dogs. You prefer the dogs to he! Cause you could ring a rock in the dogs, you could do that, but you couldn't ring a rock in *he*. He more dangerous than the dogs! So we approaching now, little before where the house is. I see he light on, I say, cause we uses to call he *the beast,* that's the name we did call he by. I say, "The beast, the beast light *on.*" So we, we shut we mouth now, easy, we passing to this side he living to this side, you know how *frighten* we is for he? Oh, yes! And he there *a-waiting.* The beast there a–waiting we.

We going quiet now we tipping, we tipping so silent them dogs can't even hear. All in a sudden I feel somebody grab on me, my arm, grab my arm tight tight. I say, "*Wha?*" When I look, is the beast–*self* grab me. I say, *Oh my sweet Jesus what this man want with you now? He gone and cut Clive, what he going and do with you now?* He make the rest a sign to the rest like that, he fist in the air. You know, *go-long! get!* So they all gone a–running. They take–off! Gone a–running and left me, poor me, left me there with this beast, this trap-man. I say, *My sweet Jesus don't let this man kill me! Don't let this man murder me tonight!* I say, and I talking up aloud to he now, I say, "What you? What you *want* with me?" He did pushing me forward, shoving me like that, big tall redman. He say, "Una walk. Una just walk. Or I going let go *all* these pon una." This time he got he pockets full with bombs, *full*. Cause it was getting to November now, Guy Fawkes time. And you know before Guy Fawkes they does start to selling the rockets, and the starlights, and the bombs and different things. Well we got to settle for little pack of starlights, maybe a bandit, pack of bandit, but this Berry, he got the works. He aunt bring it from town for he. This Berry got he pockets *full* with these bombs. You know the bombs you does hit down? The ones with the flint? When you hit them down that flint hit you all up in you foot. And I did frighten for them things so *bad*, so *harsh!* I say, "What you going do with me? When them children come back, you would let me go home? You would let me go home with them?" Cause I know they had to come back going the next way. He say, "Don't ask me nothing. Don't ask me what I going do with you, you just wait and see." I say, "If you kill me they would find me tomorrow, and them children know you is the body carry me!" I start to wriggle now, wriggle-out, he say, "Don't you wriggle neither. Don't you wriggle neither or you going wriggle in two of these. *In* you backside I going put two of these bombs!" Bombs with the flint, oh my Jesus that thing does hurt so, scorch you all up in you foot and thing, when he hit them down.

Bolom, I just want to get way. I did fraid so bad when them other children leave me, and I just want get home. I say, "What you going do better start doing now, cause it getting late." He say, "Got to do in the patient." I say, "*What?*" He say, "Got to do in the patient now." I say, "You, you wouldn't patient with me already! What you going do, do *now*. And let me go. Cause when them children reach home they would tell my grandmother where I gone, and she would call police pon you!" He say, "I ain't killing nobody." I say, "Look how you got me holding! I ain't give you consent to touch-up me!" He was walking me straight, direction of them canes. I say, *Where this man carrying you? He going kill you in these canes?* We reach in the dark now, this where the canes start. He say, "Stop." I say, "What you stopping for? You going shoot me?" He say, "You see I got gun?" I say, "I ain't know what you

got, nor I ain't *want* to know neither." He say, "You know what I want."
I say, "I ain't know what you want, and you better, you better don't
touch me!" He say, "You done touch aready." I say, "Done touch already,
but never by no vagabond like you. Never by no beast!"

Cause Bolom, I didn't had much of experience, not much, but I had
enough to know sex is the firstest thing they does go for. The firstest
thing. I accustom to that already. But truth is, I didn't think that's what
Berry did want from me. I didn't think that for minute, not one second. Amount of bright-skin girls going at the high school would give
he that? And anyway you don't does be fraid for that. You more fraid
for he to do you some *meanness,* cut you up beat you like he done
Clive. Cause you know them people with money, always want to beat
up the poor ones like that. They always doing like that. Berry say now,
"You going give me trouble tonight?" I say, "I ain't going give you no
trouble. But if I give you anything, make this the first and the last.
Cause me and you ain't no company." He say, "Oh, yes. You very easy
to say make it the first and the last. You want to get way." I say, "Yes, I
want to get way." He say, "Why you want to get way from me? Why
you want to get way from me for?" I say, "You is no good, you does
beat up people, you unfair!"

We reach in the canes now. Deep in the deep of them canes. I can't
see where I going, just walking in the blind wherever he push me,
shove me. I say, *Ain't no cause to fight he. Big tall redman. Just let he do what
he want, then you could go home.* So then, then he stop. He lie me down,
lie me down in them canes. You know, things happen, he just do he
business and that is that. Wasn't no pain like the first time, that terrible
pain searing. Wasn't nothing this time. Nothing to not-like nor like neither. Just what you got to put up with. What you got to bear. And you
getting accustom to that already anyway.

So he finish, he get up, I get up, I want run now. But still he holding me, holding my arm. He say, "Where you run and going?" I say, "I
going home." He say, "You expecting to go cross that road by youself?"
I say, "More happy going by myself than going with you." He say, "After
what happen you ain't trust me?" I say, "No. That could happen to anybody. That ain't nothing. That's just something *got* to happen." He say,
"You's a stupid woman." Just like that. I say, "Well I like to be stupid."
That's all I did answer he, "Well I just like to be stupid."

So we walk. We walk in them canes, he holding my arm. He ain't saying nothing, nor I ain't saying nothing neither, only, "When I get home I going tell my grandmother, that's all." He say, "Well you tell you grandmother and let *all* you cousins hear what you do, then you name going be out in the street. Ain't nobody would bother with me, but they all going talk about *you*." And that's the truth too. Cause you know when a girl do anything like that, when people hear, they call you *nasty*. Oh Lord they does call you so bad! You got to keep that thing in the secret. Cause Bolom, you know everybody doing like that. They all doing like that. But what people like to do, they don't like to hear they do. Don't like to *hear* how they do. They only like to say that about other people. Oh Lord you got to keep that thing in the silent. I say, "But if I don't tell them, if I don't tell nobody, *you* would tell them. You would tell them cause you's a *slut*." He say, "You ain't got nothing to say to hit me with, who you calling a slut?" I say, "You." Just like that. He say, "When I going see you again?" I say, "You ain't *never* going see me again. Never. Me and you ain't no company." I say, "Why *me*? All we going up crossroads together, other girls there and thing, why me? Why you *picking* pon me? Is cause my family can't, cause we can't come up? Cause we poor?" He say, "It ain't money. It is people. People. You understand?" I say, "That ain't true you know better than that. You and me ain't no company. And you ain't *never* going see me again." He say, "When you going up crossroads tomorrow, going at needleworks, you stop me from seeing you. Try and stop." I say, "Alright, see you tomorrow. Just let me go home, and I would see you tomorrow."

3

So he left me go now, left my arm go. I run home. I gone. And I ain't tell nobody, not my grandmother nor nobody. I too shame to tell. I *can't* tell. Just like he say, I can't afford for my name to be out in the street. I just go to the pipe for water and I bathe. I bathe and I scrub that piece of soap so hard, wash he out from my skin. Next morning I got to go at needleworks, I play sick. I tell my grandmother something, my belly bad or something. I play sick for two weeks. Cause Bolom, I ain't going back at needleworks for he to hold me again. Mistress Bethel send to ask my grandmother what happen with me, how I just start out and learning the needleworks so good and thing, what happen that I stop so quick? My grandmother say I claim sick, but she ain't know what happen, cause I ain't sick. She did know wasn't nothing wrong with me. Onliest thing is, I can't *tell* she that. How I fraid to go at needleworks cause fraid for this man to hold me again.

I stop from going at my needleworks that I did learning good too, that I did learn already most everything Mistress Bethel had to teach me. So quick. I take to that thing so quick. How to cut the patterns and sew them out pon that Singer machine, and what can't stitch pon that machine, I know to stitch by hand. I already had my scissors and my thimble too, that I did buy. Cause Mistress Bethel pay we a weekly in that needleworks too, never mind we learning still. Dollar a week. When the garments sell. She pay we a weekly, that I did save most six–seven weeks already. Six–seven dollars, that I take and I spend at the hardware store pon my scissors and my thimble. Cause I buy the *biggest* sewing scissors that they had selling in that hardware, and my thimble. I didn't even *need* to do that, cause I could use Mistress Bethel own. Mistress Bethel had all the things there for we to use. But Bolom, I did already start to making my plans. How I going do. I was there only about six–seven weeks, and I did making my plans already. I say I would start with the scissors and thimble, and I going save my money and I going buy my *own* Singer machine. That was my dream and I did dream that already. A new shining Singer machine, bigger and better than Mistress Bethel own, that I could do the needleworks for myself. Collect all the money for myself. But Bolom, I only reach to the scissors and thimble of my dream, cause now I ain't going back at Mistress Bethel no more. Now I *can't* go back, not for that man to hold me again.

I get a job ironing out the clothes with my Uncle Arrows. He father is Mr Bootman the Panama Man, and Mr Bootman got he business to wash out the clothes for the sailors. Sailors that come in off the ships. American and English ships. Cause whole lot of American and English ships uses to come in in Corpus Christi then, come in from the war. That war that they had going with Germany then. Mr Bootman would pick up the nuniforms from off the ships in the harbour, and he bring them back in he car for Arrows to wash them out. So Uncle Arrows would mind the machines turning to wash and dry the clothes, but then he got to iron out the seams. I tell he I could do that. I say, "*Chups!*

Arrows, man, I could do that!" Was one of them heater-irons he had, you know, the kind with the coals. So pon my way in the morning I just buy two pound of coals, light the coals, and when them catch up good, cover it down. Cover that iron down tight tight. Cause it could go a long time like that. That's one them *big* iron I could tell you, with handle, and *heavy*. I could scarce even pick up that thing. Bolom, you know the amount of pants and thing I scorch and had to throw down in the toilet before my uncle miss them, and Mr Bootman!

4

So I ain't seeing Berry again. Must be about three–four months. I ain't going at crossroads so ain't *got* to see he. But this Berry making it he business to come in now, come in by Sherman where I living. He get to know a fellow name of Lewey, this Lewey live facing my grandmother house. Lewey grandmother and my grandmother house facing one another. This Berry he would come early pon evenings and, you know, cook and different things with Lewey. They playing drafts and thing. Making a racket. But still I ain't had no confrontation with the beast as yet, not since the first time. I didn't even uses to be at home most the time pon evenings.

Cause my grandmother, she uses to go at church regular pon evenings. Church meeting, or choir practice, something so. You know she always doing something in that church. My grandmother go with she boyfriend, Lambert, and I uses to go with them and visit with my cousin whilst they in the church. Cause I would go to church with them pon Sundays, but not pon evenings. Children didn't uses to go church pon evenings. But my cousin living cross from the church, the big Baptist church, and I could visit with she. So when ten o'clock come, and my grandmother and Lambert going home, they call me out from my cousin house, I just run and catch the bike and I go long. Cause Lambert uses to drive bicycle, and he would, you know, put my grandmother to sit pon the front, pon the crossbars, and he riding the pedals and they going long like that.

So I there talking with my cousin, it getting late, past ten now, and I hear *glerring! glerring!* Lambert pon he bell. My grandmother call, say, "Time to go home!" I was just waiting to hear she voice, and I bawl,

"I coming!" and I run out to catch, you know, hold the fender and running behind. I ain't notice nothing particular, my grandmother sitting pon the crossbar, she wearing she broad-hat that she uses to wear at church, and Lambert driving the pedals. Onliest thing is, they moving a speed tonight, *fast,* but I could run fast too, so I just catch the fender and running behind. Quick now Lambert shift in the dark. Shift in the dark quick quick like that, dark of them canes side the road. I say, *This very strange, that he shifting in the canes? What Lambert going in them canes for?* Una could suppose maybe my grandmother want to use the toilet, you know, something like that. But una ain't thinking nothing particular, just hold pon that fender and running behind. All in a sudden I notice, I say, *Well my grandmother looking very big tonight. She looking very big and tall tonight.* When Lambert stop, and my granny hold, hold pon my arm tight tight. Bolom, when I look up in my granny face, I see this vagabond. Is Berry *self* dress up ganga! And there driving the bike is he friend Lewey. I say to Berry, "Wait! Is you, you again!" Berry was wearing he own grandmother broad-hat, he had on this wig that he get from someplace, he wearing this wig. He got on earrings, and bracelet, rings pon he fingers, pon the little white gloves of he fingers. He wearing he grandmother long-dress, oldfashion long-dress with them big pump-sleeves, big apron, so that could fit he like that. Big tall redman like he, dress up in he grandmother clothes *ganga!*

Well I say to Lewey now, cause I know Lewey he living cross the street from me, I say, "Lewey, man, why you drive this man bike for me to hold on like that? You know I ain't want nothing to do with this beast." Lewey say, "He pay me to do it. He give me money pay me and you know with money, anything goes. You *know* that!" Berry jump off the crossbar now and Lewey gone, was Berry bike Lewey did driving. Lewey gone and he take-off like that, left me there with this vagabond. I say, *This man gone and hold you again? You got to go through this thing again?* I say, "I ain't talking with you. Ain't talking with you no matter *what* you do me." He say, "Wait! I go through all this to get to you, dress up myself in ganga, and you ain't going talk with me?" He say, "You think that I would go through all this, and let you go so easy?" I say, *Well you can't fight with he, big tall man like he, and strong.* I say, "Talk then. Talk then what you want cause I can't fight with you."

So then he talk talk talk. He talk. But I ain't answering he nothing.

I ain't speaking a good time. Last I say, "You does bully everybody to talk with you like this?" He say, "No. I don't does bully people." I say, "Well what you doing with me now then? You don't call this bullying? This is bullying, this ain't love." He say, "I does feel something for you." I say, "Well I ain't feel nothing for you. I just feel when I look in you face hatred like I want *kill* you! Or you going kill me!" He say, "You just keep quiet, or let me cuff you in you mouth." I say, "I know you going cuff me in my mouth that's all you could do is cuff." He say, "Why you keep telling me them things? Why you keep telling me them things make me mad, and running from me? Why you keep running from me for?" So I say, "I fraid for you to cuff me." He say, "Not so easy. Not so easy." I say, "What you going do with me now?" He say, "I ain't going do nothing more than I ain't do already." So I say, say like the last time, "Well you just do it quick and let me go. Cause onliest thing I want is to get way from you." He didn't answering nothing to that, and I didn't talking nothing no more neither. He just pushing me walking through them canes, push me deeper in them canes. So now I say, *Well look, you could just give up. Cause he so tall, and strong, you can't do nothing to get way from he.* And plus I say, *Well if he could put heself so low, so low as that to dress up heself as woman, dress up heself as ganga, only to get to you, maybe something there? Maybe something there in that?*

Then he lie me down again pon some dead canes, he find someplace soft in them canes for we to lie. Now he start to feeling me up, but not so rough, more gentle this time, and I kind of relax. I say, "Leastest thing you could do is take off that wig. That broad-hat and them earring. You look like a *fool.*" He did embarrassed now, so he take off he ganga-clothes, he start up again. I just relax more into it, don't fight with he too much, and I did start to like it this time. You know, he was feeling me up but gentle, gentle now, and I just go soft inside. Down there. I just go all to waters. Deep blue and purple warm *wistful* waters, and he raise up and he go deep inside, he, whole of he warm deep inside, and I just melt down soft into it like that. Easy. Not fighting now. And it did feel good this time. And he did know I was liking it too.

When he finish, you know, he laugh and thing, I laugh, I feeling good now. Not so bad. We talk and thing, we laugh little bit, he ain't holding me no more but I ain't running neither. We say, well he ask me if I want to go in town. I say, "No. I can't go in town. I ain't got no

money to go in town. What little few cents I could catch from the ironing got to give my granny. Or take and buy the things that I need. I
ain't got no money to go in town. You know how it is?" He say, "Well
I could give you money to go in town. You could be my girlfriend." I
say, "Don't you, don't you *laugh* at me!" He say, "Ain't laughing at
nobody." I say, "You and me is different kind of people. Where you
come from and where I come from is different kind of people. So you
got to look for you kind of people, and I got to look for my kind of
people. That's just the way." He say, "Who is my kind of people?" I say,
"People that got money. Got education. People that go at high school
and got car and big house and thing." He say, "It don't be money. It
don't. Is just people, understand?" He say, "Just let we, just tell me if you
would be my girlfriend, and you could see me. I ain't want to dress up
in ganga-clothes all the time to look for you." Well I laugh at that. I just
had to laugh at that. He laugh too. We laugh so hard! We laugh till we
belly hurt. Now we ain't saying nothing a time. A long time. Just sitting
there in the silent. Listen in the silent to them breeze brushing through
the canes, all them canes a-creaking, *kerrack, kerrack-kak,* and smelling
green, and earth wet. And feeling the cool. Feeling far off. Like we did
far off from everybody. Last he say, "Man, do, say something!" I say,
"Alright. Alright then. I could be you girlfriend. You ain't got to walk
behind me dress up ganga, but you, don't you *bully* me!" He say, "I ain't
going bully you. I ain't. You going see. I going be alright." So then we,
we do it again. He ain't hold me this time and I ain't run this time neither. We do it again and I hold *he*. Hold on tight to melt in them warm,
wistful waters. And I did like it good enough this time.

5

So he tell me where to meet he and I go. We meet. Time to time. You
know, I still did doubt, I still did had it pon my mind. I ain't in love with
the man so good as yet. But then he did behaving heself ok. The beast
did behaving heself ok. I start to like he. Well, *more* than like, and he too.
Time come when I just couldn't miss he out from my eyesight. Nor he
couldn't miss me out from he eyesight neither. We did going together,
a time, we go in town a Saturday evening, take in a picture-show, movie-
show, things like that. And we go in the canes, always in the canes.

But then my grandmother get to find out, find out about we. Sweet Jesus! My grandmother give me so much of *struggle,* so much of struggle over this man. Tell me I hang my hat too high, and when I go to reach it down it going fall and hit me pon my head. I trying to come up too much, I should mind my station. All them kind of thing. My grandmother say, you know, he too big for me and thing. And then he father get to find out, Berry father did. Well he was more worse than my grandmother. He tell Berry I ain't no good, no class, I ain't no class for he. Berry father say I's low-down people, call me monkey, molasses-monkey, all them kind of thing. Oh Lord we get the *works.* So much of struggle. He get it from he side and I get it from my side. When I leave in the night, when I go in the canes at night with Berry, my grandmother shut me out the house. Lock me out. I got to sleep under the cellar. You know that house was standing pon posts, groundsels, and underneath open. We call that the cellar. And that place so damp, and so cold. When I sleep under the cellar my eyes swell up. Catch cold in my face.

So when Berry come to see me the next morning, he bathe and dress and walk over to see me, come from crossroads, you know I can't come out. My eyes swell too much! And then my little cousin, my little cousin Clive run out and he say, "She sleep under the cellar last night!" Thing like that. I can't see Berry no more, I too shame. But then one time Clive run out and he tell Berry, "She sleep under the cellar last night and she face swell!" But Berry call me still. He call me to come out and he standing there waiting till I come. He say, "You must *tell* me. When she shut you out like that." I say, "What I going tell you? I can't go telling you things that happen to me about my family. I got to *bear* with it. Cause you and me ain't no company. We ain't no company." I say, "If you treat me bad, kick me or anything so, you know what they going say? They going say how I *deserve* that. How I hang my hat and thing. And they going be right. I can't bring my troubles before you. Cause I ain't got no *right* to be with you!" Berry just stand there and he shaking he head, say, "Just you tell me when she shut you out. Just you tell me so."

We meeting in the canes about every night now, sexing all the time, and feeling good. Reach a point we ain't want to go home not for nothing, he to hear from he father, me from my grandmother. One night we stay out most the whole night, and didn't get scarce no sleep neither. That morning I scorch up must be about a dozen the sailor pants. You know I was working two heater-irons now, two going at the same time, steaming up, ironing out the seams. I smell this thing scorching and I turn round, I throw off the iron quick quick and sprinkling water pon this pants, time as I turn round again, *next* pants a-scorching! On and on again and again till I must be scorch up about the entire American Navy! Me one. And is not Uncle Arrows come in that morning to find me, is *Mr Bootman the Panama Man.* When Mr Bootman the Panama Man come in to find me with all these sailor pants a-scorching, near went after *me* with them iron! He say, "Man, you know who nuniform this is? You know who nuniform you got the privilege to hold in you hands? This garment near *sacred.* You don't play with Uncle Samson like that already!" I just take-off and I running. Take-off and I ain't looking back.

6

Now I got to find more work. I say, *What you could do? Ain't nothing you could do.* So then I watch at my grandmother. She does work estate, work in the fields doing labor. Not cutting canes, is the mens does do that, only the mens got the strength to do that. She work pulling grass, pulling grasses from between the canes, keeping the canes clean. I say, *You strong as she. You could do that good as she.* I ask my granny, say, "I want to help you in the field." Granny Ansin say, "I ain't want you coming behind me. I ain't want you nowhere *near* behind me. I ain't even want you in my house!" She say it to me just so.

But I go behind she still. I say, *Them's the whitepeople canes. Them don't belong to she. I got as much right to work them canes as she.* So I follow behind, and when she look back, I dodge in the canes. I watch at she how she doing, and I doing just the same, and when she look back I dodge in the canes again. Time as lunch come I near fall down about four times. That work so *hard!* I so tired, and mouth so dry! But I keep on. I just keep on the whole day. When I reach home that evening. Well Ansin, she reach before me, and when I reach home Ansin was there waiting, she say, "Girl, you look like a ghost, you turn black like a ghost. Look you face black already and you turn more black still, black like a

261

ghost!" She say, "You go outside and you bathe before you come in here." I say, "I too tired to bathe. I going rest awhile, and when night come I would bathe." Ansin say, "You get pay?" I say, "No." She say, "*What?*" I say, "Ain't sign so ain't get pay. Ain't nobody tell me to sign." Granny Ansin say, "Girl, I ain't know if you more black or more stupid. I ain't know *what* you is." I say, "Well you don't worry cause I know what I is. I is human being. And tomorrow morning I going sign and I going get pay."

So things carry on like that. I work two weeks and then I rest awhile. Cause that's hard work you working them canes, you can't go like that all the time. I rest and I work some more. They pay me sometimes three dollars, three-fifty for two weeks. That can't buy you scarce nothing that three-fifty. Maybe couple yards of cloth to make a dress. Jar of cream, Pons Cold Cream, something like that. Two weeks for jar of cream. But that's the only work you could get, so you got to do it. Berry, he ain't want to hear nothing about me working in them canes. Cause that's poor people work, that's the work for poor people. And plus he know when I in the canes working all the day like that, I ain't going back in the night. I say, "*Chups!* Man, next thing I be *living* in them canes." I say, "I tired, man. I too tired!" But he know I still like it good in them canes. Like it good enough.

7

Then one time my grandmother went pon excursion, church excursion. You know how the church have excursion to visit some other church and thing? We call that mission day. Well this mission day was my grandmother turn to cook. You know, preacher give she money to make the picnic. So my grandmother bake and cook and all kind of thing, and she make this big picnic basket for this excursion. *Big* basket. I wasn't going, but I tell my grandmother that I would carry the basket for she, with all these cokes and food and different things. I know me and Berry would get chance to be together the whole day cause my grandmother ain't going be there. I say, "Ansin, let me carry the basket. This a big basket and I could carry it I stronger than you. Let me carry the basket up the hill." So she say I could carry the basket. I raise it up pon my head to carry, we walking with them other women going up crossroads to catch the bus. I tell my grandmother, "You go-long. Go-long up in front and catch the, you know that bus would come soon so you go-long and catch and I would come up fast behind."

So I walking long and I reach up my hand throwing out the cokes now, two for him and one for me. I throw out some sandwich, about six–eight sandwich, cakes, about three different kind of cakes I throw out, coconut cakes and chocolate, different fruits and thing. He did hiding in the canes, following behind me but sticking to the canes, and when I throw out, he just run and he collect-up. The things I throwing out. One time like my grandmother, like she catch me, she wait for me to come up and she say, "What happen with you? You very far back." I say, "Feel so *tired.*" She say, "You go-long home! Give my basket and you go-long home." I say, "No. I going carry it to the bus." Cause I did feel too shame now to give she back that basket. She say, "I feel something going happen with you today. I got a presentiment for that." I say, "Ain't nothing going happen with me. You go-long have youself a nice time in the picnic." This time I was feeling so bad for doing that. So *shame.* Anyway, bus come, my grandmother gone, she climb up in the bus and she gone. Ain't even notice the basket empty. Near empty. When this man come out the canes now! So many things I throw out, near about *everything* was in that basket. Well we running we can't scarce carry all this food and cokes and different things, can't scarce wait to get weself inside them canes. So then we sit down and we start and we eat. We *eat eat eat.* Eat cakes and different things, eat banana, we must be eat about six banana each. Now we take a break and we do little something, we do little something and then we eat some more, eat some sandwich and drink a coke, take a break and do little something more, eat some more, eat a coconut cake, or chocolate, off and on and off and on like that *whole* morning long. My sweet Jesus *that* was picnic we make that day! We did start from early morning, about eight o'clock, and this now two o'clock, we doing just how we feel. *Everything!* So reach now about two o'clock, I say I going home and bathe and change, he say he going home and bathe too, and he would meet me back there in the canes about four o'clock.

So I going home now, but before I go and bathe I pass by a friend of mine cause I did feel so *thirsty.* After we eat so early and so much,

eat till all finish, cause we ain't stopping till ain't nothing more to eat.
So this girlfriend of mine, where she living had plenty coconut trees,
tall coconut trees. Coconut trees with water-coconuts. Them trees so
tall the coconuts stand and get big big, you know everybody fraid to
pick them coconuts cause they fraid to climb up so high. But Bolom,
this day I feeling I is boss. I is *boss,* and I going climb up them tree. I
put this big ladder up in the tree, and I start to climbing up in that tree
till the ladder get a belly like, a belly of sinking, but I keep climbing.
I keep climbing, and just when I get at the center, just when I reach
in the center of that belly, *plaks!* the ladder break, and all I know now
is I flying. Bolom, I *flying!* Flying through the air. Ain't even know
when I hit, when I hit the ground. Cause all I could remember is that
flying.

My girlfriend run and she call uncle of mine, my Uncle Arrows, that
same Uncle Arrows. He had car, well he daddy Mr Bootman the
Panama Man had car, and Arrows come in he daddy car. Uncle Arrows
say, "What she gone and do now? She always playing man, playing like
if she a man. Always hop pon trucks and all them kind of thing." This
time I can't scarce see he when he talking, Uncle Arrows. I did *flashing.*
Like I see he face now and then it go to dark and then he face come
back again. In and out and in and out like that, and *confusing.* Like I was
far away. Very far. And lot of, whole bunch of things was coming out
from my mouth. Like waters. Like spitting up. But the thing I could
remember, thing I could remember good is it had in *colours,* them
waters. All different kind of *bright* colours. Like pieces of colour glassbottle, coming out from my mouth. I could remember. But couldn't
talk. When I try to say the words the words just wouldn't come. Onliest
thing that come out is them piece of colour glassbottle. Blue and green
and yellow and red and purple glassbottle, every time I want say the
words. Like I say *I,* and it come out a green glassbottle. I say *he,* and it
come out a yellow glassbottle. Like that. I must of fall? Bolom, I ain't
know. But if that ladder had in the belly, and I was in the middle part,
I say I must of fall about thirty–forty feet. Forty feet is the least, and
land pon my back, *plaks!* Cause if I did land pon my head or anything
so from such a height, I could never live like that. *Never.*

So they carry me in the hospital now, the big hospital in town.
Uncle Arrows carry me in he daddy car. Meantime somebody tell

Berry, you know, how I fall out this tree, how I gone in the hospital and thing. Well Berry run and he jump pon he bicycle and he gone too. Get there *before* we! And that was about three miles to town from crossroads where he living. He home and he get there *before* we, so you know how fast he did driving? How fast he did driving he bicycle to do that? Well we reach in the hospital now, me and Uncle Arrows and my girlfriend. I trying to talk and can't talk, only glassbottle coming out, and still flashing, and ain't want to lie down neither. I just want to get up, sit up. But I can't move. Can't even lift up my foot. Orderly come and taking me out the car, and he, I hear this Berry saying, "Oh, no! I would carry she out the car!" They bring the stretcher and everything, but he ain't letting me ride in that. He just hold me up in he arms, and he talking to the doctor too. Same time. I ain't know what he tell the doctor cause I couldn't say nothing. I want to talk but the words can't come. I want to reach out to here with my hand and can't, just can't raise it up. I just sitting there like that. Cutting in and out. Flashing. And feeling like my whole body so *full,* puff, you know, puff-out? And this thing coming out from my mouth. That spitting, all them bright glassbottle colours. I can't remember even if I had pains, if I had any pains, or, I only know they put me in the doctor bed, and doctor give me needle, and I out. I *out.* Just like that.

8

But then when I wake up, well I ain't know how long I was out, but had to been a good time to wrap all that plaster. When I wake up and try to sit, *voom,* fall straight back. Straight back down again. So *stiff.* Like I did get beat or something. Like I did get beat pon my whole body. I had the plaster up to my neck, and going right down, right down to my foot. Ten days I had to remain there in that hospital, government hospital. So Berry come and he look for me, he stand pon me, Berry did. I didn't had much to say neither, but still he come. He come every day. And sometimes them nurse tell me, you know, how he wouldn't left that phone down, wouldn't left that phone from ringing. I say, "*Chups!* Mean that vagabond?" I did want to laugh at that. But you know them patients in the hospital there, them other womens in the ward round me, they get friendly with me, say, "He a *handsome* man!

He like he out the pictures! Where you get he from?" I ain't saying
nothing. Cause I ain't in love with the man so good as yet. I ain't saying nothing to them. But he was a handsome man in truth. He *handsome,* yes, backfire, gone more back to bright. He mother was a
whitewoman, I think she was a English, or something. But he father
dark. So he come out bright like that. Backfire. We call that backfire.
And he got this long nose, and hair red. Pretty and thing. And *freckle.*
He with he freckle.

So Berry come and he look for me. I in the hospital, my grandmother and them ain't come to look for me, nor Mistress Pantin. Nor
my Tantee May, cause I didn't even know where she was now. They
ain't want to hear nothing about me. I say to Berry, "Well tell my
grandmother I coming out." He say, "You got clothes for you? You got
clothes to come out in?" I say, "Yes. Them clothes that I had on. That
I reach in." Then he ask how I getting home. I say, "Ain't got no money
for no taxi. Nor you ain't got money for taxi neither. I would have to
go in the bus." He say, "You would go in that hot sun with all them
people clustering to catch the bus?" I say, "I going try. Onliest thing
that I could do is try." So next day he come with this hat. Went and
buy this hat. Well I just laugh! I just *had* to laugh at that, onliest thing
is, I couldn't even laugh so good. Cause you never see hat like that in
you life. Big broad white-hat, with roses pon it. Red roses. Whole
bunch of red plastic roses. And big long piece of gauze-cloth to tie up
under, you know, tie up under the neck. Tie in bowtie. Hat like that
same hat Miss Bacall did wearing for that Humgart man in that picture. You know, that movie-picture, *To Not Have and Have Neither,* I
think it call.

Berry say, "You laughing at the hat, but this hat would shade the sun
out from you head." And in truth, that mid-day sun was hot. So I put
it on, tie up the cloth under my neck. But Bolom, when I try to stand,
when I put the pressure pon my foot, *voom,* near fall over! My foot
just couldn't take the pressure. I say, "My Sweet Jesus what I would do
now? I can't walk nowhere." He say, "I would carry you." I say,
"What?" He say, "I would carry you in the bus." I say, "You can't carry
me like that. That bus *far.*" He say, "Never you mind I would carry you
in the bus." So he take me up in he arms and he carry me just like
that. I holding with my arms round he neck, my feet sticking out to

this side, that big broad-hat with all them plastic roses sticking out the next side. Well them poor patient, they near *kill* theyself for laughing at we. They catcalling and thing, say, "*That* is Hollywood, papa!" They clapping pon they hands applauding we like we out the pictures in truth. When we walk out like that from that ward. But he just couldn't care. He, like that make he to feel more proud still. He take me up and he just carry me straight through that hospital. I say, *Oh my sweet Jesus where you going with this man? He like he got you under he control. Like you can't say, can't do nothing to save youself from he.*

When we reach by the busstand now, we meet up this whole big crowd of people. Whole big crowd of people there waiting. Cause it had in races now, pon the garrison, and you know how all them country people clustering up to catch the bus? They *clustering*. I say, "What I going do now? How I going get up in that bus?" He say, "You ain't to worry," and he put me in the shade under the chenet tree to sit down. He say, "You sit down right here. Don't move." So when this bus turn to come in in the busstand now, you should of see all these people running to catch the bus. But this Berry big and tall, all he do is take a stride, just one big stride and he hold on, hold onto the bus coming, and he swing in through the door. He sit down right there. I sitting under the chenet tree, and he preparing the seat for me now. So when this bus start to getting full, he start to curse, curse and get on, say, "I got somebody to bring in here inside this bus boy don't you *frigging* sit down pon this seat!" Thing like that. So everybody getting scared. He left the seat now to come out for me beneath the tree, and he lift me up pon the bus put me to sit down pon he lap. He say, "Anyone una that up inside here," cause we was sitting at the end of the seat, the rest up inside, he say, "Anyone una that want to get out before we reach in Sherman get out now! Una make sure! Get out now and let we to get up inside! Cause she sick, and I can't be moving she all the time like that!" So nobody didn't getting out, and that is that.

Where the bus drop we now is still a long way from home. But he carry me the whole way, with all them people watching up at we too. He just carry me the whole way home, and he went and knock at my grandmother house. When she see me, say, "*You!* You there!" Cause this time I was looking so *bad*. I fall off from my weight, everything, look so bad, so different. She say, "You there!" and now my granny start up pon the man, pon this Berry. Ansin say, "You ain't coming in here! You ain't coming in here not for nothing!" Berry say, "She can't walk." Ansin say, "Where you come from? Why she ain't in the hospital? She did very good in there!" He say, "She get a discharge." So Ansin didn't had no choice but let he to come in, and he put me down pon the bed. Berry tell me he going home, and he would come back to stand pon me. I say, "She ain't going let you back in here." He say, "I ain't know, when I come back we would see."

When this Berry come back now he carrying two chickens, done kill from out he yard, he had some eggs, milk. Cause he had a cow home he milk the cow, bring the milk and eggs and chickens. Tell my grandmother boil the chicken in soup for me, and give me the eggs and milk. So my granny come and she tell me, "The boy bring these things for you." She holding these two chickens hanging and eggs and bottle with milk and everything. She say, "Like he a nice boy. Like I did treating he wrong." I say, "I know he gavering nice to me. He gavering nice to me a time." So my granny tell he to come in, cause he give she the things and just sitting there pon the front step, looking up pon the door. She let he to come in and he come in, and Bolom, now I feel so shame to talk with he front my family. He looking down at me, and I looking pon he face, that long nose with them freckle, I say, *Well let you look at he real good now. Look at he good, cause you only ever see this rat mostly in the night, darkness of them canes.* He looking at me now, and holding my hand, say, "I just want you to live." I say, "What you want me to live for? So you could kill me? If I dead now that ain't nothing." He say, "What I would kill you for I want you to live. If you ain't live I ain't know what I would do." I say, "You just telling me that." I say, "You just saying that to make talk." He say, "I ain't telling you that. I mean it. So hurry up youself and let we go out and do how we uses to do before in the canes!"

9

So every day I feeling better and better. He coming to stand pon me and I feeling good, getting back pon my feet. You know he bring eggs, and malt, iron, build back up my nerves. He buy block of iron, you know that black thing? He just chip-off some in the milk, and milk start and turn just like iron. Taste *shew!* real bad, but it good for you, good for the nerves. So I start to getting back pon my feet now. Everybody saying like I pregnant and gone up in that tree cause I gone crazy, I want to throw the child. Berry father say I did want to kill myself, cause I pregnant and he family don't like me. Say he feel sorry, he feel sorry for doing that. But truth is I wasn't pregnant then. I sure about that. I sure I wasn't pregnant then. Cause that come *after.* Maybe about three, that came about three–four months after the tree. After that fall. And when I start and find myself pregnant now, when I find myself now with baby for true, Bolom, that's when everything turn to bad. Not for Berry. He did happy enough. For everybody else. Granny Ansin and he father. For them two things turn straight to bad.

My grandmother turn bad pon me again. Treat me so harsh. Worse even than when she uses to lock me out the house, and I got to sleep under the cellar. Worse even than that. Then one day I went up cross-roads, catch the bus, I went up crossroads and Berry father hold me front everybody. Hold me and curse me front everybody. Say, "I would give you one kick in you belly kick that child through you mouth!" Say, "Get you whoreself way from my son!" Say worse than that. Oh my Jesus I did feel so *bad,* so shame. And Bolom, I did crying. I cry so much for that. I say, *Lord, what I gone and do? What I gone and do to get this?* I tell Berry, I say, "Look man, you just go about you business, and forget, let me go about my business." Berry say, "You can't tell me that. You *can't.* Cause that what you got in you belly that belong to me too. We just got to make out. We just got to make out together."

10

So Berry gone now and he apply for fireman. Gone and apply for fire service. You know you got to sit exam to do that, cause that's govern-ment thing. So Berry sit exam and he come out all As. All *As!* Cause he very very smart, he very smart and he could write so *pretty.* They tell he he come out all As. So he gone and he drop from the high school, cause he going join in the fire service now. Hat and cape and everything. We find weself a house to rent. Pay down the first month. Six dollars. Was a one-room board-house, and small, but it had in bed, and had in two chairs, and little table.

Bolom, we had it plan. How we did do. You know Berry gone and he buy the bucket, water bucket, and I gone and I buy the cup for we baby. Little white metal cup. And little spoon. Little cup and spoon and water bucket. Oh we did think we own the sky! We did think we own sky and earth both, so much of things we had! So next morning when Ansin go in church, and Berry father out driving the bus, we move in all we things inside the house. That little house. But Bolom, wasn't so small. Cause you know what Berry tell me? He say, "Vel, the thing I like mostest of this house is the yard." I say, "*Yard?*" I say, "Onliest thing we got for yard is the street. Pothole and puddle!" He say, "I talking about the *back*yard. You ain't notice the backyard?" He say, "We got the whole world of canes for we backyard."

Scourge and Blight

1

So then we get Junie. My first girlchild name Junie. I did had sixteen
years then, and Berry, he did had eighteen. Junie born right there in the
little house, side the field, canefield. When time come Berry jump pon
he bicycle and he gone for the mid. He bring back the mid that she
could tend to the birthing of this child, with Berry in front driving he
bicycle to show the taxi where is this house hide away up in the bush,
he sounding pon he bell *glerring! glerring!* like he leading a politician
parade. But wasn't no parade, no celebration. Not this time. Not in the
way birthings does celebrate usual, with plenty people, and eating, and
laughing and so. Cause was only we three in the house. Me, and Berry,
and that mid. But anyway that little house couldn't scarce hold but we
three. So when things start in, and them pains start to coming regular,
and I see Berry face turn in preoccupation now, I say, "Man, why you
don't go for some waters for you? You turn red like a lobstart!" I say,
"You red already, and you turn more red still. Red like a lobstart!" He
say, "I got to be here case you meet with any trouble. Case I got to

carry you in the hospital." I say, "Man, you done put me in this trouble already. You go long for you waters, that the mid could tend to me proper."

Time as he reach back, I already holding this little girl. Well Berry near drop them things he was carrying. He say, "Quick so?" I say, "You easy to say that, *quick* so. You ain't here to see the mostest of cumbruction I go through!" He did buy vanilla cake and couple cokes, and he share them round, we taking a drink each from he waters too, we toasting to the birthing just like that. I ain't even know if I drink liquor before, before then. But Bolom, I didn't care! I just didn't care cause I was so *happy*. And Berry too, least till he see the child belly. When Berry see the child belly, see how the mid cut the navelcord short and tie with a piece of twine, fishingtwine, Berry start up to curse and carry on with this mid, poor mid. He say, "Woman, you ain't to touch that! That navelstring bound to drop for itself, that I could bury it in the yard, name the child proper. Like you want put blight pon this child already! Scourge and blight! Pon all we!" I say, say to Berry now, "What you know about baby? You ain't know *nothing* about baby, so you could just shut you mouth. Still with them old-time obeah and thing." I say, "Mid do like that cause that's the way. That's the modern way. This the modern times, you ain't know?"

But Berry gone and he search through the garbage pail still, that mess, till he find the navelcord. He say, "I going in the yard, and I going bury this navelcord under 'Lizabeth, after my mother." I did vex now, I say, "You ain't even *know* you own mother! Never even *meet* she! And you going put this child under some English whitewoman you never know?" He say, "Well what you would call her by?" I say, "Ain't know." He say, "Well you better know quick. Cause this damn woman done cut the cord already." I say, "This June. She could name June. Junie." Berry say, "Alright. Alright then. I going in the yard, and I going bury this navelcord, and I going bury it under Junie." Now Berry take up the child, cause I had she holding, wrap in a fresh towel. He take up the child and he gone outside, and he was walking rickety already with them waters. Well me and the mid, we just couldn't help weself to laugh at that, and I couldn't even laugh so good. We watching at he through the bedroom window. Berry gone beneath the dilly tree, pour out some of he waters pon the ground, and he bury the navelstring. Then he raise up the child high up above he head, and he speech out some Africa *walla-walla* prayer-speech, I ain't even *know* where he get it from. He pronounce she name pon she. *Junie.*

And so we get Junie. My first girlchild. We did meeting life so good then, a time. You know he was doing good in that fire service, start to move up, get promotion. You know everybody like he. They put he to drive the truck, big firetruck, cause he had plenty experience from driving he father bus. They put he to drive the big firetruck, and that's near the top now. Berry, he love that! Cause he could drive that truck fast fast, fast as he want, fast as he could go. And Berry, Berry is a man that love speed. He love to drive a speed. And clang-out the bell. He love that. He clanging *ca-clang! ca-clang!* and driving that truck a speed, you know he can't wait for the next fire to call. Berry begin at two dollars, next thing he get raise to three-fifty, next thing five dollars. Five dollars a week! Bolom, we didn't know what we going do with all that amount of money, what we going buy. One Saturday morning we spend the whole morning discurting. He say he want to buy a music-radio. I say, "*Music-radio?* What we want with music-radio? So we could dance in here? We ain't got room enough to walk in here, and now we going dance with music-radio?" I say, "This child need a cradle-bed for she. She can't be sleeping with we all the time like that. I fraid for she to get crush." So he gone and buy the cradle-bed, little cradle-bed, and we put Junie to sleep in there. You know it had the trellising all round, that she wouldn't fall, and paint in pink. But then one time I had a bad dream about the first child, the boychild that dead. I had this terrible dream, of ants, and I wake up and searching all in the bed for Junie, and can't find she. Then I remember that cradle-bed. I remember that little cradle-bed, and I smile. I did smile so much for that.

Pon mornings I would iron out Berry cape fresh for he, he firesuit. He wearing he hat and thing. He did look so tall, so handsome. Them other womens, near went a-swooning after he. He passing with he cape? Send them near a-swooning after he. But I didn't mind. I didn't jealous for he. I was more proud. Cause you know he did had *me* walking tall too. Sometimes pon evenings I would dress up Junie nice in she long-dress, she little white cap and she little white shoes, bootie-shoes. I dress up Junie nice and I dress up nice too, and we gone in town to meet with he at the firehouse, after work. We gone for promenade in town. Take in a picture-show. Bolom, I was walking so tall beside he. Then when we ain't going in town I cooking to make the dinner ready for he, waiting for he, and hot like that. We would eat rice and stew-beef one day, float-and-accra the next, foofoo. Flyingfish. We eat and then I feed the child and put she to sleep, and we go in the canes awhile. We did always go in the canes. That's why we did never want to live in town, live with neighbor beside. We more happy living in the country by weself, long as them canes there. Cause you know long as them canes there you could always get way. You could escape little while. All the green. Cool of them canes.

2

Then time come for the Firemen Ball. That was a big big thing, that Firemen Ball, cause that's a ball for all the wealthy people in town too, that they could raise funds for the station like that. Cause you know that station could never run with government only, they got to get funds from private too. Well anyway Berry say he want to go in this Firemen Ball. But I say, "Well I can't go in no Firemen Ball. I ain't got no fancy gown, nor no highheel shoe that I could go in Firemen Ball." He say, "This ball ain't to wear gown. That's the bestest thing. This is *costume* ball. You know, masquerade, disguise." I say, "Well what you disguising as?" He say, "I going as woman. I going as ganga, like how I do in the canes." I say, "*You don't! You never! Not in front the people!*" But he say yes, that's just what he going and do. So he gone at he house in crossroads, and he thief all he granny things again. He sneak through the window thief he granny long-dress, she big pump-sleeve dress, he thief she wig with all the ringlets, she earring, broad-hat, everything. Then he come home and he start to costume heself. He draw on my lipstick, put powder, my nailpolish paint pon he fingers. He say, "You ain't getting ready? You ain't getting ready for you?" I say, "I *can't!* I too *shame!* To go in public with you dress like that, ganga like that!" But I was laughing too, I was laughing so *hard,* cause he was looking funny in truth. He say, and he talking in he ganga-voice now, he in he ganga-man voice, say, "I going find me a thweetman, and I going catch me thome breads tonight!" Bolom, I laugh. I laugh so hard! I say, *Well if he could masquerade as woman, then you could masquerade as man. That's all it is.* So I decide I going masquerade as *he.* I put on he firesuit and he big boots, he cape and hat, everything. Onliest thing is that suit was so big pon me, I had to pull it in and roll the cuff, with that cape most dragging pon the ground still. But I didn't mind, cause I was laughing at myself too. We *both* was laughing. So we leave Junie to sleep in she cradle-bed, and we gone and mount he bicycle, he working the pedals and me riding the crossbar, and we go-long to this Firemen Ball. Bolom, we near dance till we drop. *That* was dance we was dancing that night! And you know they had things to eat, like cakes and cokes and different things, waters for the mens. So we eating and we drinking, we dancing, you know we doing just how we please. We styling up with all them rich people, them brightskin people, they styling and we styling just the same. *Everything!* Such a good good time we had in that Firemen Ball.

I was so happy when I reach home that night, I tell Berry he got to go and buy that music-radio. I say, "I can't stop from dancing now. Not now. Not after tonight!" So next day he gone and he buy the music-radio. Little music-radio, with batteries inside. We did dance for that little thing too. Berry tune the station, you know he find a nice song, like Sinatra, or Ella-Fitz, he find a nice song and we dance for that music-radio too. But not inside, we could never dance inside the little house. Just like I say, we didn't have no *room* to dance inside. Bolom, we dance in the yard. Put Junie to sleep, and we take we little music-radio in the yard, we dance in the yard. We just didn't care. We just didn't care about nothing, cause we was so happy then. I say, "Good thing we ain't got no neighbors living beside, cause they would say we crazy in truth. They would send we in the mental first thing!" He say, "Hush you mouth, girl." He say, "You taking me from my waltzing rhythm." I say, "You could show-off too! You ain't know waltz from foxtromp neither!" And we carry on like that, dancing like that. We did living life so good then. That time.

3

Then like Berry father want to make trouble. Like he father want to make trouble for Berry and me. He tell Berry he could bring the child home, little Junie, Berry father say that he could bring little Junie home to *he* house. And he tell Berry he would give me money too, whatever money I want, that Berry could bring Junie home like that. Bolom, I lash out! I say, "You can't do that! This girlchild ain't yours, that you could take she way. Cause boychild belong to man, but girlchild always belong to *woman*. *Everybody* know that!" Berry say he only telling what he father say, about the money and all. I say, "Well you better don't get no ideas about that. Cause this girlchild *mine*. You can't take she neither, not even for money-self!"

Next thing Berry father, he trying to *tempt* Berry home. He trying to tempt Berry to come home with temptation. He find heself some brightskin girls, younggirls. You know he driving he bus in town, he dropping these girls to school and thing, you know he could meet plenty younggirls like that. Berry father say he got a son home. Say he got a *handsome* son home, that they could meet with he. I suppose he must be give them money too, and presents. Cause you know that's the way, buy them a cream or box of powder. Or maybe just give them the cash. But anyway he had this amount of brightskin girls waiting in the house for Berry, must be about three–four. They still dress in they school nuniform, cause you know them girls that go to school in town, private school, they does wear nuniform. Next thing Berry ain't coming home pon evening, he going at he father house. Left me and the child there, and not saying nothing. I didn't know what happen. Cause I only get to find out that *later*, when things write-up in the news, but I didn't know nothing then. And I did worried plenty. I say, *Lord, please don't let he catch in no fire! Don't let no fire catch in he!*

This time Berry only carrying on with these schoolgirls. But then when Berry go with these girls, he want beat them after, after he get through. You know, put lash pon them, slap them up in they mouth. He tear up they dress, they nuniform. Them girls gone running to he father, say they can't be with he. Not like that. They tell Berry father he must drop them home, and he must pay out the damage. Cause them girls smart too. They smart like that. They say he must pay out the damage, or they going to police with that. And they had the marks to show too. Cause them was brightskin girls, they flesh soft that they mark easy like that. You know them girls only about twelve–thirteen, something so. The news write *juveniles*. And that's a *serious* business, you a grown man and you going with *juveniles* like that, and police find out. That's *child-molest.*

So Berry father didn't have no choice but pay them out and drop them home. But then one of them girls *father* get to find out, find out what Berry do, how this girl get these marks pon she leg and thing. What happen that she nuniform tear. This girl father get to find out, and he went to police with that. Them police lock-up Berry. Lock-up Berry for three days, you know, waiting for the case. That's when everything blow up, newspaper and everything, and plenty talk. But that case never reach in court, cause that girl father gone and drop the charge. He gone and drop the charge, so Berry get a dismiss. I ain't even know what happen, cause that girl father was vex enough. He could never drop the charge so easy. So easy as that. I suppose Berry father must be pay money for that one too, pay-out the girl father too. Cause Berry father was scared *plenty* for that, I could tell you. And Berry.

When he reach home I tell he get out from in here. I say, "You don't think that you could do nastiness like that and come back in here! You get!" He say, "How you could know what I do?" I say, "I know cause it write in the news. Picture and everything." I say, "You don't think that you could do anything like that there and people not to know? You got *money.* Everybody looking at you!" He say, "That's just the reason why they put that thing in the paper. That make-up thing. All them lies. Cause they trying for money, that's all." Next day he dress in he cape and he hat ready to go in the firehouse. I say, "You don't feel shame? You don't feel shame to do how you do, and dress in that firesuit? That cape and that hat?" He say, "Woman, you going hit me with that again? That's all lies. Untruths. I tell you that already." But I know it wasn't just lies. I know that. Was something more. Cause Berry near lose he job for that, in the firehouse. Onliest thing is, they couldn't do he nothing, cause Magis done dismiss the charge. They couldn't pin nothing pon he. But still, I know there had to be something in that.

So we go back to living good awhile. Berry behaving heself good awhile. Junie growing good and she doing good. She did reach about eight months now, a year. Next thing I pregnant again. I didn't so happy about that, cause I still had it pon my mind about them girls, them schoolgirls. But Berry, he was glad enough. He was glad enough for that. I say, *Well the first one come out the next one could come out too. That's just the way.* But then I did had this presentiment, this feeling, something, of wrong.

4

Berry friend Lewey join in the firehouse now. Berry give he schooling to take that exam, and still Lewey had to sit that exam two different times. But he get through, slide through. So now Lewey there in the firehouse with he, Berry turn in bigshot. He wasn't like that before. But now he turn in bigshot, and Lewey too. You know Berry is a chief now, firechief, plenty big badge and everything, but Lewey, he just firehand. But that don't matter, cause they could *both* be bigshots like that. They could both be bigshots together, these two. They get in a habit now of going in town at night and beat up prostitutes. Cause you know here in Corpus Christi had all this amount of prostitutes left over from the war. Before the war wasn't no prostitutes. But when all them American and English soldiers come, they turn them girls straight in prostitutes, they turn them in prostitutes first thing, to go with the soldiers from off the ships. All them girls do like that. So now the war finish and ships gone home and leave all them prostitutes behind. Cause them girls can't go back so easy. They take you and they put you in prostitute, give you plenty money and you living life a style, plenty big style, you can't just go back. Not so easy. Onliest thing is, ain't no more soldiers now. They all gone home. So what them girls could do? Onliest thing is walk the streets. Dress up in they fancy clothes left over from the war and walk the streets.

So Berry and Lewey get in this habit now of beating up these prostitutes. Cause you know there in Corpus Christi too fireman is just like policeman. They most the same, police and fire, and they could put you in arrest and take you to jail just like policeman. Or beat you up just like policeman. That's why they got badge and they got bootoo, you know, stick. They got bootoo just like policeman, least Berry did. So they a gang now, Berry and Lewey. Truth is, I was surprise at Lewey for that. Not Berry. I know Berry did always like enough fighting, and brute. I know that from the start, from the time when he beat Clive. He got that brute stripe pon he. But Lewey, he did different. Cause I know Lewey a long time, even before I know Berry. Lewey did living cross the street from my grandmother, so I know he did different. Least before. Now he turn in vagabond just like Berry. Lewey and Berry. Berry and Lewey. They a gang now.

Get in this nasty habit of going in town every night and beat up prostitutes, now that government turn prostitution to illegal. Cause government didn't saying nothing before, when them soldiers come with all the money. But now when them soldiers gone home, government turn prostitution to illegal. They always doing like that. Government is. So that put Berry and Lewey in the right. They could do just how they please, with these prostitutes, lock them up in jail or just beat them, however that they want. But mostly they just beat them. I know they did going with them prostitutes too. I know that for sure, cause that's just the way with Berry. He go with them and then he beat them, after. That's just the way he do, that brute stripe that he got pon he.

Now Berry ain't coming home at night. Sometimes he ain't coming home a whole week. Then when he come home it's only to fight with me, put hard words pon me, and then sleep. He sleep for three days, and then he gone. He ain't bringing home that money again, money for the child, little Junie. Ain't no more food in the house. No more money and no more food. Junie hungry and I hungry. She crying and I crying. We crying together. I say, *What you going do? You got to do something, cause this child going dead pon you hands. And next one in you belly preparing to come too.* I did think to go back home, home to my grandmother. Least then Junie could get something to eat. But I can't do that. She would never take me back, my Granny Ansin. Cause I didn't have no *right* to do how I do, leave without saying nothing, move out, after she take me up and raise me and everything. I can't go back. I got to *bear* with it. Somehow I got to bear with it.

5

So I go and I get work in the canes. I put Junie in a basket, that she could be by my side, and I get work in the canes. But that work ain't so easy to get again, not like before. Cause now the sugar price did start to drop, in the tradings, now there ain't so much of canes left again. But them overseers know I does work hard. They know I does work harder than all them other womens, most the mens too. So I get work again picking the grasses between the canes, cleaning the canes. I work a few days catch a few cents, take a rest and I catch a few cents again. I didn't telling Berry nothing, about my working, cause I know he would make plenty noise about that. He would want to beat me for doing that. But I *got* to do it. Least me and Junie could get little something to eat now. Little something. Least we ain't in no starvation now.

Then Berry and Lewey get in trouble. They beat up one the womens so bad she had to go in hospital, one the prostitute womens. They near *kill* she! Bolom, if you could of see the picture of this poor woman they print in the news, and write-up. If you could of see she! So they get lock up for that, and trial pending. Everybody say the book going read for them two. Magis going read the book for them two. When I tell you the amount of talk was circulating on that thing, that trial. But I say Berry father must be pay-out that Magis again. I say Berry father must be *bribe* he, that Magis, cause they get off very light. Magis fine Berry twenty-five dollars, or three months in jail, and Magis take way Berry badge, he firechief badge. Lewey get ten dollars of fine or month in jail, and he lose he job in the firehouse too. So Berry father pay-out he fine for he, but Lewey, Lewey had to serve out he sentence in jail.

Berry come home now and he say he sorry. Say he sorry for that, and hanging he head dog low. I say, "Well I more sorry than you. Cause I did pregnant for somebody. Now I pregnant for nobody." He say, "You calling me a nobody?" I say, "Yes. Only you worse than a nobody, cause you got brains. All them brains the Lord give you and you can't use them. You *worse* than a nobody. You a *fool!*" He say, "Well you going see I ain't a nobody. I's a somebody, and I going get a new job and I going be a somebody again."

So I take he in. I always take he in. Berry gone and he get a new job driving taxicar. They give he taxicar to drive. Berry start to get back proud again, he holding he head high again, but you know, in the good. He take care that taxicar so good. Always shining it up, and wiping out the seat. You know that's one beat-up old motorcar, that taxicar, but he get it to shining still. He rub that car and wax, and buff it up till that car shine. Bright like wet glassbottle. And that was one *big* taxicar too, that thing, light blue to bottom and white to top, and bloat. You know, *puff-out, bloat,* like a piece of bread that soak in water. Fat like that. Sometimes we go for a drive in that taxicar pon evening, after dinner. I dress up Junie and I dress up too, and we go for a drive pon evening, in town. Or I put Junie to sleep and we go for a drive in the canes. He park the car and out the lights and we do little something in the backseat. Or we find someplace soft in them canes to lie. Sometimes we just go in the car in front the house. We in so much of hurry we ain't got time to drive nowhere! And we laughing. We laugh for that! But in truth, that backseat was most as big as we bed. That backseat was *bigger* even. Onliest thing is, I getting so big now, with child, I so big *I* couldn't scarce fit in that backseat neither.

6

Then Berry decide he want to move in in a two-bedroom house, that the children could have one bedroom and we could have the next. Cause he was making enough money now driving the taxi, making most as much as the fireservice. Only not so regular. Cause one week he would make seven dollars, next week two, three. But I could suppose he was making most the same as the fireservice. I didn't want to leave the little house, nor I didn't want to leave the canes neither. Cause if we move in in a two-bedroom we would have to leave the country, move in town. Cause wasn't much of house to rent in the country. Only we little shack-house. But I did love that little house good enough! I say, "Why we want to leave this little house? We did meeting life good enough in here. We did happy enough in here. Most the time. What we does want for more?" I say, "And now you got the taxicar that we could be in the backseat pon evening too. We like we got two bedrooms already anyway." He say, "I tired living rat-in-hole. That's what we is, rat-in-hole. And just now we going be four rats together." I say, "Well I born a rat I could stay a rat." He say, "Well I ain't born no rat. And I ain't going accustom myself to living like rat neither." I say, "I going miss the canes!" He say, "That's just what we got the taxicar for. That we could visit back in the country when we want. Go for drive in the canes when we want."

So we move in in the two-bedroom in town. This one rent for fourteen dollars. Bolom, I near drop when I hear that. *Fourteen dollars!* For

281

a *board-house!* That's more money than I did ever see in one hand. That's more than *twice* what the little house did rent. And this two-bedroom didn't have scarce no yard at all. Just a little piece of dirt, with all them neighbors living most on top. You sleeping in you bed and you hearing them neighbors discurting, they sexing with theyself, whatever, but you hearing every word. And sometimes they does talk so *dirty!* You go in the yard at night to use the toilet, them neighbors there. You lighting you fire pon evening, them neighbors there. Cause this two-bedroom had in lights, had stove, electric stove. That electric stove was outside, under a piece of roof, but I ain't using that. Cause that thing don't *heat* proper, you know, don't put out no heat, like *heat.* I can't cook pon that. I can't do *nothing* pon that. I just build a fire beside, how I know, and I cook. Them neighbors laugh so much when they see that, call me country-bookie. But I don't care! I say them people ain't got *nothing* to laugh for, if they could laugh for piece of fire, cook-fire. I say they life must be dread in truth.

So that two-bedroom had in electric lights, must of been about two–three, but water in the yard, toilet in the yard, and kitchen. Onliest thing is, that toilet and kitchen can't scarce even fit. Everything jam-up together, in that little piece of dirt. Toilet, shower, kitchen, and then my fire. Everything jam-up together. Bolom, I did feel more space in the country. The *feeling,* of that little house. I did more happy in the country too. I say to Berry, "You paying fourteen dollars for a couple lights, and God give you all the light that you could need for nothing anyway!" He say rat-in-hole.

7

Time soon come for the birthing now. Berry wasn't at home, he was out driving the taxi. But I know he had to come home for dinner, so I wasn't worried. When Berry reach I was already good into that birthing. I tell he go for the mid, go for the mid *quick.* So Berry jump in the taxicar and he gone again, but most an hour pass and still he ain't come back. Now I start to worry. I say, *Where Berry and that mid? Like they ain't want to come at all!* I was worried plenty. Then when Berry reach he come with this bunch of people. He had about four–five mens with he, and two womens. He had that car load to the max with these people. I didn't know not a one. I see some of the mens before, see them round the place, but not to know. They all laughing and passing the bottle and they talking a rate. I call Berry, and I could see how much of waters he had already. I say, "Man, where the mid? Where the mid for me?" He say, "Ain't know." I say, "*Ain't know! Ain't know!* I send you for the mid and you come back with all these people and *ain't know!*" He say, "She walking over. Cause that car full. I tell she to walk over." Bolom, I lash out! I lash out at he. I say, and I did screaming now, screaming like a madwoman, I push myself to sitting up in the bed and I screaming, "Get them *blasted* people out from in here! Every one! You get them out and you get out too!" He say, like he was laughing at me now, laughing at me through the waters, he say, "Oh-ho! This woman going born the child for she*self* now! Oh-ho!" I say, "You ain't no help to me anyhow you get out! You get out! And carry them *blasted* people too!" So he clear out. And laughing. At what? Them fools laughing at what?

Bolom, is now them pains start to come. Is now the pains start to come heavy, and ain't nobody in the house. Nobody except Junie, little Junie. She sitting pon she little stool in the corner and she crying. Cause she was fraid to come close. She watch at my face and she was fraid to come close. You know I can't get up out the bed to go to she neither. Junie sucking pon she finger and she crying. Well that mid reach just in the last minute, the last *second*. I couldn't say nothing, cause my head did swirling. My head did *swirling* then, with that pain. But that mid take care of everything, and she born the child just like that, a girlchild. My second little girlchild. Joyce. I name she Joyce, even though in truth she come with more sadness than joy. But I say if I put that name pon she, you know, things going get, bound to get. I name she Joyce still, my second little girl.

Well that mid stay with me through the night, cause you know that man ain't coming back. Mid stay the whole night, tending to me, she sitting up in a chair side the bed. She feed Junie and quiet she down, put she to sleep. She tending to all three of we together. Cause I was plenty tired after that birthing. I could scarce sit up in the bed to hold this child, little Joyce. I could scarce sit up to hold she, less the mid help me to rise. But she stay and she tend to me, and she come the next three–four days too. She come every day to stand pon me, see how things going. Such a good good woman was that mid, and so kind. Even though she was little bit off-standish. You know she very fair, fairskin, and dress so neat in she nursing nuniform with the kerchief tie pon she head, and watch pin pon she breast. She was a little bit off-standish, Mistress Russel. But I did love she plenty. I did love that woman very much.

When Berry come home now must be about five days after, a week. He ain't saying nothing, nor I ain't saying nothing neither. I don't want to fight with he. I too *tired* to fight, after the child and everything. And plus that child had me feeling so *happy,* little Joyce. I didn't saying nothing to he. Then one time I walk in the bedroom, find he talking with Joyce. He holding up Joyce in he arms and he talking soft with she, you know he couldn't see me cause he back was turn. I couldn't hear he neither, what he was saying, but I just smile. I couldn't help to smile, cause he voice was speaking so soft. I say, *You smiling pon this varmint? You know he for varmint and you smiling pon he still?* Cause Berry had he soft stripe too. He had he brute stripe, but he had he soft stripe too. And you know I's a person could forgive easy, forgive too easy. You kick me one minute turn round treat me nice the next, I just forgive. Like when I hear Berry talking with this child so soft, my heart near melt. Bolom, my heart near *melt* for that. Forgive and forget. That's just the way with me.

So I take he in. I take he in again. We go back to meeting life good again, ok. Little while. He driving he taxicar during the day, and he coming home pon evenings. Come home for he dinner. He hold one child that I could feed the next, then we switch off like that. Or sometimes I just put the two to feed same time. Cause they was both at teat then, and you know sometimes they would get jealous. But that thing does get you *tired,* you feeding two children all the time like that. Berry he bring the iron for me, he chip it off in the milk and stir and he give me to drink. That iron give me strength, and them girls give me strength too. Strength to stand up by, persevere by. Cause Bolom, I could tell you one thing, I could tell you one thing life learn me. You got a baby at teat, and ain't nobody could touch you. Say what you want *before,* that you ain't want the child, you want throw the child. But *after,* when the child *come,* when you look in that child face and you got that child to teat, Bolom, you could *never* do without then. Never. And ain't nobody could touch you then. Nobody.

8

Now Berry say he want to married. Say he want to married with me. Just so. He come with this thing just so out the blue. But Bolom, I ain't want to married. I did never even *think* about married! Cause you don't think up that for youself. That does come mostly from the parents, they tell you that. But I ain't got no parents. Nor I don't trust to married neither. I don't trust that not at all. I say, "What we going married for? So much of fighting we go through, and bad, what we want to married for?" But he say he want to married. Berry give money to the needleworks woman, that she could make the dress. Needleworks woman come at the house, she say, "You got to pick the cloth for you. You got to pick the pattern." But I say I don't care. I say, "You could pick the cloth and you could pick the pattern. Cause I don't care." I did had this feeling still. I did had this doubt. Well more than doubt. Needleworks woman send word with she little boy, that I must come in the shop, come that she could do the fitting. But I ain't going for no fitting. She send word again but still I ain't going. I say, "Tell she I got the babies to tend. I ain't got time for no fitting." But I did know that was just excuse. That was just excuse cause I just didn't want to go.

9

Then one morning this woman come at the house. Was that same prostitute woman Berry beat up and send in hospital. Cause I did recognize she *straight*. I did recognize she from that newspaper picture, first thing, from cross the street, even before she come inside the house. Berry wasn't at home, he was out driving the taxi. This woman come straight inside the house, boldface so. She open the door and she come straight inside, say, "You see you? You see you? You going have the ring, but I going have the man!" She say, "You going have the ring, but I going have the man, cause he would be with me *every* night!" She just say it like that, hit it at me just like that, and she gone. Cause Bolom, I couldn't say nothing. I couldn't answer she nothing. Onliest thing that I could do is sit down in a chair, cause I was feeling dizzy, and I cry. I cry so much for that!

When Berry come home I fix the dinner. I fix the dinner for he, he eating. He say, "Woman tell me send you to fit the dress, needleworks woman." I say, "What dress?" Just like that. He say, "*Wait!* You ain't going married again?" I say, "I want the ring and I want the man. I ain't want the ring and not the man. Whoever get the man could have the ring too!" He say, "Woman, where you get that from?" and he start pon me. I say, "I get it from that same woman you send in hospital. She come in here say it right to my face. But I ain't want to fight with you. If you want to go with that prostitute woman you could go with she." Well Berry in a rage now. He up and he gone. Jump in he taxicar and he gone.

When he reach back I see he shirt wash with blood, *wash*. I say, "What you do? You kill she?" He say, "Ain't kill she. Cuff she up in she mouth." I say, "Well you ain't had no *right* to do that! Cause you as much to blame as she, you the prostitute same as she!" Now he haul back ready to cuff me too, strike at me too. I say, "You *don't!* You better don't. Cause you cuff me and that's it. You ain't *never* going see me again, nor these children." So he hold back. That time. He didn't strike at me then, not yet. He just tear off he shirt and he ball it up throw it straight in the corner. He throw it like a ball of wet rag straight in the corner, and he sit down bareback at table, he with he waters. I say, "And you come in in here with that shirt? That shirt wash with the woman blood? You should have *never* do that." I say, "You's a *fool!* Police come now and they find you in here with that shirt, they going *lose* you in jail. Lose you fast enough!" But he don't care. He ain't pay me no mind. Only to throw more words at me, hard words, and say he going and sleep, he going in the bedroom and sleep.

So I like a next fool gone now and I bury the man shirt. Cause that thing could never rinse like that, amount of blood that it had. I gone in the yard and I bury he shirt. So much of things I do for that man. So much of trouble I put myself over he. I dig a hole in the yard and I bury the shirt, and I put the two concrete blocks on top, with the wash-tub on top the blocks. That washtub and that scrubbing board. I say,

Them police could never think to look there, inside there. They could never find that shirt like that.

But them police never come. Cause this woman never *tell* them nothing. Cause if she say anything, you know them police would come to question, that's the leastest thing they would have to do. But she never tell them nothing. And Bolom, if you could have see this woman face! How Berry did mash-up she. Bust she mouth open and mash she all up in she face. Berry beat she so terrible, I did even catch myself to feeling sorry for she. I think awhile and I begin to feel sorry for she, and *shame.* I feel shame for Berry and she both. But she wasn't shame. Not like you would think, expect. She was *proud* for that. She was proud, cause she take that beating for sign, sign that he did care for she, that Berry still did care about she. Cause they got plenty womans does think like that, in this place. They so accustom to getting beat, things get all twist-over in they mind. Things get twist-over backwards, and they start to think that's what it is to be a woman. They start to expect that, look for that. And you got to feel *more* sorry for them now, Bolom. You got to feel sorry for *all* we. In this place.

Cause this woman was out walking the street the next day, even with she face swell like that. She ain't even put on no hat to try and cover, you know, little powder or something. A dark glasses. She out walking the street just so, boldface so, before everybody. Like she did *boasting* pon that. She must be say, *Well I got the man now! I got he!* Cause you know what she do? She come up to me again. Was only about two weeks after that beating, that she come up to me again. And this the *worst* one now. This the worst thing ever. I was there waiting in the grocery store to buy some food. I holding Joyce in one arm and Junie in the next, waiting in the grocery line to pay-out my things. It was a Saturday morning, so that grocery store was full up with people, full. Then I see this woman, this same prostitute woman that Berry beat. Cause she face was still a little bit raw from that beating, even after two weeks. I didn't looking for no confrontation with she, not in front the people. I just hanging my head low, tending to the children, minding my business. She see me and she come up straight to me again, *straight,* and she speaking *loud,* say, "You man eat me last night till I can't see!" She say, "He eat me last night till I can't *see* straight!" Bolom, I run! I

287

near *vomit* when I hear that! I can't answer she nothing. I grab up the children and I take-off. I did so *shame*. For her to say that nastiness to me front the people. I did *worse* than shame, cause that thing near send me in the mental. It did went to my nerve. I near went in the mental for that. I say, *Berry never do that nastiness to you! Never!* When I reach home I take down all the cups and dish and I start like I going mad. I take down the child cup and the child bowl, and I scalding, *everything!* I scalding! And what can't get scald I throwing out.

10

Berry come home and find all the things in the yard. Chairs and bottles, clothes. He find all the things in the yard, say, "What happen?" I say, "Get out! Get to hell out from in here!" He say, "You can't put me out this house ain't yours. Is I got to put *you* out." I say, "Well I going then and I going for good, so don't you come looking after me. Cause I ain't want to see you face never again!" I tell he what happen, what the woman say. He say, "You lie, she ain't tell you that. She could *never* tell you that. Cause that's the worstest thing, that's the worstest *possible* thing a woman could say about a man!" I say, "That's just to show you what you dealing with. Look what the woman tell me front the people! I so shame I can't go back in town." I say, "And you, you *deserve* she! Any kind of man could do that nastiness deserve a woman like she!" Well Berry haul back let loose one cuff in my face. That blow send me to the ground, *flat,* bust my mouth wide open. Little Junie see me and she cry, "Mummy! Mummy!" and trying to raise up, raise me up, little thing. She could scarce stand sheself and trying to raise me up off the ground. I sit, and I hug she so tight to my breast, little Junie, and making a soft sound, "*mmmmm! mmmmm!*" cause I couldn't talk with that kerchief holding to my mouth. Holding for the blood. Cause that man ain't stopping to look to me, see to me. He jump in he taxicar and he gone again. Back to this woman. He in a rage and he gone to give she more beating, cause that's the onliest thing he does like, beating, and brute. He gone to beat she again, una could suppose, cause I ain't know. I ain't waiting for he to come back, bury he shirt again. I ain't worrying nothing more about he, nor this woman neither. I say, *You got to feel for yourself now, do for youself now. You got to get out.* So I gone in the yard wash out my mouth, my face. I change my blouse that soak through with blood, I collect up what few little things that I could carry in a brownpaper-sack, I take up the girls and I gone. I gone to wait in the busstand, and I catch the last bus to Sherman that night. Back to my granny.

Cutlash-collect-dump

1

Granny Ansin say she ain't got no place for we. She say, "You can't come in here. I ain't got food for these mouths I got already, and you want give me three more." She say, "You go back where you come from!" But I tell she I *can't* go back. I tell she I going and find work. She say, "Where you going and find work from?" I say, "In the canes. I could go in the canes." She say, "In the canes, the *canes!*" And she laugh, say, "All these years I working them canes and can't get work again, and you going in the canes?" I say, "I going try. Onliest thing that I could do is try."

Cause things did get very bad then, in the canes, very bad. You know everybody get a layoff, same as Ansin. She get a layoff even after working that estate most she whole life. She did had more years pon that estate than the overseer-self, than the landowner even. Ansin begin that work most as soon as she could walk. Soon as she did big enough to pull a grass, to know what is grass and what shootling. Cause in them days everybody had work, big and small. You want work you could have work. Everybody. But they ain't bothering to pull grasses no more pon them estates. They ain't worrying to keep the fields clean, nor nothing like that. They hiring as few workers as they could, and only field-hands, and they paying out the half, less than half. And still them estates going bust, bankrupt, left and right. Most of them estates done bust already, things did get so bad in the sugar tradings, so low. They say things get so low they couldn't even turn a profit. They had to sell for loss.

But I tell Ansin I going and find work still. I tell she, "You mind the children tomorrow, and I going try." She say, "Well I would give you three days. And if you don't find work then you got to go. That's all." So I gone the next morning and I get work, cause they was ready to start crop-season now, and I say I going cutlash the canes. Overseer tell me, and he laughing, say, "You can't do that. Only *mens* does do that, cutlash the canes." I tell he, "Well you watch at me. You watch at me good. Cause I going in them canes, and you watch if I don't cutlash more than every *one* of them manhand." I take up my cutlash and I gone. Just like that. I don't give he chance to answer nothing. I gone. I tie up my dress at the side, my skirt, and when I start to swing my arm like it can't finish. Like it can't rest. I swing that cutlash till my whole body sweating. My clothes soak right through, my skirt and my blouse, my head-tie. But still my arm swinging. I only stop to take up my bundle of canes, the canes that I did cut. I carry and I dump my bundle in the cart, donkey-cart, and I gone back to swinging straight. Cutlash-collect-dump. I going all the morning like that, and don't even stop for breakfast. Come two o'clock when all them hand stop for breakfast, my cutlash still swinging. I going like a motor, like a steam engine. Cause I *can't* stop. I got to show that overseer that I could work, work good as the men. I got to make out. Cutlash-collect-dump. That's all that I could think, do. I saying it over and over again, I saying it a-loud, with every swipe of that blade. "Cutlash" *swipe* "collect" *swipe* "dump" *swipe!* "Cutlash" *swipe* "collect" *swipe* "dump" *swipe!* Well them manhand stand up and they watch at me like they seeing a ghost. Cause they never seen nobody work like that before, much less a woman. They watch at me like they seeing a ghost, only they never seen a ghost so black neither, a black ghost.

When my bundles count at the end of the day I had seventy-five. Seventy-five bundles! Cause you know the average bundles a person could collect is twenty-three, twenty-seven bundles. But I collect seventy-five, in one day, and you know that's some kind of record. Must be. And then again my bundles weighty too. They *full* bundles. Cause most of them manhand they try to strimp by, you know, they bundles strimpy, but not mine. My bundles was full bundles. When overseer reach the count, my count, he near drop. He say, "Woman, like you want make these men in ganga. Like you want make ganga-men in *all* we." I say, "No, sir!" I say, "I ain't want make nobody in nothing. Nor woman nor man. I just doing for my*self* now."

He count out my money that was three dollars even. Three dollars! In one day! Well I take that money and I buy all the food that I could carry, and I still had little few cents left over. I buy three–four fowls, I buy a big bag of carrot, and potatoes, sack of potatoes. I buy bunch of okras, onions, hand of green-figs. I buy sack of rice, flour to make bake, two cans of pigeonpeas, *everything*. Everything that I seeing I buying, one time, *all* the food. Cause you know I was hungry too, *hungry*. I ain't eat since evening before, since *two* evenings before, and working all day like that. I carry the things home say to Granny, "Ansin, hot the fire. Hot the fire *quick*. Cause I want see that pot a-bubbling. I want see that big black pot a-*bubbling* tonight!" Well granny near jump. She say, "Where you thief these things from? You rob the store? You reach one day and want put me front the Magis already?" I say, "Ain't thief nobody. I *buy* this. From money that I make. And I going back tomorrow and I going buy *more* food." I say, and I laughing now, I near crying at the same time, cause I was so happy and so hungry and so tired, I was all three together. I say, "More food more food more food!" I say, "*Food food food!*"

2

Well Ansin didn't say nothing more about me leaving. Nor Junie nor Joyce. She didn't say nothing more about we can't stay in the house. Cause that was the only money coming in now, that money that I was making from the canes. But that money was enough. Whilst the canes did last. That money go to feed all we: four girls, three women, and three babies. Cause my sister she already had one child, and she didn't even reach to fifteen yet. And my cousins was still living in the house, Tantee Elvira girls, four girls. Tantee Elvira pick up with some man and gone to Trini, leave she girls pon Granny Ansin floor like that. They between the ages of four years and nine years about, them girls, at that time. But Clive wasn't living with Ansin again, my cousin Clive, Tantee May boychild. He gone and living with tantee and she new husband in town. Cause Tantee May and Uncle Charpie was never married, but now tan gone and married with this new man, Uncle Charpie move out all the things from they little house to the side. He take out windows and doors and everything, most the floorboards, and it just fall down. That little house just rot and fall down. So we don't see he round the place again, we don't see none of them. I say my Tantee May did *shame* for we front she new husband, cause he was a brightskin man and rich too, I say she did shame for we. And that did hurt me very bad, that thing. That does hurt me still up to now.

So that was six girls and three babies living with Granny Ansin in that two-bedroom board-house. And Bolom, that old house most ready to drop. That house had holes in the roof, that galvanize, had holes in the walls, holes in the floors. You know holes, like *holes,* big holes. And patch. Them walls more patch than they was walls even. When rain pelt you getting most as wet inside as out. And so many people you can't get from underfoot. Onliest thing that you could do is hold on to a next body and stay warm, try and stay warm.

So I send for my cousin Arrows, that he could bring Mr Bootman car and we could go for the children beds. Joyce and Junie little cradle-beds, cause they wasn't too big for them beds yet. Arrows say, "Is not me to go in *that* man house. Not till hell catch fire!" I say, "Arrows, man, that ain't nothing. Long as he taxicar ain't park in front, you know he wouldn't be inside." And anyway I did know he was living by that woman now, that same prostitute woman that he did beat. Cause I had a friend tell me Berry was living by that woman now, in she house. But Arrows say he ain't going in, he would drive the car, but he ain't going inside the house. I tell he not to worry, you drive the car and I would go in. So we gone the next evening and I take up the girls cradle-beds.

I see most of Berry things was still in the house, but look like he ain't been in there a good while, good few days. So I take up the girls clothes and they toys and everything of theirs and mine that I could find. I carry the cradle-beds home, and I put them in the room with Ansin and me. I say, *Least my babies would have a bed for theyself now. Least they would have a proper place to sleep.* Cause I did had them pon the floor sleeping, put a blanket and wrap and put them pon the floor sleeping. Cause you know them beds full up with people, three–four sleeping to each, and you just can't put a baby to sleep in a bed with four people. But I didn't like my babies sleeping pon the floor neither, cause sleeping pon the floor like that scorpion would come in the night and bite them. You got to be very watchful for that, very watchful. *Plenty* scorpions in that old house, especial when the rains fall.

But when my sister see the little cradle-beds, and pink and everything, I could see she was jealous for that. Cause you know she had she baby sleeping pon the floor too. She didn't say nothing, but I could see she was jealous for that. So I take a dollar from my pay, the next three–four days, let the rest go to buy the food and I keep a dollar back. I buy my sister a next cradle-bed that she could have for she baby too. I do the same and hold back some money and I buy my granny a dress, buy she a nice clip for she hair. Things like that, little things. You know every week I buy somebody something, little something. Cause when you ain't got nothing, when you living with nothing, them little things could mean a lot, could mean a life even. Sometimes I buy some special food for the house, like ham-bone for soup, or apple. One time I buy everybody a apple, big red shiny apple, and wrap in a box with straw. Apple that they bring from away, bring from America. They call that apple a *Cincinnati Red,* and I say that must be someplace beautiful in truth, to make them apple so pretty. That name uses to ring like a dream in my ears. *Cin-cin-nat-ti.* And them children, you know most of them children never *seen* a apple before. And grapes. One time I buy bunch of grapes, big purple grapes. That was so much of cumbruction them grapes we had to stop and divide them round that each person could take out four, four purple grapes each. But then them children in so much of hurry they want eat all the grapes same time, push all four in they mouth and near choke! We near lose half the family for them grapes.

Then one evening I was walking home from the field and I get a pre-sentiment. I say, *What happen when them canes finish? You know them canes going finish soon, and then what?* I say, *You need some kind of insurance for you. You got to buy some kind of insurance for you, and you family.* So that same afternoon I gone and I buy my insurance. I buy Sue. Sue could be my insurance. She was a little piglet, but I know by the markings pon she that she going grow big, and fast too. That's one thing I know about is pigs, cause I learn that from my Uncle Charpie. I raise with pigs. I know pigs. And I did know Sue going grow good. Well if you hear them children scream when I reach in the house with this piglet, when I walk through the door holding up Sue in my arms like a little baby, a little doll. Them children scream so much for Sue, cause she was so *pretty!* They jumping in the air trying to hold Sue, they want play with Sue. So I let go Sue in the yard, and them children gone running after Sue, screaming after Sue. Them children near scream till they burst. When night come they want to have Sue inside the house to sleep with them. Well Granny Ansin, she near had conniption for that. She say, "Pig! Pig now! *We going live in the house with pig now!*" I tell Ansin not to worry sheself. I say, "You know it's only for the night, couple nights. Cause them children going forget Sue fast enough."

But I don't forget Sue. Sue was my insurance, so I got to take care for she. I did think I could use she to breed, when the canes finish, use Sue to breed pigs, raise pigs. I clean out one of Charpie old fen, one of Charpie old shack-fen that he had side the house to keep he pigs, and not too rotten. I put Sue to live in there. I keep that fen so clean. Sweep it out every evening, whilst Ansin cooking the dinner, and I let Sue run round little bit. I take care for Sue like she was one of my own children. You know pon evening I would buy a big sack of carrot and bring for she. Every evening, cause she did love that. I carry a chair out in the yard and I put Sue to lie at my feet, and I feed she the carrot, one by one. I watch at Sue eating she carrot, one by one, and I watch at Sue grow. *Fast,* she grow so fast. But the thing Sue did love the most. You know the rind from watermelon? Watermelon rind? That's the thing Sue did love to eat the most. Bolom, if you could have see she eating that thing, that watermelon rind! She eat that with so much of *pleasure,* that was *pure* pleasure she did eat that thing. Cause Bolom, you might say a person could never love a pig, you might say that. But you ain't never see Sue eating she watermelon rinds. You sit down and you watch at Sue eating she watermelon rinds, and you could love a pig too. You could love a pig for that.

And that summer was the summer for watermelons. Seem like people was most living pon watermelons that summer, with all the rinds wasting, throwing way. So I just stop by the fruitstand every evening pon my way home and I just collect-up all them rinds they had throwing way. I fill up a big crocusssack full, full to the top, sometimes two big crocusssack I full with them watermelon rinds, and carry home for Sue. And Sue eat every one! Eat to the last one, cause she ain't letting a *one* of them watermelon rinds go to waste. Well in no time at all Sue grow so big she can't fit in she fen no more. She grow *bigger* than the fen now, so I can't keep she in there. I tie she with a rope and I keep she beneath the mango tree behind the house. Cause Sue come tame too, very tame, and she would never run way like that. But then I say, *What now if somebody come in the night to thief she? You know this big pig out in the open, and valuable, and so friendly too, you know they could just hold the rope and walk way with she.* So I decide I going keep Sue in the secret. I find a place in the bush, and near the river so she could get enough water to drink, and I carry Sue tie she up there, keep she there. Sue was my secret. My secret and my insurance.

I was working every day now, to cutlash the canes. Sometimes I get very tired, but I just push on. I drink plenty water, cause you know sometimes the mouth does get so dry. I just carry a big jug with water in the field and I drink, and that water taste better than anything, you working hard like that. I take iron and I take salts, give me strength, and I just push on. I work everyday except Sunday, cause they don't work the fields Sunday. Sunday I sleep. Whole day. I ain't getting up not for nothing. Not even for church service that I did love so much, cause I had to sleep. Granny know I did had to sleep too. She trying she best to keep all them children quiet, but you know she can't keep them quiet. You know that. Them children making so much of noise, and carrying on like that, but I sleep still. Cause I was so tired. Granny rouse them out early, she dress the children carry them long to church whilst

I sleep, that I could sleep. She know next morning I up before day again, cause I got to go in the fields to cutlash the canes.

4

Then crop-season finish. Just like that. We reach in the far corner of the far field, and wasn't no more canes to cut. I stand up and I straighten my back, and I look up in that sky for seem like the first time in four months, longer. And that sky was grey.

Crop-season finish. *Everything* finish, cause overseer say he ain't planting again. Say it don't pay he to plant again. But it was crop-over now, so ain't nobody worrying about that, ain't nobody even *stop* to think about that. Cause it was crop-over now, that big celebration we call crop-over, in Corpus Christi then. All them people drinking and they eating, they firing plenty waters, and making music. They making music and they dancing, in the big dance. But I ain't dancing. I say, *Let them dance what they want, drink they waters. You go home and you sleep.* I just didn't feel to be in that crop-over. I just didn't want to be in there. I did had this presentiment, now the canes finish. Now them canes finish for good. I say, *You just go home and you sleep.* Onliest thing is, I couldn't sleep then. I reach home and find the house empty, not even the babies there, everybody in town celebrating that crop-over. I lie in my bed and I can't sleep. That house was too *quiet.* I ain't accustom to sleeping like that, in that silent. That house like it *dead,* it was so quiet, and I couldn't sleep.

So I say I going and feed Sue. I did bring home a big bag of carrot for she, cause wasn't no watermelons left now to get the rinds, so I take up the carrots and I gone to feed Sue. I could just hear the noise coming from town when I enter the bush, that music in the distant coming from that crop-over. And that music had me feeling so lonely, and sad. I ain't know why. That music just make me to feel sad, and lonely, so I hurrying though the bushes now. I carrying my big bag of carrot and hurrying through the bushes to Sue, my Sue. When I reach the spot, that place where I had she tie, and I look, Sue gone. She ain't there. First I did think maybe I mistake the place, then I look good and I *know* that's the place, that's the tree where she was tie, that's the place

297

where I put soft for she to sleep, but no Sue. *No Sue!* I say, *Maybe she get-way?* I say, *She bound to get-way. Cause you know nobody could thief she like that, hide up here in this bush. They could never find she here.* I drop the bag of carrot, and I run down by the river where I uses to take she to drink, the little stream, and I calling, "Sue! Sue!" I calling and I looking all in the bush, and can't find Sue. She ain't there! She ain't there at all! Now I start like I going mad. Start like I going mad now. You know there was a lot of bramble there by the river, them bramble have plenty thorn. Plenty big thorn, and sharp. But I searching through them bramble still. I just didn't care. I cutting all up pon my legs and my knees, scraping pon them bramble and bleeding, but I didn't care. I like I going mad for true. I say, *Please Lord don't let my Sue lose! Don't let my Sue lose from me!* I calling out, loud, near bawling now, *"S-u-u-u-e! S-u-u-u-e!"* and searching through the bush. Then I realize she was thief. I say, *She must be thief! Cause you know she was tie good. And she would never run way neither, tame as she was. Somebody must be thief she. Somebody that know.*

I hurrying through the bushes again, cause I was heading for town now. And you know that's a *long* walk, all the way to town. That's a good hour in the least, even when you walking brisk. But I walking more than brisk, I near running now. And I counting in my head, all the while. *One carrot, two carrot, three carrot, four carrot.* Till I reach a hundred. Then I start again. I hearing that music louder and louder, and I reach in town in no time. I reach in near half-hour. I didn't know where I was going, I was just *going,* going in a rush. Cause I did had this *feeling.* I pushing through the people, shoving my way, I moving towards that ring where they have the dancing, and music. Then I see, but I can't be sure. There off to the side of that music-ring. But I can't be sure was my Sue. It was a gang of youngboys, sixteen–seventeen years of age, like that, and one them youngboys was my sister boyfriend. Cause I did recognize he, and I see she there too. These youngboys all bareback, and they carrying on a rate, they drinking and they shouting, waving they jersies in the air. They had a big fire roasting, *big* fire, so I pushing closer now that I could see, that I could know. And I did know *straight.* Was my Sue! Roasting pon that fire was my Sue!

I fall down pon the ground pon my knees, right there in the circle, that dance-circle, right there in the dust. You know my knees was all cut-up bleeding from them bramble, but I didn't care. I fall down pon my knees and I cry. Cry like a little child. Them people stand up and they watch at me but I just didn't care. I cry for Sue. Lord how I cry for Sue. I didn't tell them boys nothing, nor my sister. What I could tell them? How they thief my pig out the bush? I didn't have *nothing* that I could tell them, cause they would just laugh at me, them youngboys. I didn't even bother to waste my breath. I just pick up from off the ground, and I gone home. I carry myself home. And Bolom, is now I sleep. I didn't even bother to clean out my knees from them bramble, my legs, and that dust. I just fall in the bed and I sleep. I sleep for three days, straight. Now I don't *want* to wake! Cause I know good enough what I did had to wake up to.

5

Now begin the scourge and blight. The second session. I just look at granny granny look at me. Wasn't nothing to say. We did know wasn't nothing to say. Them few dollars that I had saving from the canes, them dollars finish before the month out. Wash from my hands before the month out. Wasn't no food left now. No more money and no more food. All we could do is scrape by best as we could. And most the time we couldn't even scrape by. I clear a field in the bush and try to plant little something, some beans, cassava. Things that grow fast, but they just can't grow fast enough. Cause you need food for seven people and three babies. That takes a *lot* to feed seven people and three babies. A lot of food. You spend two weeks growing some beans, them beans eat the same night. Just can't grow fast enough. Sometimes I get a job cleaning house for one the white mistress in town, or Granny Ansin, we get a job for couple days, we eat for couple days. Then it's back to that starvation again, near starvation. Them jobs just don't last. Cause you know everybody was living pon them canes, one way or another. Now the canes gone everybody feeling that, rich and poor together. Black and white. Everybody. We might get lucky get a job for couple days, eat for couple days, but then it's back to that starvation again. And you know that's a terrible thing, that's the most terrible thing in this life, you children crying for hunger and you ain't got nothing to give them. Nothing but water. You give them water try to fill up they belly with water. You got a little sugar you could sugar the water, or squeeze an orange. But you know that water ain't nothing, when you belly crying for food. That water same as air, to a hungry belly. Bestest thing when you could catch few cents is buy a sack of rice. That's the cheapest and bestest thing that you could do. Buy a sack of rice and try to ration the rice. Stave off the rice. Long as it could go. Most of the time you ain't got nothing to eat it with you eat it white. White rice and water. Seem like that was the mostest thing we did living pon.

6

Then one day Berry come at the house. I wasn't there, cause I had a day-job I was cleaning one the whitelady house in town. Neither was Granny Ansin there. She went in town looking for work too, leave the children watching with my sister. Cause you know Ansin would never let that man in the house, that Berry. Ansin was always mistrustful for he, from the first, and she was *right* too. But Berry come to the house when I wasn't there, nor Ansin, so he could just walk in like that. And he come with presents. He bring presents for the children. Was a big bag of candy, and he bring this firetruck for Junie to drive. I ain't know where he buy this thing, but could only be the whitepeople store in town, cause poor people don't have toys like that for they children. Poor people could *never* have toys like that for they children. This firetruck had in pedals, that Junie could sit inside and turn the wheels, and it had in steering. This firetruck had in bell to clang, just like real firetruck. But Junie did only reach about three years then, you know she could scarce drive that thing. She could scarce turn the pedals even. Mostest that she could do is clang-out the bell. But doesn't matter, cause them children all gone wild for this truck, they fighting over who is the first to drive and they bawling. They carry the truck out in the yard, cause wasn't no room for that thing in the house. They carry this firetruck in the yard and turning the pedals and pushing and trying to drive. But you know that thing couldn't scarce move in that dirt neither, in that dust. Cause didn't have no pitch-road near the house, nor pavement. Nearest pitch-road about half-mile away, by where the standpipe was. But them children don't care. They pushing in all the dust and they screaming and they clanging-out the bell. They going like they wild.

I reach home before Ansin that afternoon. I reach home from my day-job, so I catch a few cents from that, buy some food from that. First thing I meet is Berry taxicar park in front the house, so I know already to look for trouble. Next I hear this amount of cumbruction going on in the yard, these children, they all screaming and bawling for this firetruck. I take up Junie, say, "What going on here? Where you get this thing from?" Junie answer, cause she was just starting to talk then, say, "Daddy bring for me! *My* firetruck!" and showing-off front the others. I say, "Where daddy is? He in the house?" Junie say, "Yeah! and with candy too!" Well I did vex too bad already. I did *vex* over that truck. I go in the house, find he sitting there at table like he is boss. He drinking he waters, and sitting there with my sister like he is boss. And I know my sister was drinking from he waters too. I say to Berry, "*You!* You can't come in here! Ain't nobody tell you to come in here!" He say, "I come to look to my children." I say, "All these months already you ain't look to these children, now all in a sudden you want look to these children." I say, "And you gone and throw way good money pon that truck. Gone and throw way good money pon that firetruck. These children need *clothes,* they need *food,* they don't need no *blasted* firetruck!" Berry say, "I bring food too," and he nodding he chin at the table was a big tin of tin ham. England tin ham. That ham mark *FANCY.* Mark *SPECIAL.* I say, "And how much of money you throw way pon that? England tin ham! This family could eat a week, probably *two* weeks pon what you pay for that! You ain't know *nothing,* about what it is to keep a family nor nothing!" I say, "You get out from in here! You carry you ham and you blasted truck you get out! Cause we don't need no presents from you!" He say, "What I going do with truck? And this big ham?" I say, "You could give them to you prostitute woman. I don't care *what* you do." But Berry say he ain't got no woman, he living at he father house now. I say, "What happen to the woman? You kill she at last?" He say, "We get a break-up is all." I say, "Well I don't care. I just want you out from my house. You *get* from in here!" But he ain't moving. He just sitting there like that. Just sitting there at table and drinking he waters like that. And my sister sitting there with he, and taking out she breasts to feed the child, but I know she was taking out them breasts for Berry too. I was so vex! I was so vex at them both!

Then granny come home. She was ready to lash-out at he too, I know that, but then granny see that ham, and she eyes just *stick*. She eyes just stick like laglee pon that ham. Granny sit down at table too, but she ain't saying nothing. Just sitting there in the quiet. And you know my granny ain't one to sit quiet. Not long. But she just sitting there quiet like that, next thing I see she crying. She *crying*, big tears, wet pon she face! I say, "Granny? Granny, what *happen?*" She say, "That, that thing is to eat?" Cause poor woman she was so *hungry*. We *all* was hungry! We ain't eat meat in two–three weeks, nor fish neither. And we never eat ham from tin. Not in *this* life. That's one thing for sure. She say, "That thing is to eat?" Berry say, "Yes. It could eat. I bring it that it could eat." Granny smile, she smiling through the tears now, say, "Well best call the children let's we eat! Let's we *eat* pon that!" So granny open the tin and I call the children, and you know them children didn't even want to leave the truck, that firetruck, not even to eat. But I call them and we all sitting there round the table, and waiting. Then when granny go to cut the ham she stop, she hand holding that knife stop poise in the air, and I see she crying again. Tears pon she face wet again. I say, "Granny what? What *happen?*" She say, "I can't, I can't!" I say, "Can't what, Granny?" She say, "I can't *cut*. Cause it too soft. This thing soft like *butter!*"

7

So Berry stay like that. He weasel he way in the house like that. I couldn't say nothing, not then, cause my heart break for granny and that ham. I couldn't tell he nothing. Berry come back the next evening and he bring food again, bring candy for the children again. I still ain't saying nothing to he. He talking but I ain't talking. Cause I still don't *trust* he. He give me too much of trouble to trust he. But he stay and he eat the dinner. Berry come most every evening, bring food most every evening, or give me money to buy food. I didn't want to take it, but you know I *got* to take it. Cause you could go hungry for youself, you could *choose* that, if you got the strength. But Bolom, you can't let the children go hungry. Man putting money in you hand you got to take it. Take it for the children. And he was treating them children good, I got to say that. He was treating them children very good, bring them toys, and candy, you know they getting to like he good too. All the children, not just Junie and Joyce. Granny, she come to like he just the same. That was the strangest thing to me, cause granny did never like that man. Granny was always mistrustful for he. But that Berry is a charmer, that's one thing for sure. He had he soft stripe, and when he play pon that, when he let that soft stripe show, he could most charm the rattles off a snake. That man.

Cause soon enough he had me charm again too. He had me falling for he again too. Soon enough. We go back to we old habit of going in he taxicar. You know, after we eat the dinner and I put the children to sleep and everything, he say, "Let's we go for drive. Drive in the canes." I say, "You know it ain't no canes left. You know that already. How we could drive in the canes and ain't no more canes?" He say, "We could drive in the bush then." I say, "Bush ain't the same. Bush ain't the same as canes." But you know we go for the drive still, drive in the bush. He park the car out the lights, we do little something in the backseat. After couple nights we go for drive again, Berry park the car and we find someplace soft in them bushes to lie. But I don't like that. Not so much. Cause that did put me in mind of them canes, and I did miss the canes. I say, "Let's we just stay in the car. We could stay in the backseat of you taxicar." So we get back to we old habit of going in he taxicar, that big old taxicar. Most every night now.

Then one time after we park, after we get through, you know we did sitting there in he taxicar park in the bush, he done out the lights and we get through, now we sitting there we relaxing. Berry start to telling me about this new housing project government did had in promotion then. Cause that was all the talk then, at that time. Was a big block of compartment houses government build, and offering to poor people to buy cheap. *Buy,* not rent. You paying the money like rent but you buying. They offering these houses to poor people with family. Government call it the Family Plannings, that promotion. And these compartment houses build from *concrete.* No board-house now, and they had in upstairs and down. These government houses had in electricity, and they had in pipes. These houses had in most *every*thing, everything except toilet. Toilet in the yard, public toilet, but you know that toilet flush with water.

I tell Berry, "*Pipes!* Pipes in the house! Only house I ever see with pipes is the whitepeople own." He say, "Yes man, pipes. We could live with pipes." I say, "And you ain't got to pay extra for that?" He say, "No. Long as you could fit the category. You ain't got to pay nothing extra." He say, "But we got to make the application *quick,* cause most of them house done grab-up already." I say, "What category? What you mean *category?*" He say, "Well you got to have one or more child, and you got to married." I say, "You got to married! You got to *married* to fit in the category!" I say, "Well we ain't fitting in no category. We ain't getting no concrete house and we ain't getting no pipes. Cause I ain't *never* going married with you! I been through too much hell already to married with you!" So we ain't discurting nothing more about them concrete government houses. That finish with that. He did know my mind was make up, and I was stubborn too. Must be three–four weeks we ain't say nothing more about them houses, neither him nor me.

8

At that time we had a big storm in the country. *Big* storm. Wasn't a hurricane, but was a big storm, and that storm last five days. Darkness for five days. Thunder. Wind cutting. Rain pelting for five days straight, and that rain pelting *hard*. We just couldn't stay dry, cause that roof had so much of holes. That galvanize so rusty and so rotten, and them walls. You know everything wet, soak down, wet right through. We keep changing the children clothes, but you know we ain't got clothes enough to change. You put a fresh jersey pon the child that jersey more wet than the one you taking out. Onliest thing that you could do is take out the jersey and wring it good, best as you can, put it back pon the child damp again. Cause you could hold a jersey or underpants with a stick over the fire, but you ain't got *time* to dry all the children clothes like that. And them children clothes get so *smoky*. After a time you just leave them wet. Everything wet. Clothes wet, bed wet, food wet. I could tell you living in that house was like living under the sea.

First four days we had food enough. Well not *enough,* but we had food anyway. Cause when that storm start we had a big bag of potatoes, most a sack of rice, some vegetables, and evening before that storm Berry bring a big piece of bacon, bag of eggs. Cause you know Berry could never come to we during that storm, not with that road wash like that. He could never pass in that road. But we had food enough the first four days. If we could of only think to cook it when we had the chance. If we could only *think* of that! But Bolom, you know when you in the middle of a storm you don't think like that. You don't say, *Well we best cook all the food before the fire finish, cause this rain ain't stopping for five days.* You don't say that at all. Onliest thing you say is, *Well that rain going stop just now and sun going shine and you could dry youself. You could be warm again.* That's the onliest thing you does say. Cause time as I tell Granny, "Ansin, we best cook all the food *now,* before the fire lose," time as I tell Ansin that, that fire near finish already. That was the morning of the third day, best as we could tell what was day and what night. Cause all was dark, pitch dark, in that storm. Bolom, when I look at that fire and I see it outing, see it smoldering that white sad smoke, and hurrying quick to poke a flame back but wouldn't come back, cause that fire *finish* now. Bolom, when I see that, I near cry! We eat the rice, rice that I cook pon the last of that fire, then we had to eat raw potatoes and raw peas. We live pon that for two days. Then we finish the potatoes and the peas. That was the end of the fourth day. Then we didn't have nothing, neither fire nor food. After the fourth day.

Them poor children! They so frighten, every time the lightning crack. Junie say, "Mummy, I want my firetruck! Cause this old house going wash way soon leave it right there in the yard!" I say, "Bestest thing could happen to we is lose that firetruck. Bestest thing! But we ain't going lose it. Cause this old house here longer than you and me, it could last out this little rain." But them children smarter than that. They know we was frighten too. Them poor children, they go through so much of suffering in that storm. That was the hardest thing, to sit and watch at them children suffer. They shaking from the cold, and teeth chapping, and you only got a wet blanket to wrap them in, wet towel. They dribbling from they nose, they coughing and sneezing. You know they want to run round the house and can't run, cause ain't no room in that house. Onliest thing you could do is hug them tight and try to keep them warm. We *all* hug tight.

We hug tight in a circle, sitting together in the middle the floor. We had a piece of clear plastic that we could hold over we heads, sitting there in the circle, and we sing. And that did sound *echoey* too, under that plastic. Sound *brass.* Like when you talk with you ears plug, sing with you ears plug. But we sing the louder still! We hug together and we *sing!* Every song that we could think, remember. School songs and church songs. Spiritual songs. Work songs and calypso songs. American songs off the radio. Every song that we could remember. And Ansin did know plenty songs, church songs, all the hymns. She was in the choir at church, so she could know plenty songs. She could sing pretty too, very pretty. Granny teach we the songs and we sing. We sing till we throat hurt, and we head was hurting too, from trying to remember more songs. And you know sometimes we would all go silent cause nobody can't think of no new songs, we go silent and after a time one them children start to cry, Joyce crying again, two children crying now. Then somebody think up a new song and they burst out. A good one. Like when Granny come out in, *Oh when the saints come a-marching!* And we been singing already two days and nobody think of that one! We could never *believe* it, that we could forget that one! We hugging tight tight and we singing, *loud,* we singing all together, "*Oh when the saints, come marching in! Oh when the saints come a-marching in!*" We must be sing that five different times. We near *scream* for that.

9

Then sun come out. That was midday on the fifth day. Rain stop and sun come out. Just like that. You stand and look up at that sun like you seeing sun for the first time. And you heart jump for that, that sun! So all the children gone out running in the sun, they playing in the sun. The yard was all mud, but they gone running still cause they was so tired from being closed-up in the house so long. Five days. I tell them to go look in the bush for wood, dry wood, look under the leaves that they might find some dry wood. But you know they gone looking for food, cause was plenty fruit pon the ground after that storm, and coconuts. I was just waiting for the sun to dry the road little bit, that I could go at the store and buy some food to cook. I was thinking to buy some macaronies and cheese. Cause them children love that, and me too! I was thinking of them macaronies and cheese, and I was so *hungry.* And I know Berry would come the next morning too. By next morning that road would be clear and Berry would come with more food. So I wasn't worried, I wasn't worried for nothing. I look up at that sun and I wasn't worried not for nothing.

I was out in the yard trying to collect some dry wood, that I could start that fire going again. Ansin was doing the same thing, so wasn't nobody in the house but Joyce, little Joyce. I leave she there to play by sheself. So I come in the house with my arms full with this wood, I see Joyce playing in the corner. She did start to taking she first few steps then. You know, hold the wall and take a step, couple steps. But mostly she was crawling, crawling pon she hands and knees about the place. So I scarce pay she any mind, I going with my wood and I see she pon she hands and knees playing in the corner. I scarce even notice she. But then I see she was playing with *something*. She playing with something there in the corner. Bolom, when I look good and I *see*, what she did playing with, I just *freeze*. I stop dead still, standing there holding my arms full with this wood. Cause just there in front Joyce pon the floor, just by the tip of she little fingers, was the biggest scorpion I ever see. *Big* scorpion! And *black!* I never see scorpion big so in my life. That thing long as a grown person thumb, and most as fat. And so *ugly!* So big and so ugly! He with he tail holding above he head ready to strike. I just stand there frozen, cause I know the slightest movement and that scorpion would strike. I must be stand there a full minute, frozen like that, before I dare call out. I call soft as I could, like a whisper, "*Joyce! Joyce!*" But she don't move. Like she don't *hear* me calling. Just remain there studying this scorpion, with she hand reaching out to touch. I call again, quiet as I could, "*Joyce! Joyce!*" But still she don't move. Another long minute. Then all in a sudden she head turn, turn to look to me, a jerk of she head, and that scorpion strike.

I drop the wood same time I running. I grab up Joyce in my arms, and she screaming now. She *screaming*, for that pain, and I hug she tight to my breast, I watching at that scorpion disappearing in a crack between the floorboards. Disappearing *slow*, cause he so big and so fat he couldn't even *move* fast! He head disappear first between the boards and then he thick black tail like a plat of hair curling round under and he gone. So big and so ugly!

I got to think quick, what I could do for this child. She screaming, but I don't stop to quiet she. I run in the kitchen I take up the knife, the short sharp paring knife, and I put Joyce pon the table and I hold she finger that I could make the cut. I make a short quick slice in she middle finger where she get the sting, I squeeze to draw blood from that finger and I suck the blood, spit the blood. I suck that little finger two–three minutes, and spitting so much blood pon the ground, trying to suck the poison. Joyce screaming so loud and she crying, but I don't worry about that. I just trying to suck the poison. I know I got to get to that poison *quick*.

Then granny come in. She say, "You got to give this child the medicine! Got to give she quick!" That was a thing from granny time, old-time thing, they call that the *medicine*. It was a big bottle with spirits, bush–rum, the babash rum, and they throw in every kind of varmint in that. Coral snake and mappapee, scorpion and centipede, tarantula and black widow spider. Every kind of creature with venom they throwing in, and they leaving it to soak years at a stretch, that medicine. So when you get sting from anything, or snake-bite, you just drink from the bottle. And we had one. I ain't even remember that thing, sitting there above the cupboard. I say to Ansin, "You know that ain't nothing, that old-time thing." I say, "This child need the injection, the *anti,* I got to get this child to the hospital *quick!*"

But Ansin ain't listening. She reaching for she medicine, say, "*Injection!* I never hear of no *injection!*" She say, "You can't go in no hospital anyway. Cause that road *wash.* You can't go *nowhere.*" Granny ain't listening and I ain't listening. My sweet Jesus! Ansin pouring this medicine down Joyce throat, intending, but Joyce only screaming and coughing up this thing, this nasty thing, spitting up and trying to breathe and coughing, and I only trying to pull way Joyce out granny hands. Joyce screaming and granny screaming and I screaming. Joyce fighting and granny fighting and I fighting. But granny get a good dose of that medicine down Joyce throat. I ain't know how but she do it, but before I could pull the child from out granny hands, she did get a good dose down. I pull way Joyce and I take off. I hug that sweet baby to my breast and I gone. *Gone.*

But I couldn't go nowhere. Cause I couldn't make no *distance* in that road. Just like granny say, it *wash.* That road hardly a road even. *Mud!* Mud high as you *knees* in spots. You got to wade that. And trees. Felled trees all in the road you got to climb over, from that storm. And so *slippery!* You slipping and you sliding every which way. I fall down in the mud get soak, my whole dress, and Joyce, we both soak in mud, cake in mud. Just couldn't make no distance. But I push on. I hug Joyce to my breast and she crying, she don't stop from crying. I hug she tight and I push on.

I was just trying to reach crossroads. Reach Berry house. I did think if I could just reach at he house, then Berry could take Joyce to the hospital in he car. If I could just reach crossroads! You know that's a twenty-minute walk when the road ain't wash. Twenty minutes is the most, half-hour, but I was walking a full hour and I ain't reach crossroads. In that mud. I hold Joyce tight and I say, *Lord, just let we reach the house! Just let we reach the house for this child!* She ain't crying no more, not all the time. Just let out a sob every, about every five–six of my steps. Then I start to feel like she hot, with fever, *hot.* This child did *burning!* With that fever. Now I was more frighten. I say, *Crossroads!* I say, *Berry house!* I say it again and again.

When I reach the house the car ain't there, Berry taxicar. He car ain't there and Berry father bus ain't park in front neither. *Nobody* there! That house was lock-up tight, all the doors and all the windows. Lock-up tight. I say, *Lord Jesus what I could do? What I could do now?* Onliest thing is walk. Keep walking. But that road was better now so I could make some distance. I could push on. My dress did soak, heavy with that mud. I raise up and I tuck in, at my waist, that my legs could walk free. And I *walk.*

Then we reach the hospital. Last we reach the hospital. I see the hospital approaching in the distant and my heart jump. My heart jump in my breast, and I burst in tears. I look down in my arms, I say, "*Joyce! We reach! Joyce!*"

But Joyce did cold. She did cold then. I could feel Joyce did cold then. In my arms.

10

That was the hardest thing I ever do. That long walk back home with this child in my arms. That was the hardest burden I ever did bear. This little child.

Wasn't before next afternoon that Berry reach at the house, come in he taxicar, and he was two hours driving in the road to do that. He bring food but I ain't eating no food. I ain't hungry for no food. I send he back again. Back for the box. Send Berry to the carpenter that he could make the box.

So granny and me dress up Joyce in she long white-dress, and we bury she that evening. Just as evening fall. We bury Joyce next to my first child, there behind the house by the mango tree, my first little boy-child. When Berry come back to the house, cause we did leave he there to finish-off. He come back to the house and find me sitting there pon the front stoop. Berry lean the shovel against the house and he sit down by my side. We sitting there in the quiet. We watching at the last of that bright sun. A long time. Last I speak. I say, "Make the application. Make the application for that government house, cause we going fit in the category."

In the Family Plannings

1

Berry say he want church-wedding. Say he want the works. Hat and gloves and everything. I say, "*Gloves!* Man, we ain't got money for no wedding with gloves. Nor we ain't got time neither. Cause you know all them houses going give way just now, if they ain't give way already." I say, "Let's just go before the Magis, that he could pronounce pon we and write-up and finish." Cause Berry and me had to married before we could apply for one them houses government was offering in the Family Plannings. We did had to married before we could fit in the category. But truth is, I didn't *feel* for no style-up wedding. Not with little Joyce just dead and everything, and me still grieving so much. I *couldn't* be in no style-up wedding. I say, "Let's just go before the Magis and finish." So Berry bring he friend Lewey that he could stand as witness, and Magis pronounce the marriage pon we. Quick so. Magis write-up certificate and he write-up birthpapers for Junie same time, cause we did need them papers to make the application too. That same afternoon we went at the Health Ministry, we make the application and we get through. We get the house.

Bolom, I was so relieve for that, I hug the little oldman they had working behind the counter. Little brown-skin oldman, and round like an egg. I reach cross the counter hug he almost knock he eyeglasses pon the floor. The oldman laugh, say, "Madam, if I had beard you would take me for Father Christmas. A brown Father Christmas." I say, "Sir, you the nearest thing to Father Christmas I ever had in my life. You Father Christmas to me!" Cause we was the last to get through, in that plannings, the very last. You know all them houses done grab-up already. All but one. They had the big map pon the wall of this Family Plannings, and the oldman stand pon a chair and he X-off the last compartment that was number fifteen, and we make the first payment that was seventeen dollars. Bolom, that was the happiest I ever feel to pay-out money. I near bounce when Berry hand over that. I tell he, "Let's we move in right now. Tonight-self! Let's we go for Junie move in in the house!" Berry say, "We ain't got beds for we. How we could move in the house and ain't got no beds for we?" I say, "Man, put a blanket. Blanket pon the floor." I say, "I don't even need no blanket. Cause I want feel that concrete against my skin. I want feel that!" I say, "We going sleep pon that concrete floor tonight!" So we gone in Berry taxi-car in the country, we collect up Junie and what few things we had, we move in in the plannings.

That compartment house did seem so *big,* for just two people and one child to live in. That house near big as granny own, with all them people and children and babies living together. You know it had the two floors, upstairs and down. Upstairs had the bedrooms, little one for Junie and big one for Berry and me, with living to down, kitchen to down. We didn't have no furnitures yet, so that house did seem more bigger still. Neither we didn't have no bulbs for the fixtures, them socket-fixtures hanging from the ceiling in every room, so I search through we things till I find a candle. I light the candle that we could see by. I take one Junie hands and Berry take the next, we walking room to room. Junie swinging from we arms and she jumping up in the air, she bawling, "*H-o-o-o! H-o-o-o!*" She bawling that she could hear the echoes off them hard walls. She say, "Mummy, this house is a manchant! We living in a manchant now, a *spook* manchant!" I say,

"Whoever hear of spooks living in concrete house? Whoever *hear* of that?" We just walking room to room with we eyes bug-out. We eyes bug-out like three toads in a bucket, we climbing them stairs.

Everything did paint in white. Everything except the floors, cause them floors was raw concrete, but everything else was paint in white. That paint did *smell* fresh too. Them walls did seem so *clean.* They so clean I was fraid to touch them, fraid to dirty them up. But you know I *had* to touch them. *Every* one. I had to feel the hardness, feel the coolness, knock to hear the sound of them walls, smell the paint! But Bolom, the bestest thing of that house was the pipe. That pipe in the kitchen, with sink below. I just couldn't left that thing alone, just couldn't left from opening to watch the water come. I must be open that pipe a dozen time. And every time that water come did give me so much of *pleasure.* Cause that ain't no ordinary pipe you opening, that ain't no standpipe away up in the bush you carry you bucket half a mile to get to. That's *you* pipe in *you* kitchen you opening, and you could cook you could wash clothes you could bathe youself, *everything* you could do with that pipe, and it right there in you own kitchen. Well Berry stand up and he watch at me like he watching a loon, loony-person, he say, "Girl, would never believe is water that pipe putting out, amount of times you turning. Would think that rusty water was coke-cola!"

That night we spread a blanket pon the floor in the living to sleep. Put Junie between Berry and me and sleep right there in the living. But I was too excited to sleep. I couldn't sleep then. I hug Junie and I close my eyes but I couldn't sleep. But the main reason I couldn't sleep was that I did start to hearing this noise. Hear this funny noise, *shrew-honk,* like that, about every minute, every couple minutes. Just when I start to drop asleep, I hear it again. Sometimes it repeat a few times, *shrew-honk, shrew-honk, shrew-honk,* then quiet awhile. That noise like it coming from the other side of we livingroom wall. I say, *How come we didn't hearing that before? How come this noise sounding all of a sudden so?* I whisper, "Berry, man, what's that? That noise?" He listen awhile and noise come again, *shrew-honk,* and that wall did even shake little bit this time. I say, "*That,* what's that?" He say, "Maybe that's people opening they kitchen pipes. Them other compartments. Cause when you open the pipe a noise does come, something like that." I say, "But so *much?* How them people could be opening they pipes so much as that?"

Berry say, he raise up he head and he look down pon me, he say, "Woman, you going ask me that? After you stand there and opening that pipe most the whole night, you going ask me that?" So I wasn't saying nothing more about that noise. Just close my eyes and think about that cool concrete beneath my cheek. I try to sleep.

2

But Bolom, next morning I wake, I feeling my cheek *cold. Cold cold.* And damp. I feeling like my cheek wet. I lying there with my eyes close still, I say, *Well you never sleep pon concrete floor before, maybe that's just how it is? Maybe concrete does sweat cold like that pon a morning?* Then I open my eyes and I see. My face was soaking in a puddle of water. That whole *floor* flood with water. But not by the window, on the other side the room. Big puddle by the other wall and reaching all the way to where we was sleeping, all the way to where *I* was sleeping, cause I was sleeping pon that side. I jump up. I say, *What the hell going on here? We had rain last night? I ain't remember no rain last night?* I look out the window and that little piece of dirt front the house was dry, stone dry. I say, *This very strange. That we ain't had no rain last night and this floor flood. This very strange.* I did think maybe that water come from the kitchen, maybe that pipe burst, or maybe I ain't shut it down good. But I check the kitchen and wasn't no water. That pipe did ok. So I quick spread some towels and sheets pon the floor to soak up, and I leave Berry and Junie there sleeping whilst I go find out where all this water coming from.

I had to pass round the whole building to get to the back of we compartment, cause we own was the one at the end and flush up against the fencing, snagwire fencing. I pass round the whole building, all the way to where we compartment was on the other side, back of we compartment. Now I confront this lineup of people. Big lineup of people. Fifteen–twenty people. I say, *What these people waiting for so early in the morning? What they waiting for, and ain't even full day yet?* Was mostly women and children, but I see couple oldmen in that lineup too. They all waiting before a door mark WC. So I ask a woman, I say, "What that does mean, WC?" Well she laugh, she say, "WC? You don't know that means *White Colonial?*" I did embarrass now, I say, "But what you *mean* by that?" She say, "Child, you look in any one them toilets, and you would know *just* what I mean."

Bolom, now I realize where all that *shrew-honking* did coming from. That come from the toilets flushing, every time they pull the chain. Now I realize where that water did come from too. Cause this WC was nothing more than a big long room full with toilets, toiletstalls going end to end, whole length of the back wall. I did count five. *Five* toilet-stalls! More toilets than I ever see in one place in my life. Even the courthouse in town only had two, one for mens and one womens. And Bolom, this WC did smell so *harsh*. This WC did *well* disgusting. Cause you know half them toilets stop-up. They stop-up and flooding over, paper and garbage all about, with good two–three *inches* of water pon that floor soaking. Nasty *toilet* water. That water collect-up and soak right through the wall. We *livingroom* wall!

I take off running back to we compartment. I grab up Junie off the floor and I say to Berry, "Man, get up! get up *quick! We* sleeping in toilet water!" Berry sit up and rubbing he eyes, say, "Woman, what you?" I say, "See this water?" and I nod my chin at the towels soaking. "This water is *toilet* water! Nasty toilet water! We sleep in toilet water last night!" He say, "What foolishness you talking now? How toilet water could be in here and we ain't got no toilet in here?" I say, "You go and you see for youself. Other side this wall is the WC. This water come from the toilets! Soak right through from the toilets on the other side!" I say, "We got to change we compartment. We can't be living in here like this, toilet water soaking through the wall. We got to go at the Health change we compartment *right now,* first thing!" Well Berry still didn't understand what I saying. He shaking he head at me like I's a loon again. But Berry dress heself and he go round the building and he *see,* and he did know I wasn't no loon.

So I dress Junie and we gone back at the Health Ministry again. Berry tell the little oldman we compartment flood with toilet water. Say he got to change we compartment for we. Well that oldman try he best to smile up at Berry, he try he best, but that little oldman was scared. He tell Berry ain't no compartments left to change. Say we own was the last to give-way. So Berry vex now, he *vex,* and Berry is a man you got to be watchful when he vex like that. Big tall man like he. So tall and so strong. This poor little oldman! Cause Berry take one skip

315

and he skip right to the other side the counter. Just like that! You know he so big and so tall, he could just skip over that counter like that. Berry look down pon he now, say, "You could change we compartment for we, or you could *eat* them eyeglasses you wearing." But the oldman only shaking he head, say, "No, sir! Ain't nothing I could do, sir! No, sir!" Now I speak up, I say, "Well you could give we back we seventeen dollars then!" Cause we could rent a *good* house for that seventeen dollars. Might not be concrete, but wouldn't have no toilet water flooding through. I say, "You could give we back we seventeen dollars then!" Now the oldman look to me, and I know he was relieve to look way from Berry face, he glasses fog and everything. He say, "No, madam. That money in the PM purse already. How I could give it back and it in the PM purse already?" Poor little oldman. I know he was telling the truth, and I did like he too. Now I frighten for what Berry going do he. I frighten for he and Berry both, cause this oldman is *government* people. I say, "Berry, man, let's just we go home. Cause you know he can't do nothing." But Berry ain't listening. He ain't going satisfy till he mash-up this little oldman. Ain't nothing Berry love more than beating, and this beating going be the finish of he now. I say, "Well I ain't standing here to watch at you put youself in more trouble again. Cause that's government property you handling. You touch this oldman and they going *ruin* you, ruin *all* we!" I say, "If you love this little girl then you could left he alone. You could do it for she!" And with that I carry Junie outside to wait in the car, and wasn't too long before Berry come, thank the Lord Berry come. I didn't telling he nothing, cause I know better than try to reason with he when he vex. Just let he go for he bottle drink it down, and by next morning he would forget the whole thing. Cause that's just the way with he. But I know good enough that even with that water pon the floor, even with that nasty toilet water washing through the place every morning, I know that compartment house was still far better than any house I ever live in my life, and I was grateful for that. I thank the Lord for that.

3

Bolom, I buy a mop, and I just get used to mopping out the floor. First thing every morning. I buy a five-pound sack of lye, that bright yellow thing, and I sprinkle the lye. Kill the smell like that, and kill the germs. Cause you got a little girl running round the house, and playing pon that floor, you got to kill the germs. You can't just mop up. I tell you some mornings that water did smell so *harsh,* so *nasty.* I just open the front door and the window that air could pass, I mop out and I sprinkle the lye. First thing every morning before Berry wake, and every evening before I start to cook the dinner, before Berry come home. Cause I can't let Berry remember that water soaking. I can't let he to contemplate that, or he going vex again. He going run the rampage again, and *I* ain't want to be in the house he running he rampage like that. Bolom, I just get used to mopping out the water, every morning and every evening, and after a time I don't even notice. I forget about that. After a time we all forget.

We forget about that, and we start to fix up we compartment house. Berry gone and he buy the furnitures, and you know he got to buy everything one time. He ain't waiting not for nothing, cause everything got to buy one time. Buy on credit. Was a couch and table and two lounging-chairs for the living, table and chairs for the kitchen, and he buy the stove. But this one was Westinghouse electric *hotplate* stove, one big plate and two small, and them plates hot so *quick.* Them plates so quick I near scorch up the food first couple times I cook. But Bolom, the bestest thing Berry buy was the bed. Two beds, cause Berry buy a little one for Junie too. Junie did reach to four years now, so she can't be sleeping in she little cradle-bed no more. She did need to have a proper bed for she. But the bestest thing Berry buy was the bed for me and him, cause this one was *foam* bed. Not fiber, cause in Corpus Christi at that time all the poor people beds was fiber beds, coconut fiber, and them beds so hard and so prickly. Last *long,* them beds could last a long time cause they fiber, like Junie little bed, but they hard and they prickly. Not foam! That foam so soft, so restful. That foam like it make from *air.* And that bed Berry buy was so *big.* Big bed, cause that man don't like nothing small, everything got to be big. That foam mattress so big we couldn't scarce get it up the stairs. We had to fold it in halves, but Bolom, that mattress like it did *living.* That mattress like it did want to *battle* we. How anything so light and so soft could be so *brute* I could never say, but that thing did want to battle we. We fold it one way it fold back the next way. We roll it one end it roll out the next end. Well we *laugh,* Berry and me. We laugh so much for that! We had to *wrestle* that foam mattress up the stairs. We had to *pounce* pon it to get it through the door. We just lie there pon that mattress, and sweating, and we laughing too. We trying to catch we breath but we laughing still. I say, "Man, you best behave youself this time, cause we ain't *never* getting this mattress out from in here. We would have to get gun and shoot it first!" Berry say, "Don't you worry about that. Cause I's a married man now, I *got* to behave. My name done *write.*" He say, "Why I going in some other bed when I got this big *foam* bed to lie in?" I say, "It ain't the bed it's who does hot the sheets." He say, "Well best bring them sheets let we hot them up right now."

4

But Berry don't behave. That good don't last long, don't last no time at all. Berry go straight back to bad again. That's why I did never want to married, why I did never *trust* to married. Cause Berry use that marriage licent as excuse. He use that licent as excuse to do just how he please, to keep me there in the house whilst he gone with other womens, gone running behind other womens. He must be say, *Well you married now so you could have youself a woman on the side. Man ain't married proper till he got he woman on the side.*

Berry come home every night, most every night, but I know he was going with other womens too. Not like before, when he come home with waters pon he head and want start discurting with me, want put lash pon me. Not like before, when he come home with he head wash and want beat me. Now Berry ain't saying nothing. Like he ain't *got* to say nothing, or tell me he out driving the taxi. Cause he was driving extra hours now, driving all the time, now that we had that house and them furnitures to pay. But not till five–six in the morning. Ain't nobody does hail cab five–six in the morning, not in *Henly.* I know Berry was running behind other womens, cause that's the *meaning* of married in this place. I couldn't say how many, but I get to find out about at least one. Was that same woman Berry was living with, same woman he beat up, send in hospital. I get to find out Berry was going with she again, but I only get to find out that *later,* when the woman

318

went in childbed to bear she baby. But that woman wasn't the only one. I sure about that.

Still, Berry come home most every night, and most nights he would give me couple dollars too. Couple dollars for them envelopes. Cause we had the two envelopes, one mark *H* and next mark *F*. I keep adding to them envelopes till we reach to seventeen dollars for the house and thirteen dollars for the furnitures. Then I seal them down. Wait for the end of the month to pay them out. Cause you know that's the onliest way. That's the onliest way we could make them payments. You know ain't no money standing in *that* man pocket. Berry got a dollar in he pocket he spending the dollar, same time, and he did know good enough too. Berry just give me the money and I collect it up, dollars and coins. I collect up in them envelopes till we make the rates, then I seal them down. Onliest thing is, them envelopes could hardly ever *seal* before the month out.

So I get a day-job too. I go at Mistress Pantin house and I clean and I cook. Mistress Pantin was some kind of relation to me, not too close, cause she skin bright and she had money too. She husband had money. He working for government. I go at Mistress Pantin and I let Junie run round whilst I clean. Mistress Pantin say she don't mind that, say she ain't got no children, and that does make she heart glad to see little Junie running round the place. Sometimes Mistress Pantin did even take Junie to the parlour-store buy icecream for she, or snowball, she carry Junie for walk in town whilst I work. She was very good to both we, that Mistress Pantin. So I was catching little few cents from my day-job, and I give some of that money to granny too, long as we make sufficient to pay-out the house and the furnitures. I give some of my day-money to Granny Ansin, cause you know she had all them children to feed and clothe and everything.

I clean at Mistress Pantin, then when I finish I carry Junie home feed she and put she to sleep. Then I cook the dinner for Berry and me. I cook the dinner and I put it aside, cause you know Berry reaching home a different hour every night. I put the dinner aside, and I heat it back when he come. We eat the dinner together, then we go upstairs in the big bed. Cause we ain't going in the backseat of he taxicar no more, not when he driving that car all day, and not when we got the big foam bed to lie in. I didn't want to go in that backseat no more anyway, not when he carrying he other womens in there. I say, *Left that for them. Give me the bed and left that backseat for them.* Sometimes Berry don't come home at all, and I just eat the dinner cold. I eat it cold, and I put the rest away. I climb the stairs and I sleep in the little bed with Junie. Cause I ain't sleeping in that big bed by myself. I did feel *lost* in that big bed by myself. I sleep in the little bed with Junie.

5

Then I find myself pregnant again. Was only a few months after we move in the plannings, and I find myself pregnant again. I was so distress for that, I did want to throw this child. I think about little Joyce and my first boychild that dead, dead so young, and I didn't want no more children. Not to go through that again, watch this child dead pon my hands again. I decide to throw it, try to throw it, cause I did hear about all kind of ways womens does do that. Cause these doctors didn't doing abortions then, not in Henly, not at that time. But these womens had plenty ways to do that. I say, *Lord, why you give me the children only to take them back again? Why you do like that?* I say, *If you want this one then take me first. Or let me give you this child now, before it born, cause I ain't never want to live through that again! I ain't never want to hold a dead baby in these arms again!* I think about Joyce and my first boychild, and I did feel so bad, so distress.

But Berry don't distress. Berry near *bounce* to hear that. He say, *"Ma-doo!"* He say, *"Pam-pa-lam-pa-lam!"* Berry say, "That's what we be *need-ing* in this house is a new popo. Cause this house too big for we three to rambling rose in here." He say, "And make this one a manchild for me. I need a *son* for me!" Berry was so happy, he did get me most to feeling good too. Cause in truth we had room and money enough, at that time. We could have a next child. And now that we had a proper house to live in, now that we ain't living in no little rotten old-shack, roof ready to drop pon we heads and scorpions running under the floorboards, now that we did have a good solid *concrete* house to live in, ain't nothing could happen to this child. This child could never dead, not like them others. Not like before. I tell Berry, "Alright. Alright then. We could have a next child. But I can't promise this child

320

could be a boy, cause the only one could say that is the one that knows." And I say, *Yes Lord, give me the child. I would bear the child. And make this one a boychild for Berry sake.* I say, *Please Lord give Berry a son for he!*

I did think that if Berry could have a son things might go back to good, we might go back to meeting life good. Cause that's the bestest thing to keep a man in the house, give he a son, the bestest thing. Cause you know girlchild ain't nothing, according to the way mens in this place think, and most the womens too. For these people girlchild ain't nothing. Girlchild the same as nothing. *Boychild* now, that's something special. I beg the Lord for boychild for Berry.

But Bolom, I could never know what I did asking for when I beg for that. I could *never* know. Cause Berry was *already* preparing to have a child for heself then. Another child, at that same moment. But I only get to find out that later, that was after *I* did pregnant already a good five–six months. Berry wasn't out driving he taxicar that afternoon, he was home in bed sick with measles. Very sick, with them measles that was passing round the place then. He in bed burning this hot fever. I was downstairs in the kitchen feeding Junie the dinner, just reach from Mistress Pantin and feeding Junie. I hear this car outside, hear this car tipping tipping pon the horn and don't stop. So I take up Junie and I rush outside, and I couldn't even move good to carry Junie and my belly already big with child too.

I rush outside, I see Lewey sitting there in he motorcar, engine still running. I say, "Lewey, man, what you tipping like that for? Why you don't come in in the house like you accustom?" Lewey say, "Want talk to Berry." I say, "Well you know he upstairs and carrying them measles. You know he can't come down." I say, "Why you don't go up talk to he like you accustom?" Lewey say, "Want talk to he private." I say, "Is business? Berry got money for you? He owing you money?" Lewey say, "Is business, but ain't money. Just tell he want talk to he private." So I say, *Well Lewey behaving very strange tonight. He behaving heself very strange tonight, but if it ain't money then can't be nothing too bad.* So I take up Junie again, I go upstairs and tell Berry Lewey want talk to he private. Berry throw on he shirt and he gone down, and he was looking so bad with them measles, fever burning a heat. Next I hear Lewey take off, he wheels spinning in the dirt. So I waiting now for Berry to come back, but Berry don't come back. I look out the window and no Berry there. He done take off in the car with Lewey.

When Berry reach back was near morning, and if he did look bad when he leave then he look the worse now. He look drain. Look *pink* now. Cause you know Berry was a red negro, he was a red black man, but he turn to pink now. He go from red to pink. Berry just drop he shirt pon the floor, he drop in the bed and he out. Just like that. He sleeping and not saying nothing, about where he went with Lewey nor nothing. But then next morning when I pick up he shirt I see this paper in the pocket. See this paper that Berry did give blood, give blood in the hospital. I say, *How he could give blood and he sick with measles? How he could give blood with measles inside?*

So when Berry wake I ask he, I say, "You give blood in the hospital last night? How you could do that? Give blood and you so sick with them measles?" Berry say, "Woman with child and want blood, I got to give she the blood. What I could do? Stand and watch she dead and baby dead same time? I got to give she the blood." I say, "Woman? What woman? What woman you talking about?" He say, "She. You know, that woman I was going with." I say, and now I getting excited. I getting excited and vex both, same time. I say, "Mean you gone and put you blood inside that woman? That same woman that you was living with?" I say, "That means you still care for she. Means that you still care for she, you to take out you blood and put inside she and you so sick!" I say, "It's *you* could have dead-up youself like that, never mind that woman and she child!"

Well Berry don't answer me nothing to that. Just lie there in the bed quiet, he head prop against the wall. But Bolom, then I start to thinking something else, and I not liking this thing at all. I say, "Well maybe that's *you* child she bearing? Maybe she pregnant for *you?*" Berry say, "Doctor people say so. *She* tell the doctor people so." I say, "Well if doctor people say so then got to be true. Cause they would never take out blood from you with measles inside less it's true. They would *never* do that!" Berry say, "You know that woman is prostitute. You know that baby could be anybody. She just trying to pin it pon me, but that baby is *prostitute* baby. He ain't got no father." I say, "Who you calling prostitute?" I say, "You the prostitute good as she! That baby is *you* prostitute baby good as she!" Berry say, "Listen woman, I ain't too sick to cuff you in you mouth. So you could just shut." He say, "That baby going dead anyway. Woman might could dead too. Least I ain't got they deaths pon my conscience." I say, and I was standing in front Berry now, and holding up my big belly in the two hands, I say, "Maybe you prefer the death of *this* baby pon you conscience! Maybe you prefer the death of *me!*" Well Berry just take a swing. He long arm. Don't even bother to sitting up in the bed. Berry just lie there with he head prop against the wall, and he take a swing. Bust my mouth clean across. My chin. That cuff knock me over backwards like big seawave, flat pon my back. I just pick up from the floor, I go downstairs at the pipe and I wash out the blood. So much of blood. Wasn't just Berry lose blood that morning, and that was only the start.

6

I ain't saying nothing more about this woman. I just trying to forget she. Just trying to forget about she. But Bolom, I had my presentiment still, from that morning, and that presentiment just wouldn't left me alone. I did had this *feeling*. Of bad. And I was right too. Cause that baby don't dead like Berry say. Woman don't dead neither. That blood Berry give them carry them through. She get through, and baby get through same time. Is *she* born the boychild. Berry first son.

And Bolom, this boychild was bright too. Bright bright bright, very bright. This child skin near *white*. Cause you know this woman was mix, like backra, she something of backra, and Berry red, so this child must come out bright. Backra plus red must equal to bright. Cause I see the child too. That wasn't even a month after Berry had them measles, after he give this woman the blood. I see she holding up she child, one evening when I went at the store to buy some food. I there waiting in the line to pay-out my food, and I see the woman. She holding up she baby high in the air like she was boasting pon he, showing off pon he. And that boychild was pretty too, *pretty!* You know she got he dress all pretty and everything, long white dress, and bonnet, little white bootie-shoes.

Woman come up to me again. Come up to me again straight, soon as she see me standing there. I waiting in the line and holding up Junie in one arm, all this food and macaronies and block of cheese in the next, with my big belly push out to here pushing up in the middle too. Well most as pretty as this woman was with she baby I was ugly, that afternoon. I trying to look the other way, but this woman coming straight at me to give me she address. She say, "That's a next black rat you got in you belly? A *black rat?*" And she laugh. She speaking a-loud for everybody to hear, she near bawling now, say, "Bring this woman a next block of cheese! Cause look she make a mis-count! She got but one, and look she going get *two* black rats to feed!"

I didn't answer she nothing. What I could answer she to that? Bolom, I just stand up tall and I keep to looking the other way. I swallow that. Swallow that like bad air. I didn't answer she nothing. I just hug Junie tight to my breast and I swallow. When Berry reach home that night I didn't tell he nothing neither, about what the woman tell me front the people. I just didn't want to *think* about she, just want to wipe she clean out from my mind. I try my best. But I *can't* forget she. Cause just now Berry ain't coming home again. He ain't coming home, and I know he was going at that woman house. He taking he dinner with she. He sleeping at that woman house.

Berry just clear out. I come home from Mistress Pantin one afternoon find all he things gone from out the house. Wasn't Berry take them, was the woman. She come with Berry key and she move out he things. Neighbour-woman tell me was a brightskin lady in the house all morning, and she carry way a lot of things. Neighbour-woman say ain't nobody could tell she nothing, cause this lady so bright and dress up such a style, ain't nobody could tell she nothing. Well I just sit down at that kitchen table and I cry. I take Junie pon my lap and I hug she tight, I just cry. Junie crying and I crying, and poor Junie didn't even know what she did crying for.

Now I think of them people already coming for money for the house and money for the furnitures. I know them envelopes empty, but I had to take them down still. I had to shake them out empty. I take out the kerchief from my pocket, my kerchief that I had tie with all my coins inside, and I count them out. Two dollars and sixty-three cent. *Two dollars and sixty-three cent.* And I owing *thirty* dollars! Then I think of this child in my belly. This child in my belly most ready to come now. I think of this child, and I go back to distress again. Only worse now. I *more* than distress now, cause it did went at my nerve. Like it did want to send me in the mental. I say, *You going stand and watch this baby dead again? Watch it dead pon you like the other two? Cause you ain't got food enough to feed youself and Junie proper, how you going feed a next child? With these people already coming to take out these floors and these furnitures from under you feet? I say, You got to do something for this child. You got to do something quick!*

Bolom, I get up next morning and I band my belly, before I go at Mistress Pantin house. I band my belly good, and I go at the chemist to buy the quinine powder. Cause chemist would never sell me that powder if he see me pregnant like that. He would know I trying to throw the child. I band my belly, tell the chemist I suffering malaria spells, say I need the quinine powder. Chemist sell me the powder, and I mix up a big tablespoon in glass of water and I drink it down. That thing taste so terrible, so *acid*. I just hold my breath and I drink it down. Three times a day. Morning noon and night.

First that powder had me nervous, had me to dropping things all the day long. I so nervous and jumpy, I chiding Junie and she don't even need a chiding. Then I start to feel light in my head. Start to feel *dizzy*. Like that powder send my head to spinning. One morning I go at Mistress Pantin house and I fall down, fall down whilst I cooking. I slip pon the porcelain tiles in the kitchen fall down hit my head against the sink, drainpipe under the sink. I must be pass out a time, cause Mistress Pantin come in find me there pon the floor with my head under the sink, and bleeding. She say, "Vel, what happen? What happen?" I say, "Ain't nothing. I just feel little dizzy and I slip pon the floor is all. Ain't nothing." She say, "You got to be more careful, Vel! You got to take care for yourself, or you going *lose* this child!" She say, "You eating proper? You taking vitamins? You got to eat proper and take plenty vitamins. B and D and C!" I say, "Yes, Mistress Pantin. I taking care. Best as I could. But you know I alone and sometimes it hard, things *hard*." Mistress Pantin say, "Well you must tell me, Vel. You need money you must tell me." Mistress Pantin take out she billfold give me extra money to buy vitamins. Vitamins and milk and eggs. *Three* extra dollars Mistress Pantin count out crisp in my hand, to buy vitamins and milk and eggs. Three dollars, crisp, just like that!

I take them dollars and I buy more quinine. I say, *Mistress Pantin, you could never know, but this child need the quinine more than it need the vitamins and milk. Quinine more sweeter than milk to this child in my belly.* I just keep drinking it down. That thing had me so dizzy, and so weak. Weak from the vomiting, cause I sure I vomiting most as much of that quinine as I swallowing. But I keep swallowing. Hold up my breath and just drink it down. I could tell you that quinine near throw *me,* near abort *me,* but it like it ain't doing nothing for this child at all. My belly only swelling the bigger, with this child only kicking kicking like it just want come out. I band my belly and I go at the chemist for more powder.

First that quinine had me nervous, then dizzy, then tired. That was the rhythm of that thing: nervous, then dizzy, then tired. Cause now I want to be sleeping all the time. Just can't get up out the bed pon morning. I was sleeping in Junie little bed now, sleeping in Junie little bed with she, cause I tell the furnitures people to carry way the big bed. I didn't want to see that bed again anyway. I tell the furnitures people to carry it way, carry *all* the things. All but the stove and Junie little bed. Them two I hold back. Junie and me like we living in the spook house again, we go back to living in the spook house again, it did so empty without them furnitures. But spook house better than *no* house. Least we still had the house. Cause Mistress Pantin advance me money for the rent. She say, "You can't be worrying about rent. You got you baby to think about, and little Junie." She say, "Don't you worry about nothing but you baby. You baby is the only thing! You baby!"

7

Bolom, that was the Friday before, Friday of the week before, and this only Friday again and I just can't get up out the bed. I was working extra hours now, work from six in the morning till most eight–nine at night, till Mistress Pantin husband reach from he office. Cause I had all that money to pay back she. And now that I had to be working all them hours, now I can't get up out the bed. That quinine powder had me so weak, so *sleepy.* Junie pulling pon the sleeve of my nightgown, she pulling pon my hand, say, "Mummy, get up! You got to get up! We got to go at Mistress Pantin!" But I just can't get up. That Friday morning I sleep till most two o'clock. When I wake Junie wasn't in the bed beside me. I call out, "Junie! Junie!" but she don't answer. I say, "*Junie come, make haste, we got to go!*" But still no answer.

So I go downstairs, I look quick in the living quick in the kitchen, but I can't find Junie. I know she can't go outside cause that front door was locked, and she can't open that. She could never reach to open that. Now I say, *Well maybe she playing in the big bedroom upstairs and ain't hear? Or maybe she hear but ain't answer?* So I gone upstairs again and I look in the big bedroom, and still no Junie. That room was most empty now, empty without the bed, but right there in the middle of the floor was my white box. My little box that I keep my lipstick and my nailpolish, my Cashmere powder. There was my box in the middle of that concrete floor where the bed uses to be, with all my things scatter. My sewing scissors and my thimble. Well now I vex, cause I did scold Junie enough times not to play with that. She always want to be going in my box and drawing on the lipstick and shaking out the powder, and I did scold she enough times for that. I calling for she loud now, I bawling, *"Junie! Junie, come!"* Then I hear she voice answer from downstairs, say, "I here, Mummy! I here!" Well I hold my belly again and I run down them stairs again. And Bolom, when I reach at the bottom of them stairs, when I look up, I near drop. Just there above the puddle of water, that same puddle that's always there pon a morning, I see this big hole in the wall, with Junie pushing she head *in* through the hole! She was standing in the WC on the other side, and pushing she head *in* through the hole! *Big* hole, in that *concrete* wall, cause this hole was big enough for Junie to climb through out to the other side. Out to the other side of that wall.

I say, *"What the hell? What the hell?"* I run and I grab Junie under she arms, I pull she in through the hole. And I could see the edge of that black toilet seat on the other side. I see the little square mirror holding in Junie hand too, my little square piece of mirror that I use to put on my lipstick. I say, "You use that mirror to scrape the hole? This big hole?" Cause I see the scrapings of concrete like mud soaking in that puddle below, little hill of white mud, with Junie cover in that white concrete too. She only wearing a panties, with she skin and she hair and she face all cake in concrete. I say, "You scrape this big hole?" She say, "Yeah, man! I do it by *my*self!" I say, and I start to crying now, tears rolling pon my cheeks now, I say, "But *why?* Why you *do* like that?" Junie say, "I hear the spooks! Hear them spooks making spook-noises! They did *stuck* inside that wall, so I let them out!"

I just rush Junie in the kitchen bathe she down under the pipe, cause she was smelling so *nasty*. That concrete had the smell inside, it did *absorb* that smell. I bathe she down, I say, *How Junie could do that? How little child could scrape a hole clean through a concrete wall?* But in truth I did notice like that paint boiling off the wall, *bubbling* off the wall, last few weeks when I mopping out the water. Like that *concrete* was bubbling off, all above where the water collect. But I ain't pay it no mind. Cause that wall was *concrete* wall, *cement*. I didn't think nothing could happen to that. I ain't pay it no mind. But that wall was rotting. It was *rotting*, with that water soaking every day. That concrete wall was rotting back to mud.

On my way home from Mistress Pantin I get a piece of galvanize. Pull it off the roof of a house nobody wasn't living in, old abandon house. I pull off a good piece, not too much of holes and not too rusty and rotten. I lean it up against the hole, and I roll a boulder out the bush. *Big* boulder. I full pregnant with my belly ready to bust, and I climbing on top old house and I rolling boulder. Roll it with my feet, through the front door and up against the piece of galvanize. I say, *Least that would keep some the smell out, some the stench. Least that would keep Junie from climbing through the hole again.*

But Bolom, that don't keep the smell out at all. Not at all! That house go to stenching worse than ever now, more toilet water flooding and more stench. I come home from Mistress Pantin, I find the livingroom soaking in three inches of water. *Stench!* I mop out and I sprinkle the lye, but that lye don't do nothing. We go from living *beside* that WC to living *inside* it. Then about ten–twelve days later, about two weeks later, I wake and I find Junie through the hole again. How that little child could roll that big boulder and pull down that metal I could never say, but she do it. Somehow she do it. I don't know, but when I wake I find Junie through the hole again. I give she such a chiding for that, so much of lash for that.

8

But that chiding and them lashes come too late. Too late, cause Junie was sick already. She sick to she belly, with cramps, belly-cramps, she running loose to she stools. Rice-water stools. Want to be using toilet all the time. We reach back five minutes, Junie say again, "Mummy, I got to use the toilet. Use the toilet again." I say, "One or two?" She say, "Two. Two again." But poor child them twos was coming more like ones. I take she up and I carry she round the building again, all the way round to that WC. Cause Junie was getting weak pon she feet now, weak from them loose stools. Only want to be using toilet and drinking water, more water. So much of water that child drink down. I stew the green guava try bind she up, mix it with milk and little sugar, and make she drink it down. But that stew green guava don't do she nothing. I boil tea with lantana bush make she drink the tea. But that lantana don't bind she neither. I can't be working at Mistress Pantin house now, I got to stay home tend to Junie. Three days I stay home and I stand pon she.

Time as I carry Junie to the hospital she was burning a fever, and so weak she could scarce stand. Doctor take one look and he say she got the cholera, bad case of cholera that was passing round then. Cause doctor say he can't *count* the people he treat already from the plannings with this cholera. Doctor say this cholera come from a place call *Asia*. But I ain't know nothing much about cholera, I ask the doctor how she could catch that. I say, "Junie never even *been* in Asia." Doctor say, "Maybe from the water, tap-water." He say, "You must boil the water." Then doctor ask, "Does Junie play near the outhouse?" I say, "*Outhouse?*" He say, "Could have Junie come in contact with human extrement?" I say, "*Extrement? Extrement?* Mean *extrement?*" I say, "We *living* in extrement! Where we *living* is extrement!" Well doctor tell me I got to get Junie way from there. I got to carry Junie way from there. He give me pills for she, and pills for me too. Tell me I must take the pills too.

I catch the bus and I carry Junie straight in the country. I ain't going back at that plannings not even to collect up we things. I carry Junie straight in the country. Straight to Granny Ansin house. I hug granny so tight, I say, "We got to tend to Junie! We got to stand pon she till she get better, cause she very sick!" I say, "But she *bound* to get better. Now that we away from that plannings and all that extrement. She *bound* to get better."

But Junie don't get better. We put she in the bed and granny and me stand pon she the whole night, granny and me and all the girls too. My sister and my cousins. *All* the family, eight–ten womens and girls and babies. Standing round the bed the whole night, reading psalms and singing hymns and saying prayers. We give Junie the doctor pills and we boil the water for she to drink them with. We press cool Limacol press pon she forehead. But Junie don't get better. Just get weaker and weaker, and more hotter with the fever, and by next morning she was dead.

But I couldn't feel that grief yet, not yet. You don't feel the grief right away. That does come *after*. I stand there at the end of that bed and looking down pon Junie, but I couldn't feel the grief then. Like I couldn't even *see* she like that. Not yet. I looking down pon she but I couldn't see she yet. I just feel daze. Feel *tired*. Granny tell me, she say, "You got to send for Berry. You got to send that he could bring the box." I say, "Not Berry. Don't send for Berry. I ain't want to see Berry." I say, "Arrows could go for that box. Arrows could bring the box." So granny do just as I say, cause she was fraid for me. She was fraid for this thing to go at my nerves. Granny send for Arrows and he bring the box. Arrows go in Mr Bootman car for that box. Granny and me dress up Junie and we bury she beneath the mango tree, mango tree behind the house. We bury Junie beside the other two. My three children.

That same night I went in childbed. The shock, mid say was the shock. The shock does do that. That shock send me in childbed that same night. Mid say I was a month early, a month is the least. That's why he come out so easy and so small. Come out in no time. Come out *tiny*. But he come out living! He was *living*, and I had to hold he! Mid clean he off wrap he in a towel, white towel, but I had to hold he. I get up out the bed and going for this child. They had to give me he to hold, they *had* to give me, cause I was out the bed already. I hold to that little thing squirming and I say, *Please Lord let he to live! Let he to live! Give me this little black rat to live!*

But then they had to take he way again. They was waiting for me to drop asleep, but I wouldn't sleep, just wouldn't sleep. I *refuse* to sleep. I couldn't say how long I was holding he. Maybe an hour, couple hours. Maybe that whole night. But then they had to take he way from me again. Mid say, "Why you don't put he down Vel let he sleep awhile?" I did *know*, but I, like I was dreaming now. Like in a dream, when you say things how you want them to be even though you know better. You say them how you want them to be. Cause I say, "Well I could just let he rest awhile. Just a little while." Mid say, "Yes Vel, let he rest awhile, and you rest too. Sleep little bit." I say, "Yes. I going sleep little bit." I did know, but I say that still. I close my eyes still, and I must be drop-off little bit. Cause when I open my eyes again they wasn't in the room. They was gone, mid and granny gone, baby gone. I get up out the bed. Maybe I did dream that too? But I could remember saying, *You got to cover! You got to cover!* Cause I was naked, and I couldn't find nothing to cover with, that room was so dark. But I could remember saying, *You got to cover! You got to cover!* I just take the sheet and wrap it round, and I go stumbling out the house. Round to where that mango tree was. I see the mid with the kerosene lantern holding and granny working the shovel, and that's when everything go to black. Go straight to black, and I *out*.

9

I ain't know what it was kill the child. Maybe the same cholera. Cause in truth I never get chance to take the doctor pills. Maybe that quinine kill he. But I did stop that since Junie dig the hole in that concrete wall. Since that morning. That was a month, that was three weeks in the least, before the child come. But maybe it was that quinine? Or the cholera? Or maybe he just come too early, come too small? Mid say *premature*. That was how she did call it by. Maybe he just come premature. Maybe all that, all that together, or maybe just the one that got things planning? That's what *I* say, what I want to believe. The one that got things planning. He planning for you, and you don't even know it.

Now I did want to sleep in truth. Onliest thing is sleep. Granny bring food for me and I eat it, then it's sleep again. I go outside to use the toilet, then sleep again. Onliest thing is sleep. I must be sleep ten days, if that could be possible. Cause I ain't know how long I lie in that bed. But I say was close to ten days. Then one morning I wake up and I was *awake*, full awake, after all that time. Wasn't nobody in the house that morning, granny nor nobody. I could hear the children playing in the yard, or playing someplace close by, but wasn't nobody in the house.

I get up and I go outside to use the toilet, then I go in the bathstall and I bathe. I see the bucket there full with water, so I use it and I bathe. I dress myself, then I carry the bucket at the standpipe to full it back again. Government put a new pipe cross the street, cause that old pipe was all the way by the main road, pitch road, but government put a new standpipe cross the street. So we didn't had so far to go for water again. I full the bucket, and I put it back under the shower. Then I take up the bottle of peroxide. Big bottle. We had the bottle of peroxide there, and I take it up. I hold my breath and I just drink it down. Fast as I could. I drink it down and I ain't stopping till I finish the whole bottle.

But Crissy was there spying pon me. Crissy was my aunt youngest girl, she did reach about six years then. Crissy was hiding under the house and spying pon me the whole time. Hiding behind the grating, where I couldn't see she. That big peroxide bottle drop out my hand *vups* and I drop pon the ground too, *vups,* pon the wet earth. Then I hear Crissy bawling, "Vel foaming at she mouth! She foaming at she mouth! Vel foaming at she mouth!" And then I out. Everything go to black again.

10

When I wake I was in the doctor bed this time, hospital bed, and I had tube in my nose and tube in my arm, tube dripping from the bottle hanging. My arms was tie to that bed too, and my feet, with Berry sitting there pon the bed side me. I just gazing up in he face cause I couldn't believe it. I didn't know if I was living or dead or dreaming or what. I say, "*You?* You there?" He say, "Yes. Is me." He say, "I come to stand pon you. Take care for you." Well I didn't saying nothing a time, just lie there in that bed like that. I was gazing up in he face and seeing the dripping from that bottle too, behind, and that slow dripping dripping of red take me far off, like it did carry me someplace distant. Then all in a sudden I lash out. I start to scream, *loud,* I say, "You *get* from me! *Get* from me! I never want to see you again! Not till hell catch fire!" I trying to sit up in the bed even with them straps tie. Doctor hear me he come running, he tell Berry he got to leave, got to get out. And that's the last I see of Berry. The last. He come back again but I tell the nurse I ain't want to see he. Again and again. Ain't want to see he. I did *never* want to look pon he face again.

Doctor tell me they had to pump that peroxide out from my stomach, but I going be ok. He sure about that. I going be ok. That doctor was the psycob, you know, trink-doctor, cause this hospital was the mental. Not that other big hospital. This one was the mental. Doctor come to visit with me everyday. He was a whiteman, English, cause he speak like English. He name Dr Bolforth, or Bolder, something so. But I uses to call he Dr B. That Dr B come to visit with me every day. He was very kind to me, that trink-doctor. He say ain't nothing wrong with me. After two days he take off them straps from my hands and my feet, cause he say I don't need that. Ain't nothing wrong with me. He ask me why I do it, why I try to do it. I say, "Doctor, when you got more grief than you could handle, more grief than you could keep up with, you got to get way. Got to put youself out the way." He say, "Never put youself out the way, Vel. Put somebody *else* out the way. Or put some *place* out the way." I say, "Who I going put out the way, doctor?" He say, "That's only the question *you* could answer." Doctor say, "Maybe you need to travel? Maybe you need to pick up and live someplace else?" I say, "That's what I would *love* to do, Doctor! I would love that very much!" But then when he leave I sit back in that bed, I drop my head pon that pillow, I say, *How you could travel anyplace? How you could ever get way from here?*

Bolom, that's how I know somebody was planning for me. Somebody did had it plan. Cause doctor tell me I could go home. Wasn't a week after I reach in that mental when doctor tell me I could go home. He say there ain't nothing wrong with me, he can't keep me in there. Doctor tell me to come back in five days, and he give me some pills to take if I feel bad, tranquils. He tell me to take the pills if I feel bad. Feel nervous. And come back in five days. But Bolom, I reach back to that doctor sooner than five days. I reach back the *next* day, cause I had to come for my health certificate!

Time as I arrive at granny house they did already receive the letter. Letter from Di. Arrows did already bring that letter at granny house from Di. She was a cousin of mine, fourth cousin I think. Cause I remember she did call my granny *great-aunt,* so that's fourth cousin. Di was working for a rich whitelady all the way on the other side the island, all the way in St Maggy. And Di write to say this lady going need a next servant. Say this lady going need a next servant, and that could

be me or my sister. Di say we must send police record, and health certificate, and recommendation, and if we could send those three things
this lady would send back the ticket for the bus.

Well that had to be me, cause my sister had a record. She did hit
granny with a stone, and granny carry she in court and she get the
charge. So my sister couldn't go. But *I* could go. *I* didn't had no
charge! Next morning first thing I go at the station and I get my
police record, then I go at Mistress Pantin house and she write me
recommendation. I go at the hospital I get my health certificate. I ask
my trink-doctor to write me out that health certificate, cause Dr B
was a doctor too, he could write me out that too. Is Dr B tell me I
must write the letter. He tell me I must write this letter to Mistress
Grandsol, how much I want the job, how much I need the job. Dr B
say, "Write *everything.*" He say that letter would be the best thing for
Mistress Grandsol to know just who is the person I am, and it would
be the best therapy for me too. So I got to do it. I sit down I write
everything, just how Dr B tell me, cause I does do whatever he say.

I put that letter and my health certificate, my police record and my
recommendation all together in a big brown envelope. I seal it down
and I post it way. Then in five days the ticket come. *Five days!*
Everything did happen so *fast.* Cause Bolom, next thing I know I
climbing up pon that bus bound for St Maggy. *St Maggy!* And I never
even been past *Henly!*

Lilla Grandsol
d'Esperance Estate,
St Maggy,
Corpus Christi, W.I.

That's all that I could hear, over and over again. All that I could see
when I shut my eyes. Them fancy letters of Mistress Grandsol styling
cross the back of that white envelope. *Styling.*

third chaplet

Bolom

BOLOM

Save your understanding for the living,
Save your pity for the dead,
I am neither living nor dead,
A puny body, a misshapen head.

Derek Walcott,
Ti-Jean and His Brothers★

★ First performed in the Little Carib Theatre, Port of Spain, in 1958

The Other Side of Sleep

1

Is that I say, Bolom. Is that I want to believe. When the book read. Fate.
Faith. However you choose to call it by. Cause in the end all those
words don't amount to nothing. Don't say nothing. Not to compare
with that feeling inside you chest sometimes. That feeling that catches
you unawares, all in a sudden, sometimes standing over a cooking pot
or listening to a child sleep, to a dog lapping water in the yard. That
feeling that takes you from behind, swelling-out, and rising-up. Bolom,
things happen in this life that you would never expect. You would never
know. Somebody planning for you, and you would never even know it.

Cause next thing I was climbing up embarking pon that bus bound
for St Maggy. St Maggy, and I never been past Henly. I climb up and I
settle in in the seat, my suitcase and all my things, my parcels, and my
heart was beating so *fast*. My heart was beating so fast, and I could
scarce breathe then. So much of excitement. Anticipation I had. But
that bus couldn't reach before evening, early evening, cause you know
that's a long way all the way to St Maggy on the other side the island.

A long way. To me that was most like crossing over from one side of the world to the next, that passage. In truth we did had to cross over the mountains of the North Range, with that bus climbing higher and higher and air so *cold,* and wet. Everything cold and wet and smelling of wet earth, and so high sometimes that bus would swallow whole inside a cloud. Bolom, we reach inside the sky in truth! Then we start to climb down again, and down, with that bus chupsing every time the driver stamp the brakes or grind a gear. It could only last till Couva, that old bus, cause you know them buses always breaking down. Bound to break down. When we reach Couva we had to wait two–three hours for that driver to get the bus to going again.

Time as we reach St Maggy it was early evening, and I was near exhausted. I could scarce even see them lights blinking. Like in a dream, when we descend the hill and I look down pon all them lights blinking round the harbour below, so many and so *pretty,* blinking pon that water, I could scarce even take them in. I was so exhausted. When we reach in the terminal and I climb down from that bus with my suitcase and all my things, I flag a taxi, I say, "Carry me to d'Esperance Estate." I did know that name was French, and I couldn't even speak that too good neither. I say it the way Granny Ansin teach me to say it, cause she could speak that French-Creole good too. Say, "Carry me to d'Esperance Estate, residence of Mistress Lilla Grandsol!" And that French name did make everything more to me like a dream still. But taxi-driver still can't understand, or don't know, so I take out the envelope that I had holding in my bosom with the stub from my bus ticket still inside, I show he that address Mistress Grandsol write out cross the back. Well taxi-driver read, and he laugh, say, "Girl, you mean Despair Estate, *Des*-pair *Es*-tate. Embassy of the WC, them French white-*culs!*" I say, "Yes it is!" Say, "Yes it is!" Exclaiming it like a fool like that cause I couldn't speak that French-Creole neither.

And don't matter anyway, cause when we *reach,* when that taxicar approach in the drive and I look up pon that house, well my heart start to beating in my breast again. I could scarce breathe again. That house did so *big,* looming like that above the drive. Looming out into the night. It was a board-house, yes, but I never see house so big as that. Don't be no houses like that in Sherman. They don't even got houses like that in *Henly.* Not so big as that. Not for people only to live in. I climb out the taxicar and I look up pon that house looming above, I stand there in the drive leaning my head back, peering up through the dark, and that house did so tall it did had me dizzy. Make me to feeling weak pon my feet, and dizzy, that house was so tall. I most fall down right there in the drive, and all my excitement and my anticipation come straight back again. When I take up my suitcase and my things, my parcels, I mount the front-porch and I knock the door. And Bolom, when that door open, when that door swing open and I look *inside,* when I see them furnishings, that fancy carpet-rug styling before the door and that big chandelier-fixture glittering above, *glittering,* pretty as those same lights round the harbour, well I did think my heart burst now in truth. Cause all in a sudden like it *stop. Every*thing stop, and I couldn't breathe neither. I did stun, I did startle by all that, and now my feet, like my shoes *stick.* Stick pon that floor like laglee, glue, cause I couldn't make them move. Couldn't *pick up.* I couldn't pick up my feet to step inside the house! I could only stand there staring. My eyes bug like a toad inside a bucket.

But I was staring at Mistress Grandsol now. I couldn't help myself from staring at she, cause she was more beautiful than any woman I ever see in my life. So tall and so poise, so *poise,* even standing there without shoes pon she feet. And she was so *young* too. Cause I was expecting a woman twice she age, older. I was expecting a older woman, and she was scarce even older than *me.* But was something else too. Something else beside she youth, and poise, that just wouldn't unlock for me to shift my eyes way. Was she gaze. This gaze that she call up. It, like it did *drinking* me. Drinking me whole inside the cool of cool waters, and I just couldn't look my eyes way. That thing, like I did know that, like it did *familiar,* that gaze, onliest thing I couldn't say from when, or whence, or how this thing could spring back pon me all in a sudden so familiar like that. It did mournful, yes, I could *see* it did mournful. Deep deep down and mournful below, far below. But up near the surface it was shining, and bright, cool and clear and bright like those same waters drinking me in. Drinking me whole. This gaze that she call up.

Next thing big tears pon my face. My cheeks. Big tears, and I couldn't even *say* why! I was so excited, and exhausted, I was so excited and exhausted both, and next thing big tears rolling pon my cheeks. Rolling. I did know Di was standing behind, standing in the shadows behind, but I couldn't look to she. Cause I couldn't shift my eyes from Mistress Grandsol. My eyes that bug and now flood with tears. Well wasn't she speak then, wasn't Mistress Grandsol speak then, was Di. Di say, "Vel? Vel, what *happen?*" I say, and I was looking at Mistress Grandsol still. I was speaking to Di, but I was looking at Mistress Grandsol still. I say, "That thing could walk? That carpet could walk pon?"

Well she smile, Mistress Grandsol smile for that. Di must be smile too, but I couldn't look to she. Cause I couldn't shift my eyes from staring at Mistress Grandsol. That gaze that wouldn't stop from drinking me up. Drinking me whole.

Di say, "It could walk. It's a carpet that it could walk."

But Bolom, I still didn't know. I wasn't sure. Cause Di wasn't standing pon that carpet, she was standing behind. And Mistress Grandsol, she wasn't wearing no shoes neither. She was standing with she feet bare. So I just step out! I just take a step and I step out my shoes just like that, easy as that. I step out my shoes and I step in inside the house. My feet pon that fancy carpet too. So soft and so plush. I stand there a moment, and I didn't even look to my feet neither, cause I was staring at Mistress Grandsol still. But I could feel it. I could *feel* that! I could feel my feet ain't even touching ground!

2

Di was my fourth cousin I think. Cause I remember she uses to call my granny great-aunt, so that's fourth cousin. But she more to the Bootman side anyway, and I more the Downs, and that's how she could be more brighter than me, more fair. She throw-back more to the Bootman side. Must be. Cause Mr Bootman the Panama Man he was a whiteman. Oh, yes. He was white. Or Spanish, Portugee, red, something so. I couldn't say for certain. But Di was a Bootman-Walker, and I was a Downs-Bootman, cause my granny uses to say she was the halfway-house to Mr Bootman-self, you know, outside child, and must be true since how else could she go by Bootman? Put my mummy and all the rest under Bootman? So we all got something of Bootman, all we, less or more, one way or the next. Onliest thing is that Downs that I got near wash me clean of Bootman, not like the Walker, and that's how Di come out more fair, and me so dark. Near black. And don't matter anyway, that's the *main* point of this history, cause Di was so good to me. Don't bother she bright. Di treat me just like a daughter, and in truth, Di say I put she in mind of she own daughter, Mistress Grandsol and Di both. Say how I could be the darker copy of Di own daughter. She only daughter name D-Ann, Dulcianne. Di say we most the same age, even got the same features, same looks. And ways too. Looks and ways too. Di say D-Ann was a girl with plenty spunks. She got plenty spunks. Just like me.

We did just wake that morning, that was maybe two–three days after I reach, and I was fixing up the bed whilst Di was changing out from she nightclothes. Cause that bed was big enough for we two to sleep together, never mind Di belly out to here with child too. We had space enough. So I was fixing up the bed neat, and Di dressing, and I say, ask, "Where D-Ann is now? She back in Sherman? I never hear of no D-Ann back in Sherman?" Di say, "Child, I ain't know where she is. Ain't even know if she living." And Di chups, say, "Last I hear of she she run and gone foreign. Gone America, Canada. But that was twelve years back, and I ain't hear a word since." Now Di turn round, she smooth the front of she dress, she take hold the belly in the two hands. She look down like if she was talking to the baby too, say, "That's why I make this next one. That I could have somebody to care for when I grow old. And *get* cared. A next child to replace the one that gone." I watch at Di and I was thinking, I say, *Well I ain't got time to replace the children wash from these hands already. Nor I ain't got the strength neither.* I say, *I happy to grow old by myself. Happy enough.* But I didn't tell she that. I didn't answer Di nothing to that.

We was both quiet a time, and I start to changing out from my nightclothes too. I start to thinking about who the father was. Who give Di this child. Cause I never hear she speak of no man, boyfriend, and she was going back to Sherman anyhow. But then I start to thinking, I say, *Well if she want me to know she would tell me, no cause to ask.* Cause I did hear the father of the first one, that same D-Ann, I hear the father was Mr Grandsol-*self.* Englishman. *She* husband. I did hear that all the way in Sherman. But he wasn't even there in the house. Mistress Grandsol was all alone. And I say that's the reason she was so mournful too, lock-up like that in she room. I say, "How come Mistress Grandsol all alone like that? Lock-up in she room?" I say, "What hap-

341

pen with she husband? He gone traveling?" Cause I know the white-people does travel plenty, least the mens does, travel for business and different things. Go England, go America, Venezuela. And travel amongst the islands too. I say, "Mr Grandsol gone traveling?" Di look to me now, but little bit peculiar, like if she don't understand what I saying. Then she see a spark. Catch a spark. Di say, "I going tell you about oldman-Grandsol proper enough. Don't you worry about *that*. But you asking after Mr *Woodward*. She husband name Mr Woodward. *Him* is the body gone traveling, traveling for *good* too."

I did startle by that, I did shock. And now I *know* how she could be so grieve. I say, "He *dead?* He gone and dead and widow she so young?" Di say, "Not dead and not widow, but gone just the same. Gone to England. The very *day* you reach. Day before. That's the coincidence of it." Di say, "And that's the reason why Mistress Lil lock-up, so sad and so mournful." I say, "He gone with a next woman? How he could gone with a next woman, and she so *beautiful?*"

Well Di sit down now pon the side the bed, like if she need to sit to think proper. She say, "Child, I couldn't tell you if is a next woman or what. But I know he ain't coming back. Cause when he, that same morning that he leave, and he come inside the kitchen to tell me good-bye, when he say, *Di, take good care of Lilla for me,* I did know he ain't coming back. Was he voice, way he say it, and I just *know*. But I couldn't tell you why. If is a next woman, or the cricket, cause he was a sports-man uses to play plenty cricket, or maybe government. Maybe government *make* he leave. Cause he uses to work for government too, building buildings and such, and I know he had problems with government. I just couldn't say."

Now I sit down pon the bed beside Di, we two together side by side and quiet a time. Last Di say, "Whatever is the reason, *even* if is a next woman, I don't judge he wrong. Cause when he tell me that, *Take good care of Lilla for me,* way he say it, I know how hard that leaving did take he. And that man was a gentleman, you hear? He was a *real* gentleman. Mostest of gentleman ever step foot in this house. I don't judge he wrong." Now Di turn to look to me, she take up my hands in she own, say, "Onliest thing I could do is feel sorry for *she,* for Mistress Lil. Child, my heart near break for she, cause I know how much she did care for that man. I know how much of hurt she feeling right now for he."

I say, "We got to help she! We got to help she to get *over!*"

Di say, "*You*, Vel. Is you got to help she. Cause I going just now. I most sure *he* didn't even know that neither, Mr Woodward. He *couldn't* have know, how I carrying this child and preparing to leave same as he." Di say, "Vel, I wouldn't be able to care for she cause I wouldn't be here. Only you could care for she in my place. Only you could help she."

I say, "Well I going do it. Don't you worry about that. Cause ain't *nobody* know that pain better than me. That loneliness." I say, "I going help she and I going care for she so good, cause I so grateful too. She to bring me here from Sherman, escape from my life. She to bring me here to live with she in this big house. Live with fancy furnishings, eat with silvers, and carpet pon the floor to walk pon!" I say, "All this a dream to me. This a *dream,* and I still floating!"

3

That same morning I make the bake I make it for she special. I ain't know how but I do it. Cause you could say a bake is only a bake, a bake ain't nothing more than a bake, ain't nothing special you could do with a bake. Only little flour, and water, pinch of salt and pinch of bacon-grease, and ain't nothing special you could do with that. But Bolom, somehow I do it. I make the bake special and I dribble the golden syrup special too. Boil the coffee special too. I fix up everything nice pon the silver tray, a fresh linen napkin I fold so nice, I climb the stairs and I knock the door. I present that tray to she special. Don't just give-over, I *present,* and I know she did sense something of that too.

Then I start to cleaning the house under Di supervision. Cause I wouldn't let she do that. Not pregnant like she was. And besides, to me that cleaning was such a pleasure. To me that cleaning was a *pure* pleasure. Like how I beat out them sofas. Them lounging-chairs, and *pouffe,* and dust them fancy press. Them fancy sidetable cover over with mar-mol. And when I finish dusting I dusting over again. Only to *feel* that cloth gliding over the wood, that marmol. Them fancy furnishings, just couldn't *finish* from dusting them! And that dining table. I say I must be wax that dining table about half-a-dozen times, in only three days, and that table was most big as a house all by itself. And Bolom, we only

343

reach to the dining and living. We ain't reach to the parlourroom yet, and entrance, and don't let me to start to talking pon that *kitchen*. I ain't *start* to talking pon that kitchen yet! Cause I would need a whole book only to discuss that, I would need a whole new *language*. In truth, I did had to learn a whole new language only to navigate through that kitchen. Like *decanters*. We had a bunch of fancy glass waterjugs in a special glass cabinet, and Di say those got to call *decanters*. I can't say *jug!* I got to say *decanters*. Coffeecup got to call *demitasse*. Bowls got to call *tureen*. I can't even say fryingpan no more! What? That got to call a saucepun. Like that, *saucepun*, my lips purse like Di own to say it too. *Please to pass that saucepun. Please to pass that decanters*. I got to purse my lips, and I got to point my nose up in the air just like Di. Onliest thing is, I couldn't even say that without bursting out laughing! And neither Di. We two there in the kitchen laughing for all the day like two foolish younggirls, we lips purse in the air laughing over a saucepun.

So let me just start with the pots and pans, that same saucepun. So *many* pots and pans. Some heavy iron, like the griddles and them, some tin, like the colander to drain-out the rice, and some pure copper. Like that saucepun, that was pure copper. You can't use steelwool to clean that. You could use steelwool pon the griddles, them iron griddles, but you can't use steelwool pon that copper saucepun. That steelwool *scratch* it up! You got to use a scrubrag to scrub that, and when you finish you got to polish. But then when you polish that copper come to *shining*. Just like that teaservice, only that teaservice was pure silver now. Pure. Silver like silver too! I could never *believe* it. I could never believe that, but then Di turn over to show me the stamp of the Queen sheself all the way in England, how she stamp sheself pon every member of that teaservice. And Di say they had a next teaservice even *bigger* than that one, come from French, onliest thing is it get thief. Well I say that thief do me a favor. That thief do me a kindness in truth, cause I would need about four more elbows in the least to polish that. Cause that teaservice I polish with elbowgrease, we call it elbowgrease, and I put elbowgrease pon that teaservice till it shine just like a mirror.

And them *silvers!* That's my favorite part. That's my favorite part of this book of the kitchen, them silvers! They stow in a big wood box big as a sweetdrink-crate, and that keep in a special press too. Keep long with the special chinas, cause we got chinas for normal and chinas for special. Like Christmas Day. Guy Fawkes Day. Just like them silvers, cause we had silvers for special and silvers for normal too. *Flatwares.* Call them the flatwares. But the *special* silvers now, they stow in the big wood box, and inside had compartments. Lot of little compartments, all line with velvet-cloth, navy-blue velvet-cloth, *plush,* and each compartment shape special to cradle a special silver. And so *many!* So many different ones. For example spoons. We could begin by discussing spoons. Well we had three different sizes of spoons. Spoons make just for soup. Spoons make only to eat cakes, eat duff. And little silver spoons only to stir sugar in coffee. Forks. We had two sizes of forks. We had one set of knives for meat and a next set for fish. We had knives only to spread bread with butter.

I dump them out. *All* the silvers! Cause there in the kitchen had a little round table for Di and me to eat at, I cover it with a soft cloth, and I dump out all the silvers in the middle the cloth. All the different ones, pile together in a big tall pile, and that pile was most big as a mountain. A *mountain* of silvers! Now I sit down to that table and I polish. One by one. I take up a spoon or a knife and I rub the polish. I wait for that polish to dry and I wipe it off. Now I buff and I buff and I buff again. Each spoon. Knife. I blow moist air pon that knife and I buff it in the skirt of my dress, cause I set aside a special dress only for polishing them silvers too, my *best* churchdress. And only after I get that knife to shining *perfect,* perfect as it could shine, only then could it go back in its own particular velvet compartment inside the box. Bolom, I polish all afternoon. All into the night. Cause one by one handling them silvers get me to feeling special too. *Me.* After a time I get to shining just like them shining silvers! I get to feeling special, and that's the first time I feel that since I couldn't remember when. And when longlast I crawl quiet in the bed beside Di to drop asleep, drop dead fast asleep, my dreams was polishing that mountain of silvers too!

4

Then one evening I was standing there at the sink washing up the wares from we dinner and Mistress Grandsol own upstairs, the very evening before Di leave. Cause she was in the bedroom packing preparing she things, and me in the kitchen washing the wares. I look up through the window I see a whiteman staring. I see a whiteman, staring in through the window looking back at *me*. Well I was ready to bawl thief! I was *ready,* but then I remember a whiteman ain't got no cause to thief. A whiteman could never be a thief. And he didn't have the markings pon he of a thief neither. He didn't paint like no thief. Standing there dress a style, and smoking slow pon he cigar, cigarette, sipping slow out the silver flask in he hip pocket. He was standing there and smoking pon he cigarette slow and pensive, and sipping, studying in through the window like if *he* is the body to be questioning *me*. What *I* could be doing my hands in them suds washing wares! Well anyhow I wasn't frighten no more, not after the primary instant, so I just rinse out that plate that I was holding, I wipe it dry and stack it back inside the cupboard. I wipe my hands against the apron, and I gone in the bedroom to call Di.

I say, "Is a whiteman looking in through the kitchen window." Di was there bending over she suitcase, she back turn, and like she ain't even hear. Cause she don't venture no response, just continue to folding she things inside the suitcase, she back still turn. Well now I speak up loud, loud enough, I say, "*Is a whiteman looking in through the kitchen window!*" But still she don't respond, not even a flex, still with she back turn bending over the suitcase. Now I start to wonder if Di gone deaf, or maybe she did deaf all the while and I ain't notice, and I was getting ready to *bawl,* bawl a third time, when longlast Di chups and she straighten she back. She let loose a groan, and massaging she back a moment down along the spine, cause in truth Di belly was big now. Di say, "Come." And I follow she back inside the kitchen.

Di shove open the window above the sink, she say, "Help me to climb up." I say, "*Wha?*" She say, "Help me to climb up, out." I say, "You can't fit through that window neither! Big as you is!" I say, and now I was frighten, now all in a sudden I was frighten for *she,* I say, "What you want outside with that whiteman for?" Di say, "Never you mind. Just you help me up." I say, "But you big as a *milkcow* even! How you suppose a milkcow could fit out through this window?" Now Di turn to me, and she smile, say, "Just what I telling you. You got to help this milkcow to climb up out through this window!" So what to do? I got to help she. Help she to climb out. And Bolom, I could tell you that climbing out was a *project,* that sink bubbling still with suds too.

Now I stand there watching at Di disappearing into the night, disappearing with this whiteman, and onliest thing I could think to do with myself is finish washing the wares. And when I finish that stack of plates I take down another, I commence to washing them too. I say I must be wash about every *plate* that had keeping in that kitchen. *All* the wares. Every demitasse, and tureen, and all the chinas normal and special both. Cause Di don't come back for a good long while. Not for a good long while, and if we had a project shoving that milkcow up out the window, you could just imagine the project we had to get she back *in.* Now Di stand there and leaning up against the sink, fanning she neck with the kerchief *sheeew! sheeew!* and me there beside waiting for she to speak, cause Bolom, is not *me* the person to touch first pon what is she doing climbing up out the window in the middle of the night to do with this whiteman? Not *me.* I there silent waiting for *she* to speak first, and not till we get back inside the bedroom do she tell me, say, "Well now you make the pleasure of acquaintance with oldman-Grandsol. Mistress Lil father." I say, and I was near bawling now. Cause I was excited. I say, "And you haveen for he? Is *he* is the whiteman you haveen for for this child? Mr Grandsol-*self!* And you ain't *shame?* You ain't shame before *she?* To go with she father and make this child with she father so easy as that?"

Well Di should have glaze with me now. She had every right to glaze with me now, me saying it just like that. But Di don't glaze. Di don't glaze in the least. She only turn round and sit down slow pon the side the bed, and motion for me to sit down beside she too. Di massage she back down along the spine quiet a moment, and she say, quiet, "I did promise to tell you about oldman-Grandsol. And I leaving in the morning, so now is high time for me to do it." Di say,

5

Child, when I reach to this house I did had only fifteen years. My mummy did just pass, not even the month before, and I did had only fifteen years. You could tell me, "*Only* fifteen?" You could say, "But fifteen years is a woman. Fifteen could never be a *only,* fifteen is a woman," and I could tell you you right. But fifteen is a girl too. Fifteen could be a girl too. And that's just how I was. Some ways a woman, and some ways still a girl. Cause I didn't have no experience yet with men. No confrontation yet with men. I never even know my *father!* And I was the only child, didn't have no brothers neither. But my mummy teach me about men. Teach me some things about men the mostest of women *never* learn. Don't misremember my mummy uses to study the sciences. Uses to work obeah. Things that *she* own mummy who was the daughter of Africa teach she, and those same things my mummy instruct me. How to give a man passion. How to take they passion way. How to give a man *potential,* and how to take they potential too. Make they seeds to dry straight up. All those things my mummy instruct me, and more beside.

But my mummy never teach me about when the white gentleman carry you under the house. She never teach me *that* one! She could have never know *sheself* about that, to teach me. Child, I didn't know what to think, do. I didn't know how to *interpret* that. What to think or how to do about that. And I was *confuse!* When I see Madam Grandsol the following morning, when she come in in the kitchen and she see *me. Madam* Grandsol, she mummy, cause Mistress Lil didn't even born yet. And I did come to care for Madam Grandsol too, so *much.* Cause let me tell you she was a firm woman, she was *firm,* know all about manding. She mand servants left and right and up and down. Learn that manding from out the cradle, right here in this house. But Madam Grandsol never mand me. Not me. Not even in the least, and I did come to care for she so much. Onliest thing is, I did come to care for he too. In a different kind of way. Maybe something like a father, if I could even know how that was. But truth is he was a handsome man then, and dignify. Oldman-Grandsol was handsome then, in them days, and he did giving me presents too. You know, on the sly. Packet of powder. Turtleshell-clip for my hair. Things like that. Little things like that. But child, nobody never give me presents like that before. My own *mummy* never even give me presents like that before. Turtleshell-clip for my hair? She had enough of struggle only to put food in my belly, clothes pon my back, how she could give me turtleshell-clip for my hair? And child, them presents leave a mark. They leave a mark, and you could scarce even see that mark fall.

So time pass. Life boil-down little bit and things carry on like that. First year. Second year. Next thing I find myself pregnant. Haveen. That was with D-Ann, Dulcianne, and now I was fraid in truth. I was *fraid,* that they would send me back home, back to Sherman. Cause you know that's how it is. Servant find sheself pregnant she got to *go,* got to go home. That's just how it is. Seem like that's the *law.* And I didn't even have a home at home left to go home to! Then my good fortune. Then my good fortune step out to shine pon me, shine pon my head, cause now Madam Grandsol find sheself pregnant too. Just in time, and just at the *same* time, most the same time. Now they decide I could stay. I could stay and nurse the two babies together, raise up the two babies together. They did even give me a little house behind, little ways off in the bush behind, all for myself. It was only a mudhut, we call that a mudhut, clay walls and caratroof, dirt floor, but I was so please with my little mudhut. Cause up till then I was living down in the cellar, I had a little room downstairs in the cellar of this house, and pon mornings that cellar so *cold,* and damp. But now I had a house all for myself.

Then when time come for the birthings and D-Ann come out ok, she born ok, madam baby was born still. Stillborn. And only three days after D-Ann! Now my tragedy again, cause now I got to go back home again. Easy as that. One minute I staying and the next I going again. Back to Sherman to a house that I ain't even got, and leave the one here that I had, and now toting a child pon my back too. But now my fortune step out to shine pon my head a second time. *Twice-*over. And I didn't even know what I do to deserve that! Cause now madam find sheself haveen a second time. That was only two–three months after D-Ann was born. So that's just how it happen. How my life boil-down for me. Mistress Lil was born not even the year later, and I raise she up longside D-Ann. Nurse the two babies together. Raise-up the two babies together.

Course the question you asking now, question you want to ask me now is if madam ever discover the two babies had the same father? And child, the only answer I could give you is maybe. Probably. Cause madam never indicate to me one way or the next. All them years. But I say she had to know. I say she *had* to know, only she close she eyes to that. Cause that's just the way with all them French-Creole families, right down the line. They see the things they want to see, only the things they want to see. The rest they blank. And that's how things carry on a good long time, good few years. The girls growing good, things going good, ok, only I make sure never to find myself haveen again. I say twice lucky is twice too many times already, and I make *sure*. I take proper precautions for that.

Seem like things did going up a long time, or holding steady anyway, then when life boil-down some more things start to change. Here pon this estate and outside in the world too. Like the whole world did getting ready to turn a tumble, and in truth, the big war was preparing to fight then. You could feel it. You could sense that, even right here. How things did start to going down, and more down, pon this estate too. All in a sudden the sugar-industry bust, sugar-tradings bust, near bust the estate same time. We pick up and we carry on, but not so good. Not so good as before. People start to call we Despair Estate. That's how they did calling we now, *Des*-pair *Es*-tate, and the person that hit hardest is madam. Madam Grandsol. She suffer that the most, start to taking to drink then. Wouldn't come down from out she room the whole day. Cause madam did know the time of prosperity too, *real* prosperity, she did know that better than any of we. But now we was all living in Despair Estate, only we didn't even know it yet, see it coming. Me? Child, I didn't see the *half*.

Now I discover he was going with she too. *He* was, with *she*. Oldman-Grandsol was going with D-Ann too, my own Dulcianne, *he* own daughter! And D-Ann was only fifteen years old. *Fifteen*. Same age as me when I reach here. Like if time did play a trick pon me, fold over backwards when I ain't looking. Like if there ain't no progress to make in this life at all, no *advance*. Like time did fold over backwards traveling backward. In *disadvance*. Cause D-Ann was worse off than me, plenty worse. I was seventeen when D-Ann was born, and she was only fifteen and pregnant already. But child, soon as I discover that, D-Ann was gone already too. She pick up one night and she gone. My Dulcianne! Run to America, Canada, and I ain't hear a word of she since. Nine years now. I was ready to *kill* he. I was *ready*, to do murder. Only I couldn't. All the world was killing up each other left and right like no tomorrow, and I couldn't murder but *one* man! If such a species as he could call a man. A human being. I couldn't do it, and I didn't know how neither. Cause my mother never teach me that. Not that. I could suppose she had ways, she science had to have ways, murder a man. But my mother never teach me that. Vel, I murder he *manhoood*.

He potential. Just how I telling you. And I kill it *dead*. I murder he manhood so he could never do what he do to me and Dulcianne *never* again. And child, once I finish murdering that, it couldn't even stand-up. Hear what I saying? Never again. Couldn't manage nothing more than pass piss.

I leave he there like that. Leave he there like that a good long time, good few years. But still my anger wouldn't side. Wouldn't side-way, ease-off. Cause I did want to see he suffer. *Me*. I did want to *witness* that, for myself. Now I call science back to my service again. Now I steep up he passion. Just how I telling you, Vel. I leave he manhood where it was, dead, and now I steep up he passion. I *steep* it up! Till he had to come a-*begging* to go with he under the house again. And child, now I take my pleasure. I take my pleasure in he *pain*. Oh, yes! And I make he to pay good money for that. Good *green* money! Look here. Let me reach . . . my bosom. . . .

Look here, Vel. Twenty-seven dollars. *Twenty-seven dollars!* Only to lie pon my back and take my pleasure in he pain. Cause child, you know what it is to be a prostitute? You know what is the meaning of that word, *prostitute?* Well I make *he* into the prostitute. He is my prostitute now, and I collect good green money for my pleasure too.

So let me put you mind to ease pon that. Let me ease up you mind and settle it right down pon that. Cause no point to tell you who is the father of this baby here in my belly. But one thing I could tell you sure as this money holding in my hand, it ain't he. Oldman-Grandsol. *He* could never be the father of this baby. Not this one. Not in *this* life.

And only one thing left to tell you, Vel. Explain. One last thing, and child, then you got to let me loose to finish my packing. Cause look morning creeping through the blinds, and my suitcase ain't *ready* to walk yet! One last thing. Concerning this last part.

Mistress Lil don't know nothing about that. She know all the *rest,* even if she mummy didn't, or close she eyes *pretending* she didn't, Mistress Lil know. And she ain't blanking nothing. She know good enough. Who is D-Ann father, and who is the father of D-Ann baby too. But she find place in she heart to understand we for that, try to understand. She find place in she heart to forgive we for that. Is *he* Mistress Lil could never forgive, oldman-Grandsol. She make it so *he* got to run from this island, just how he do to Dulcianne, and Mistress

Lil make it so he can't come back neither. Put a charge pon he head before the magis. A *hefty* charge, that thing call *embezzlement*. That if magis catch hold of he tail he would lose in prison. He would lose and throw-way the key too. You know them whitepeople don't skylark with that embezzlement already! She settle that long since the mother pass. Long since Madam Grandsol pass, and she marry with Mr Woodward, and this estate pass over to she hands. Despair Estate. What was left anyway.

Far as Mistress Lil know the father long gone. Far as she know, he long gone and living in America. Years now. And he did too. He *run*. He run like he tail catch a fire, and he *gone*. He was gone a long time, three–four years in the least, but somehow he come back. *Snake* back. And living here as fugitive. Living here in the hiding. And child, soon as I start to count up my money and make plans to go back to Sherman, to build my house and make my life for me, whatever remain, he appear again one evening just like tonight, watching at me through the window whilst I washing wares. Child, I say that's my fortune stepping out to shine pon my head again. A third time, and this time I could *count* it too. Count it out in good *green* money! Cause now is time for he to give me back my house again. Time, Vel. My life longlast.

6

One morning I catch a vaps. Just like that. It was going on six weeks already that I was living here in the house, and one morning all in a sudden I just catch a vaps. Cause Di did already gone two weeks then, and I was here with she four weeks before Di had to leave. So six weeks, that I was living here with Mistress Lil, and we did scarce even speak a full sentence to each other yet. She to me nor me she. Mistress Lil did lock-up all that while, and taking she meals upstairs in she bedroom too. Ever since I arrive she did only come out to descend the stairs two times a week. Once every Sunday morning to unlock the front door for Di and me to walk to town for service, we prayer meeting. And once again every Wednesday morning for Di and me to walk to market, then me alone, buy whatever food for the house that we need. And when I reach back a couple hours later and I knock the door, like Mistress Lil was standing there behind it waiting all the while, listening, cause I don't even get chance to take down that basket from off my head before she open again. And straight back upstairs in she bedroom to lock-up. Lock-up again.

Course, *I* didn't lock-up. Even though every door in the house was shut drum-tight, and she had the only key, a special *gold* key! Cause Bolom, you don't suppose a house like this one here could open with no ordinary *iron* key? *What?* It got to open with a solid *gold* key, that Mistress Lil could wear that key pon the black ribbon round she neck just like a necklace. Oh, yes! But I didn't lock-up. Not in the sense that she would let me out anytime I ask, if I only ask. Like couple times I wanted to go in town to mail Ansin a letter, send she few dollars from my salary, I only ask Mistress Lil and she let me out. But I didn't even have hardly reason to ask. I was so content being here in this house, and it so spacious, I didn't even *want* to leave neither. Wasn't me I was worried for for all this lock-up. Was *she.* I was fraid for she to take to drink, like Di tell me the mother did. And Di say that drink went to Madam Grandsol liver to kill she too. But Bolom, I know about drinking. I raise with drinking. Even though I never hardly take a drink in my life. And I know from one glance pon Mistress Lil pon a evening that she ain't doing that. Not yet. Onliest thing is, I was fraid for she to start. I say it ain't no good for she to lock-up like that, all the time like that. Ain't no good.

One morning I just catch a vaps. I did already present to she the tray with she bake and she coffee, and I did already take it back from she empty too. I was just starting in to waxing that dining table, waxing when it don't even call for waxing, cause six weeks now and ain't nobody even sit to that table to eat. Then all in a sudden I catch this vaps I take off mounting up the stairs. I didn't even think to put down that buffing pouch neither, cause that pouch was still in my hand holding when I mount the stairs and I knock the door. When Mistress Lil open, and I find myself looking in she face that was paint in perplection now, cause this the first time I ever knock the door outside the appointed times. All in a sudden I find myself staring into Mistress Lil face, and I didn't even know what to say. What I was planning to say. Just stand there in the silent, a *long* minute, with me only wondering what we two could be doing all in a sudden after six weeks staring face to face, and wasn't even the appointed time for that!

Last Mistress Lil say, "Yes? Yes, Vel?" But Bolom, I still didn't know. I was only standing there thinking how *beautiful,* even with she face paint in perplection like that, only now I was thinking, *Well you better speak up quick. Cause just now that flood of tears coming to paint up YOU face again.* Then I start to talk. I just start off to talk and talk and talk like I eat parrot, and ain't even thinking what. I say, "I was just wondering Mistress Grandsol if you don't mind for me to walk barefoot whilst I working? Whilst I cleaning the house? I mean, long as ain't no guests to serve at luncheon nor nothing like that. If you don't mind for me to walk barefoot?" I say, "Mistress Grandsol, truth is I did never take much to wearing shoes. Not much. Ever since I was a little girl. Ever since then I just kick them off, slip them off. First chance I get. Even in church, Mistress Grandsol. *Especial* in church! Church more than anyplace else. I just stretch my legs under the bench in front, pew, I just stretch out my legs under the pew in front and I just slip-off. Now I press my feet against the cool of that cool concrete floor, that I did love so much. I just can't feel comfortable with them shoes pon my feet! Can't feel comfortable that I could celebrate my*self* proper, that I does go to church *for.*" I say, "And Mistress Grandsol, being in this house is like being in church for me. That's how I does feel in here, like being in church. *Better.* Cause being in here is the feeling of church and quiet too. Quiet. No preacher to preach nor choir sing, and no congregation to testify nor tongues talk. That's good for Sundays, but a person needs quiet to celebrate theyself too. Just quiet. And Mistress Grandsol, I been waiting on this quiet a *long* time." I say, "I just can't be in here in no shoes!"

Well that take she back a little. You would expect that would take she back a little, good few seconds. Me talking so much, and all in a sudden like that after six weeks in the silent. But she say, "Of course, Vel. Of course you can go barefoot." She say, "I always do myself, Vel. Always detested wearing shoes myself. Ever since I was a little girl." And we just leave it there at that. She smile and I smile, and she close back the door, and we just leave it there at that. But we did both know was plenty more than that.

Next morning first thing I wake to the sound of knocking pon *my* door, and wasn't even full morning yet. I jump up out the bed I scramble to the door, find Mistress Lil standing there in she housedress. And this the first time I see she wearing more than a dressinggown since I reach, that first evening and now. She was smiling again, only now was something little bit wicked behind she smile. Little bit. Hidden behind. And she was *excited* too. She say, "Quick Vel, *shoes!* Gather up all you shoes and come with me!" I say, "*Wha?*" Mistress Lil say, "*Shoes!*" I say, "We going to the shoe-cobbler? How we going at the shoe-cobbler, and ain't even morning yet?" She say, "Never you mind, Vel. Just gather them up and come with me. *Quick!*" I say, "Don't I got time to change from out my nightdress even?" I say, "I would *shame* before that cobbler me in only my nightdress!" But she was already past me then. She did already grab up one pair of my shoes from under the bed, and pulling out the drawers of the press one by one searching out the rest. Well she find them in no time, there in the bottom drawer. Three more pairs that I had and two more Di give me before she leave. With half these shoes tumbling out from Mistress Lil arms, and me grabbing them up off the floor fast as I could, tumbling out my arms now and grabbing them up again, scrambling behind Mistress Lil with both we arms hugging to we chest all the shoes that we could carry, tumbling, grabbing-up, scrambling into the dining.

When I reach I find the big table covered over with a cloth, red table-cloth, and pile up top that cloth was a mountain not of silvers this time, but *shoes.* Old shoes. A *mountain* of old shoes! Pile up tall as that chandelier-fixture hanging above. More shoes even than the Clarks store in town, than the cobbler shop. I see womens highheel shoes, crepesole shoes, platform shoes and pumps. Clip-on shoes, button-up shoes, zip-out shoes and lace. I see Chinee slippers, esparilles, go-forwards, washykongs. I see mens hardback shoes, loafing shoes, jesus-boots and rubber. I see the pink dancing slippers of a little girl. With Mistress Lil piling up all *my* shoes now top the pile! Grabbing up the four corners of this red tablecloth, and hefting up with a loud *ha-rumph* this big bundle up top she shoulder bigger than a Father Christmas sack!

Mistress Lil hefting this big sack out the dining through the kitchen, out the back door. With me scrambling behind, stumbling over my nightdress, scarce even able to keep up! She hefting this big sack cross the gallery, down the back steps, cross the yard that was still a *yard* then Bolom, not bush yet. Hefting under the big flamboyant tree, through seaoats, through brambles, burrs, down over rocks *ha-rumphing* over mangrove banyans down onto the slippery shore. Mistress Lil at last letting go she Father Christmas sack to drop behind *plaps* at my feet, *plaps* in the wet mud. Spreading out the four corners of this tablecloth, and Mistress Lil taking up a cream-colour highheel shoe holding by the heel. Now she smiles to me, wicked, reaching she arm right back to pelt this cream-colour highheel shoe tumbling out over the glittering sparkling water, *plash! Plash* up against the big red sun that wasn't even up out the water yet. Next she takes up a green Chinee slipper. Mistress Lil looks to me again, smiling, bawling now, "Come, Vel! Pelt!" And she lets fly the Chinee slipper. *"Pelt!"*

So what I could do, Bolom? I got to do as Mistress Lil tell me, I got to pelt, and I could *feel* my cheeks already smiling ear to ear for that pelting too! I take up a esparille by the strap I swing it round in the air three times, I *cata-pelt* that esparille. Next I go for a washykong. Jesusboot. I pelt a shoe and Mistress Lil pelt a shoe and we both pelt shoes together. *Pelt, plash! Pelt, plash! Pelt, plash!* Every single shoe that had holding in that big Father Christmas sack. Till we couldn't pelt not another shoe if we try. Till we couldn't pelt even a go-forward. Till we was both exhausted, and sweating, standing there in the knee-deep water with my nightdress near soaked, and she daydress, both we laughing for all the day like two wicked younggirls. Laughing for all the day and looking out over a sea of floating shoes. A glittering sparkling *sea* of floating shoes!

7

Time as we reach back to the house we was so exhausted, most we could manage is mount the three back steps and drop each in a rocker right there pon the gallery. She in she daydress dripping and me in my nightdress soaked straight through, cause we was too tired to change. Too tired to laugh again, or talk, or manage nothing more strenuous than doze straight off asleep. Both together. And we must have sleep like that a good couple hours, cause time as we wake the sun was riding high up in the sky, shining full in we faces. And Bolom, let me tell you that's a sensation a body could appreciate. That's a sensation a body could *splendour* sheself by, that feeling of waking with the sun shining warm and tingling pon you face. And that's the first time I could

356

remember feeling that in my life. Now we both was hungry. *Hungry,* both together. So I ask Mistress Lil what she would want for she breakfast. Breakfast, cause now was long past the time for bake and coffee. Now was the time for breakfast. Mistress Lil say what she would care for most in the world is fricassee chicken, and white rice, and steam christophine. Well I say she could have the rice and christophine, and she could have fry chicken, or bake or broil or brown, or she could have chicken in stew or chicken in pelau, but she can't have no *fricassee* chicken cause I could scarce twist my tongue to *say* that, less still to know how to cook it! Mistress Lil say she could cook the fricassee chicken for *me.* And is just so she do.

Mistress Lil brown the molasses and she cook the fricassee chicken in the French-Creole style, and I boil the rice and I steam the christophine. Now I tell Mistress Lil what I would care for most in the world is some bake yam, so she say in that case I must bake some yam. And is just so *I* do. Now we sit down together, but we don't sit down only to eat. We sit down to *dine* now, cause we was sitting at the big long dining table with that chandelier-fixture glittering above. Mistress Lil say today is a holiday. She say, "Today is the fifteen of June, Emancipation Day!" I say, "Well you know better than that cause 'Mancipation Day is first day in August." I say, "If today is 'Mancipation Day, onliest thing it could be is 'Mancipation *Shoe* Day!" And Mistress Lil say I am exactly right.

So that's how we pronounce that holiday pon weself, Bolom. Easy as that. And that's how we celebrate weself for that holiday too. She sitting to one end of that big long table and me sitting to the other, with that chandelier-fixture glittering between. We dining pon the special chinas with the special silvers too. But Bolom, I couldn't believe it. I just couldn't take it in, absorb that, and I could only sit there peering down that long shining table, peering up at that fixture glittering so *pretty,* and I could only say to myself, *You got to be dreaming! You got to be lying in you bed dreaming all this, cause how else could you be sitting here at this table dining pon fricassee chicken with special silvers too, and you wearing in you nightdress still?* I say, *You got to be dreaming this!*

But wasn't no dream. I wasn't dreaming then. Cause that following afternoon and *every* afternoon after that day we eat breakfast together. Mistress Lil and me. And every evening after that day we eat dinner

357

together too. Course, we don't eat in the dining with the special chinas and silvers. We eat sitting together at the little round table at the back of the kitchen. We eat pon the normal chinas, and we eat with the flatwares. All except Sunday callaloo. Sunday callaloo we eat at the big table in the dining, soon as I reach from my prayer service, and that callaloo we drink out *tureens.*

But the rest of days we eat breakfast and dinner together in the kitchen. Sitting to the little round table at the back. And every afternoon after that day we take tea together in the parlourroom too. Mistress Lil she special English tea call *darjeelings,* that I could scarce twist my tongue to say it proper even after all these years, and she drink she tea out a Castleford cup and saucer. Me, I take my bushtea same as always. Kooze-maho or caraili, and same as always I drink my bushtea out a tin cup. Bushtea just got to drink out a tin cup, and that's that. But Bolom, it's the company now makes the tea special. Every afternoon at three o'clock. Every afternoon of we life together. The company that makes the tea. And every year after that day going pon ten years now, the fifteenth of June we celebrate a holiday. Same as Christmas, or Guy Fawkes Day, or the Queens Birthday. We celebrate Emancipation Shoe Day. That's we own holiday that we pronounce pon weself, and we mark it down special in we memory for always.

Bolom, that's when I start to getting fat too. Oh, yes! Fat like a butterball turkey. Cause we did eating pon them butterballs *regular.* Every time that American ship arrive in the harbour. Every time we hear the loud *phaaamph!* all the way here in the house, and we mouths start to water. We got to go at that American ship buy weself a butterball turkey. And not three apples, six, we got to buy weself a whole *crate.* Them Cincinnati Reds! That's the first time in my life I find myself eating three meals a day, not just one, plus tea and Dutch tinned biscuits every afternoon on top. First time in my life I find myself getting fat, and I wasn't pregnant for no child neither. Cause that fat was pure me. Me one. Me alone. My thighs and my hips. My *bamsee.* I could feel that fat right down to my toes. And that fat was my pure pleasure too. I tell myself, I say, *Vel, well now you know what is the meaning of happy. After long last, all these years, cause ain't no way a fat person can't be happy. You got the physical proof right here in you bamsee.* I say, *Happy is you fat bamsee!*

We did enter into a phase of serious feeding then, Mistress Lil and me. We did enter into a feeding *delirium*. That's how I did call it. And Bolom, I couldn't tell you why. I couldn't say what was the reason, or how could be the particular psychology behind this thing. This delirium. All I could say is we was eating *serious*. Eating all the day long. And when we ain't eating we resting up from eating, dozing-off in the parlourroom, or dozing-off each in a rocker pon the back gallery. Lazing it off after a big feed. Or back in the kitchen again cooking up a storm getting ready to feed some more. But Bolom, we delirium was a *controlled* delirium. Wasn't nothing haphazard about it. Wasn't nothing haphazard in we delirium at all. Cause let me tell you we eat slow and we eat *pensive*. Spend time with every mouthful. Like we could dedicate three hours only to eating a breakfast. Three hours only for a plate of float-and-accra. Three hours only for a bowl of bulljhol. We eat slow and pensive and we eat purposeful. We purpose was we pleasure. Cause we didn't eating for need, hunger. You eating two three-hour meals every day, plus bake and coffee in the morning, plus tea and big handful of Dutch tinned biscuits every afternoon, you ain't eating for no hunger. *What?* Hunger don't even enter into the picture then! You eating for pure pleasure. And we *was* too, me and Mistress Lil both. Sitting there together at the little round table at the back of the kitchen. Three hours, only for a helping of haveinadash.

And Mistress Lil did eating even *more* than me! I couldn't believe it, and she neither. Cause she say she was always a fussy eater. She did always eat *fussy,* pick-a-pick at she food. Mistress Lil say she did never have much of appetite in she life. But now she was eating even more than me. One evening I sit there I watch at she eat a whole guava duff all by sheself. A whole duff! We did already finish we dinner of rice and fricassee chicken, cause that was my favorite now too, way Mistress Lil cook it. When we finish we dinner of rice and fricassee chicken and christophine and yam and cassava, I say I full. I *full*. Say I suffering the macajuel syndrome. That's how we does call it Bolom, like a big macajuel snake after he feed. He swallow up a lappe, agouti, can't do nothing but lie there three days digesting that. Well Mistress Lil say she suffering the macajuel syndrome too. She *say* that, say, "Me too, Vel. Not another morsel! Not another bite!" Then I watch at she eat a whole duff. *Entire.* She eat a whole entire guava duff all by sheself. I say,

"Mummy," cause that's how I did calling she now, most the time. I ain't even know how I did take up that habit, but I say, "Mummy, good thing you suffering only macajuel syndrome and not 'popotamus. Cause if you was suffering 'popotamus syndrome, you would have to eat the whole *house!*"

Onliest thing is, I was getting fat all by myself. Cause no matter how much she eat, Mistress Lil always stay trim. Stay just the same, tall and trim, now matter *how* much she eat. Not me. Now I was fat like a butterball turkey.

That's how it was, Bolom. We first years together. My first years in the house. If I was to remember that time, thing I remember best is that feeding delirium. All those three-hour breakfasts together. Cooking together. Eating together. And dozing-off together after pon the back gallery, parlourroom, each in a rocker. One day I was dusting that marmol table in the living, I catch myself looking in the big mirror above. I catch myself smiling, my fat cheeks, *fat,* and I say just how Di uses to say it, *You life boiling-down girl, but you cheeks blowing-up just like a butterball. A black butterball!*

Bolom, that's when I start to learn something about life too. About good and bad, sad and happy. Them two things. I learn how the bad moves through time slow. Like poverty, despair, hunger. Moves through time *slow.* My first twenty-three years of life did last long as three lives together. Twenty-three years that could equal sixty-nine. Three times sixty-nine. But the good moves through time fast. Just the opposite of what you would think *then,* whilst you in the midst of that good. Whilst you seeing that good pon all quarters, whilst you eyes *blind* for all that good, you would believe that good could last forever. But Bolom, I did start to learn that's only a trick of time, how Di say. Of good and bad, happy and sad. Them two things. *Happy?* Time as you stop to remember that, time as you turn round to contemplate that, that happy done slip from out you grasp already. So easy. So quick. Ten years in ten minutes.

8

One Wednesday morning I watch at Mistress Lil loading a sack of rice in the backseat of the Ford, I say, *Wait. Wait just a minute.* I say, *What going on here?* Cause she had to fold down the top to fit that sack of rice in. She had to fold down the top! So much of food we did had already pile up in the trunk, pon the backseat of that Ford. All in a sudden I watch at Mistress Lil loading this sack of rice in the backseat, I say, ask to myself, *You know how much of money she spend for all that food? How much, of money? And she spending that every week too.* I say, *That money could never last. Not like that. No matter how much she got, that money could never last like that.*

It was the first time I stop to consider it, first time since I arrive in the house, and that was four–five years already. How long could Mistress Lil money last? *We* money. Cause I was living off that money too. Not just food every week, but Mistress Lil did paying out my salary. Fifteen dollars every month. My salary that I was sending mostly to Granny Ansin, cause I didn't need that, and Ansin had all those mouths to feed. I just take out three dollars for myself, just in case, the rest I send to Ansin. Every month. I didn't even need for those three dollars that I was taking out neither, cause I didn't have nothing to buy, nothing I wanted to buy. Mistress Lil did buying all that I could need and more still. Like when we go to Brisons, she buy a creme for she-self, she buy a next one for me same time. Two Pons Cremes and two Cashmere Powders, same time, one for she and one me. Only once I could remember I had to spend those three dollars that I did holding back from my salary, one month. I had to buy myself some shoes! Cause we did pelt them all in the sea, and I did need at least one pair of churchshoes. One pair, that I could at least *arrive* in, then I could stretch out my legs under the pew and slip-off. I could press my feet against the cool of that cool concrete floor. And I could slip my shoes on again after to walk out. Cause Bolom, I did too *shame* to arrive in that church barefoot. You can't arrive in church barefoot, you could slip-out once you reach, but you can't arrive like that. I spend my three dollars at Clarks pon a pair of churchshoes.

But other than that one time, Mistress Lil did paying out money for all we needs together. Money that I *know* she had stash somewhere in she bedroom. Cause I went with she in the bank the day Mistress Lil close up she affairs with them, Barclays. That was the first year after I arrive, when we went in the Barclays Bank, and she carry home all she money in a brownpaper-sack. Cause Mistress Lil say she don't want to think about money again, say she ain't never going back inside that bank again. She carry she money home and stash somewhere up in she bedroom. A *lot,* I could only suppose it was a lot of money, judging from the heft and bulk of that brownpaper-sack. That afternoon when I watch at she mounting the stairs with that sack perch under she arm. But I didn't stop then to think no matter *how* much, it can't last forever. I didn't stop to consider that till the Wednesday morning I watch at she loading that sack of rice in the backseat of the Ford that had to have the top *down,* so much of food we had pile up in that motorcar already. I stand there watching at Mistress Lil, and I say for the first time after four–five years, *No matter how much, that money could never last like that.*

Right then and there I decide I got to bust my way inside she bedroom. Somehow, when she ain't in there, when she don't know, I got to bust my way inside so I could find out how much money she had stash. How much she had *left.* Before we run out. Before we meet in *tragedy.* Cause I know she ain't bothering she head with that. She ain't bothering she head in the least with that. And I say I got to thief she gold key. That's the only way, so I got to do it. Sometime when she dozing-off pon the back gallery, or in the parlourroom, I got to slip-off that black ribbon with that key from round she neck. Or I decide better still I could snip it off with the scissors. I could snip it off, and I could thief that key and bust inside she room and search-out she stash, and I could count it up and tie back that ribbon round she neck before she could even wake. But Bolom, now I notice something that I never even notice before. Something *peculiar.* Now I notice that every time she doze, *every* time, she doze-off with that key holding in she hand! Tight tight. Every time. Cause I was vigilant for that over a month. Two–*three* months. And I couldn't thief that key not for nothing.

Then I get my chance. *She* give me my chance, Mistress Lil, and I didn't have to do no thiefing neither. I didn't even have to do nothing dishonest at all! Well not much. Not so much. Cause Mistress Lil put that key straight in my hand. Just like that. One night out the blue, Mistress Lil decide now she going mail that key to England to she husband, that same Mr Woodward. She lock-up all the doors in the house, including she bedroom, and she decide now she going mail that key way to England to Mr Woodward. She give it to me to mail! Hand it over to *me* to mail, and she was *anxious* to present me with that key too! I couldn't understand it, Bolom. I say, *What Mr Woodward would need for for this key? He ain't even living here in this house?*

9

Took me three weeks of searching to find that money. Where she had it stash. Three weeks, and then I wait another two before I give she back she key again. So five weeks. Five weeks in all, cause I wasn't in no rush neither, now that I had the key. And I get waylaid. Most every night when I bust in inside she room to continue my search, I get way-laid from that. Cause she was sleeping downstairs in my bedroom now, both we together in my little bed, those five weeks. And she was sleep-ing *sound* too. Mistress Lil don't just snore, she *donkey-weezle,* that's how I does call it, donkey-weezling. All through the night. I just slip out the bed and I tip quiet up the stairs, I lock myself inside Mistress Lil bed-room with she golden key. And that's the first time ever that I step my foot inside there. I lock myself in every night, most the *whole* night, that I could continue my search for she stash. But most every night I get waylaid.

First I decide I got to give that room a proper cleaning. Cause it was a *mess!* That room was a proper mess, with dust thick like a blanket pon them bedstand tables, and mildew growing green up the walls that I got to scrub with lye. First I get waylaid from my search for all that clean-ing, then I get waylaid for she diary. Mistress Lil diary, that I happen to stumble pon in the drawer of she bedstand table. There together with she passport, and my same application parcel that I did send she when I was applying to come as she servant. My parcel with my recommen-dation, and police record, my health certificate and my long letter that I did write she.

Was Mistress Lil diary waylay me the most from my search. Bolom, I just couldn't *help* myself from reading that. Every night. All into the night. Despite that I know reading in she diary was little bit dishonest. Little bit. But I just couldn't help myself cause she writing was so *pretty,* stying like that cross the page. And anyway the passage I did like best was the last one, and that one concern *me.* It was the last and longest passage she did write in she entire diary, which concern Mistress Lil

363

reflections pon the very evening I reach here. That same evening I reach here in the house. Cause she write how after that passage she ain't recording no more of she life in that diary. It was the last and longest passage and it was the prettiest, and I read that passage *every* night. Every night for five weeks, and sometimes I read it two–three times over again in a *single* night. Mistress Lil reflections pon that first evening when I reach here, when we begin we life together. Bolom, I read that passage till I didn't even need the diary no more to read it. I could close my eyes and see those words just like a dream, styling cross the page of my memory clear as writing. Mistress Lil diary that waylay me from my search.

Last I find the stash under she bed. Right there in the most *obvious* place, and that's why I did take so long to find it. Cause it was right there hidden beneath a loose floorboard under she bed, and still in the same brownpaper-sack. And Bolom, now I could relax a little. Now I could calm myself down a little, cause I count up that money and she had 300 dollars left. I say that's plenty, plenty money. And plus, the next night when I bust in inside she room, I put *my* 180 dollars that I had save inside the brownpaper-sack too. I add my money to she own. That 180 dollars that I had save from my salary every month, those three dollars that I did holding back every month now for five years. So that was 180 dollars that I had, plus 300 that she had, to equal 480 dollars that we had together. And Bolom, I could relax now, cause I say 480 dollars is plenty money, plenty. That's more money than I ever see in my life. Than I ever *dream* to see! I say we could live for three–four years in the least pon that. We could live four–*five* years pon that money, especial if we ration. Start to ration. I fold up that 480 dollars in the brownpaper-sack and I fix it back beneath the floorboard under Mistress Lil bed. We stash. And I relax myself little bit.

Now I wait a couple more weeks. I say I could wait a couple more weeks, cause it would take at least five weeks for this letter to post to England and return again. Now I steam back she gold key back inside the envelope. Just how I see Mr Tracy do it in that detective movie. Just the same, how I see Mr Tracy do it, cause you could steam the envelope open and steam it back closed again and that person would never know. Least Mistress Lil didn't. I put that envelope with the key inside a *next* envelope, I stick the stamps like if that key done cross the sea to

England and come back again. And just how Mr Tracy do it in the movie too, I use a *typing-machine* to write out that address, she address. Otherwise Mistress Lil would *recognize* my hand! She would know my writing, just as easy as I could know hers. Bolom, I ain't so fool as to write out that address with my hand. I do it just how I see Mr Tracy do it. I use the funny little typing-machine that I find downstairs in the cellar, and cover in dust. And I say that thing must be Mistress Lil *toy* to play with long since she was a younggirl, cause that typing-machine was so small with my fat fat fingers mashing them little keys left and right. But I manage, I type out Mistress Lil address pon the second envelope. And that same morning I go inside my bedroom I wake she up still asleep in my bed, she donkey-weezling, I say, "Look, Mummy! Look at what the mailman just shove under the door!"

10

But Bolom, that money don't last. That money don't last and that good don't last neither. No time at all. Even though I start to ration. I start to put we *both* pon a serious regiment then. I say, "Look here, Mummy. We two come like two butterball turkeys bouncing-up in here. One white and one black. Bouncing-up in here." I say, "We got to put weself pon a serious regiment!" I say it like that, even though I was the only fat one in the house. But Bolom, my fat was gone again before you could blink. Cause I take we back to one meal a day, plus coffee and bake in the morning, and I cut out all them blasted Dutch tinned biscuits from we tea too. I make the food that we was eating in one week last two, last three. I put we both pon a serious regiment, and I start to put my salary back inside that brownpaper-sack too. Every month. Back in that brownpaper-sack inside Mistress Lil bedroom. Soon as she hand it over I put it straight back, cause I ain't sending that money to Granny Ansin again. We can't *afford* to send that money to Ansin again. Now I send *she* the three dollars, and the remaining twelve I put in the brownpaper-sack for Mistress Lil and me. Every month for most three years. Every month when she hand me over my salary, I tuck that money in my bosom and I wait for she to doze-off in the parlourroom, and I climb out through the window above the kitchen sink. I climb up the drainpipe and I climb in the window of Mistress Lil bedroom.

Every month I fold my salary money back inside that brownpaper-sack. I shove it back under the floorboard under she bed.

One afternoon I was unfolding the sack I say I better count out we money. I wasn't worried, cause wasn't even three years yet since we start to ration, and I know that amount of money could last four in the least. Four-five years in the least. Before we even got to *start* to worry. Most the time I didn't even bother to count it out, cause most the time I was in too much of hurry. I was mostly always in a flap, to get back down that drainpipe in through the kitchen window again before Mistress Lil could wake. But one afternoon I was unfolding the sack, I say I better count out we money. Bolom, we had but thirty-three dollars left. *Thirty-three dollars!* Including the twelve that I just put back from my salary. And Bolom, when I climb back down that drainpipe I was in a stupor. I was in a *stupor,* when I climb back in through that kitchen window. I say, *Vel, what we could do now? Now all the money all but finish?* I say, *What you could do? What YOU could do now, and whatever it is, you better do it quick!*

I was still in a stupor couple evenings later when I start to washing up the wares. The wares from me and Mistress Lil dinner that wasn't hardly any wares at all. Cause we didn't even hardly eat any dinner. Handful of white rice and little piece of bacon each. I didn't hardly cook any dinner for we to eat, that evening. I look up through the window I see a whiteman staring. Looking in through the window staring back at *me.* But this whiteman wasn't oldman-Grandsol. I couldn't *believe* he could be oldman-Grandsol. Cause he didn't come back at the house not since Di leave, all those years since Di leave. And he didn't dignify like oldman-Grandsol, nor style. This whiteman was a bacra-johnny. What we call a bacra-johnny. Vagrant. Wastrel. Dress in he clothes all raggedy and filthy, and he was drunk too. Drinking out he bottle of babash, the bush-rum. I was ready to bawl thief. I was ready, then I hear he sing out. Low and brass, like how a toad does sing into the night, "*Dul-ci-anne! Dul-ci-anne! Dul-ci-anne!*"

I rinse out that plate that I was holding. I wipe it dry, and I stack it back inside the cupboard. I wipe my hands dry against the apron.

When the Book Read

1

Dream youself flayed open like a fish. Gutted. Sewed back up.

Dream youself falling and falling inside a deep dark water-well. Black. Falling and falling.

Dream youself a flayed fish. Gutted. Sewed back up.

Falling and falling inside a deep dark water-well. Black. No bottom to reach, hit. That ice-cold water. Just falling and falling inside the dark empty silent.

Falling and falling.

A flayed fish.

Dream youself letting go. Just letting go. Falling backwards out the tall flamboyant tree.

Dream youself waking up in this room. This bed. She here beside you.

Dream youself running through the canes. Faster and faster. Canes slicing past you face, screaming inside you ears. Faster and faster.

A golden key.

Dream youself flayed wide open, like a fish. See in you dream the point of the fishknife fitted careful inside the small pinched hole below, down there, in the soft underbelly place. Cutting-edge turned up. Feel the icy hollow stab of the fishknife shoved all the way in up to the wood handle. Up to you *throat*.

Feel you underside severed in two from the soft underbelly place where the small hole *was,* up between you breasts all the way up to you throat. Flayed wide open. Feel you insides severed through, you guts spilling, you warm blood sloshing like seawater inside tall rubber fishboots.

Feel you stomach tied to the bottom of you string of guts ripped joint by joint from the inside notches of you spinecord. Ripped way from bone. And stopping, all in a sudden. Just before ripping out the feathery orange gills tied to the top of the string of guts just below you throat, stopping. The fisherman changing she mind. The fisherwoman changing *he* mind? Stopping. All in a sudden at the last moment, and shoving the warm guts back in. The warm wet glistening living guts. Mixed-up living guts, ripped way from bone and shoved back in. Sewed back up. Blood squeezing out warm and thick between the stitches. Drying cold and stiff, colour of wine against you black skin. Black against the white sheets.

Dream youself waking up in this room. This bed. She here beside you.

Dream youself waking up to find the key tied round *you* neck. Tied together pon the same fishingtwine with Ansin little silver cross and the piece of obeah-mirror. The golden key.

Remember in you dream mounting up the stairs in she arms. She carrying you weight, carrying you up. Cover in blood now too.

Remember she putting you to lie down here in she bed. Gentle. "There, Vel. There, now. *Shuuu . . . shuuu. . . .*" And you bawling, still, "Please don't send me home, Mummy! Nothing for me home!"

Remember she looking beneath you dress wet with blood, flipping it up. Seeing the bindings. And rushing out the room coming back a moment later with the same scissors, the big sewing scissors. Stain with blood like a fishknife.

"There, Vel. There, now. *Shuuu . . . shuuu. . . .*"

"*Aye aye aye aye aye!*"

Beginning to cut through the bindings. Gentle. Careful.

Black.

Remember in you dream waking up to find youself naked in the bed, *he* here too. Whiteman. Doctorman. Listening through he listening-cup press against you belly. The underbelly part. Shifting. Pressing. Listening. The shiny top of he head. And you trying to sit. Struggling to sit up. Black.

Wake and feel youself tumbling backwards over the bed. Something beneath? Shoved beneath you bamsee?

Wake and feel you legs spread wide open, the little shiny-head doctor pressing up between, doing *something*. Something? He hands inside the soft place pulling and pinching, pulling and pinching. *Sewing?* And you looking over at the side to see all them doctor-instruments. Silver but *not* shiny. Pinchers and clampers and crushers and such. Line up in a perfect line pon the green cloth just here beside pon this bedstand table. And all in a sudden thinking, saying, *No!* All in a sudden, after all *that*. After obeah and quinine and bush-medicine and throwing youself out the flamboyant tree. After that sewing scissors. After all that, all in a sudden you heart and mind swinging together the other way. The contrary way. Now that it is too late. Now the thing is done. *Ended.* Looking up at the little shiny-head doctor pressing up between you legs, and thinking, saying, *No! No! No!* Trying to sit up. Struggling. She pressing you down.

"*Aye aye aye aye aye!*"

And black.

A flayed fish.

2

Waves of pain. Pon the surface. Rippling like water cross the surface of sleep. Slow-dissolving sleep. Not a harsh pain. Not deep inside. Not to compare with that other, the pain of birthing. A series of sharp stiff cuffs down deep in you belly to take you breath way. Oh, no! Nothing to compare with that. Just a humbugging, stinging surface pain. The after-pain of scorched skin. A burned finger held beneath the pipe. Coming in waves. With the soft seabreeze brushing in through the blinds to ease the pain way. Cool the scorched skin. Lie here with you eyes closed still and feel the seabreeze brushing in soft through the blinds. Hear the waves turning over gentle pon the shore down below. Over and over.

And think how long since you stop to listen for that sound. How, when you first reach here in the house, you couldn't sleep nights only for listening to the sound of the waves turning. Over and over. How you didn't *want* to drop asleep, only for fear that somehow that sound, and the waves turning, and the sea sheself might go way. Turn back into fields of ruined canes. Villages of smoking rubbishheaps, and dust, and falling-down patched-up shacks. You fear of losing the sea! And listen first thing every morning before you open you eyes to make certain, that sound of the waves turning over gentle pon the shore. Still there. Still sounding, breathing. And smile. Remember feeling you cheeks smiling against the pillow, even before you open you eyes. And think how for so long, years now, since you forget to listen for it. Forget to remember. Like all good things, important things, after a time you forget to remember.

Lie here with my eyes closed and listen to the sound of she breathing soft beside. And smile. Listen and smile.

Lie here with my eyes closed and listen to the rhythms of my own body. My own breathing. The scorching pain, rippling cross the surface in

370

waves, coming in waves. Lie here and feel myself tumbling backwards over the bed, something shoved up under my bamsee. Feather pillow? Pillows? By the little shiny-head doctor? Soaked through with sweat, blood? Lie here and feel my hips shoved up in the air, my spinecord bent backwards over the pillows. But easy. Reposeful like this, comfortable, cause that doctor *know*. With you so exhausted-out and busted-up you couldn't shift a muscle anyway. Couldn't lift a limb. Lie here and feel my thighs spread wide open to swallow up the cool seabreeze. Ease the pain way. The soles of my feet pressing together below like hand-palms praying, warm and comforting like this. Comfortable, press together like this by that knowing doctor too. Feel my fingertips tingling, undersides of elbows, waking up, coming back to life. A cool damp tingling running cross my forehead. Lie here with my eyes closed and listen to my body deep deep down. Deep inside, like a deep dark cave, waiting for a voice to call. To sound out the echo. Listen deep down for the pulse and quiver of the child that is gone way, given back, drown in the waves of the sea. And try to remember the name that has lived pon the edge of you tongue so long, five months. Name of a lover. Enemy. And wake one morning to find the enemy-lover gone way, you life all in a sudden vacant, insides hollow, the name no longer there waiting pon the edge of you tongue to pronounce it. First thing before you open you eyes. A name turned to a piece of blue seaglass that all you can do is swallow. Try and swallow. Lie here with my eyes closed and feel the flood my eyelids could never hold back. Salt tears. Rolling and rolling from beneath my shut eyelids like the sea. Tears of lamentation. Tears of forgiveness. Wet pon my cheeks and rolling down soaking up in the soft foam mattress behind my head.

Till there's no more tears left to pass.

Lie here like this longer still, and open my eyes. Slow, very slow. Look up into the early morning darkness. Wait for my eyes to grow accustom, to focus pon the grey ceiling up above, pon the dark patches of moss and mildew, the shadows in stripes running between the grooves of galvanize. Black circles of rust at the leaks, and bubbling-off paint. Look up at the moss and mildew growing in hairy patches long the rafters, dripping down the wood walls. And catch my glimpse all in a sudden over there in the corner, so big I must blink my eyes twice before I could *believe* it. *What?* Like a giant tree-fern! Bushing out,

371

breathing out between the rafters like the top branches of a cedar! Like a big grey ghost, hovering down to settle pon Mistress Lil makeup table. Settle there just beside the framed picture of she mummy, Madam Grandsol, dress in she fancy wedding gown dragging down the steps like a next grey ghost. Looming out in the dark. With the tall dressing-mirror there behind the makeup table in three silver-grey sides. And over pon the bedstand beside Mistress Lil the open bottle of Limacol I can tell straight off by the smell, like the sickness of old West Indian people. A big envelope-parcel I know straight off too by its size and tatter, and wonder what Mistress Lil could be doing with *that* out in the middle of the night? Less she had to show the doctor my health certificate? Less she was reading through my letter like how I uses to read through *she* diary? Like how I would do right now if I had the light to read it by. The concentration to call it up. Those words styling cross the pages of memory like out a dream.

And Mistress Lil sheself, sleeping here quiet beside. She white white skin throwing off a kind of glow in the dark. Not harsh like a ghost, but soft soft glowing just like an angel. How I does call she sometimes, my white angel, lying here bone-naked in the bed like an angel too. Cause she don't sleep in no nightdress, she don't even *own* a nightdress! Sleep naked just like that, and even *more* peculiar, don't wear no slip beneath she daydress neither! And strip down naked in one to go swimming at Huevo Beach, don't even bother if people watching. Just how she feel like doing, how Mistress Lil does do. Cause that's just the way with she. Lying here bone-naked pon she back and so beautiful, beautiful to *me,* in my eyes, cause I know she could scarce recognize that in sheself. Tall and thin and so poise, even asleep. Lying here with she long legs cross at the ankles so narrow. She hand-palms press flat to she chest with the long arms cross at the narrow wrists, cross between she small shapely breasts. Shapely, and beautiful, younggirl breasts. Too *pretty* to call tottots! Not like my own. Not like I could even remember my own. Not after suckling four babies and almost a fifth. Almost, almost a fifth.

Shift my eyes now in the direction I don't want to look. Direction I can't scarce bear to look. Shift my eyes now and look *up* at my own rolling-backwards tottots. My full, heavy, preparing-to-almost-suckle-again tottots. Rolling backwards on top me now with my bamsee shoved up top the pillows. Lie here and look *up* at my heavy tottots, at my belly behind like a big black cannonball rolling down to crush me. Mash me like a crab in the night against the pitch. A bundle of canes waiting to crush beneath the big stone wheel.

Look up like that for a full minute. At my big black cannonball-belly rolling down to crush me. And now, all in a sudden, like somebody shaking me awake out a bad dream, like hitting the hard icy water at the bottom of the well, like looking out from the dark tunnel of canes into sunlight. Now, all in a sudden, looking up to *see* it. My own big round belly. And say, *Wait!* Say, *Wait-wait-wait!* And before I can even get *chance* to question it further, feel the child pelt a kick! One hell of a blasted kick against the insides of my belly like I'm the biggest fool in the world. One hell of a blasted *joyful* kick, like I'm the biggest, happiest fool in the world. *You*, Bolom! Living still. Living stronger than *me*. And think, say, *But how? How could it be possible?*

Turning my head quick to the other side to see that the bedstand table beside me is empty. No doctor-instruments. No pinchers nor clampers nor crushers nor no piece of green cloth. No *nothing* pon this bedstand table beside me but a blanket of fingered-up dust. Cause Bolom, I could *remember* them instruments lying there, even after that doctor left the room. And straining now to lift my head up off the mattress, stretching my neck to look down over the side of the bed. Peering through the dark pon the floor for all them balls of blood-soaked cottonwool. That I could *remember* in my dream the doctor pelting there. Remember *good* enough, Bolom. A dozen little balls of pink cottonwool pelted top the heap of my own blood-soaked dress, all them bindings of ripped bedsheet. Right *there.* Peering down through the dark pon the floor and not finding *nothing.* Nothing but air. And smelling now in the very air itself for not even the *scent* of that doctor. He doctor-scent that I could remember in my dream harsh as pitch-oil in a piece of gauze shoved up my nostrils. Gone, Bolom! Not a trace of he left in the room! He doctor-scent absorbed like a white moth into the night by this Limacol-soaked kerchief, fluttering down from my forehead now to the empty floorboards beside me.

And letting my neck go soft, in one, letting loose the straining muscles of my neck for my head to drop back like a dead weight onto the mattress. Drop with a soft cuff, *poff,* onto the soft foam mattress. And thinking, questioning, asking to myself again now, *How in all the world? How pon God green earth?* And getting my answer now from *she*. First from you Bolom, and now she. Mummy. Mistress Lil. Answering my question with a flash of gold at the very instant of that *poff* onto the foam mattress. Right before my eyes right between my own back-wards-rolling tottots! And reaching there quick quick to grasp a-hold and feel it heavy and cold and precious between my fingers. Hold it up before my eyes and see it glitter even in the dark. Right here tied round my own neck pon the same length of fishingtwine with Ansin little silver cross and the shard of obeah-mirror. The golden key. *We* golden key. We life together, hers and mine and yours!

You golden key, Bolom!

Feeling the cold metal heavy and precious between my fingers. In my closed palm. And smile. Close my eyes and smile. Lie here exhausted and beat-up and happy. Listen to she breathing soft beside me and the waves rolling over gentle down below, only a moment longer, and let myself drift back off into sleep.

3

7 May 1948

Yesterday's was to have been my last entry into this diary. Yesterday was to have been the day I'd anticipated with both fear and longing for so <u>many</u> days. Weeks and weeks now. Playing out my role as the stronger one. The one denied the luxury of weeping. A role relegated to me without my choosing it, ever since the evening we two happened to chance upon one another high at the top of a samaan tree, in the midst of my own too-boisterous dey-boo. A role relegated to me with-out my choosing it, in the very instant in which I looked up from that letter back-rolled into the darkness of that tiny typewriter, and found Daisy standing there before me. Dressed in his cricket whites, victori-ous, and bent-over and beaten. In the very instant in which I imag-ined I saw his lower lip tremble slightly, and reached up to take him into my arms. To console <u>him</u>! Taking up in that instant a role already prescribed for me years before without my knowledge or consent. My wretched role as the stronger one. Denied even the luxury of weeping.

Of breaking down and crying hysterically like a lost and frightened child. An abandoned and abused child (according to her own self-absorbed reading of the world). A thoroughly spoiled child. Suddenly truly orphaned. A grown woman twenty-three years of age waiting for the husband she loves to leave her forever.

But no. I would not allow myself to weep. I would play out my role to the bitter end. <u>Then</u>, I told myself, <u>then at last you can die in peace!</u> So long. So many hours, days, weeks. Denied even the compensatory pleasure of weeping. Till yesterday. Or so I'd imagined. So I'd believed for so long. Because yesterday was to have been the day of Daisy's departure. And, by my own calculation and choosing, the day of Vel's arrival. I'd counted it out carefully to make sure. But, true to form, I'd counted out the days incorrectly. <u>Miscounted</u>. And though yesterday <u>did</u> see Daisy's departure as planned, Vel did not arrive till today. Tonight. Only a moment ago. And now, at this moment only a moment later, as I hurry this pen cross the page of my memory shaping words my mind wants so to outrun, to fly off the page into the future. Forward. Beyond memory. Into the unasked-for and unfathomable future. As I sit here writing this I cannot help but believe that this day is not the last day of my life, but only the first. The first day of <u>our</u> unexpected, unasked-for life together.

But this has not been my first surprise during these nearly two days. My first surprise came yesterday, on the morning of the awaited yesterday—which <u>ought</u> to have been recorded in my long-anticipated <u>final</u> diary entry <u>yesterday</u>—though, as it turned out, I found myself far too busy yesterday to take time out for such an entry. Because immediately after watching Daisy disappear behind the puffs of exhaust spit from Sir Eustace's horrid little Ausin Healy, I climbed the stairs and locked myself straight away into this room. Twisted shut the blinds, sat down dutifully upon this bed, my back pressed against the pillow against the headboard—just as I sit here now to write this— my eyes closed, awaiting the longed-for luxury of weeping to arrive. To overwhelm me. Consume me thoroughly and utterly. That long-anticipated pleasure of letting my life loose, of breaking down and cry-ing hysterically, which I'd promised myself like a secret gift for weeks and weeks. <u>It did not come!</u> I <u>could not</u> shed a single tear, no matter how hard I tried to do so. Suddenly, quite to my own surprise—and *dismay—all I could locate inside was a sense of relief. Not that I was in any way relieved that Daisy had gone, of course not, not at all. Simply that the singular <u>event</u> of his leaving, the very incidence and occurrence of it, was over. Finally and irrevocably over. And all I could feel inside was a sense of relief. No matter how foolishly I endeavored to conjure up feelings of sadness, despair, loss. No matter how hard I <u>struggled</u> to make myself weep! Quite to my own surprise, and dismay, all I could feel inside was a sense of unburdening. Till I began to feel <u>frustrated</u>. Sitting here with my back propped against the pillow against the headboard, my eyes closed, trying my hardest like a chupidee to break down weeping. Only feeling more and more frustrated. And in my frustration, without realizing in the least what my hands were doing—otherwise, truthfully, I should have to consider myself the most atrocious woman alive—I began doing something which I'd not done in months and months. Which, in fact, I'd not done in over a year. Since the very day of my pilgrimage with Di to the little black madonna in Maraval. In my frustration, quite unconsciously, I began rolling beads! Of course, I'd not a chaplet to hold in my fingers upon which to roll them. That chaplet I'd offered up to the little black madonna. What I found myself fingering instead, with my right hand, and without my even realizing it, was the golden skeleton key. Which I <u>did</u> happen still to be holding! Fingering <u>it</u> with my eyes closed as though it were the golden beads of my chaplet. My golden chaplet. Worn like a necklace round my neck. Or the little black pempem seeds of the chaplet worn round my neck all the years of my childhood. My lips unconsciously whispering the words of a Holy Mary, rolling beads for the first time in months and months. Over a year! And not yet an hour after poor Daisy'd left the house!*

Of course, when I did open my eyes—when I <u>did</u> become fully conscious of what my wicked hands were doing, my wicked <u>left</u> hand (<u>Let not thy right hand know</u>, et cetera, et cetera . . .)—when I did become fully conscious of what my wicked left hand was doing, completely without consent of my right, I was not simply shocked, I was quite measurably <u>repulsed</u>. Yet I could not stop. Could not possibly bring myself to stop. No matter how hard I tried. As though I'd lost control now of my own hands! As though, as absurd as the notion may sound, as though the key itself were now controlling <u>my</u> fingers. The golden

376

skeleton key itself! Because suddenly I could not possibly put it down. Could not bring my fingers to let it go even for an instant and put it down to rest here on this bedstand table beside me. This golden skeleton key meant as a gift for Daisy, but which—as I realized now with a sudden procession of ants <u>streaming</u> up my spine, a sudden buzzing between my trembling thighs like a batchaks' nest—this key meant as a present for Daisy, but which I realized now was actually a gift for myself. A gift I would give to <u>me</u>! Because I could not possibly bring my fingers to put it down. And once I acknowledged the futility of my trying to do so—once I accepted the physical impossiblity of trying— all I could do was give myself over. Let loose my life! Break down, utterly and absolutely, but in a way in which I could not possibly have imagined only an hour before. Permit myself to break down in a way which, initially, I'd found both shocking and repulsive. Till I acknowledged the absurdity of harboring those notions too. After all, what possible harm could I bring to the world? A woman, locked-up in her room, alone with herself? Rolling beads. Even if the world would have her weep?

4

I was still rolling beads the following afternoon when Di knocked on my door saying that Vel, the younggirl, going be here just now. Which is <u>not</u> to say I'd <u>not</u> put down this key for an instant since the previous morning; that I'd been rolling beads uninterruptedly without even a pause for a breath of air for twenty-four or thirty hours at a stretch! Of course not. I'd slept much of the time. And of course, I'd let go the key to eat the meals Di brought to my bedroom on the silver tray. The meals which, peculiarly enough, I'd eaten with a <u>ravenous</u> appetite. Actually stuffing the food into my mouth with my <u>hands</u>—for the first time, I can assure you, ever in my life! Because sitting here in the bed with my back propped against the headboard, the tray balanced precariously upon my lap, I found the silverware far too awkward to operate. How much more economical to take up a leg of chicken and swirl it round in the fricassee sauce with my fingers, and how much more <u>pleasurable</u>! Not to mention my newly discovered delight in prodding my fingers directly into the sauce without the intervening chicken leg, and sucking them one by one quite audibly afterward! After all, there's not a living soul here in my bedroom to witness. To critique my bad table-manners. (And, fortunately enough, there's no one but me to read in this secret diary and be shocked by my wicked writing-manners either!) Other than the pair of Amerindian lovers hanging cross from my bed—and they're far too taken up at the moment with themselves, with their own overwhelming, impending history—to be much bothered by me. My delightful finger-smacking! Not to mention my scooping up handfuls of rice or mashed-potatoes with my curled flippers like a turtle scooping sand, shoveling it into my mouth. And plucking away afterward the excess paste or all the fallen grains of rice stuck to my chin, and neck, and twittering tottots. And more than once even to the golden skeleton key itself (which I now wear on a black ribbon tied round my neck), placing _it_ in my mouth along with my sticky fingers. Smacking _it_ clean and shining too. More than once having to douse _myself_ down in the shower after such a meal!

Another surprise during these nearly two days—my peculiarly ravenous appetite, since I've always been a fussy eater. Particularly after all those years in the convent. All _those_ awful meals—that awful porridge morning after morning _in saecula saeculorum!_—a sour-faced nun scrutinizing our bowls afterward, making sure we licked down the last scrap. Oh, no. My new appetite—or, rather, my newly discovered pleasure in eating—was still another discovery during these nearly two days. Two pleasures: one newly discovered, the other freshly recovered. And for these nearly two days, other than my spats of sleep, I've been sitting here with my back propped against the pillow against the headboard, doing little else.

The truth is that still I have not wept. Not a single solitary tear. Much to my own surprise and dismay. Still I have not—if I am to be entirely honest with myself—still I have not felt a moment of despair. Of anguish. I have, however, felt more than a sense of relief. More than a sense of unburdening. There _have_ been moments, stretches even, during which I have felt not despair or anguish; nothing so ennobling or profound—but only the slow surfacing of a deep sense of loneliness. Only in moments. Perhaps even stretches. Welling slowly up from down below, from someplace dark and deep inside me. It is not new, this sense of loneliness. On the contrary, it stretches back before the

time of Daisy. Back before my time spent in England, before the happy
year or so spent living with mummy together in this house, stretching
back even before my years in the convent. Back to my earliest child-
hood. An acute feeling of loneliness which has surfaced in varying
degrees during the various periods and stages of my life—the unpleas-
ant times and the pleasant, the sad and the happy—but which I have,
with varying degrees of success, managed to keep shoved-down.
Submerged deep within. It is a loneliness I have always been aware of,
all my life, at least in some vague way. An acute and profound sense
of loneliness, which I have felt in distinct moments during these nearly
two days. Felt even for stretches. Welling slowly up toward the surface.

5

But I can assure you that I was not contemplating that loneliness
when Di knocked upon my door saying that Vel, the younggirl, going
be here just now. I was rolling beads. And quite pleasurably at that!
Nevertheless, I got up from my bed and dutifully dressed myself for the
first time in nearly two days. Went downstairs for the first time in
nearly two days, into the parlour to wait with Di for Vel's arrival. The
bus from Henly was due in in St Maggy at 3:30 this afternoon. Di'd
estimated another twenty or thirty minutes by the time Vel flagged
down a taxi to carry her from the terminal in town out to the estate.
But when eight o'clock arrived this evening and Vel still had not, I
decided to return to my bedroom upstairs. Perhaps, I reasoned, she'd
missed the bus? Perhaps, despite recommendation and health certificate
and police record—despite that letter sprawling on and on for pages
and pages of which I've still not found the strength to read more than
the first two sentences!—perhaps the younggirl has decided she does
not want the job after all? Perhaps the want-a-wallop sister has hit her
over the head with a big stone, as she'd done the grandmother, and Vel
is lying in a hospital bed in Sherman recovering from a profound con-
cussion? If Sherman even has a hospital?

That is what I was wondering when I started up the stairs to return
to my room, and I heard Vel's timid knock at the door. Di'd heard it
also, because as I bent over to fit the key into the lock to open the front
door, I could sense her approaching behind me from the back of the

house. I swung the door open, standing there waiting for my eyes to adjust to the darkness outside, still holding the key in my hand. Still holding the golden skeleton key in my hand, and trying, as my eyes slowly focused—for the <u>second</u> time in nearly two days—to pierce the blunt point of it through the center of my transparent palm. The gift of this golden skeleton key which I could not bring myself to let go and hand over to Daisy only thirty-four or forty hours before, but which, after a single <u>instant</u>, I was struggling to hold <u>onto</u> now. Because I wanted so to give it to her! Immediately. Without a second thought. After a single instant I wanted to give it over to <u>her</u>. And the only possible way I could prevent myself from doing so was to press it blunt-pointed into the center of my palm, struggling to keep my hand from disobeying me once again.

This younggirl was Dulcianne! The same Dulcianne of my childhood whom I'd not laid eyes upon since I was the age of twelve or thirteen, ten years ago! But she was no longer a younggirl. This Dulcianne was a woman—just as my imagination should have pictured the woman Dulcianne would grow up to become. Only my imagination should have fallen short. Should have been inadequate. Because <u>this</u> woman taking shape out of the darkness before me, this Vel, was more beautiful even than I remembered my beloved Dulcianne had been. More beautiful and stronger, her skin darker, richer still than Dulcianne's. Even more alive, more <u>real</u>. More a part of the tall cedar trees and the glittering river and the smoky musty smell of the forest. Stronger and more beautiful and more vibrant with life, because now she'd matured into a woman. And now, after leaving me for ten years, she'd returned.

I could not move. Suddenly my feet felt stuck like laglee to the silk Persian rug beneath them. I could only stand there staring, gazing into her beautiful dark eyes, trying with all my might to pierce the blunt point of the key through the center of my palm. This key which I wanted so to surrender without a second thought! Gazing into the eyes of this woman I had known for only an instant, but whom I felt sure I'd known all my life. Whom I had always believed was my own twin sister. My opposite. My own inverted mirror reflection separated from me only by the pane of glass. The pain of glass. And now this woman offered me proof. Now, as I stood there locked into the gaze of her beautiful eyes—as suddenly powerless to look away as I was physically incapable of piercing the key through my palm—now she wept for me. In my place. Wept as I had _not_ been able to do for the previous thirty-four or forty hours. _She_ wept; for _me_; in _my_ place. Just as I had not been able to do. Had found myself physically incapable of doing. Because as I stood there, in that moment, I realized that in truth I'd not wept in ten years. That, in truth, I'd _forgotten_ how to weep: willfully forgotten. Neither for sadness, nor joy, nor even for physical pain. Not even the physical pain of a lipstick-canister shoved up brutally inside me. Not then or after. Not once. Not a single solitary tear, in ten years. Not since the night before my departure for the convent. Not since the very last time I'd laid eyes on Dulcianne. Both of us standing there beside the washstone at the side of the house, me gazing up into her face half-hidden by darkness, she still holding the coiled-up lasso she'd just used with all her strength to lash me cross my face. That lasso meant for the capture of the half-human, half-animal lagahoo disguised by the darkness of a child's imagination, and uncovered in the last moment of a lost childhood to reveal her own monstrous father. That last moment in which I stood gazing up into Dulcianne's face half-hidden by darkness, the tears rolling down my cheeks, weeping, watching her turn from me now and disappear into the night.

She had come back, unasked-for and unexpected, and more beautiful even than my own imagination could call her up again out of darkness. She had returned, and now she was weeping in my place. Weeping for all the sadness, and joy, and all the physical pain _I_'d not been capable of weeping for myself in ten years. Such real human emotions as I'd made myself incapable of feeling. Willfully forgotten. Ever since that night ten years ago. That moment in which I stood beside the washstone peering into the darkness through a wash of tears. Looking behind my beloved Dulcianne disappearing into the night.

Di said something. Standing there in the shadows somewhere behind me. And now she said something, this woman who called herself Vel and came from the village of Sherman, and who was even more beautiful than Dulcianne. Who had returned to me even more beautiful than Dulcianne. Returned, I knew—or believed, hoped with all my heart—this woman who had returned to teach me the simple *necessity of weeping. Teach me how to remember. Even if it should take me another ten years to learn.*

She said something, asked something, Vel did—about shoes and walking and the rug—but I could not decipher it. Could not answer. Locked-up as I was in the gaze of her dark eyes. All I could manage was a weak smile which felt silly, but was not ingenuine. She stepped into the house. And then she turned round to take up her suitcase and her various things, parcels, and Di stepped out of the darkness behind me and bent over beside her to take up some of her things too; and then they both walked past me. Leaving me standing here staring out the open front door, into the dark night. Standing here feeling the pain of this key still pressing blunt-pointed into the center of my palm, the sting of that coil of rope lashed with all the hatred of an abused race and gender cross my face—which I could feel as acutely ten years later as the instant in which I received it, looking out into the same night which ten years ago had swallowed up my life. And now, ten years later—or so I want to believe, so I hope with all my heart—has returned my life to me again.

6

Lie here and feel the waves of pain. Stinging cross the surface. Rippling like water cross the surface of sleep. Coming in waves. Lie here and feel the cool seabreeze brushing in through the blinds to ease the pain way. Hear the waves turning over. Listen down deep inside my body for the pulse and quiver of the child that is living still. Better, stronger than me! And pronounce the name in my sleep like a prayer for waking. For waking up inside a sweet dream. *Bolom. We Bolom. We sweet Bolom.* Lie here and listen to the waves rolling over and over pon the shore down below, to she breathing soft here beside. And smile. Lie here with my eyes closed feeling the key cold and heavy and precious in my closed palm, and smile. Lie here and smile.

Open my eyes and look up into the early morning darkness. Up at the patches of moss and mildew growing like clouds cross the grey galvanize sky. Black circles of rust at the leaks. Bubbling-off paint. Look up studying the hairy patches of moss and mildew growing long the rafters like a multitude of miniature islands. A whole Caribbean of islands, drifting cross the sky like clouds reflected pon the sea. Slipping off the sky and sliding down the wood walls, floating tranquil pon the sea.

And think how long ago since you bust you way inside this room to give it a proper cleaning. Well, to search out the *stash,* the money that she had stash. But then when you see the *state* that was in this room, all the dust and all the filth, you get waylaid. Waylaid from you search for she stash. That was five years back, five years in the least, so no wonder this room could be in a state again. And think now, say, *First thing, Bolom! First thing this morning soon as we could get sufficient light, soon as we could catch sufficient strength. Up pon that ladder and scrub-down that galvanize. All them rafters and all them walls. Scrub with lye, that Ajax bleach. And plant that blasted tree-fern out in the yard where she belong! Up top that flamboyant if you want, but Bolom, this time we climbing up with the ladder. This time we climbing down with the ladder too!*

Lie here saying that, thinking that, all them plans, and all in a sudden remember my body all busted-up. Exhausted-out. Scarce even able to shift a muscle. Lift up a limb. Lie here in this bed with my hips still shoved up top the pillows, my rolling-backwards tottots and cannonball-belly preparing to crush me. And say, *Well leastest thing we could do is little dusting. These bedstands and Mistress Lil makeup table, and beat out that big old bagging-down chair. That's the leastest thing that we could do, Bolom. First thing this morning. Little dusting.* Lie here looking up into the early morning darkness. And think of all those nights, five weeks of nights, busting my way into this room with the thiefed key, and give this room a proper cleaning. Get waylaid for that cleaning, and the diary, waylaid from my search for she stash. That money that Mistress Lil had hiding up in here. And then stumbling pon it after long last right there in the most obvious place, right here beneath this bed under the loose floorboard. Right here in that same brownpaper-sack that I did watch she tuck under she elbow to walk out from Barclays. And Bolom, counting up that money and feeling such a rush of relief. Such a rush of my relief from all my mounting preoccupation, when I count it out, them 300 dollars that she had remaining. And then the very next night adding *my* stash to she own inside the brownpaper-sack. That money that *I* had saving from my salary evey month, 180 dollars, cause I did saving that money a *long* time. Most five years.

So that was 180 dollars that I had, plus 300 that she had, to make 480 dollars that we had together. That we had stash together in the brownpaper-sack right here under this bed, under the loose floorboard. And Bolom, now I could feel the rush of my relief. Cause 480 dollars is plenty money. Plenty plenty money! That's more money than I ever see in one hand in my life, than I ever *dream* to see. Less still to look down now in my dream and see that this hand belongs to *me!* I say we could live a *long* time pon that amount of money. Four–five years, especial if we ration. I say we could live four–five years in the least, before we even got to *start* to worry.

And I take we back to a serious regiment too. And every month I put back my salary inside the brownpaper-sack. Every month. Soon as Mistress Lil hand it over. I tuck it way in my bosom straight, and soon as she drop asleep dozing off pon the back gallery after breakfast, or in the parlourroom, I climb up again straight out the window up over the sink. Straight up the drainpipe in through Mistress Lil bedroom window, and I tuck my salary money inside the brownpaper-sack beneath the floorboard. Here beneath this same bed. So *many* times, climbing up and down that drainpipe, up and down, and always in a hurry to get back inside before Mistress Lil could miss me. So many times that after a time I didn't even bother to count it out no more. Cause we did had so *much,* and me always in such a flap to get back down. After a time I didn't even bother to worry my head with that.

But then one afternoon I catch myself unfolding the sack, I say you better count it out. You better count it out, however much money we got left, cause it's a *long* time now since you ain't do it. Bolom, we had but thirty-three dollars! *Thirty-three dollars,* left from out the original 480, and that's including the fifteen dollars from my salary that I just put back! And Bolom, when I climb down that drainpipe again that afternoon I was in a *stupor.* When I climb back in through that kitchen window. I say, *What you could do now? What you could do, and whatever it is, you better do it quick.*

I was still in the same stupor couple nights later, standing there before the kitchen sink washing out the wares, cause I didn't even get chance to wake up yet. Wake up out from my stupor. I didn't even get chance to think out proper what I could do, all the *amount* of things that I could do, to bring in some cash. Like get a day-job with one the wealthy white mistress in town, cooking and cleaning and watching over the children. And if Mistress Lil don't like that, she don't want me going out the house doing that, I could take in some extra laundering right here. Clothes and linens and such, for people that need extra laundering. Cause we got that big Maytag machine that don't even hardly turn for just she and me. And that electric iron standing mostly idle. Or I could do needleworks. I could do needleworks cause I learn that from young, and I could still remember too, still got my scissors and my thimble from my needleworks. But Bolom, I didn't even stop to think that, think it out proper, cause I still didn't even get chance to wake up yet from my stupor. My shock that I did had. That night only a couple nights later, when I was standing there before the sink washing the wares, and I look up.

See oldman-Grandsol staring. Staring back at me through the kitchen window. And he ain't even been back at the house not since Di leave. That I could *know* about anyway, cause I ain't lay my eyes pon he since then. Ever since then. And Bolom, that was so long back I could scare even *recognize* he. And he did change too. Change inside-out. Cause this oldman-Grandsol turn in bacra-johnny now. How we does call them, the poor whites. Vagrant. Wastrel. Dress in he clothes all raggedy and filthy, and he was drunk. Oh my Jesus he head was *wash!* Wash clean through with babash, the bush rum. He head was so wash he did take me for D-Ann, Dulcianne, Di daughter. Cause Di say he uses to go with she too, go with Dulcianne too. Di say how this oldman-Grandsol even get Dulcianne haveen with child. Get she haveen so she didn't have no choice but take-off running for America. And now he was back, oldman-Grandsol. Taking me for she. Standing right here beneath the kitchen window, taking *me* for *she,* and singing out low and brass like a toad into the night, "*Dul-ci-anne! Dul-ci-anne! Dul-ci-anne!*"

But that haveen that he put pon Dulcianne was long before Di work she science. *Long* before. That was long before Di murder he manhood, he potential, that Di say she kill dead for *always,* and long before Di steep-up he passion too. But Bolom, truth is that I was scarce even thinking that. All that. That evening when I was standing there before the sink washing the wares, and I look up to find oldman-Grandsol looking in staring back at me. Cause I didn't even wake up yet from my stupor of two days before. I was only standing there, my hands still in them suds, and not even listening to he toad-voice singing neither. Cause I was listening again to *Di. She* voice, singing out to me again in my same dream, *"Twenty-seven dollars! Only to lie pon my back and take my pleasure in he pain. Twenty-seven dollars!"*

But Bolom, it wasn't no pleasure. Not for me anyway. Least not till he hand over the money! Wasn't no pleasure, and it wasn't no pain neither. Wasn't no *nothing.* Not for me, cause I just close my eyes I shut them tight tight tight. After I did follow he under the house. After I follow he round the concrete steps of the back porch stoop, and we bend down to crawl in under the gallery. Crawl in pon some blankets that he had there, some old crocusssack, spread out there cross the dirt. And I just lie down pon my back. I just shut my eyes tight tight tight. Cause I didn't even *know* what was preparing to happen then.

Nothing. Most of nothing. That take place between him and me under that gallery. I could feel he moving above, moving about in the darkness above. Like he did doing something to heself, nasty, like you could just imagine, but I didn't even *want* to see. To know what. Course, he did touching me up too. Little bit. My tottots. But then when he reach to touch me down *there* I just grab-on he wrist, tight, like I *mean* it, I just push he hand way and he don't try that again. Not again. Next thing I smell he babash-breath beside my face, at the side, that stiff babash smell, and next thing I know he did sleeping. He did *sleeping,* right there, and scarce any time at all since we did climb up under. And Bolom, no sooner do I catch he sleeping when I shake he straight awake again. I shake he awake, say I got to go, got to *go.* Not even two minutes after he drop asleep, when I go crawling out and he come crawling out straight behind. Now he hand me over the money, hand me over a fistful of raggedy bills that he pull from he pocket, and I tuck straight in my bosom and I gone. Don't even *stop* to count it out, cause I gone. Not till I climb back in through the window back in over the sink, back inside my room with the door shut. Twenty-seven dollars! *Twenty-seven dollars,* only for doing nothing. Most of nothing. Nothing but lie pon my back and close my eyes, and make pretend that I was Di daughter. Dulcianne. Make pretend that I was *she.*

7

Then one day Berry come at the house. That was a time after I did start this business of going under the gallery with oldman-Grandsol. This prostitute business, how Di say it, only he was *my* prostitute now. Maybe five–six different times. Six–seven. That I did go under with he. And Bolom, it was so *easy,* so quick and so easy, like getting paid just for doing nothing, that I didn't even worry my head to think up nothing else. Day-job, or taking in extra laundering and ironing, or needle-works. I didn't even worry to confront with Mistress Lil about looking for nothing else, didn't even worry my head to think about that. Then one day Berry come at the house.

I wasn't there, cause it was a Sunday I was in town to my prayer-meeting. He did know it too. He did *plan* it like that, cause he know I wouldn't let he in the house. Not till hell catch fire! He wait till I wasn't in there, and he disguise up heself too. Disguise up heself as ganga, dress up heself as ganga, like a woman. Same old tricks exactly how he uses to pull. Mistress Lil answer the door and Berry say he is my Granny Ansin, come all the way from Sherman to pay a visit pon me. Well I ain't know how Mistress Lil could fall for that. I ain't *know* how, cause he was so *ugly.* But Bolom, truth is that man did pull that same old trick pon me once pon a time too. Once pon a time, that Berry come dress as ganga and bearing gifts of England tin ham, and Mistress Lil open the door easy as me, easy as that beautiful fairy-princess out the story-book open up for the wolf. That same wolf dress up in heself ganga. She let he to come in straight. Straight inside the house, and she put he straight to dine at the dining table pon that *whole* big jorum of callaloo that *I* had cooking inside the kitchen.

Bolom, when I reach back, when I reach back in the house from my prayer-service, and I find he sitting there in the parlour all dress-up ganga looking such a *fool,* all the fingertips of he little white gloves stain to dasheen-green from sucking pon them crabs, well I just let-loose pon he. I just let-loose! Don't even give he chance to answer nothing. I say, "*You?*" I say, "What the hell you think you doing in here? What the hell you think you doing coming in here inside this house?" I say, "This house *sacred!* This house is sacred ground, *blessed,* so what you doing coming with you nasty self inside to foul it for?" I say, "You *get out!* Get you blasted self to hell out, and don't you *never* come back to foul the sacred ground of this house again!"

I return to Mistress Lil waiting for me in the kitchen, I say to go and lock that front door proper how it belong. And don't let he to come inside here never again, don't care if he come carrying a *cow.*

But he come back. That same night. He come back that same night and he don't bother to knock the door neither. He climb straight up the drainpipe, in through Mistress Lil bedroom window, and he take way that key that she had wearing round she neck pon the black ribbon. He lock-up Mistress Lil inside she room, and then he descend the stairs to come in here inside *my* bedroom now. Right here, use the same key to lock-up *we* here inside my bedroom too.

Well I did startle. Startle and vex both. To find he in here. I sit up in my bed and still half-asleep, I say, "What the hell you doing in here?" Berry say, "I come for you." I say, "*Wha?*" He say, "I come for you, back for you. That we could go back to being together again." Well Bolom, I should have laugh. If I wasn't so vex, and glaze, and sleepy still, I should have laugh straight in he face for that. But I don't laugh. I say, "What you talking about? You drunk? You head wash?" I say, "You head *must* be wash, for you to come in here and talking that foolishness!"

Now he sit down pon the side the bed, not even boisterous, more quiet like, and he say, slow, "I got some waters pon my head, but my head ain't wash. Ain't wash. And what I got to say I been planning and thinking out a long time." He say, "I come to carry you back to Sherman. Carry you back home, that we could be back together again. Just how we uses to be." He say, "I been thinking plenty Vel, and I going change my ways. I going turn over. You watch. I going turn over a new leaf pon my life, and we could go back to living good. Just how we uses to be."

Well I sit there a moment taking this thing in, this address that Berry prepare to give me. And when I answer I don't answer vex. I don't answer glaze. I answer he in the patient. I say, "Berry, what you remember? What you could remember of we life? That good that we had, how we uses to be together?" But he don't answer now. He don't answer now cause he *can't* answer. He could only sit there in the quiet, and now I answer my own question to *me.* I say, "Well let me tell you what I remember. Of all that good that we had. I could remember waiting in the night for you to reach home, and you don't never reach. Night after night. I could remember bearing the children by myself, raising the children by myself. I could remember *struggling* for them children, and I could remember watching them children suffer too. Watching them go hungry, that starvation, and not a thing in this world I got to give them. To do for them. Don't even get chance to think pon my *own* suffering, my *own* hunger, the hardship of my *own* life, for watching at them children suffer." I say, "But Berry, the thing I could remember most, the thing that I could remember the hardest, is watching them children dead pon my hands. Four children! One after the next! And Berry, when they all was dead, when they all four was dead and bury, and I get chance for the first time since I could even remember to feel my own suffering, my own pain, that pain was so harsh I couldn't bear it. Couldn't carry, cause my shoulders and my body and my *mind* wasn't strong enough. And all that I could do was take my own life. Try and take." Now I stay quiet a moment, a moment of quiet, I say, "And you want to carry me back *there?*"

Now we both sit quiet a time. A long time, in the quiet. He looking pon me and me looking pon he. And truth is, I couldn't help but think how handsome. Never mind how vex and how glaze I was with he only couple minutes before. Cause just as brute as that man was, just as beast, he was soft and he was good-looking. The two sides. And I couldn't help myself from reflecting little bit pon the other side. How handsome he was, sitting there bareback with he red skin, and so tall, strong, he muscles a-rippling, with he orange hair and them freckles pon he nose just like a little schoolgirl. I couldn't help but smile. Little bit, cause truth is I did always hold a soft spot for he, no matter what, and he me.

Last he smile too, he say, "Well I know you ain't going send me home empty-handed. I know that. You ain't going let me come all the way here, dress up myself in ganga, and send me back without a little something." But I wasn't listening to he good, cause I was drifting off in someplace distant, quiet. I say, "What?" He say, "You could give me little something, to go home with, like how we uses to do in the canes." I say, and not even bawling. Cause I was talking quiet still. I say, "You *get out*. You hand me over that key, and you get you blasted self to hell out. And don't you *never* come back in this house to soil this sacred ground again!"

I did think that was the end a he, Bolom. I did sure, but then one morning maybe two–three days later, when I was dusting inside the parlour, dusting off them side tables, I see beside the chair a big red handbag. Big red handbag, and *ugly,* and I say I never see Mistress Lil carrying this thing before. I never even see Mistress Lil carry no hand-bag before. And then when I look inside I find a lipstick, a compact-powder, and two little white gloves with all the fingertips stain a dasheen-green. But I ain't shut it yet, cause I find a little clip-purse too. One them little clip-purse, like to carry coins in. And roll up tight inside this little clip-purse was a roll of bills amounting to eighty-four dollars. I say thank you Berry! Thank you Berry and thank you Lord for that! And I tuck that money safe inside my bosom.

When I fold out the brownpaper-sack and I make the count we was up to 212 dollars. 212 dollars, from the original thirty-three that we had when we first meet with crisis. That crisis before the tragedy. When I first feel the fall of that crisis pon my head, me and Mistress Lil eco-nomic crisis. But all I could feel now was the rush of my relief, the drain of all my mounting preoccupation again. Cause we was back up to 212 dollars. And I say too, right then, I say now is the moment to confront with Mistress Lil. Now that we got a space of calm, and secu-rity of cash. Now that we got that insurance of 212 dollars, now is the moment for we to confront pon we future life together. Whilst we still *got* a future. I say tomorrow afternoon after tea. Tomorrow afternoon, after we sit down to take we tea. I going tell Mistress Lil the complete entire history of that brownpaper-sack beneath she bed. All this secret scrambling up and down the drainpipe. And that prostitute business beneath the gallery too. Oh, yes! That too. The complete entire history, no matter how painful the telling is. The hearing of it. We secret his-tory, that carrying on now for months and months. Years. I *swear* myself to it. I say *tomorrow afternoon, after tea,* we going confront pon we future life together. Whilst we still got a future life to confront pon.

But then that night I was there in the kitchen washing the wares, and I did had this funny feeling. Of bad. Like a premonition like. I did just want to finish them wares quick quick and scramble off to bed. I did even *know* what it was, this premonition that I was feeling, cause I wasn't looking out through that window above the sink not for nothing. I just didn't want to look. And anyway I ain't hear he call, he frog-call, how he does always do. Nothing more than them crickets in the night cracking. Crick-cracking. And now I start to feeling little better. Now I wasn't hardly paying no mind to my premonition no more. Not till I stack the last plate inside the cupboard, wipe my hands dry cross the apron, and I turn to leave. I catch a glance of he through the window.

Standing there smoking slow pon he cigar, cigarette, and I say that's a peculiar thing, for he to be smoking pon that. Peculiar for he *not* to call-out, how he always do. And peculiar for he to be smoking pon that cigarette. Cause I ain't see he smoke pon that in all these times since the first. That very first time, when Di was still in the house. And now he did appear different too. Not so much of bacra-johnny. Now he appear like that first time, dress back a style, and he face shave clean. Like he did gain back he dignity again. Somehow. And Bolom, this thing did had me *fraid*. Had me fraid and worried both, both at the same time. I stand there staring out the window, watching up at he staring back at me, and I say, *Vel, don't! You don't got to do it so don't do it!* But then I was hearing a next voice too. Sounding out at the same time. Singing out to me at the same time in the midst of my same dream. Di say, *"Twenty-seven dollars! Only to lie pon my back and take my pleasure in he pain. Twenty-seven dollars!"*

I notice something else different too, straight off, even before I could get myself out through that window. I notice he didn't drinking. Not now, not tonight. I notice he didn't drinking and he didn't drunk. He head didn't wash. Cause he was *helping* me to climb out through the window! He reach up and he take a-hold of my weight and he lift me down, help me down, and he never do that before. Not never. Not a *once*. Cause most the time he was too drunk even to stand up for heself, less still to lift me down out the window! And this night he was strong too.

I lie pon them crocusssack and I shut my eyes tight tight tight. I shut my eyes tight, cause I didn't even *know* what was preparing to happen then. I didn't know what he do. What it is he do to heself. To gain back he strength. Maybe he take tonic? Dose of bois bandé? Maybe he pay a obeahwoman to unwork the work Di do? *Unscience the science?* Or maybe just drink, the *lack* of drink. Plain and simple. Maybe just the fact that he didn't drinking no waters and he head didn't wash. This night. Cause when he hold me down. Strong, cause he was a big man too. When he hold me down, all he strength, and he force heself pon me with all he strength too, he potential wasn't dead neither. Not for nothing. Not for life, nor death, and not for no longer than the animal grunt of a split-second. Not no longer than that bullet-blast of life to signify my own death.

9

Is *waters* steep up the passion. Is waters kill the potential too.

Maybe. Maybe it was only the *lack* of alcohol that he *didn't* drinking that night. To give he back he strength, he potential. Maybe he take tonic? Dose of bois bandé? Or maybe he pay a obeahwoman to unwork the work Di do? Unscience the science? That night of my nightmare underneath the gallery. My nightmare that I wouldn't wake up from not for another five months.

Now in my dream I hear Di calling out again. She voice, over and over, "*Servant find sheself pregnant she got to go, got to go home. That's just how it is. Seem like that's the law!*" Now in my dream I climb up the pipe to get in Mistress Lil bedroom, but not to put back money, put in money. Now I climb up that I could *thief* the money. Thief the money to go at the pharmacist and buy quinine powder. I tell Mistress Lil I walking to town to mail Ansin a letter, and Mistress Lil say she would carry me in the Ford. She say she glad to do that. I say I *walking* to town and I walking by my*self,* I say it just like that, harsh like that, and I walk to town to the pharmacist to buy more quinine powder.

Then one Sunday in service I see a oldwoman looking cross. Looking cross. Every time I raise up my head out the prayerbook. Then when I was going to leave, even before I could get out the church, this oldwoman come behind me. She say, "You looking to throw that what you got carrying inside you belly?" She come behind me and she say it, just like that, even before I could get out the church! Bolom, I run! I take-off and I *run.* I say, *How she could know what I got carrying? How she could know that?* And following Sunday she come behind me again. This same oldwoman. She say, "Thirty dollars. For you to throw that. Thirty dollars." Bolom, I take-off running again. I *run.*

But following Sunday I had the thirty dollars tuck in my bosom. Thirty dollars that I thief from beneath Mistress Lil bed. She carry me to she house that wasn't nothing more than a falling-down shack press together amongst other falling-down shacks. Not even a door to it. Just a crocusssack curtain that she close behind. Now she count out seven drops of something inside a glass of water. Seven drops of something that smell like pitch-oil, cause I *know* that smell, know it good enough. And she give me the glass of water with this pitch-oil inside to drink. Now she put a tin basin with more pitch-oil pon the dirt floor in the middle the room, and she light the pitch-oil. She throw in little bit of something to make it smoke up even *more,* like some crushed leaves, smoking up in a big smoke of black sooty nasty-smelling smoke. *Harsh.* And now she make me to raise up my skirts and squat down over! Squat down over so this black smoke could go all up inside *there,* all up in my clothes and my skin. Till I start to cough and cough and she had to take me off the basin and put me to lie down. Give me a next glass of water to drink. Cause I was ready to pass right out, after breathing in all that sooty smoke! Now she tear off two piece of the same bed-sheet that I was sitting pon she bed, coconut fiber bed, she roll up the two piece of bedsheet and put them to soak in the same basin of pitch-oil. Now she light it back again, a blast of that black sooty smoke, and then after couple seconds she out the fire. Tell me I must wear each under my armpit. Them roll of burn-up sooty-up bedsheet, each one press under my armpit. I got to wear them all day and I got to sleep in the night like that too. And come back the following afternoon. Every afternoon for seven afternoons straight. Same foolishness.

Now I got to bind my belly. I *got* to do it! First thing every morning before I carry the tray upstairs for Mistress Lil with she coffee and she bake. I got to do it, cause my belly was showing big already. I trying everything, everything that I could think, that I could know. I drinking down the quinine day and night. I drinking down the bush-medicine, them stews of green pawpaw and castoroil and womb-fruit, and ain't doing nothing but make me to run loose to my stools. I wearing them obeah-burntrags under my armpits day and night, even though I know that oldwoman thief my thirty dollars. Thief the money from me that I thief from she. From Mistress Lil. Binding up my belly every morning so she wouldn't discover this big black cannonball growing inside preparing to explode. *You*, Bolom. Binding up my belly every morning so Mistress Lil wouldn't discover about *you*, and send we both way. Send we back home to Sherman. Cause Bolom, I know good enough that would be the death of you. I *know*. I been through that four times already. I know it's far more better to give you back now, *before*, than have to watch a fifth child dead pon my hands again. I *know* Bolom, and that would be the death of me too.

Last I make up my mind to confront with Mistress Lil. The *second* time. I say that's the only thing that I could do so I got to do it. I got to confront with Mistress Lil pon the secret history of you, Bolom. *Everything*. Cause I say maybe she know something that I don't. Some other way that I didn't try. Maybe them French-Creoles got they own way, some special way that I ain't never hear nothing about nor never try. And I say too maybe she know a doctor in town, could do me an abortion. Make me an abortion. Pon a black woman. Maybe she know something about that.

After we New Year Day feast. I say that would be the best time, to confront with she. Right after we New Year Day feast that we did planning most two–three weeks already. Cause we didn't eating like that again. To spend *that* kind of money pon that kind of food again. Not no more. Not for months and months, years now. But this New Year Day Mistress Lil say she want to make a feast. She want to eat a *feast*. Like she did know the end was close at hand, know what was coming. Somehow. Like she did sense that. And I say that might even be the best thing, for we to eat a last feast together, cause I wouldn't be here in this house to eat no feast like that never again. We did plan it all out. How we going eat the fricassee chicken that Mistress Lil going cook, that was both we favorite and we ain't eat in so long. And I going cook the split-pea soup with the hambone, pigeonpeas, the white rice and steam christophine and bake yam that I did love so much too. We even plan to eat a guava duff! A guava duff, that we plan to eat for we desert.

And we *eat* it too, *all* that, for we New Year Day feast together. All but the duff, cause I was just then in the kitchen steaming over the duff. You know, steaming it over little bit to warm it up. When I look up out the kitchen window and I did feeling so sad, so frighten, thinking about what I was preparing now to tell Mistress Lil. I was feeling distress, standing there like that, looking out the window up at that tall flamboyant tree so sad too, not a single red petal pon it. Just then I remember something. Something that I ain't remember in years and years. I remember a story about a cousin of mine back in Sherman, how she did jump out a coconut tree to throw she child. Ellis. She did name Ellis. Dorine sister. I was standing there looking out at that sad flamboyant tree off in the distant, when I remember Ellis, hearing about Ellis. How she did throw she child.

All in a sudden I find myself climbing up out the window again. But not in no hurry, even though that duff was still there steaming. Cause I just leave it there steaming just like that, when I find myself climbing out the window slow. Calm. Walking slow cross the yard that was gone to bush then, now, weeds and brambles and them castoroil bushes, that I was picking my way through. Over towards the tall flamboyant tree. And now I was climbing up. Slow. One branch after the next. One branch after the next. My same nightmare that I did dreaming now for five months. I climb up till I reach to the tip top. And now I rest. I rest there a moment, getting ready to let loose. But now all in a sudden I hear like Mistress Lil calling after. Calling behind, and now she did climbing up behind too! Now all in a sudden I start to feel confuse, cause I couldn't *believe* it. I say Mistress Lil could never be climbing up in no tree, not Mistress Lil! I say she could *never* be climbing up in no tree. And now I *know* that I was dreaming, all this, my life, it was all only a *dream,* cause Mistress Lil could never be climbing up in no tree like that. Now all in a sudden she was right here, right here beside, and now I watch at she in my dream reaching out slow to touch. Touch to my shoulder, she finger to my shoulder. And when I feel the touch I did know that was my signal in my dream, cause it was all impossible, and I just let go. I just let loose my arms and my legs both, let loose from my life, my nightmare, and I *fall.* I feel myself fall and I feel myself hit the hard ground, *bram,* and straight back up pon my feet! *Cause I couldn't even wake up!* I throw myself out the tip top of that flamboyant tree and I fall and I hit the hard ground, *bram,* and I couldn't even wake up out from my dream. My dream of my life. Cause now I was walking back towards the house.

I was still dreaming five days later when Mistress Lil say she going upstairs for she nap after we take the tea, after we did finish taking we tea that afternoon. I think it was five days after that flamboyant, but maybe it was four, or seven, cause I did lose all track of time then. I was sitting there with Mistress Lil in the parlourroom that afternoon after we finish taking we tea together, just like every afternoon of we life together, when Mistress Lil say she going upstairs in she bedroom to take she nap. I watch at she get up, walk out from this parlourroom, and I hear she climbing up the stairs. I hear the metal scraping together of that key turning inside the lock, and I hear the door close. Now I say I going in my bedroom and do the same. Cause in truth that quinine powder did had me so *sleepy* then, and tired. I did reach to the tired-ness phase of that quinine powder then, and I say I going same as Mistress Lil in my bedroom and take a nap.

But then when I reach inside the room I didn't lie down pon my bed. I didn't lie myself down to take no nap. Cause all in a sudden I was searching all in the drawers of that big press, searching for something. But I didn't even *know* what. I was feeling my hands all about in them drawers, all amongst my clothes, my underclothes, all them belts and hats and handbags and all the different things that I had in there. Now all in a sudden I was pulling out, dumping out. All the clothes and all the different things pulling out with both my hands at the same time, dumping out in a big heap pon the floor. One drawer after the next. Like all in a sudden something just *snap.* Inside my head. My mind. Like something did go straight at my nerve, *straight,* cause all in a sud-den I was dumping out with both hands like I was going mad. Like a madwoman, all my things in a heap pon the floor looking for some-thing, and I didn't even know what it was.

I rush inside the WC I start to pull down all the things out the cab-inet. That medicine cabinet behind the mirror, all them bottles, boxes of powder, all them tubes of makeup and toothpaste and all my bottles of oils. I pulling out the cabinet dumping out in a heap pon the porce-lain floor. Now I rush back to my bed I start stripping off the bed. I pull off coverlet, sheets, pillows. I strip off that bed everything all tum-ble up in a big tumble pon the floor. I throw off that mattress! Throw it off the bedsprings with such brute strength in one direction that I throw *myself* in the next direction, slamming up against the wall, my shoulder. And now I slide down slow long the wall to sit in a heap pon the floor. Sweating, my dress soaked straight through, my headtie. All these bindings tie-up round my middle so tight I can't even breathe. Can't *breathe!* With these bindings. And now I feel the tears rolling out pon my cheeks. Sitting here with my back press flat against the wall, sweating, trying to breathe, tears rolling out pon my cheeks burning inside my eyes.

Now I look up I see under the bedsprings the white box. My white shoebox. Now I crawl over pon my hands and my knees, I pull it out. Dump it out pon the center of the mattress there beside. Spools of different coloured threads and pieces of different coloured cloths, pins and needles and my thimble bouncing up off the mattress rolling cross the floorboards.

My big sewing scissors.

10

Waves of pain. Pon the surface. Rippling like water cross the surface of sleep. Slow-dissolving sleep. Just a humbugging, stinging surface pain. The after-pain of scorched skin. Like a burned finger held beneath the pipe. Coming in waves. Lie here with my eyes closed and feel the soft seabreeze brushing in through the blinds to ease the pain way. Cool the scorched skin. Lie here and listen to the waves turning over pon the shore down below. Over and over. She breathing soft here beside. Lie here with my eyes closed and listen down deep inside for the pulse and quiver of the child that is living still. Better, stronger than me. And pronounce in my sleep the name like a prayer for waking. For waking up inside a sweet dream. *Bolom. We Bolom. We sweet Bolom.* Lie here with my eyes closed and feel this key cold and heavy and precious in my closed palm. And smile. Lie here and smile.

Open my eyes slow now, very slow, and see the first light of morning breaking in through the blinds. Lighting up all the petticoats of that big tree-fern rustling she skirts in the early morning breeze, early morning sun. Spreading out slow cross the galvanize sky. Lighting up all that multitude of miniature islands growing long the rafters. A whole Caribbean of islands, floating tranquil pon the sea of the sky, lighting up, coming back to life. Waking up again in the early morning.

Lie here and feel my own body waking up. Slow. Slow. My busted-up, exhausted-out body that feels five-hundred years old! Waking up after a sleep of five-hundred years. A nightmare lasting five-hundred years long. Or maybe only five months. Five hours, minutes. But waking up! After long last. Lie here with my bamsee still shoved up top the pillows. My spine still bent over backwards, my feet still pressing together below like palm-hands saying prayers. Lie here looking *up* at my rolling-backwards tottots. My preparing-again-to-suckle-again tottots! My big black cannonball-belly rolling backwards to crush me. But comfortable like this, happy, and scarce even able to shift a muscle anyway. Lift a limb. And making plans. Making plans anyway. To *spite* my five-hundred-year-old busted-up body. Oh, yes! Plenty plans. How we going do, Bolom. Me and you and Mistress Lil, you next mummy. Cause you got *two* mummies to confront with, make the plans with. Soon as we could get sufficient light. Soon as we could catch sufficient strength. Soon soon.

Up pon that ladder to scrub-down that galvanize. All them rafters and them walls. Scrub with lye, that Ajax bleach. Plant out that blasted tree-fern up in the flamboyant tree where she belong. Dust out these bedstands, Mistress Lil makeup table, beat out that big old bagging-down chair. *Open up all the doors!* Oh, yes. Every one. Open up all the doors and all the windows. All together. Get some *air* to blowing through this old house. Some fresh air.

And we got to confront pon we future, Bolom. Make plans. How we could get some *cash* to coming in. All we three together. You and me and you next mummy, Bolom. Mistress Lil. Cause we got to work this thing out together. We enter in it together, we got to work it out together. How we going do. Whether it going be extra laundering and ironing. Or the needleworks. Cause Mistress Lil could sew good too. Well I ain't know how good she could *sew*, but she could do that fancy *crocheting*, with the two needles. Pretty pretty. Doilies and such. And bootie-shoes, Bolom! She could crochet you a pair of them little baby bootie-shoes! Pair for you to wear and more pairs for we to sell, and baby-bonnets. Cause Mistress Lil learn that fancy crocheting when she was in the convent-school, long since she was in the convent-school. Like how I learn my needleworks, ever since I was a younggirl too. Still got my scissors and my thimble for that needleworks.

So we could do the needleworks, or the laundering, or we could convert this old house in a boarding-home. Oh, yes. That's *exactly* how we could do. Cause we got so much of *room* in here, this big old house, for just we three to be living in. We could get weself some extra beds, them *foam* beds for the comfort, and extra linens and towels and such. Convert this big old house in a boarding-home for women. Women, or women with children that ain't got no father, no husband. And we could serve the meals in the dining at the big dining table, cause that table plenty big enough, and we already got all the silvers and all the chinas that we could need. Tea could serve afternoons in the parlour-room. And Bolom, we could *dance* too! Oh, yes! We could host the dances pon evenings for we guests in the boarding-home. We could use the big old music-radio in the parlour. Or carry that big old gramo-phone and all them records out pon the back gallery for we to dance. That we could dance. Looking out over the glittering sea beneath a big fat moon. And una could suppose if the mens want to come round to dance with we little bit, we could let them come. Let them dance with we if they want. Little bit. But then when they finish dancing they got to *go*. That's all it is. They got to carry theyself, cause this boarding-home is a boarding-home for women and children. Where we could be together, live together, celebrate weself with weself together.

Happy-ever-after, like a story out the pictures! That's just how this story bound to end, Bolom. Like a story out the pictures. How this story bound to *begin*, cause truth is we only reach the beginning part. We go through all this commess only to reach the beginning part. The happy-ever-after beginning part. I *know*. I could *feel* it, cause I got the golden key right here in my hand holding. We golden key. Hers and mine and yours, Bolom. And I could raise it up before my eyes right now and see it glitter. Glitter like pure gold in the early morning sun. Glitter like a prayer for waking. For waking up inside a sweet dream.

I say *Amen!* to that. Say, *Amen!* And put this golden key inside my mouth that I could *taste* the taste of pure gold. Give *you* a taste, Bolom. Cold and heavy and precious and so sweet. And let we to pronounce it together again. The happy-ever-after beginning of this prayer. Let we to call it out loud, and this key in my mouth that we could taste it too. Same time. Together. Say, "*Ah-mum! Ah-mum! Ah-mum!*"